STARGATE SG·1

HALL OF THE TWO TRUTHS

Susannah Parker Sinard

FANDEMONIUM BOOKS

An original publication of Fandemonium Ltd, produced under license from MGM Consumer Products.

Fandemonium Books
United Kingdom
Visit our website: www.stargatenovels.com

STARGÅTE
SG·1

METRO-GOLDWYN-MAYER Presents
RICHARD DEAN ANDERSON
in
STARGATE SG-1™
MICHAEL SHANKS AMANDA TAPPING CHRISTOPHER JUDGE DON S. DAVIS
Executive Producers BRAD WRIGHT MICHAEL GREENBURG
RICHARD DEAN ANDERSON
Developed for Television by BRAD WRIGHT & JONATHAN GLASSNER

WWW.MGM.COM

Print ISBN: 978-1-905586-77-6 Ebook ISBN: 978-1-80070-036-9

For Mom and Dad
See you on the other side.

Historian's note:
This novel is set after the episode 'Red Sky', the fifth
episode of STARGATE SG-1, season five.

You have not departed dead; you have departed alive.
— Egyptian Pyramid Text, Spell 213

PROLOGUE

ANTICIPATION was not a sensation to which she was much accustomed. When one had lived for millennia, little remained in the universe which inspired the heart to quicken its pace — or so NebtHet had believed. Certainly she had not expected this peculiar feeling of restlessness or this inability to remain still. The whole experience was quite novel — right down to the nervous knot in the very pit of her stomach.

Well, not *her* stomach, technically, although she and Eshe had been blended for so long it was nearly impossible to remember existing as two separate beings. Unlike the Goa'uld, who disgustingly suppressed their hosts, or the Tok'ra, who insisted that each maintain their individual identities, the Djedu shared complete and perfect communion with their *akana* — their vessels. Two minds merging. Two organic bodies becoming as one. Eshe was as much within her as she was within Eshe.

So really it *was* her stomach which tensed expectantly at each sound that echoed in the great hall, just as they were her legs which restlessly paced before the chaapa'ai, waiting for the first groan of the ring which would bring this insufferable wait to an end. Although if all went as she hoped — as she had so carefully planned — it really would not be an end but a beginning. And it was that thought which made her hearts beat faster than they had for a very long time.

NebtHet nodded absently to others who passed through the hall. She had shared this with no one, yet. It was too soon. If Aset returned with disappointing news, the others would be none the wiser. Too many had already accepted defeat. To raise what remained of their hope and then destroy it would be the final blow.

The lowering sun through the high windows cast the chaapa'ai's great round shadow at her feet. The Djedu had brought many items through the great ring over the centuries — a treasure-trove of technology from races long extinct. Not one had brought them the knowledge they sought. Still, they might yet have some usefulness. She would know only when Aset returned.

As if in answer, NebtHet felt a slight vibration beneath her feet. The inner ring of the chaapa'ai began to move and the lights around the perimeter came to life.

Finally.

Willing herself to be calm, NebtHet stood just out of reach of the blossoming wormhole and waited as a familiar robed figure stepped through the shimmering wall. Always difficult to read, Aset's demeanor revealed nothing as she strode down the incline to where NebtHet waited.

"What news?" She kept the eagerness out of her voice. With Aset, a dispassionate discourse was usually the better approach.

Aset made no reply but simply withdrew a small leather pouch and dropped it in NebtHet's hand. Within was a small green vial of liquid, their entire future in a slender tube of glass.

"He has done well." NebtHet held it up to the light. As small as it was, its contents only filled the bottle half-way. "But is this enough?"

"Your novice claims it is." Aset's tone was matter-of-fact. "Only a drop or two per person is required. He said it was all he could procure. Any more and it would have been missed."

"He must not jeopardize his place among the Tok'ra. It is vital, for our plan to work." NebtHet returned the vial to its pouch and secured it in her pocket. "Is everything else proceeding, then? Has he secured the necessary position within their hierarchy?"

"So he assures me. Although some time will be needed to set events in motion."

"Then we must prepare." NebtHet took a deep breath. She felt oddly at peace. Gone was the restless anticipation. Determined purpose had taken its place. "After all these years, finally, the time has come."

Aset sniffed. "You expect too much, NebtHet. Especially from these Tau'ri. They will not give you what you need."

"I will not turn back from this course, Aset." She had not devoted her entire life to the Djedu to accept failure now. Aset's skepticism would not deter her. Nothing would. "This plan will go forward, with or without your approval. Our destiny awaits, and SG-1 will play their part — willingly or not."

CHAPTER ONE

AS PLANETS went, P4C-679 was better than most. The climate was temperate, although if Sam had to guess by the size and nature of the coniferous trees that surrounded them, the region most likely spent at least half its solar year covered in snow. That it wasn't winter now, she was grateful. She'd developed a bit of an aversion to bitterly cold conditions over the past few years. At least they wouldn't be fighting the weather.

It had taken SG-1 the better part of an hour to reach the ruins. There hadn't been much of a path — a sign that the Stargate wasn't something that got much use here. If not for the previous trail cut by SG-16, Sam was sure they'd have taken more than a few wrong turns, even with the map the Tok'ra had provided.

The ruins themselves were not terribly impressive. She wondered how the Tok'ra scouts had even discovered them. The only parts of the original structure still standing were no higher than her waist, and the rest of it lay half-buried in the tall grasses that had long ago claimed the area. Daniel was going to be spending a lot of time crouching.

At the moment, though, he was simply standing in the midst of a large semi-circle of rubble, looking slightly confused.

"Daniel — is there a problem?" Sam trudged up the small hill to join him. The mass of the planet was undoubtedly greater than Earth's. Everything seemed to weigh more here, including her kit.

Daniel was gazing off into the distance. "I thought the Tok'ra said there were settlements here — people."

Colonel O'Neill answered before she could. "According to SG-16, the closest village is about ten klicks that-a-way." He pointed in the direction of some small hills dotted with more cone-bearing trees.

"Really? Well that's disappointing; I was hoping to meet some of them."

The colonel took off his cap and slapped it against the side of his leg to knock off some dirt. "We didn't come here to make new friends, Daniel." Adjusting the cap back into place, he gave the brim an extra hard tug. Sam glanced at Daniel, hoping he'd pick up on the warning sign of the colonel's irritability and let the matter drop.

"I know." Daniel remained oblivious. "It's just that sometimes there are local legends about ruins that often hold a grain of truth. It would have been helpful to ask someone from around here what they know about this place."

"Yeah. Well. Looks like we're fresh out of local tour guides this time around — which, for the record, is fine by me. So you're on your own."

"Not everyone lives in towns and villages, Jack."

Sam tried to catch Daniel's eye to warn him off, but he didn't look her way.

"Maybe after you and Teal'c set up camp you could look around to see if you can find someone who lives nearby —" By then Daniel must have realized he'd crossed some invisible line and let the sentence fade away. "Or not," he stammered slightly, answering his own question. He indicated the ruins behind him with a jerk of his thumb. "Why don't I just —?"

"You do that," the colonel shot back. "Carter — you too." He motioned her toward where Daniel was unpacking his gear. "We've got forty-eight hours on Planet Pointless here. Make the most of it."

"Yes, sir." Sam dropped her pack to the ground and began unloading her own gear. From the corner of her eye she could see the colonel and Teal'c heading back to the campsite. Setting that up would keep the two of them occupied for a little while at least. The colonel was always happier having something to do. Waiting around for Daniel and her to assess the ruins for the next two days certainly wasn't going to improve his mood.

Maybe getting him to track down some locals wouldn't be such a bad idea after all.

Although, considering what had happened on K'tau, maybe it was. Things had been going smoothly so far — mission-wise, at least. She hadn't infected this sun or doomed the planet to extinction, so keeping the colonel away from the indigenous population might be for the best. If they continued to avoid any major catastrophes, this mission might actually turn out to be a success.

What exactly defined 'success' in this case, however, Sam wasn't entirely sure. The ruins had been brought to their attention by one of the Tok'ra, who believed them to have some connection to the Ancients. Daniel had confirmed this after SG-16's recon photos, but aside from investigating a lone device that looked as though it might crumble at a mere touch, Sam doubted there was any more to be learned on-site than what the photographs had already revealed.

But General Hammond had insisted, and in spite of the colonel's strenuous objection that their time would be better spent doing just about anything else, here they were.

Daniel already had his notebook out and was sketching a rough lay-out of the ruins. It didn't take Sam long to locate what she was looking for. In the photographs, the domed apparatus appeared similar in size and shape to the one they had found on Earnest Littlefield's planet. Now that she saw it in person, she was even more convinced that it had to be tangentially related. At least it wasn't as fragile as it had seemed in the photos. What she had mistaken for decay was nothing more than some indigenous lichen that had attached itself to the surface.

Based on what Sam could see of Daniel's sketch, the device was situated directly in the center of what once must have been a circular structure. Given its position, it was possible the building's sole purpose had been to house it — whatever *it* was. Sam felt a momentary rush of excitement. If the device itself was the very reason the structure had existed, then maybe that was an indication of its importance. This might not be such a wild goose chase after all.

Not that she was ready to share her theory with the others. Yet. Better to err on the side of caution. The colonel would never let her live it down if it turned out to be nothing more than a glorified Ancient drink dispenser. One more thing to add to his list of her screw-ups lately.

Sam heard the whirr of the focusing lens to her right as Daniel began an in-depth photo-documentation of each piece of stone. She'd need to remind him to take detailed pictures of the device as well. In the meantime, she better get to work.

With only a brief glance in the direction of the colonel and Teal'c, Sam opened her toolkit and began.

"Damn it!"

Daniel looked up from the section of wall he'd been studying and blinked. Sam was venting her frustration over the device she'd been working on for — he checked his watch — wow, four hours. For the first time he realized that the sun had dropped considerably toward the horizon and the temperature was cooler than before.

"You okay?"

Sam was sitting back on her heels in front of the apparatus, staring at it. From his vantage point, Daniel could see she'd been working on a small tray of crystals. Their assorted colors caught the low-angled light of the sun, reflecting small rainbows on a nearby stone wall.

"There's no reason this shouldn't be working." Her aggravation was evident. "Every crystal is in perfect shape. They're all here. I'm even getting a power signature from them, which means they haven't burned out. But I can't get the damn thing to turn on."

"Um, maybe that's not a bad thing? I mean, since we really don't know what it is yet —"

She stood up and dusted off her pants before joining him.

"I was hoping maybe you'd have a clue about that. Anything?"

Daniel rose to his feet and flipped back a few pages in his notebook.

"Actually — no. I mean, not yet," he amended when he saw Sam's brow furrow in disappointment. "However, this is really very interesting because what I'm finding here is not only Ancient, but a second set of writing as well."

"A second set?"

"Yes. It's much newer than the Ancient stuff. If I had to guess, I'd say it's probably the indigenous language of the people who live here. It looks like a derivative of Akkadian writing, which evolved from the original Sumerian —" Sam was looking at him as if he were actually speaking it. Right. Keep it simple. "Point is," he continued, "if I'm translating it properly — and there are subtle differences in the —" She had that blank look again. "Anyway, if I'm translating it right, it says 'the ones who came before have blessed us with great power' and they — the ones who came before — have given them the ability to make 'the gods of the sky dance at our bidding.'" Daniel shrugged.

There were so many ways one could interpret that, he was going to need a whole lot more to put it into context.

"Whatcha got, kids? Anything worth writing home about?" Jack had come up behind Sam, startling her. "Daniel's got a partial translation on some —" She looked to him for help.

"Akkadian derivative."

" — text he's found."

Daniel reread what he'd just translated for Sam. Jack looked only mildly interested.

"'Great power,' huh? So, we're talking about that thing, I presume?" He turned to look pointedly at what Sam had been working on. "Guess that means it's your turn, Carter." Jack looked at Sam expectantly. Daniel saw her redden just a bit. Or maybe it was the evening sunlight.

Sam walked them both over to the device. The tray with the crystals was still open and she slid it shut.

"It should be working, sir. Everything on the inside checks out. All the controls up top seem to be intact. I can't find any loose connections. But—" she pressed two or three of the panels on top without anything happening. "I'm at a loss as to what to do next."

Jack didn't seem very disappointed. Daniel had the sense he'd merely been humoring them.

"So, no 'Idiot's Guide to Ancient Devices' included, I gather?" Jack's back was to Sam, so he didn't see her wince at his smart-ass remark.

"Sir." There was a slight edge to her tone. "This is a very complex piece of technology and you can't expect—"

Jack spun back around. "Oh relax, Carter. No one's saying you couldn't figure it out, given enough time." He leaned on the device with exaggerated casualness. The panel under his hand sprung to life.

"How did you do that?" Sam hurried to look at the now glowing section. "What did you do?" she demanded, half-glaring at Jack, who'd pulled his hand away as if he'd touched a hot burner.

Sam pressed a different panel, but nothing happened. She tried a third. Still nothing.

"Sir, try another one."

Jack looked skeptically at the device and then a bit suspiciously at Sam before he tentatively reached out and pressed a different square. It too lit up.

"I must have the magic touch," he quipped with a sheepish half-grin

Sam, however, was not smiling. "Daniel, you try it."

Obligingly, Daniel pressed one of the two remaining unlit panels. Nothing happened.

"Hey, at least we know it's not just you, Carter."

Daniel glimpsed Sam's face before she turned away to check

the readings on her scanner. Seriously, was Jack going out of his way to be an ass, or was he just being stupidly oblivious?

"Jack—"

There was a click. Jack had pressed yet another panel.

"Um, maybe we should quit while we're ahead," Daniel cautioned. "After all, we still don't know what this thing does. I think we've learned that lesson enough times, don't you?"

But he was too late. Jack had pressed the remaining panel and the device began to vibrate slightly, as some internal mechanism creaked to life. Two panels slid back above the control pad and the dome-shaped core, about a half-meter in diameter, slowly rose through them, humming loudly as it broke the surface and stopped. It was hard to tell with the sun still visible, but the dome seemed to be glowing with small pinpricks of light. It began, very slowly, to rotate.

"Pretty," commented Jack. Daniel and Sam both ignored him. Sam was walking around the device, studying it from all angles, consulting her scanner. Jack waved his hand over the top through the minute rays of light.

"Should you be doing that?" asked Daniel, warily. Jack withdrew his hand at once.

"It should be safe. As far as I can tell it's just—light," reported Sam, puzzled. "No radiation at all, that I can detect. No other kind of energy, either."

"Not like that other light-thingy—the one that made us all a little nuts?" Jack asked. Daniel had just been thinking the same thing.

"No, sir. This is just—light."

They all stared at it.

"So. I'm thinking, Ancient disco ball?"

Daniel rolled his eyes at Sam, only she was giving Jack a peculiar look. He recognized a light bulb moment when he saw one.

"I'll be right back!" She took off at a quick jog toward camp, returning a few minutes later with a tarp, and Teal'c trailing behind her.

"Daniel, how high do you think this building was originally?"

He thought for a moment. "Based on the size and shape of the stones, I'm thinking it was—"

"Domed," she supplied.

Daniel nodded, surprised. "Yes. How did you know?"

"Just a hunch. How high, would you say?"

Daniel did some quick figuring. "Probably about six meters, give or take, at the center."

Sam was nodding. She began unfolding the tarp, giving each of them a corner. At her direction they held it over the top of the device and then stretched it out, lifting it over their heads.

"Carter?"

"We can't simulate the building exactly, sir. We don't have enough height, obviously. But this should test my theory. Or, your theory, actually."

Jack looked surprised. "You mean it really *is* an Ancient disco ball?"

Sam smiled the first genuine smile Daniel had seen on her all day.

"Not exactly, sir. But close. This would probably work better after it's completely dark but—Everyone hold it as high above your head as you can."

Daniel stretched his arm up over his head, and for good measure balanced on his toes. The others did the same.

"Now, look up," Sam instructed. Daniel did his best to balance his position and tilt his head back. The pinpoints of light were shining on the underside of the dark green surface, but not in a random pattern or a perfectly ordered one, for that matter. Instead, they were clustered in different groupings. It looked familiar. He'd seen this before.

"Constellations," he said. Then it dawned on him. "It's a planetarium—or, at least, the Ancient equivalent of one." Of course. If the roof were domed it would be exactly like the ones on earth. The slow rotation of the device showed the progression of the stars as they ran their course in the night sky.

"A planetarium?" repeated Jack, incredulously. "We came all this way to look at a planetarium?"

"So it would seem," replied Teal'c, calmly.

"What about the 'great power' and 'gods doing our bidding' thing?"

"Well," Daniel replied. "I mean, it's pretty obvious isn't it? To an unsophisticated civilization, the ability to reproduce the stars and emulate their movement across the heavens would have seemed like making the gods of the sky — the constellations — bend to their will. They would have probably considered that fairly powerful magic."

"It's a *planetarium*," complained Jack.

"I know. To you and me, nothing remarkable, but to them —"

"Fine. Great. We came. We saw. We missed the gift shop, but that's okay. If we pack it up now we can be back to the gate in an hour. Tonight's *Simpsons* is not a rerun."

"Sir —"

"Jack —"

"Carter. Daniel."

Daniel looked at Sam and knew she was thinking the same thing.

"We can't leave yet, Jack. There's so much more here that I haven't even begun to try to translate. General Hammond gave us forty-eight hours."

"General Hammond didn't know it was a planetarium, Daniel. Besides. What more could we possibly learn from this?"

They'd let go of the tarp and it drifted over the device.

"Well, first of all, it's obviously Ancient technology," began Sam, pulling the tarp off to uncover it. The ambient light was fading rapidly and the pinpricks of light were becoming brighter. "And I still don't have any idea how you turned it on. Studying it may help us, if and when we encounter future Ancient tech. I'd like a few more hours with it, sir, especially now that we know what it is."

"And I've only begun to decipher the Ancient writing on these walls, Jack. Yes, I know I can take lots of pictures and do it back at the SGC," he forged ahead when he saw the objection forming on Jack's lips. "But that's never as good as doing it on-site. Besides, we're running out of light and I can't finish taking pictures until morning now anyway. I get too much reflection with the flash."

"Night is quickly approaching, O'Neill," Teal'c pointed out. "It would be difficult to navigate a return to the Stargate without adequate light. The path to this location was quite circuitous."

There. If nothing more, they had a practical reason to remain, but Jack was still hesitating. For a minute Daniel thought he was going to order them back to the gate anyway, but finally Jack threw his hands up in the air.

"Fine. Fine. We'll stay." He turned his back and walked away. "But tomorrow," Jack waggled his finger in the air, "we're out of here by noon, and not a second later. So, translate, study, take pictures — whatever. Just be done."

Daniel shot a satisfied look at Sam, expecting her to share his relief, but her eyes were following Jack's retreating back, and there was a troubled expression on her face. A moment later, though, it was gone, and she turned her attention back to refolding the tarp.

Noon. Daniel figured that would give them about six hours of good light. At the very least he could finish photographing and mapping the ruins. Even if it *was* just a planetarium, the Ancients must have had some reason for building it.

Six hours. It probably wasn't enough time, but it was what he had and it would have to do.

Teal'c walked silently beside O'Neill as they followed the path back to camp. It had been a wise decision not to attempt returning to the Stargate now. He did not know if this planet had any orbiting bodies, but at the moment no moon was present and the darkness was swiftly descending. Trying to find their way by means of the poorly marked trail would have been hazardous at best. Remaining at camp for the night was the correct choice, even if it made O'Neill less than pleased.

"A planetarium." O'Neill was muttering in a low voice, his head shaking.

"You do not think it is a valuable discovery."

O'Neill glanced over at him. "On the list of really cool things I'd like to have from the Ancients, it's near the bottom. Right after 'toaster oven' but before 'electric toothbrush' — although, come to think of it, an electric toothbrush would probably still be more useful."

"Perhaps tomorrow will yield a new discovery." Teal'c saw O'Neill give a cursory look over his shoulder at the two shadowed figures that still moved amidst the ruins.

"Yeah. Well. Let's just say I'm not holding my breath."

"You have been reluctant to come on this mission from the very beginning."

"You noticed," O'Neill said dryly.

"I do not understand why."

"Would you like the short list or the long one?" O'Neill pushed aside a low hanging branch with so much vigor that Teal'c heard it snap.

"Is it because you did not believe there was anything of benefit to be found here?"

"You said it, not me." O'Neill took point as the path narrowed. "And for the record, I was right."

Teal'c followed his silhouette through the underbrush. "Are you no longer confident that we may someday discover alien technology to assist us in the fight against the Goa'uld?"

"The only thing I'm confident of is that this whole thing is a huge waste of our time." He grunted. "SG-16 was already here. Hammond should have sent them back to finish the job. They could have done it with their eyes shut."

"Do you not believe the expertise of Daniel Jackson and Major Carter were required on this mission?"

"It's a planetarium, Teal'c. Not rocket science. Hell, she can't even get it to work half the time."

"I do not believe the fault lies with Major Carter."

"I'm just sayin'—there are better things we could be doing than wasting our time on this half-ass Tok'ra wild goose chase." Teal'c heard another branch snap, as if to emphasis O'Neill's point.

"It is my understanding that it was the liaison to the SGC from the Tok'ra High Council who provided the information about this planet, and that their interest was more academic than strategic."

"Anise's experiment with those damned bracelets was supposed to be 'academic' too, and look where the hell that landed us."

"I do not believe there is evidence to suggest that these circumstances are comparable, O'Neill."

"Hey, just because they haven't dropped the other shoe yet, doesn't mean they won't. Trust me. There's more to this than meets the eye. With the damn Tok'ra, there always is."

"I find it difficult to believe that General Hammond would have agreed to the mission had he not felt it had merit."

Ahead of him in the dark, O'Neill muttered something, but the only intelligible words Teal'c made out were "Daniel" "Carter" and "geeks". Even so, the context did not sound especially complimentary.

"Have Major Carter and Daniel Jackson displeased you in some way?"

He had noticed, for some time now, that O'Neill's attitude toward his colleagues had become increasingly critical. Now seemed as appropriate a time to address it as any.

"What are you talking about? No. Of course not." The response was immediate and vehement, which Teal'c found telling. It was his experience that the more fervently humans denied something, the more likely it was to be true.

"Your recent behavior toward them would seem to suggest otherwise," he countered. "Especially Major Carter." For months now, ever since Major Carter had nearly perished by O'Neill's own hand, his manner had been brusque and distant. Teal'c had his suspicions as to why, but those were best kept to himself.

O'Neill was silent for a moment. "Look, Teal'c." There was a hardness in his voice that Teal'c knew hid deeper feelings. "Sometimes you've just gotta do the job, you know? You can't let other stuff get in the way. It makes things… complicated."

Teal'c considered how best to choose his words in response. It was usually best, he had discovered, to be direct with O'Neill, particularly on personal matters. Yet in this case, perhaps a more subtle approach was required.

"When I served as First Prime of Apophis, we were not permitted to keep our same lieutenants for more than a few campaigns. The Goa'uld feared that we would become too attached to them and that our loyalty to our brother Jaffa would outweigh our loyalty to our god."

"Makes sense, in that 'me-first' Goa'uld kinda way."

"Nevertheless, many of us still forged deep and lasting bonds that made us as brothers, even though we knew that if death did not tear us asunder, our god most assuredly would."

They emerged into the clearing where they'd set up camp. The small fire Teal'c had started before leaving to assist Major Carter was nearly out. Only a few glowing embers remained.

O'Neill pulled up short and faced Teal'c, cradling his P-90. "And your point?"

"If we fear to lose that which we hold most dear, then it is, in fact, already lost — as are we."

"And your point?" O'Neill repeated, testily.

Even in the dark, Teal'c could tell from his stony expression that it was futile to pursue the issue further. So he simply said, "I believe my point is quite clear."

"Of *course* it is," O'Neill snapped sarcastically, before wheeling around and stalking away. "Don't give up your day job,

Teal'c," he called over his shoulder. "I don't think Dear Abby is quite ready for you."

Teal'c watched his friend's back disappear into his tent and shook his head sadly. If only he had Bra'tac's skill at bringing out what was in a man's heart. But he did not think that even the Rite of M'al Sharran would induce O'Neill to acknowledge the truth that was within him.

"Say again, sir? I think we had a bad connection." At least Jack hoped that's what it was, and that Hammond hadn't just said what he'd thought he'd said.

Through the tinny radio speaker, Hammond repeated himself. Jack winced. Nope. Just what he'd heard him say the first time. Damn it.

"But sir, it's *just* a planetarium."

"*Which is why it's of such interest, Colonel.*" Hammond's voice was firm. "*Apparently it's the only one of its kind ever discovered. We'll redial in ten. Be prepared to receive your guest. And I hope I don't have to remind you, Colonel, to play nice.*"

"No, sir," Jack muttered, kicking the grass at his feet as the Stargate's blue puddle shimmered out of existence. Wonderful. Just how he wanted to spend his last few hours on this rock: hosting the very people who'd sent him here in the first place.

Or person. When the blue puddle reappeared, a lone figure stepped through. He was young for a Tok'ra, probably not far into his twenties. Of course, that was only the host. God knew how old the snake inside his head was.

"I am Jenmar, of the Tok'ra," he said, walking up to Jack and bowing slightly.

"Jack O'Neill," he replied curtly. "And this here is Teal'c." The big guy returned Jenmar's bow with his own precisely timed head nod. Birds of a feather, in an odd sort of way.

"It is an honor to finally meet you both." Jenmar smiled. "Your exploits are legendary among the Tok'ra."

Jack raised his eyebrows. "Legendary, you say?"

Jenmar's smiled broadened. "Quite. And now that you have discovered the Dome of Anu —"

"Excuse me?. 'Dome of Anu'?" Jack frowned. "Where'd you hear that?"

The smile on the Tok'ra's face froze for just the blink of an eye and Jack didn't think he was imagining that the guy suddenly looked just a bit nervous. That nagging feeling that had been flitting around in the back of his head ever since this whole thing began was starting to get a whole lot naggyer.

"I… I was only recently able to decipher some of the writing in photographs your General Hammond so kindly provided me," Jenmar explained, apologetically. "The study of languages is something of a specialty of mine." Funny. Jack didn't recall Daniel making any mention of the Dome of anything, although he might have missed it. He tended to tune Daniel out quite a bit these days. Still —

He nailed the Tok'ra with his best suspicious look and noticed that the guy wouldn't meet his eye.

Right.

"Yes. Well. It's a hike, so we better get moving." Jack waved the guy toward the trailhead with the barrel of his P90. Jenmar scurried behind Teal'c, who took point. Jack brought up the rear so he could keep an eye on their guest. That nagging feeling was still there and if he'd learned anything in all these years, Jack knew better than to ignore it. No matter what everyone else thought.

"So. How long you been with the Tok'ra?" Jack said after they'd walked for a while.

"I have been Tok'ra all of my life, since I was spawned of our beloved queen Egeria, millennia ago."

Jack was confused. If Jenmar was the snake, where was the booming baritone voice?

"You do not choose to speak as most Tok'ra do?" Teal'c took the words right out of his mouth.

Jenmar smiled slightly and shook his head. "We do not. Keyleb and Jenmar speak as one. Our blending is… unique."

"Sounds like a Goa'uld," Jack grunted. "No offense." Something about this guy didn't read right. Maybe this was why.

"I assure you, Colonel, I am no Goa'uld. But to answer the question I think you meant to ask, I am Keyleb, formerly of Wasir, and I have been host to Jenmar for what would amount to about seven of your years."

"I am familiar with Wasir," remarked Teal'c. "Was it not destroyed in a battle between the forces of Ra and Cronus?"

Jack saw Keyleb — Jenmar, whoever — tense slightly. "It was. Very few of us survived. I was among those who were mortally wounded. The Tok'ra found me and saved my life."

That always gave Jack the creeps. Sure, he was grateful that Selmak had saved Carter's dad. He'd come to like Jacob a lot and he knew how much having him involved in their work, even as a Tok'ra, meant to Carter. But to willingly let a snake into your head, even a supposedly good snake? Personally, he'd die first.

"So, if you don't change your voice, then how do we know which one of you is talking?" Jack wasn't sure what bothered him most, knowing he was talking to a snake, or not knowing if he was talking to a snake.

"It is quite simple, Colonel. Both of us are speaking."

"Right…" Somehow Jack didn't find that reassuring. Just another reason to keep his eye on this guy. Guys. Whatever.

They didn't bother to stop at the camp. It wasn't there anymore anyway; just their kit remained, bundled up and ready to go. He hadn't let Carter or Daniel anywhere near those ruins until everything was packed. Daniel had complained loudly about wasting valuable morning light, but he'd complied eventually. Carter had said nothing.

In the distance Jack could see Daniel peering at one of the ruined wall sections and writing in his notebook. Carter had her head inside the base of the planetarium thing, her body twisted in an awkward position that made it look like she was being eaten by the darn thing.

"Look, kids. Company," Jack called out to them as he, Teal'c and Jenmar slogged through the high grass. Carter extricated herself from the Ancient device and stood up. Daniel finished his writing before joining them.

"This is Jenmar, of the Tok'ra. He's come to check out all the fun he's been missing." Jack plastered an exaggerated smile on his face.

Jenmar did that bowing thing again.

"I merely wished to see for myself what a great discovery this is. When General Hammond told me that you would be returning early, I asked if I might be able to come in time to see it."

"I'm not sure I'd classify it as a great discovery," Carter observed. "Interesting, certainly, but not terribly useful, I'm afraid. Especially since we can't get it to work consistently."

"Pish, Carter!" Jack chided. "Don't you know you've been tinkering with the infamous Dome of Rectu?"

"Anu," corrected Jenmar. "Dome of Anu."

"Yes, that." At Daniel's puzzled look Jack added, "It seems Jenmar here speaks the same language you do, Daniel. Or, you know, languages, I guess."

Daniel's features resolved into recognition. "Dome of Anu — yes! I did find that somewhere." He started flipping back through his notes. "Which makes sense, when you think about it. Anu was the Akkadian's god of the sky. There's a —"

"Great!" Jack slapped Jenmar on the back, much to the Tok'ra's surprise. "The two of you go knock yourselves out. Just remember, we're out of here in —" He checked his watch. If he didn't know better, he'd have sworn time ran slower on this planet than anywhere else in the galaxy. Who knew? Maybe it did. It was all relative, after all. At least according to Carter. "Three hours," he told them, holding up three fingers for emphasis. "Don't make me wait!"

"Sir—" Carter hurried up to him as Daniel took Jenmar off to look at some rocks. She was somewhat dusty and her hair was every which way from having been inside the base of the planetarium. Not that he noticed.

"What is it, Carter?" He readjusted his sunglasses. There wasn't a cloud in the sky this morning.

"I've been thinking."

"I'm shocked."

She looked more annoyed than amused. "I think we ought to consider taking this device back with us. Or, at the very least, sending a team of engineers back to retrieve it."

Jack studied her. "I thought you said it wasn't such a great discovery?"

"From a utilitarian point of view, it's not." She spoke quickly, a sign she was nervous. "But I still don't know why it won't work for anyone but you. And any chance to study Ancient technology, even if it is just a device for displaying the stars, shouldn't be wasted. The scientists at Area 51 would have a lot more resources to figure this thing out than I do. Especially given that I'm on the clock," she added, in a half-accusatory tone.

Jack studied the device. "Well, it's too big to cart back with us now, but give Hammond your recommendation and—"

He thought he heard a sound, an all too familiar sound. Glancing at Teal'c, Jack knew he'd heard it too; Teal'c was already assuming a defensive stance as he scanned the skies. A heartbeat later Carter picked up on it as well. She dove for her weapon, which she'd left lying next to her backpack by the Dome.

"Daniel! Jenmar!" Jack shouted, unslinging his P90 and flicking back the safety. "We've got company! Take cover!"

The two men looked up, confused, until they heard the distinctive whine of the engines. Daniel grabbed Jenmar by the sleeve and hauled him off into the nearby brush. Carter too was scrambling for cover. Jack followed her lead and hunkered down behind a pile of Ancient rubble. Teal'c alone stood unprotected, his staff weapon raised in anticipation.

"Teal'c, get down!"

Teal'c ignored him and Jack could see the crackle of energy at the tip of his weapon as he took aim.

The first death glider strafed the ground around them, kicking up jagged bits of stone and dirt. A large chunk of shrapnel hit the rock just by Jack's head and he ducked reflexively. Coughing, he swung out from behind the boulder and took aim at the second glider coming in from behind the first one. Jack could hear the pings of his bullets ricocheting off the ship's hull as it zoomed overhead.

From the pitch of the sound, Jack knew they were circling around for another attack. He'd heard the sharp staccato sound of Carter's P90 as she fired too, but her weapon was as worthless as his against such an attack. Only Teal'c had any chance of bringing down the ships.

Jack assessed their options. They were sitting ducks out in the open like this, but if they all made a break for the tree line they'd never make it before the death gliders swung around again.

They were screwed.

The hum of the gliders' engines was growing louder again. They were coming, like two great predatory birds. Jack gauged the distance to the tree line one more time. Maybe if he gave the ships a specific target, the others might have half a chance.

"Carter!" She looked over her shoulder at him while reloading her weapon. "When I say so, you, Daniel and Teal'c run like hell for those trees." He'd almost forgotten. "And take the damned Tok'ra too."

Her brow furrowed. "What about you, sir?"

"Just do as I say, Major. That's an order."

Throwing him a look of belligerent resignation, she radioed the message to Daniel and Teal'c. The big guy had finally taken cover near the center portion of the ruins, crouching behind his own pile of stones and brambles. His head snapped up sharply and he frowned at Jack when Carter's message came through, but finally he nodded and acknowledged the order.

Good. He didn't need last minute heroics from any of them.

Jack picked his destination. There was a small cluster of pines maybe a hundred yards from his position. It wouldn't be much cover, even if he made it, but it was at a right angle from the flight path of the gliders. They'd have to bank sharply to follow him, and that would take both their time and attention. Carter and the others could escape to the tree line in the opposite direction and, if he were lucky, he'd make cover before the pilots actually got him in their sites. Throw in the fact that the run of the mill Jaffa was usually a lousy shot, and he might just survive this.

Emphasis on *might*.

Spotting a better location from which to launch his sprint, Jack scrambled to a nearby mound of rubble. Amidst the screech of the oncoming gliders, he heard what sounded like a zat, but that didn't make any sense.

Unless they were being flanked by ground troops as well.

If that were the case, then they really were screwed.

Jack hesitated. There was no point in running decoy if he was just as likely to get a staff blast in the back for his troubles. He clicked on his radio.

"Carter, did you —?"

There was no need to finish. He heard the zat fire again. Grasping his weapon, Jack leaned around the pile of stones just in time to see a blue arc strike Carter from behind. His brain registered a motionless form where Teal'c had been and no longer any sign of the top of Daniel's head. Crap.

Jack heard it before he felt it, even as the strafing from the death gliders started spattering the ground again. His body half-tensed in anticipation a split-second before the zat blast set his nerves on fire. There was a jolt of acute pain paired with a flash of self-loathing, and then Jack's vision faded to black.

CHAPTER TWO

"WE'D LIKE to go back, sir." The determination in Colonel Reynolds' voice belied how weary he and the rest of SG-16 appeared. "And I'd like to request a UAV. SG-1 might just be out of radio range."

"I've already authorized the UAV, but, for now, I'm suspending any further search and rescue." It was the last thing Hammond wanted to do, but based on the evidence of a Goa'uld attack, he wasn't about to put another team in harm's way. Not until he had a better idea of what had gone wrong on P4C-679. "Get some rest, Colonel. All of you." He dismissed them with a nod.

Back in his office, Hammond watched SG-16 slowly file out of the conference room. He understood their frustration. He shared it. This was supposed to have been an easy, no-stress mission for SG-1. Something that would ease them back into the saddle after the debacle on K'tau. He'd meant it as more of a team-building exercise than anything else.

So what the hell had happened?

To make matters worse, he also had a missing Tok'ra. Hammond didn't relish making that call to the High Council, although maybe they would be able to shed a bit more light on why they'd proposed the mission to '679 in the first place. Jenmar had presented it as an opportunity to explore newly discovered Ancient ruins, but maybe Jack had been right, and there was more to it than that. Considering his people had been missing for nearly eighteen hours now, Hammond was inclined to think so.

"The UAV is ready to deploy, sir." Sergeant Harriman was standing in the doorway, waiting expectantly.

Hammond nodded. "I'll be there in a moment, Sergeant." He supposed it was too much to hope that they'd find SG-1 safe and sound in a nearby village. That just wasn't their kind of luck, lately. Maybe he should have heeded Dr. Fraiser's advice and given them some leave time. If he had, they wouldn't be in this fix — whatever it turned out to be.

Walter had retreated only as far as the conference room and was waiting for him. Sending the UAV was more of an exercise in hope than expectation, Hammond was sure. He was already steeling himself for what came next.

"Walter, when we're done with the aerial reconnaissance, I'm going to need to make a call."

"Yes, sir. Local or long distance?"

"Very long distance." Hammond sighed. "Better start looking up the area code for Revanna."

Everything ached.

And by everything, Jack meant, *everything*.

Although maybe that was a good sign. At least it suggested he was more or less in one piece. Even if all those pieces hurt like hell.

Now if only he could figure out where he was. And how he got there. Because by the way his head was pounding, all signs pointed to a first-class hangover.

Or the after-effects of a high-powered zat.

"Crap." Now he remembered. Well, parts, anyway. There'd been that Tok'ra, whatever his name was, and some ruins. And a couple of death gliders shooting at them.

"Crap," Jack repeated, rolling onto his back and digging the heels of his hands into his eyes. If his head would clear, then maybe he could think straight. What he wouldn't give for a couple of aspirin about now.

Tok'ra and gliders and zats.

Oh my.

He dug his hands in deeper. One of Maybourne's steel drum bands seemed to have taken up permanent residence inside his skull. They were playing their entire repertoire. He pressed even harder. Had he ever mentioned he hated Calypso music?

Focus, damn it.

The memory of Carter dropping to her knees in the glow of blue zat-fire came to him. Vividly. That was all it took. The cobwebs cleared. Everything came back.

Jack's hand went instinctively to his holster. Empty. Of course it was. No self-respecting bad guy would have left him armed. Still, he double-checked, just to make sure.

Nope. They got all of it.

Pushing himself up on his elbows, Jack looked around. Dirt floor. Rock walls. No visible exits, although the light was so dim it was hard to say what he might be missing. What little illumination there was came from a few anemic torches that burned far out of reach above him. Their flickering light danced across four other motionless forms laying nearby.

Four?

Oh yeah. The Tok'ra. How could he forget?

Well, good. At least they were still together. That was one less thing he had to worry about.

His eyes rested on the body nearest to him.

"Carter —" He could make out her blonde hair even in the half-light.

Ignoring the fact that his muscles felt like Jell-O, Jack managed to crawl over to where she lay sprawled on her side. "Carter!" Rolling her onto her back, he reached past her collar to check for a pulse. Beneath his fingers her skin was warm and he could feel her heart beating steady and strong.

He started to breathe again.

"C'mon, Carter. Wake up." He shook her by the shoulder and she stirred slightly. Good, but not good enough. "No sleeping on the job, Major." He shook her again. Her eyes struggled open and she blinked at him, recognition finally kicking in.

"Sir?"

"Trust me, it wasn't the tequila." She was still too fuzzy to get his joke. It had been a lame attempt anyway. "How's your head?"

"It hurts, sir." She winced.

"Yeah, zats'll do that. I've gotta check on the others. You gonna be okay?"

She nodded, still a bit unsteady. He patted her gently on the shoulder. "Don't go anywhere. And don't doze off on me." She blinked again, wide-eyed, still trying to shake it off.

Daniel was next. He was easier to rouse, a sign that the effects of the zat were wearing off. By the time he was sitting up, rubbing his eyes, Teal'c was already standing. A moan from the last unconscious form indicated that the Tok'ra, Jack still couldn't remember his name, was coming around as well.

"Any idea where we are?" Daniel squinted into the darkness. Jack spotted his glasses on the ground and handed them to him. "Thanks. That's better. Or not."

"It appears to be a cavern," Teal'c remarked. "Possibly underground."

"Spread out," Jack told them. "The light doesn't go very far. Let's see what we can find." He eyed the Tok'ra, who appeared rather pale. "Maybe you'd better just stay here." The guy nodded, looking grateful. Great. Of all the Tok'ra they *could* have been captured with, they had to get the one who probably didn't know which end of a zat was up.

Carter and Teal'c fanned out in opposite directions and were already exploring the unlit space. Daniel was moving more slowly, his attention focused on the sconces. Jack could see that vague look of curiosity on his face, the one that suggested that, if they hadn't been imminently in mortal peril, he'd find this place incredibly interesting — just like at the ruins. Which only went to prove that, if they'd left when Jack wanted to in the first place, they wouldn't have ended up in this mess. He hated to say "I told you so" but —

Jack turned to stare at the Tok'ra. Come to think of it, things had been just fine until he'd shown up. That was one hell of a coincidence.

"You wanna tell me who the hell those guys were?"

Jenmar — Jack remembered the name now — nearly jumped out of his skin.

"What?" The Tok'ra's voice quavered and he shrunk back slightly as Jack advanced toward him.

Oh yeah. He had something to do with it, all right. Jack could smell it. The Tok'ra were up to their old tricks. Damned if he hadn't been right.

"You know very well what I mean." Jack gestured upward. "The Jaffa in those death gliders. Whose were they?"

Jenmar was shaking his head. "I — I don't know."

"Like hell you don't," snarled Jack, getting right up in Jenmar's face. He was sick and tired of being a pawn in whatever game the Tok'ra were playing. "There had to be some reason you wanted us on that planet. All that 'You ought to see the ruins, they're lovely this time of year' bullshit was just the bait to get us out there. Now I want to know why!" He reined in the urge to throttle the guy. He wouldn't let it be Brother Malchus again.

"I s-s-swear — I don't know anything." The young Tok'ra was visibly shaking now. Good. Let him be scared, the lying little sonofa —

Jack didn't see Daniel until he was practically between him and the simpering little snake head.

"Jack —" Daniel was pleading in his best diplomatic voice. Jack scowled at him too.

"This was a set-up, Daniel. Right from the start. I told you we couldn't trust them."

"The Tok'ra are not responsible," whimpered Jenmar, taking a half step back to give Daniel more space, and taking advantage of Daniel's size to partially hide behind him.

"Jack, listen." Daniel's palms were up. "If he was behind this — if he set us up — then why would he be here with us? He was knocked out right along with the rest of us. He swears he didn't do this, Jack. I believe him."

"Sir —"

The 'I found something' tone of Carter's voice aborted Jack's response to Daniel. Right. There were more pressing issues than how they'd gotten here. He wasn't done with the Tok'ra, but it could wait until later.

"What is it?" He glared at both Daniel and Jenmar for good measure before turning around to look for Carter. Jack could barely make her out in the shadows.

"I think you'll want to see this."

"Whatcha got?" When he reached her, Carter was pointing downward, scuffing the dirt with her boot. It took some effort to see what she was showing him, but finally he saw it: a faint and definitely metallic arc inlaid into the floor.

Rings.

"Well, that would explain why there appears to be no way in or out," said Daniel, coming to look too.

"I'm guessing there's no panel around here that's going to let us use them?" Jack figured there wasn't, but he felt compelled to ask anyway.

"If this is indeed a prison, then you are correct, O'Neill. We will find no means to activate the rings from within this cavern."

Jack automatically looked to Carter. It was almost Pavlovian, after all these years. About now was when she usually came up with some brilliant solution to get them out of here. She glanced up and caught him staring at her. Damn. He hadn't meant for that to happen.

"Sorry, sir. I'm afraid I don't have any answers either."

"Didn't expect you to, Major." He'd meant to let her off the hook, but by the crestfallen look on Carter's face, not to mention the glare he was getting from Daniel, apparently it hadn't come across that way.

Jack looked back down at the rings. "At least now we know where the front door is."

"Which gets us what, exactly?" Daniel frowned.

"I don't know, Daniel. Someplace to lay out the welcome mat." He hated not knowing what was going on. It made him irritable. So did this damn headache.

"Everybody just—" Jack waved them away from the rings. "Go see if you can find a panel somewhere." He cut off Teal'c before he could speak. "I know. There probably isn't one. But humor me."

Jack watched them scatter. The odds of success weren't great. Zero, in fact. But it sure as hell beat sitting around waiting for the next damn shoe to drop — or his head to explode. Whichever came first.

The others had regrouped in the center of the cavern by the time Sam joined them. She'd made one more pass around the perimeter, but hadn't found a thing. Of course, without even so much as a flashlight it was possible she could have missed a well camouflaged panel. But she tended to agree with Teal'c. They were trapped in this place until someone decided to ring them out.

"The good news is that they obviously didn't put us in here with the intention of killing us," Daniel pointed out. "They could have done that easily enough on the surface."

"Well, *that* certainly brightens my day." The colonel was making no attempt to conceal his bad humor. Sam avoided looking at him. His earlier remark still stung — as if she really needed further proof that he'd lost confidence in her. It wasn't as if she wasn't trying to figure a way out.

If only her head would stop pounding. It was hard to think around the pulsating, red mass of pain that made her brain feel like it was about to be split in half. She was usually pretty good at ignoring physical discomfort, but, as far as headaches went, this was off the scale.

It didn't help, knowing the rest of them were waiting for her to conjure up some kind of brilliant idea. Sam could feel herself tensing, defensively. What did they expect, after all? It wasn't like she could make a control panel appear out of thin air.

"I guess all we can do is wait," she said finally, watching

as their faces registered disappointment. Well, Daniel's and Teal'c's, anyway. She still wasn't looking at the colonel.

"So it would seem." There was a hint of resignation in Teal'c's voice. He adjusted his stance as if he intended to remain in that pose for quite some time.

Out of the corner of her eye Sam saw the colonel shove his hands deep into his pockets and let out an exaggerated sigh.

"Awww, Hammond'll be looking for us by now. We're way past due. I think." His hand covered the empty place on his wrist where his watch had been.

"Who's to say we're even on the same planet?" Daniel observed. "We were unconscious for a long time; at least it feels that way." His brow furrowed in concentration. Or maybe it was pain. "Much too long for it to have been just a zat."

Sam hadn't considered that before, but Daniel was right. And it would explain the headache. "You think we were drugged?"

Daniel shrugged. "I don't know, Sam. But I think we all felt pretty awful when we woke up. If it was only a zat, then it certainly wasn't any ordinary one."

That was true. And it made sense. They'd all taken plenty of zat hits in their time and none had incapacitated them as long as this one obviously had. If whoever captured them had used the Stargate, or had a ship in orbit, who knew where they could be this many hours later?

Her head throbbed all the more, just thinking about it. Sam couldn't help herself — she pinched the bridge of her nose, trying to make it stop.

"Carter?"

Apparently her gesture hadn't gone unnoticed.

"Sorry, sir." She didn't mean to wince, but just moving her eyes in the colonel's direction sent waves of pain rippling through her head. "Still have a bit of a headache."

"You too?" He cocked one eyebrow at her, but his tone was surprisingly sympathetic.

"Me three." Daniel, raising a finger to be counted.

"As have I." This from Teal'c, who had never remarked on pain in the four and a half years Sam had known him.

They all turned toward Jenmar, who was standing a little apart. He looked up, suddenly aware of their attention.

"What?" He looked expectantly from one to the other.

"Are you experiencing any physical discomfort in your head?" Teal'c asked.

"You mean a headache?" He hesitated. "Well, maybe — just a little."

"Oh trust me," the colonel snapped. "If you had one of these babies, there wouldn't be anything 'little' about it." He rubbed the heel of his hand against his own temple and grimaced. "Drugs, you say?" The colonel had directed the question at her.

"It's just a guess, sir."

"Oh, hello —"

All eyes turned toward Daniel. He was examining something on his fingertips. Before Sam could ask, he reached his hand back behind his left ear and brought it out again. In the dim light she could see there was discoloration. It was blood.

"Daniel, let me see." She found the spot on his head easily. There was no wound per se, but a patch of reddened scalp and some blood-matted hair testified that something round had punctured the skin.

Sam pushed her hair aside and probed behind her own left ear. Her fingers touched a tender spot and she winced as it shot more arrows of pain through her head. She felt dampness in her hair and when she pulled her hand away found the same faint traces of blood.

"Sir —" But the colonel and Teal'c were way ahead of her, both of them displaying fingers smeared with drying blood from their scalps.

"Well, that can't be good," Daniel observed dryly. He tensed suddenly. "And neither can that."

They all felt it now. A familiar hum was reverberating off

the stone walls. Behind them, a sudden column of bright light pierced the darkness.

The rings.

Sam reached reflexively for her weapon and saw the colonel do the same. They both came up empty. She could practically see her own mental curse mirrored in the colonel's dangerous, dark look.

Within the hazy glow of the hovering rings, two humanoid females appeared. Both were dressed in long white robes adorned with only a single sash. Despite their understated wardrobe, there was an unmistakable air about them, even if Sam hadn't already begun to sense the presence of their symbiotes.

They were Goa'uld.

As soon as the rings vanished, the chamber was plunged once more into twilight. But only for a moment. Before Sam's eyes could re-adjust, the taller of the two women touched her bracelet and the anemic torchlight flared into a steady, high flame.

With unconcerned casualness, both women stepped forward. There was no mistaking that the one with the bracelet was in charge. The shorter woman followed in her wake.

Beside her, Sam felt the colonel tense. She was sure he'd been expecting something like this all along.

The first woman surveyed them with a self-satisfied smile.

"SG-1." The name rolled off her tongue with a slight accent, but to Sam's surprise, her voice was normal. Maybe they were Tok'ra. "How nice to finally meet you. I feel as though I know each of you so very, very well."

Before anyone could reply, the woman stepped in front of Teal'c. She was tall enough to practically look him in the eye.

"Teal'c, of Chulak. Father of Rya'c. Student of Bra'tac. Former First Prime of Apophis. Loyal now to the Tau'ri. Welcome." She bowed slightly before moving on to Daniel.

"Dr. Daniel Jackson. Husband of Sha're of Abydos. Archeologist, linguist and foremost expert on Earth's ancient past."

"Well, I wouldn't exactly say that," Daniel muttered, half under his breath.

The woman was bowing again. "Welcome."

Sam was next. She felt herself stiffen. In spite of the fact that this seemed to be proceeding in a congenial manner, appearances could be deceiving. She could sense the colonel's unease mirroring hers. The woman, however, smiled pleasantly. Sam saw that there had once been a kind of beauty there, but it had faded long ago.

"Major Samantha Carter," the woman continued. "Daughter of Jacob Carter, host to Selmak. Air Force officer. Brilliant astrophysicist. Yourself once host to Jolinar of Malkshur." She bowed once more. "Welcome."

Sam said nothing. It was obvious the woman had at least a little intel on each of them. She wondered if it was mostly for show, or if it ran deeper than that. She watched as the woman moved on to the colonel.

He cocked his head at her, one eyebrow raised, expectantly. Her smile broadened.

"Colonel Jack O'Neill. Formerly husband to Sara and father to Charlie." The colonel's face went stony at the mention of his son. "Air Force Special Forces. Conqueror of Ra. Destroyer of Apophis. Friend of the Asgard. Leader of SG-1. Welcome."

Sam cringed as the woman spoke. So maybe it was more than a *little* intel. She glanced worriedly at the colonel.

"And you are —?" he asked icily and without preamble.

The woman stepped back and surveyed all of them once more.

"I am NebtHet a'Eshe. This is Aset a'Teneb. We have come to welcome you to Duat."

"Duat," repeated Daniel. Sam could tell the name had some meaning for him.

"Daniel?" The colonel beat her to the question.

"Duat." Sam could practically see Daniel processing the facts in his head in order to explain them coherently. "In Egyptian mythology, it was a place where the gods dwelt. Sort of like the Greek's Olympus, except that the Egyptians believed that it was actually, physically located under the earth." Sam saw him study NebtHet a moment before he continued, more slowly and thoughtfully. "Duat was also the underworld, a treacherous place that those who died had to journey through in order to reach the Hall of the Two Truths, where they would have their heart weighed to see if they were worthy of entering the Afterlife."

"I thought that was Ne'tu?" The colonel frowned.

Daniel shook his head. "Ne'tu was eternal damnation. Duat was the place they had to survive long enough to reach final judgment." Daniel pushed his glasses back up his nose. "The Egyptians believed that a spiritual representation of their physical body — what they called the *Ka* — remained behind in the tomb, while the *Ba* — which they considered to be like a soul — traversed through the perilous underworld on its way to the Final Judgment. Assuming it was successful, the Ka and the Ba would be reunited and become an *Akh*."

"A what?" The colonel's brow furrowed even deeper.

"An *Akh*. It —" Daniel sighed. "Never mind." He turned back to NebtHet. "Duat is also the realm of Osiris, isn't it? Is she — he, whatever — the one who's behind this?"

"You are indeed well versed in your mythology, Dr. Jackson," replied NebtHet, her admiration, or at least some well-acted admiration, for Daniel quite obvious. "And no. Osiris has no place here. None of his kind do."

Sam couldn't help but wonder what exactly NebtHet meant by that, especially given the edge of disdain in her voice.

"But you were right about one thing," NebtHet continued. "Duat is indeed the underworld. And you each have a journey to make here."

Something about the way she said it made Sam shiver. There was a look of keen anticipation on NebtHet's face as she added, "It is time, now, for you to begin."

Her moves were smooth and swift. Sam didn't even see the

zat until its blast struck Teal'c full in the chest. Aset had drawn a zat as well and fired seconds after NebtHet. Teal'c dropped to his knees and sank to the floor.

He was dead.

Sam barely processed what was happening. It was devastatingly fast, yet excruciatingly slow. She heard the colonel roar in rage and lunge at the two women, but he seemed held back by something. Sam vaguely registered that Jenmar was restraining him.

In horror, she watched NebtHet turn her zat on Daniel. Aset followed and Sam saw her friend fall, just as Teal'c had done. The colonel, still struggling to break free from Jenmar, swore violently. Something in Sam ignited. Fury. Grief. Fear. She dove for NebtHet herself.

The first zat blast caught Sam in the midsection. The too familiar sensation of having touched a high voltage wire shuddered through her. She barely felt the second shot when it hit. For the briefest moment she thought she heard the colonel cry out in anguish.

And then — nothing.

When the second zat turned toward him, Jack felt only relief. Teal'c. Daniel. Carter. Hell. He was already dead. Dying would just be a technicality.

Aset fired.

He hardly felt a thing.

CHAPTER THREE

"YOU MEAN to tell me, the Tok'ra are *not* the ones responsible for our people being on that planet?" Hammond looked back and forth between the two individuals who sat across from each other at the conference table. Both wore the same schooled expression that every Tok'ra he had ever encountered, save for Jacob Carter, seemed to have perfected. It made it hard to get a read on them, which perhaps explained why Jack never trusted them much.

"*I assure you, General, we are not.*" Anise's tone was defensive, as usual.

"The planet of which you speak would never have been considered for a Tok'ra base, as it is inhabited," Aldwin clarified.

Hammond's message to the Tok'ra that Jenmar had gone missing on P4C-679, along with SG-1, had resulted in the swift arrival of Aldwin and Anise. He wished Jacob had been available, but apparently Major Carter's father was deeply embedded in Goa'uld territory and unreachable.

So he was left with these two. Anise he was only too familiar with, although he had not seen her since the tragic events surrounding the death of Martouf. Aldwin, he knew only by reputation. 'Rigid' was the word he believe Teal'c had used to describe him in a report. They were quite the pair.

For the moment, however, they were the only pair he had. Hammond resisted the urge to sigh, but he did clasp his hands even more tightly on the table in front of him.

"And what about the Ancient technology that's there?" he asked. The two of them shared puzzled glances, which, as far as Hammond could tell, seemed genuine. It was Anise who finally made the connection.

"*Perhaps you are referring to the Dome of Anu?*"

The look of confusion resolved on Aldwin's face too.

"The Dome of Anu?" repeated Hammond.

"On Teranu — what you designate P4C-679 — there are ruins of what once was a planetary mapping station," Aldwin explained. "It contained a device of the Ancients that no longer functions. Years ago our scientists speculated that it perhaps was designed to chart the stellar drift as part of the mechanism for updating the coordinates of the Stargates. It was deemed insignificant and no further attention was given to it. Perhaps it is of this which you speak?"

It certainly sounded like it, based on Jack's report. But the rest of the story did not match what Jenmar had told them. Hammond told them as much.

"Jenmar would most certainly have had access to our records about Teranu. But why he would think the device or the ruins worth further exploration, I cannot begin to say," Anise replied.

"Did you not think to question his motive?" Aldwin asked, disingenuously. Hammond stifled a harrumph and refrained from pointing out that when it came to the Tok'ra, their motives were always in question. Somehow he did not think such a response would benefit the present discussion.

"As he was your liaison, we had no reason to," he replied instead. "We took a recommendation from the Tok'ra at face value. Something which, in retrospect, was ill-advised." He didn't get the sense that either of them had gotten his subtle jibe. Jack was right. They did have an innate arrogance that allowed them to shed responsibility like a duck did rain.

"We regret that yet another *Tok'ra life has been lost."* Anise's accusatory tone matched her glare. She closed her eyes for a moment and when she opened them her face softened. "And we offer our condolences on the loss of your people, General. I, for one, was very fond of the members of SG-1." Freya spoke this time. She sounded sincere.

"That's jumping the gun a little, I think." Hammond didn't bother to hide his irritation. "We still haven't drawn any final conclusions as to what might have happened on that planet. That's why you're here. We need your help."

"I'm not sure how we can assist you," Aldwin glanced at Anise. "At the moment our resources are extremely limited. All of our efforts are committed to establishing the base at Revanna as quickly as possible."

"Then how about just some good, old-fashioned intel on this 'Dome of Anu'. Do you have any idea why the Goa'uld might be seeking it? Or want to destroy it?" There was always a possibility that what had happened to SG-1 simply might have been an instance of bad luck and bad timing. Deep in his gut, though, Hammond didn't think so.

"As we have said, General." There was an edge of impatience to Aldwin's voice. "It is a place of no consequence. If or why the Goa'uld might have taken an interest in it, we do not know."

"And what about this Jenmar? Why would he want to send SG-1 there?"

"I cannot say. There are none among the Tok'ra who know Jenmar well. He has always kept to himself — even more so since his blending with Keyleb." Freya exchanged an odd glance with Aldwin and added, "I truly am sorry, General. I am afraid there is very little we can do to assist you in finding a motive behind Jenmar's actions, if indeed he is responsible for this."

Hammond sat back in his chair and studied them both. His instincts told him they were holding something back, but he wasn't sure what. He'd just have to dig a little deeper — and push the right buttons.

"I'm fairly sure you're not going to like what I'm about to request," he said in preamble. "But I should warn you that if I don't get your cooperation, I am willing to go as high up the ladder as it takes to get what I need."

"*What is it you would ask of us, General?*" Anise was back.

"Access," he replied. "To anything and everything Jenmar owned or worked on. He *is* responsible for my people going missing and I want to know why."

The two Tok'ra communicated silently through another exchange of looks before their mutual nods indicated they'd reached an agreement.

"Although, as you are aware, it is our policy not to share information with outsiders," began Aldwin.

"We agree that it is in the best interest of all concerned if we cooperate with you on this matter," finished Anise. *"If Jenmar had an agenda of his own, it would be beneficial to both of our peoples to discover what that may be."*

"And you'll share everything with the SGC," Hammond reiterated. He needed to make sure they were quite clear on that matter. Anise bowed her head slightly. When she raised it, it was Freya who spoke.

"You have our word, General. Everything."

Hammond nodded. Now they were finally getting somewhere.

"Good. Then we have a deal."

"Explain." NebtHet tried not to snap at Jenmar. What happened on Teranu had not been his fault, but this was a complication she had not anticipated. "How was it that you came under attack by the Goa'uld?"

She was half-way out of the hall before she realized he was not at her side. Instead he stood where she had ringed him out of the subterranean room, gaping at the pillars which rose high above them and taking in the morning light that bathed the chaapa'ai in a golden glow as if he'd never seen either before. Had he? Was this his first visit to Duat? That hardly seemed possible, but perhaps it was.

She felt she ought to know these things. He was her acolyte, after all. Today, however, was not the day to admire architecture. Hearing her call his name, Jenmar looked immediately penitent and hastened to catch up, trotting next to her long, purposeful strides. She repeated the question.

"I do not know," he answered, somewhat breathless from

keeping pace. "Their arrival was completely unexpected."

"I do not appreciate things which are unexpected. We have worked for millennia for this moment. Having the Goa'uld interfere, even tangentially, is troubling." She came to a sudden halt and studied Jenmar. "You must go back," she decided. "You must go back and learn everything you can about the attack. I need to know who they were and how it was they came by their information." She set her jaw resolutely. "I will not allow our last, best hope for ascension to be lost at the hands of the Goa'uld."

Jenmar was very still. He looked exceedingly pale in the bright sunlight. The Tok'ra and their tunnels: they were like rodents who never saw the light of day.

"Returning will be... difficult," he stammered. "I do not think I will find a welcome among either the Tok'ra or the Tau'ri, and certainly no help."

NebtHet dismissed his comment with a wave of her hand.

"I have no doubt you will be your usual resourceful self. I have complete trust in you, Jenmar. You have not failed me yet." She reached into the pocket of her robe and withdrew a small bronze sphere. She had brought it in case the rings in the dungeon had failed. They had not been used in many years.

"Take this." She placed the communication orb into his outstretched hand. "When you have news, contact me."

Jenmar looked as if he wanted to speak but changed his mind. He bowed instead, and hurried back through the portico toward the hall of the chaapa'ai. NebtHet paused to watch him go.

Perhaps she had been a bit abrupt with him. The truth was, she could not have gotten this far without his assistance.

When Jenmar had sought her out, seeking to join the Djedu, she had been hesitant. There had been no novices to the order for centuries. But his earnestness had been compelling and his position among the Tok'ra too strategic an opportunity for her to pass up. Without him, she never would have learned of the advancements of the Tau'ri and the potential of SG-1.

And she wouldn't be here now, on the threshold of revelation.

She owed him much more than even he, perhaps, realized. And when the time came, she would gratefully pay that debt.

The sun was warm on her face as it dipped low behind the Great Hall. For a moment she closed her eyes and tilted her head so that its rays completely enveloped her. Three thousand years of expectations had brought them to this one, single moment. It was impossible not to feel the magnitude of it.

Now it would truly begin.

NebtHet took a deep and steadying breath.

The time had come for her to awaken the dead.

Jenmar all but staggered back into the chamber of the chaapa'ai. Whatever beauty it had held for him mere moments before was lost now. He leaned against one of the great pillars and stared at the orb in his hand.

NebtHet wanted him to go back. Back to the Tok'ra and the Tau'ri in search of answers. How could she ask such a thing, after all he had done? Did she not comprehend what his fate would be? By now his role in the disappearance of SG-1 surely would have been suspected. The only thing that awaited him back on Revanna was questioning and incarceration. Perhaps they would even hand him over to the Tau'ri. He had heard of their dungeons. Underground places, where sunlight was forbidden. He would be left forever in the dark and cold — as he had been on Wasir, before help came.

He had risked everything for NebtHet. Believed in her. Followed her. All he ever wanted was peace. An escape from the turmoil of this life. A transcendent path where there were no dark places, no pain, no loss. The Djedu had been his salvation. Their quest was his quest. He longed only to join them.

"How fares our spy today?"

Jenmar had not heard Aset approach. She must have been lying in wait for him in the shadowy corners of the vast hall.

He slipped the orb into his pocket, out of sight.

"Hmmm." She eyed him critically. "You appear troubled, Jenmar. Has NebtHet said something to distress you?"

He could not hold it in. "I am to return to Revanna. She wishes me to discover who was behind the attack on Teranu."

There was a strange glimmer in her eyes. "I hardly think you will be welcomed with open arms by the Tok'ra."

Finally. Someone who understood.

"I fear this is true."

"Then why go?"

Jenmar bowed his head. "Because I am sent."

Aset shrugged. "Why not refuse?" She leaned in closer. "Is it because you fear NebtHet will deny you the great secret of ascension once she has discovered it from the Tau'ri?"

Jenmar's shoulders drooped. "My Lady Aset knows I have never secured such a promise, although I live in hope."

Aset laughed out loud. It echoed through the hall. A few passing Djedu turned their heads.

"Hope, Jenmar, is for those who are too timid to take command of their own fate." She lowered her voice, conspiratorially. "Besides. It's quite the fool's errand, isn't it? Since I already know who was behind the attack."

Jenmar looked at her in gratitude. If she had this information, then he would not have to leave.

"We must inform NebtHet!"

Aset narrowed her eyes. "We could," she mused languidly. "And would that lessen the sting of her betrayal? Would it take away the brutal fact that she has not only used you to make this experiment possible in the first place, but now wishes to send you back to the very people you betrayed in her name?"

Every word Aset spoke hit its mark. She had given voice to what burned within him. NebtHet had betrayed him, nothing less. Resentment replaced dismay.

"And do you think," Aset continued, when he made no reply, "having tried to be rid of you this way, and failing, NebtHet will proceed to share her secrets with one she obviously deems unworthy?"

He knew it would not be so. NebtHet had revealed her true self. To her, he was only a means to an end. How had he ever allowed himself to believe she would help him ascend? His hope had indeed blinded him.

"I will tell you no lies, Jenmar. I will share with you the secret of who attacked the Tau'ri on Teranu." Aset leaned closer to him. "I know you, Jenmar *a'Keyleb*." She whispered his full Djedu name in his ear. "I know why you sought out the Djedu, what you seek in ascension. And I tell you this: NebtHet's plan will fail. This is her last, desperate grasp to attain the unattainable." She walked behind him and leaned in toward his other ear. "The Tau'ri have no answers for her. But that doesn't mean they cannot yet help us — you and I, and those who understand that the peace you seek comes not from transcending to another plane of existence, but by assuring an end to the constant conflict on this one." Aset stepped back, offering him a knowing smile. "It doesn't mean running away from who we are, but embracing it — and assuring the success of one mighty enough to bring a final and enduring peace to the entire galaxy."

Jenmar flinched. "You mean, a Goa'uld."

"A peacemaker," Aset insisted. "More powerful than any System Lord. When he comes to rule, I assure you, there will be no more wars. No more fighting. There will be peace — the very peace you are so longing for."

Peace at the hands of a Goa'uld? The part of Jenmar that had been Tok'ra his whole life rejected such an idea.

But perhaps this was the best he could hope for. And if no planet ever again suffered the fate of Wasir, if no more Tok'ra perished fighting a battle that could never be won, then maybe that was not a bad second choice after all.

Jenmar straightened his back. "What must I do?"

"It's quite simple, really." Aset smiled. "Make a delivery to an old friend."

She pulled a small wooden box from her sleeve and handed it to him. "This is a gift. Tell him it is a token of my good faith." From a pocket she pulled a blue data crystal and held it up. "This contains my request." From her other pocket she brought out a clear crystal. "If his master agrees to grant my request, then you may give him this." Before he could take it from her hands, she pulled it back. "If he refuses, you are to destroy this. Is that clear?"

Jenmar nodded.

"I would do this myself, of course, but NebtHet has enrolled me in her little drama. So I am counting on you to be my wise and cunning representative."

Jenmar accepted the box and slipped the crystals into his pocket with the orb. "Who is this old friend I am to visit?"

He did not find Aset's smile reassuring.

"Oh, I think you will be in for quite the surprise."

The planet was too warm for Jenmar's liking. The heat and humidity pulled at his lungs the moment he stepped through the chaapa'ai. Neither did he enjoy the sight of a half-dozen staff weapons pointed directly at him. Still holding the small box, he raised his arms.

"I have been sent by Aset," he called out. "My name is Jenmar. Tell Tanith I am here."

CHAPTER FOUR

THE FIRST sensation of which Teal'c became aware was the hardness of the surface on which he lay. It pressed against his back without yielding and was solid beneath his head. It was also cold. He felt as if all the warmth from his body had leeched into it, as though it were sponge made of solid rock.

Rock. Now he recognized it. And with recognition came memory. A cavern. A Goa'uld. A zat'nik'tel. And pain. The pain of death. Because there had not been one zat'nik'tel, but two. And he had died.

Or not.

Cautiously he pushed himself up into a sitting position. His attire was unfamiliar to him. He wore thin linen pants and a tunic and upon his feet were strapped leather sandals. Little wonder he had felt the dampness so acutely.

The stone slab he had been laying on was in the middle of a large, empty room with a single arched doorway. Surrounding him were walls of great hewn stones. Their smoothness and precision showed evidence of having been fit together by master hands. Teal'c had seen such craftsmanship before. The palaces of the System Lords were similarly built, with the sweat and blood of many Jaffa slaves.

Teal'c tried standing. The room swayed for a moment but then righted itself. He did not recognize this place, although there was very little to distinguish one Goa'uld prison from another. But was it a prison? The archway marked the only way out, but he could see no door or bars to keep him from leaving. Perhaps there was a force shield.

He approached the opening cautiously. He could discern no ripple in the air, hear no thrumming of any energy. A temperate breeze brushed by him, unimpeded, and he caught the faint scent of fresh air and greenery.

Through the opening Teal'c saw only forest and brush and a single path that led from the doorway into a thicket. There was nothing to prevent him from leaving and no one else was in sight.

Neither was there any sign of O'Neill and the others.

The vaguely unsettling memory of dying returned. Perhaps the rest of SG-1 had met a similar fate. Yet he did not appear to be dead. All aspects of his physiology seemed as it had been before, including the presence of his symbiote, content within its pouch. This was not death as he understood it.

At least, he did not think so.

Teal'c's eyes rested on a long, thin object leaning against the wall in the shadows. He recognized it at once. It was his staff weapon. Teal'c eyed it suspiciously. Why would his captors return his weapon to him? It was most strange, unless —

Careful of a booby-trap, Teal'c hefted the staff. In weight and balance it felt as it should, and when he activated it he heard the thrum of its power at the precise frequency he knew was his. Examining it, he could discern no tampering. All was as it should be.

Nevertheless, it was peculiar to find it here.

On the ground, beside the weapon, was also a knapsack containing food and a skin filled with water. The food was nothing Teal'c recognized, but evidently was meant to be nutritious and an adequate substitution for more traditional meals. After sniffing the water, he drank a small amount. It had a pleasant, fresh taste.

The stone bier. His clothing. The tokens of food and water. The staff weapon — his most treasured possession. He understood, now, why there was no guard. He knew what this place was.

It was a burial chamber, similar to those used on Chulak by the ancestral Jaffa before the Rite of Burning had taken the place of entombment. But if this was Chulak, how had he come to be here? Had the others brought him here, presuming him dead?

Perhaps he was indeed dead, after all.

That would explain much. Would not his spirit long to return home, if given a choice? Was this his *calak's* journey through darkness to everlasting life?

There were no answers to be found in this tomb. If he wished to discover the truth, he had no choice but to follow the path into the forest. Either he would learn what had become of O'Neill and the others or he would endure the trials of the dead on his path to eternity.

Accepting the gifts of food and water, Teal'c grasped his staff weapon firmly in his hand and stepped through the doorway.

Whichever fate awaited him, he was prepared.

Daniel stood in the doorway, blinking into the blinding sunlight. He was relieved to leave the chamber and its claustrophobic air behind him. Even the sand-colored walls had been incapable of banishing the shadows which had reached out for him from its unfathomable corners. He had been reminded immediately of Abydos and the pyramid which housed the Stargate, except this was on a smaller scale — and without a Stargate.

Although the view might have fooled him. How many times had he stood atop the steps of the Abydonian pyramid and gazed across the endless stretch of sand and dunes, feeling the same dry wind and relentless sun? If he hadn't known better, he might have believed he stood there now.

Except, he did know better.

It just didn't *feel* like Abydos. He'd lived there long enough to recognize the subtle differences of air and gravity which separated it not only from Earth but from every other planet he'd visited. This was not Abydos. Although it was close. Very close.

If only he could sort out exactly what had happened. He was clearly alone. There was no sign of Jack or Sam or Teal'c anywhere. The small pyramid behind him could not have housed any other chambers besides his own. He had been the sole occupant of the tomb.

Tomb. That was exactly what it was like. Especially when he considered how he was presently dressed. The plain woven linen pants and tunic reminded him of ancient burial shrouds, and considering that he'd been laying on nothing less than a stone bier —

Perhaps someone had thought he was dead.

Or maybe he was.

NebtHet. Goddess of the Dead.

The full memory returned with searing clarity. Had he been shot twice? He had no memory of the second zat. But considering what they'd done to Teal'c, he could only assume he had.

Which meant that he ought to be dead. But if he was, this wasn't like any death he'd ever imagined.

Although if there was any place in the universe he would have considered close to a concept of heaven, it had been Abydos. At least, while Sha're had been alive.

Daniel corralled those thoughts before they could go any further. The last thing he needed was to open the door to those memories. It had taken him long enough to get to the point where thoughts of her didn't ambush him daily. He'd finally made an odd sort of peace with it. Knowing Shifu had helped. But he couldn't afford to go back there. He had to think clearly — rationally — and figure out what was going on here. What all of this meant.

Daniel scanned the horizon, looking for a sign of anything but the blowing sand. There was, he realized now, something of a pathway that began at the base of the steps and traveled up over a distant ridge. He hadn't noticed it before. Its visibility seemed to come and go with the shifting winds.

The way did not look particularly inviting, but it wasn't as if he had any other options. He had already scoured the walls of the chamber behind him and found nothing there to enlighten him. If it was a tomb, it was a fairly austere one. The custom in

Ancient Egypt had been to bury the dead with their worldly possessions, or at the very least, symbolic representations of them, to assure their comfortable journey to the Afterlife. However, the only contents of this tomb, aside from himself, had been a small knapsack, filled with some sort of food, a full canteen of water and — this was the odd thing — his own small, leather-bound notebook.

"Not exactly a pharaoh's treasure," he muttered aloud, retrieving the paltry assortment of belongings.

He absently rifled through the pages of his journal before stowing it in the knapsack. Wishing that whomever had thought to pack for him had also included his hat, Daniel took one last, quick glance over his shoulder into the darkness behind him and a cold shiver ran down his spine.

Maybe he really was dead. Maybe this was some whole other level of existence.

And maybe he just didn't have a clue what he was talking about.

"A journey of a thousand miles," he mused. Okay. So maybe he was mixing cultures, but some truths were universal.

With a dubious glance at the distant ridge and only the briefest hesitation, Daniel took the first step.

"You've got to be kidding me."

Sam's voice blew back at her on the harsh wind that swirled snow like brittle needles against her face.

It was a blizzard.

No wonder she'd been half-frozen when she woke up. Especially considering that she was dressed in only the thinnest of linen pants and top. Exactly how she'd come to be wearing them, Sam really didn't want to think about. Better to focus on more immediate problems. Like getting out of the doorway and back into the comparative warmth of the inner chamber, even if it was as gloomy as a mausoleum. Not even its polished white, marble walls could dispel the intrinsic desolation of the place.

Shivering, Sam retreated to the low, stone platform in the center of the room. As much as she disliked the idea, staying put for the time being was her only viable option. She'd be dead in a matter of minutes if she went outside. Not that her prospects in here were necessarily much better. She might not be as exposed to the elements, but it was only a matter of time before hypothermia set in. She was just postponing the inevitable.

Which made no sense to her whatsoever. Because if whoever, or whatever, had put her here wanted to kill her, then why not just leave her dead in the first place?

At least, she was fairly sure she'd been dead. The Goa'uld had killed Teal'c and Daniel so swiftly, she'd barely grasped what was happening before the zats had turned toward her. She had a vague recollection of a distant, anguished shout, and then nothing. Until she woke up here, alone.

But if she had been revived, maybe the rest of the team had too. All it would have taken was a sarcophagus. Not that she much liked the thought of having been inside one of those things, but still, it was better than the alternative. Of course there was the grim possibility that they had only revived *her*, but she refused to consider that for more than a heartbeat. It was better to stay positive.

Granted, that would be a lot easier to do if she weren't freezing, or if whoever had brought her here had given her some decent clothes. They had left a knapsack, but the only useful thing inside it, besides some food and water, was her scanner, which worked, except for a curious malfunction in the date and time mode. No amount of fiddling with it would give her anything but the same error message. She had no way of telling how long it had been since they'd left the SGC. It could have been hours or days — maybe even weeks, if they'd been keeping her drugged. But why? All she had were questions, with no hint of an answer in sight.

A gust of wind swirled an eddy of snow through the open doorway and into the corner of the chamber. The mystery of why she was here would have to wait. Basic survival came first and what she needed most right now was a fire. Outside the tomb were any number of trees, half-buried in the snow. With no little effort she could probably find some fallen branches that were relatively dry for fuel. Igniting them, however, was another matter.

Sam turned the scanner over in her hand. If she could manage to pry open the back she could access its inner circuitry. A few crossed wires and, if she were very lucky, she'd get a spark or two. As long as there was some dry tinder around —

Linen. It was dry. And a natural fiber. It would burn easily.

Sam plucked at a few stray strands of the fabric on her pants until one unraveled. Before long she had a small pile of threads which she carefully tucked into the knapsack to keep them from blowing away.

Unfortunately, that was the easy part.

The only means of getting inside the scanner was to break it open against the marble slab. She hated doing it. It meant giving up the only piece of technology she had and she couldn't shake the feeling that she'd come to regret it later. Still. Technology wasn't going to do her any good if she froze to death. It was a necessary sacrifice.

Her arm was in mid-swing when she stopped. She just couldn't. Not yet. The catalyst, after all, was the very last thing she needed. There was no point in destroying the device until she was sure she had wood dry enough to burn.

Which meant going out to search for fuel. In the snow. In her thin clothes.

Her body recoiled at the thought. She'd had enough bad experiences with snow and ice. Just once it would be nice to get stranded on a tropical island.

Sam sighed. That was the colonel's line. She could almost hear him in her head, grumbling good-humoredly. That is, when he used to be good-humored. But for some reason he had changed in the past few months, especially toward her.

Now she felt like she was treading on egg-shells every time she was around him.

She missed how it used to be between them. The colonel never hung out in her lab between missions anymore, or joined her for meals or, for that matter, talked to her about anything other than work. If even that. And certainly whatever feelings they had agreed to keep in the room during the za'tarc testing no longer seemed to exist. At least, not on the colonel's part.

Sam took a deep breath. Going down that road wasn't going to get her anywhere. She needed to focus, to make a plan. The simple fact was, she needed to go out into the cold if she were to have any hope of surviving. And she needed to survive if she was to find out what had happened to the rest of her team. Staying on task was crucial. She could not let her feelings get the better of her.

With determination, Sam returned to the doorway. The wind had changed direction and seemed to have lessened in intensity. If there ever was a time to act, this was probably it.

"Right," she said aloud, taking a deep breath. She could already feel the sharp wind slicing through her thin garments. Her sandaled feet were nearly numb. Would it have killed them to at least given her a real pair of pants and some shoes?

Fueled by the warmth of her irritation, Sam stepped out the door and into the full force of the wind. She figured she had ten minutes, tops, before frostbite set in.

Time to start the clock — if only she had one.

"One-one-thousand," she muttered to herself and lunged forward into the snow.

"Carter?"

Jack half expected to hear her voice, his usual lifeline to consciousness. It was only when his brain finally kicked in that he actually remembered.

There'd be no answering "Sir." Not now. Not ever.

And no Teal'c. And no Daniel.

Maybe consciousness wasn't all it was cracked up to be after all. Being dead had been a whole lot easier. Living was what hurt like hell.

Jack lay there and let it. What was the point in getting up, after all? He'd already tried that. The room had spun a few dozen times and then he'd hit the floor. That had been some time ago, judging by the dried blood that was crusted on his upper lip. He had no desire to repeat the process.

In spite of himself, however, he opened his eyes. A black cylinder was pointed right at his nose. The barrel of a P90.

Crap.

With more energy that he'd thought he could muster, Jack rolled out of its way and into a defensive crouch. He'd been right, it was a P90. In fact, it was *his* P90 — he could see that now — resting on the floor next to him. There was the telltale scratch from when he'd used it to fend off some over-zealous, knife-wielding Jaffa a few months back. Siler had wanted to fix it, but Jack had said no. There was nothing like a visual reminder of one's own mortality to keep a guy on his toes.

Too bad he hadn't remembered that earlier. He should have ordered his team back to the gate instead of giving in to Daniel's whining and Carter's technology fetish. The job of protecting them was his and he'd screwed up. Again. The Goa'ulds might have pulled the triggers, but he'd put the weapon in their all too eager hands.

Jack eyed the P90 for a few moments before reaching for it. Next to it was some kind of backpack and a canteen, neither of which were his. But the gun was. Even without the evidence of the scratch, it had a more than familiar feel.

Ignoring his slightly protesting knee, Jack got to his feet. No spinning room this time, which was a start. He prodded the sack with the tip of his gun, but it seemed to be as advertised. Hooking the strap of the canteen, he lifted that next. Nothing happened. Either whoever had left them was the world's worst booby-trap setter, or the stuff was as benign as it appeared.

Since he was still in one piece, he'd go with the latter.

There was food in the backpack and water in the canteen. Seeing as how someone had gone to the trouble of leaving him with the bare essentials for survival, he figured the least he could do was to oblige them by getting the hell out of there.

Having emptied the contents of the sack on the ground to see what else it might hold — which was nothing — Jack squatted to repack it. He didn't even hear the footfall until a split second before a hand rested on his arm. The sensation of having been pricked by something sharp was forgotten a second later as he leapt to his feet to face this new threat.

Except —

He blinked.

"It's me, sir."

"Carter?"

She stood there. In flesh and blood. Alive. And smiling at him.

"Yes, sir."

Jack was suddenly light-headed, and happier than he had any right to be. He pushed aside the impulse to hug her and grasped her by the arm instead. She felt warm and solid beneath his fingers.

"But how?" Not that the details were important, only that she was there. "I thought you were dead."

The gigawatt smile faded into a sympathetic, almost pitying look. "I am, sir," she replied gently, her eyes locking onto his. "But then, you see, so are you."

CHAPTER FIVE

"I'M DEAD."

"Yes, sir."

He pointed at her. "And you're dead."

"Yes, sir." She sounded rather matter-of-fact about the whole thing. And here he thought he was the one who'd taken a blow to the head.

"No offense, Carter, but you look pretty damn healthy to me."

She shook her head. "I'm not sure how, Colonel, but I don't think this is really us." She closed her eyes for a moment as if sorting through her thoughts, and then opened them. "I mean, it's us, of course, but not us like we're used to being us."

Okay. Now she was starting to scare him. Cryptic wasn't Carter's usual M.O.

"Come again?" he said, eyeing her. She tried once more.

"Okay. It's almost as if the essence of who we are has somehow been manifested into a form that physically resembles how we used to be, so we're able to talk and walk and do everything we could do while we were alive. But I don't think these are our real bodies. In fact, I'm pretty sure they're not."

Jack touched the gash on his lip — the source of the dried blood — and winced. "Oh I don't know. Feels pretty real to me." He saw a bemused smile tug at her mouth as she half-shrugged.

"I don't pretend to completely understand it. But think, sir. You saw me die. We both saw Daniel and Teal'c zatted to death. Odds are, they killed you too. And yet, here we are."

That part, at least, he couldn't deny. Still. Carter getting all metaphysical on him? It was weird. Too weird. "Well, here some of us are, anyway." He looked around. "Where's Daniel? And Teal'c?"

She shook her head. "I have no idea. When I woke up, you were the only one here. But you were unconscious, so I checked outside. I didn't see any sign of them."

"And that's when you came up with this 'theory' about essences and stuff...?" He hated doubting her. It was like questioning whether the sun would rise each morning. But this stuff was way out there. He couldn't imagine even Daniel coming up with it.

"Well, it's not exactly *my* theory. Here, I'll show you."

Jack followed her to the doorway. Already he could hear the gentle patter of rain on leaves and the singular smell of wet vegetation. Sure enough, a steady drizzle was falling. A heavy fog obscured everything farther away than twenty meters, muffling both sight and sound. It was like being wrapped up in a thick, gray blanket.

"There."

She pointed at markings that had been engraved on a plaque on the exterior wall of the building. He looked at her askance.

"And you can read this?"

Carter nodded.

"So — what? Suddenly you're channeling Daniel?" He hadn't meant for it to come out quite so snide. Carter seemed not to notice.

"I can't explain it, sir. But when I look at it, I just — I don't know, I understand it. It's as plain as English."

Considering he'd once been capable of both writing and speaking Ancient — or so he'd been told — he wasn't exactly in a position to doubt her.

"Okay. In that case, what does it say?"

She reached out and ran her fingers over the text.

"*Oh you who sleep, awaken and send forth your soul. Fear not for the shell that remains above, for in its stead your Ba shall journey through the realm of the gods. Through Duat shall your shade journey unto the Hall of the Two Truths and upon the scales shall your deeds be measured. In Duat you will be tested and the truth of your heart laid bare."*

He couldn't help staring. He was used to Daniel spouting that kind of stuff. Not Carter.

"And that means —?"

"Well, it's pretty clear, I thought." She traced a line of symbols with her finger. *"Fear not for the shell that remains above —* that would be our physical bodies, I'm guessing. And this part about the *Ba* journeying in its stead — Daniel said that it was the *Ba* which undertook the trip through the underworld, and Duat is the name of the underworld. I recall NebtHet telling us that."

"And this is why you think we're, you know, dead?"

"It's the only thing that makes sense, sir."

Jack pretended to peruse the plaque to give himself time to think. He wasn't buying it. Carter foregoing a scientific explanation for a supernatural one? It just didn't feel right. None of this felt right. Especially when there was a much simpler explanation.

"Or, they could have used a sarcophagus. They're Goa'ulds, after all. I thought those things were practically standard issue."

He waited for her response, watching her mull over his suggestion. He could practically see the wheels turning in her head. That much, at least, was familiar.

"A sarcophagus does make more sense," she said finally, nodding thoughtfully. "I guess I hadn't thought about that, sir."

And there it was. A sarcophagus should have been the first thing Carter came up with, not some farfetched Ancient Egyptian mumbo jumbo. Sure, she'd been through a lot the past few months. Maybe she just wasn't completely back on her game, but this was *Carter*, for crying out loud. She was usually miles ahead of him, not running to catch up.

Those warning bells in the back of his head were really going off now.

Forcing levity he really didn't feel, Jack grinned. "Good. Then it's settled. We're *not* dead. I feel better already."

Her answering smile was hardly one of relief. If anything, she seemed a bit disconcerted. Something was definitely off with her. He'd only seen her this way once before. It had ended up with her eyes glowing and the damned snake in her head calling his name from behind a locked cell door.

Maybe he had good cause to worry.

"Come on," he said, brusquely. "Let's go." He would need to keep his eye on her, but, for now, they just needed to get out of here and find Daniel and Teal'c. As much as Jack knew it was probably a trap, there was really only one destination of choice.

"Go where, sir?"

Picking up the knapsack and handing her the canteen, Jack gestured toward the plaque. "Wherever it is whoever put us here obviously wants us to go — the Two Halls."

"The Hall of the Two Truths."

"Yeah. That. The sooner we get there, the sooner we figure out what the hell is going on." Not that he had any illusions that their journey would be straightforward. Someone had thought to leave him his P90, after all.

Jack paused to look up at the sky. The drizzle had turned into more of a mist, but he could still feel the dampness soaking into his joints. "Just once," he sighed. "Just once, I swear, it's gonna be a really nice tropical island."

At first he thought it was a mirage. Daniel had spent enough time in the desert to know that a combination of sun and shifting sands could create illusions that messed with one's head. And if that were the case, then his brain really was screwed up, because of all the millions of illusions it could possibly have concocted, this was the last one he ever would have thought of. Or wanted to think of, for that matter.

Except it wasn't in his head. It was real. As real as the last time he'd seen it. A lone tent in the middle of nowhere, its black-spired top rising high above its golden sides. At the four corners, banners of black and gold fluttered in the constant breeze as the late afternoon sun glinted off the standards atop the canopied entrance.

It was the tent of a queen.

The tent of Amaunet.

Funny how he remembered it so clearly. At the time it had hardly registered. But seeing it again — or, at least, something that looked like it — he knew it instantly. He had died there. Once. And also he'd begun to live again. Slowly. So maybe it wasn't too much of a stretch that he should find it here, of all places, where he'd died and yet, also, somehow seemed to live.

If that's what was happening to him. Which he still wasn't sure of quite yet.

Reaching the tent took longer than expected. He'd never been good at judging distances. Jack had long ago taken that privilege away from him on missions. Sam was the go-to person for figuring out how far it was between point A and point B. And Teal'c would have known precisely how long it would have taken to get there.

Daniel wondered if they were dead. Teal'c, he knew, had gone down, but what about Sam and Jack? Maybe they were already in the tent, waiting for him.

Alone, Daniel felt vulnerable. Trudging across the valley to the distant ridge he wondered how many pairs of eyes were following him, or how many staff weapons might be trained on him. When the others were with him, he rarely gave such things a second thought. It was odd being on his own like this. Almost like part of him was missing.

The sensation wasn't exactly new. He often felt like this, even when the others were around. Jack had been such an ass lately, it was having an impact on all of them. But it was more than that. Daniel had been feeling this way for quite some time, as though the others were heading in one direction and he in another. Like he was walking through a valley all alone, taking a path toward some unknown destiny.

An apt metaphor, given the circumstances. Or, come to think of it, were these circumstances the direct result of what he'd been feeling lately? Now there was a conundrum. If he was dead, was this all a creation of his own thoughts and fears and beliefs? Or was it completely serendipitous that he found himself in an actual, physical representation of exactly where his thoughts and emotions had been lately?

Frankly, it seemed too coincidental. And, for better or worse, he'd learned from Jack that anything that looked like it was a little too convenient, probably was.

Although that would mean he was dead, and part of him still wasn't ready to go there. Not without a little more evidence. Besides, it would most likely mean that the rest of his team were dead as well, and that surety was something he really did not want to deal with.

The woman standing beneath the striped canopy seemed to materialize from nowhere. Daniel had merely looked away for a moment and suddenly she was there. He was still too far away to see her face clearly, but it didn't stop his heart from lurching against his chest. The color of her hair, her slight build, and her flowing Abydonian robes: they were all he needed to tell him that what he'd hoped, or perhaps feared, was true. After all, if this were any sort of afterlife, she would be there.

"Sha're!" He ran toward her, his feet trying to find purchase in the soft sand. When she didn't turn around, he called her name again, but the wind only blew it back toward him. Determined, Daniel ran faster until he reached the crest of the hill and the place where she stood.

"Sha're!" he said again, panting with exhaustion. He touched her arm and she turned around, her own ringed hand covering his. Daniel felt a slight burning sensation but he barely noticed because the woman was not Sha're after all, but a stranger. Daniel stepped back, yanking his hand away.

"Who are you?" He had been so certain it was her, that to

discover it wasn't was like a physical blow.

She looked momentarily confused, but then stepped toward him, her hand outstretched. "It *is* I, Dan'yel. It is your Sha're."

He was about to deny it again, but the words died on his lips. It *was* her. He could see that now. How had he ever thought it wasn't?

Daniel pulled her into his arms and held her. How many times had he dreamed of this? Finding her this way, free from Amaunet? But, of course, she had been free, for a very long time now. And while part of him simply reveled in the joy of feeling her in his arms, another part of him couldn't help the dozen or so questions that peppered his thoughts.

He finally broke their embrace and stepped back, holding her by the arms so he could study her.

"Sha're, I don't understand. How is this possible?"

Her smile was as dazzling as he remembered and her eyes danced playfully, just as they had in that passionate year they'd shared before Apophis had come.

"It does not matter how, Dan'yel. All that matters is that you are here now." She wrapped her arms around his neck and kissed him. For a moment he let himself be lost in the sensation of her soft lips pressed against his. No one had ever made him feel the way Sha're had. She'd awakened in him aspects of himself he hadn't even known he possessed, or thought anyone, let alone a beautiful woman like her, would ever find appealing. Their life together would have been rich and full, had it just been given the chance.

But it hadn't. It had taken him a long time to come to terms with that. And while it sounded cliché, he had, with great effort, moved on at last. Sha're's Daniel was someone who no longer existed.

Gently he pulled away from her kiss and disengaged himself from her arms.

"Dan'yel?"

He tried to smile. "I'm sorry. It's just — I don't understand what's going on, how you're here like this." He indicated the tent. "I guess I just need a lot of questions answered first."

"What kind of questions? I am here. We are together at last. What more do you need to know?"

He remembered how her simple, straightforward view of the world had once been such a delight to him, like a breath of fresh air to his overcrowded, over-analytical mind. But he needed answers before he could just accept the premise of what lay before him.

"Well, first of all, where is here, exactly?"

"Here is… here." She shrugged, puzzled. "It is where I have been waiting for you. It is Duat."

"Duat," repeated Daniel. That's what NebtHet had said before she'd killed them. "The Egyptian underworld, the place through which the dead must travel to reach the final judgment."

He waited for her to contradict him, but Sha're merely gazed at him, as if expecting more.

"So, you're telling me I'm dead. That we're both dead."

"You already know I am dead, Dan'yel. You were there the day Teal'c killed this body and released my soul from the demon that possessed me."

"Yes, I know." Teal'c had done what he had to. Daniel had never blamed him for that. He was certain Sha're wouldn't have either. "But does this mean that I'm dead too?"

She smiled and reached her hand up to caress his face.

"I have waited long for my husband to join me in this place, so that we might journey together to the great Hall and stand side by side for our hearts to be weighed. If you are beside me now, then yes, Dan'yel, you are dead. But only to the world above. Here with me, you will live forever."

Sha're spoke with such conviction it was difficult not to believe her. Of course, the Abydonian belief system was rooted in Earth's Ancient Egyptian culture, so it would be natural for her to interpret whatever was going on here in that context. Whether it was actually true or not, well, maintaining a certain amount of skepticism on his part would probably be a good idea.

"What about Sam, Jack, and Teal'c? Are they dead too?"

Her look was sympathetic.

"I do not know what fate has befallen your friends, Dan'yel. I am sorry. If they too have died, then they will each have a separate journey to make. I am here only for you."

"I see." Actually, he didn't. Not completely, anyway. But he knew it was pointless to press Sha're too much.

"Come." She took his hand and pulled him toward the tent.

A moment of misgiving caused him to resist. "Why?" He wished he didn't feel like he barely knew the woman in front of him.

"Because I have prepared food and drink for you," she explained, plaintively. "And because there is shelter from the sun. We must make preparation for the journey ahead."

"The journey?"

Sha're's smile was patient. "I told you, Dan'yel. We must travel to the Hall of the Two Truths. It is a far distance. And I believe we may face many difficulties along the way."

Going by what he knew of Duat, 'difficulties' might well be an understatement. Daniel didn't necessarily care for their destination either; the Hall of the Two Truths was where one's worth was ultimately decided on the scales of Maat, the arbiter of Truth.

Daniel was liking the sound of this whole thing less and less.

Sha're misinterpreted his hesitation. "I know it has been a long time, Dan'yel, but surely you remember that a desert is best travelled in the cool of the night," she chided him gently. "We will start out once the sun has set. Until then, let us at least rest in the shade for a while."

Of course she was right. He'd already done the trudging through the sand in the heat of the day thing anyway. Travelling by night was certainly the sensible way to go.

If he went. Because he also knew *how* one's worth was determined in the Scale of Truth, and quite frankly he'd rather pass. Dead or not.

At the moment, however, his options seemed to be limited. Short of striking out on his own, going with Sha're really was his only choice.

She was waiting, her hand stretched out to take his.

With a reticence akin to picking a scab off an unhealed wound, Daniel reached out and took it, glad, at least, that there was as yet no scale nearby to reveal the heaviness of his heart.

CHAPTER SIX

TEAL'C had been tracking them for some time. Two individuals: one larger, the other smaller both in stature and weight. They moved at a steady, although unhurried pace, no more than a quarter hour ahead of him. They were not people he knew and most certainly they were not members of SG-1.

With minimal effort he could overtake them, but for now he was content to merely follow. As much as he desired answers to his many questions, Teal'c knew he must exercise caution in obtaining them. Until he could assess his situation more thoroughly, keeping a secure distance would be his most prudent choice. And perhaps whomever he followed would lead him to where the answers would become clear.

Distant voices brought Teal'c to an abrupt halt. He listened. Two people conversed, in all likelihood the same two he followed. Their voices did not fade, which meant they had stopped. Perhaps the time had come to learn more about them after all.

With great care, Teal'c advanced until the voices were nearly intelligible. The path took him around a towering, dense bush and into a wide clearing. Here a river flowed just a short distance away, and lofty trees cast tall, blue shadows along both banks. On the near shore, in those shadows, Teal'c's eyes finally found two men deep in conversation.

He knew they saw him the moment he emerged from the brush, but their body language registered neither surprise nor alarm. The smaller of the two remained seated, his features obscured by the shade, but the other individual stepped forward as Teal'c neared, a gauntleted hand reaching out in welcome. An errant piece of metal pricked Teal'c's forearm as the stranger grasped it.

"Did I not tell you, Rya'c, that he would come?" The stranger called over his shoulder to the other. To Teal'c, he said,

"*Tek'ma'te*, old friend. It is good to see you at last."

For a hairsbreadth of a moment, the shadows revealed a face Teal'c did not know. But then he blinked and saw, indeed, that it was Master Bra'tac standing before him, eyes warm with friendship and understanding.

"How is this possible?" Teal'c looked at the youth who had come to join them. It *was* Rya'c. He pulled the boy into an embrace. "I have missed you, my son."

"We have been waiting for you, Teal'c," Bra'tac said heartily. "Come. Sit." He gestured toward large boulders along the embankment. "There is much to discuss."

"What is this place?" Teal'c had too many questions to be able to sit just yet. "Are O'Neill and the others here as well?"

He saw Bra'tac and Rya'c exchange a furtive look.

"Teal'c, what I am about to tell you will be difficult to accept. But you must believe me when I tell you that I speak the truth."

Something in Bra'tac's voice made Teal'c's chest constrict. "I have never doubted your words, old friend."

"Then hear me, Teal'c, when I tell you that this is Duat, the underworld. The place where the dead must journey to meet their final judgment."

Teal'c allowed himself a moment to absorb Bra'tac's words. So it was as Daniel Jackson and the Goa'uld woman had said. Which meant, he was, indeed, dead.

But if he was dead, then —

Anguish gripped his heart as he looked with alarm at Rya'c and then back to Bra'tac. He knew by the look in his old friend's eyes that his worst fear was true.

Bra'tac and Rya'c were dead too.

"No —" He could not keep the grief from his voice. "Tell me, Bra'tac. Tell me that this is not true. My own death I can accept, but not you and Rya'c both."

Bra'tac smiled at him sadly.

"I am sorry, my friend, I have no solace to offer you, unless it is that we are now on this journey together."

"How?" It was the only word Teal'c could utter. Bra'tac was right. There was no comfort to be found in mere words. Rya'c had so much life yet to live, so many years awaiting him. It was impossible to think it had been taken from him this soon. Teal'c's heart broke at the thought of it.

"A powerful Goa'uld, I do not know who, attacked the planet where we had sought refuge. There was no warning, no opportunity to fight back. Many were killed where they stood. Very few, I think, survived."

"Drey'auc?"

"I am sorry, Teal'c, but I do not know her fate. She is not here. That is all I can say."

Anger churned within him. To target women and children — such an attack was the act of a coward. Yet he could not deny his own hand in this. Were it not for him and the cause for which he had so fervently fought —

Bra'tac must have read the self-loathing in his eyes. He reached out and put a steadying hand on Teal'c's arm. "Even if you had been there, Teal'c, there was nothing you could have done."

Teal'c looked at Rya'c. The boy looked somber and would not meet his eyes.

"Can you forgive me, my son?" His voice broke. "I never meant for any of this to befall you."

Rya'c looked up at him, traces of the little boy he had once been still evident on his adolescent face. "Then give me my life back, Father," he said, with just a hint of confrontation in his tone. "I'm not supposed to be here."

Teal'c turned to Bra'tac, confused. The old man nodded.

"What he says is true. Rya'c should not be here." He rested his hand on the boy's shoulder. "Since arriving here my eyes have been opened to a great many things, and I understand in ways I never dreamed possible. Do not ask me how, but I know, in my heart, that Rya'c's presence in Duat is a grave error. He still has many years of life remaining. He must not stay here. One of us needs to take him back."

Joy and confusion in equal measures overwhelmed Teal'c. His son's death was not meant to be, but how was he expected to be returned to life?

Bra'tac seemed to sense his bewilderment. "These are not questions I can answer at this time, Teal'c. They can only be discovered on the journey ahead."

"Father — please." His son's earnest voice was like an arrow through Teal'c's heart. He had always been willing to die for the boy. He would gladly face whatever lay ahead to give Rya'c back his life.

"You have my word, my son." Teal'c brought the boy into his embrace again. "I will do everything in my power to restore you to life."

The good news was that Sam had finally managed to find some moderately dry sticks and twigs beneath the sheltering limbs of a nearby tree. The bad news was that the wind had kicked up again, creating an absolute whiteout. If the mausoleum was nearby, Sam couldn't see it. She couldn't even follow her own footprints back. The wind had obliterated them as well.

Squinting against the snow, she thought she might be able to catch a glimpse of the building between gusts, but all she could make out was the shape of a nearby tree and —

Something moving.

Sam blinked back the wind-induced tears and tried to focus again. Maybe she'd imagined it, but she'd thought she'd seen —

The warmth of adrenaline rushed through her. There *was* something there. Something large. And it was coming directly toward her.

Her hand went to her thigh without thinking — but, of course, her zat wasn't there. She could see the shape better now. It was a person. They were leaning into the wind, slogging through the deep drifts and heading her way.

Her first hopeful thought was that it was the colonel. Or maybe Daniel or Teal'c. Somehow they'd found her. But it wasn't. She could tell, even though they were bundled in a long, hooded coat and wore protective goggles. None of her team was built that slight.

It was pointless to do anything but wait. Even if they were responsible for her being here, it would be better to be recaptured than to die of exposure. The thought of simply being warm again was worth whatever the accompanying risk might be.

Still, Sam tensed. It was hard to be a sitting duck.

When the figure was about two meters away, it stopped, offering her an object it carried. It was a coat. Without even thinking, Sam reached for it. She hadn't realized how badly she was shivering until it took two attempts to slip her arm into the sleeve. The coat's warmth instantly enveloped her and she nodded gratefully.

She could see now that, although thin, the figure was male. He motioned her to come, before turning back into the wind. Stepping in his boot prints, Sam followed. Even though he was no more than a couple of meters ahead of her, she occasionally lost him in the renewed blizzard.

The building was closer than she'd thought. It appeared out of nowhere, looming before her in the gray light. It was an oddly comforting sight. Her guide reached for her hand, assisting her over one last enormous snow drift and onto the steps.

The mausoleum was not as Sam had left it. A small fire was crackling in the middle of the room, setting macabre shadows dancing along the white walls. Near it waited a pair of fur-lined boots, identical to the ones her rescuer wore. He gestured her toward them.

"Th-thanks," Sam stuttered, moving to the fire and bringing her hands as close to it as she dared. They tingled painfully.

The man removed his goggles and unwound his scarf, but his hood still concealed much of his face. When he spoke, she didn't recognize his voice.

"Please, allow me to see your fingers."

Before she could protest, he reached for her hand. His touch caused her fingers to sting like a pinprick and she yanked them back.

"Who are you?" Rescuer or captor, she needed to know.

Slowly he pushed back his hood. "Surely you haven't forgotten, Samantha. It is I, Martouf."

Sam blinked. For just a moment she hadn't recognized him, but now, with the full firelight on his face, she could see it really was him.

Which was, of course, impossible.

"No." She shook her head and glared at him. "Martouf is dead. I ought to know. I'm the one who killed him."

His gaze was kind, if sad.

"A necessary act, given the circumstances. You did what you had to do, Samantha. I have never held it against you."

Sam continued to shake her head. All her logic insisted that the man standing before her could not be Martouf. This was some kind of a trick. It certainly wouldn't be the first time the Goa'uld had tried to make her believe something that wasn't true. Maybe she was hallucinating, or they'd drugged her water.

"I don't know who you really are," she told him, "or how you're doing this, but you can just stop it, right now, because I'm not buying it."

A slightly pained look crossed his face as she spoke. It was a look she'd seen before, a look Jolinar had known too well. For just a moment it stirred something within Sam. A memory of feelings that were not her own.

"I knew this would be difficult for you." His tone was gentle. "You depend so very much on your science and your logic to explain everything. But they cannot explain this. This requires that you set your preconceived notions aside and take a leap of faith, Samantha. And I know only too well that this is something you are not accustomed to doing."

The last time she'd had a conversation like this she'd ended up with a psych evaluation and that creep, Simmons, breathing down her neck. Not to mention having to buy a new toaster. But even Orlin hadn't tried to make her believe something she knew, fundamentally, to be untrue.

"So, if you're Martouf, then just what, exactly, is 'this' supposed to be?" Maybe if she just let him play his part, she could gather enough information to figure out what his game was.

Although that hadn't worked especially well with Orlin either.

The mausoleum had warmed quickly with the fire. Sam moved away from it, taking a seat on the nearby stone slab. She kept a watchful eye on 'Martouf'. Beneath his now unbuttoned coat she could see the familiar Tok'ra attire, including a sheath from which the handle of a knife protruded. She filed that information away for future use.

He sat next to her. Close, she noticed, but not too close.

"On your world, Samantha, do you not have any sort of belief system that prepares you for life after death?"

"We have several, actually. Many of which are quite different from one another."

"And is there none among these to which you subscribe?"

She wasn't the one who really needed to be answering questions, but it was clear he was leading her somewhere with this line of inquiry. It might be useful to know where.

"I did. Once. A long time ago." Sunday mornings in the base chapel with her mother and Mark emerged from a dusty corner of her memory. Ankle socks and patent leather shoes as shiny as her father's best dress ones. Mark's hair plastered to his head, his tie never quite straight. It ran like an old eight millimeter movie in her mind.

Sam pulled out of her reverie. Martouf was waiting for her to continue.

"Heaven," she explained abruptly. "It's called heaven. But believe me, it's not supposed to be anything like this." She gestured at their surroundings. This place was about as far from heaven as one could possibly get.

"Do you make no journey to get to this 'heaven' after you die?"

Sam shrugged. "It depends. Some people think there's a place you go to beforehand. A place where you atone for all the mistakes you made in your life."

He was nodding now, and she could finally see where he was going with this. Not that it was going to convince her one bit.

"And is it not possible that this could be such a place, a place of atonement and self-discovery?"

"Theoretically, I suppose so." She wasn't going to get sucked into this. "But it's not. I'm sorry."

Martouf sighed with disappointment.

"Samantha, why do you not trust your own senses? Did you yourself not witness the death of the others? Teal'c? Dr. Jackson? Colonel O'Neill?"

Sam's stomach gave a sickening lurch at their names. She studied her hands so that Martouf wouldn't be able to read her face. No matter what he said, she still had hope. She had been revived. The others may have been too. She wasn't going to give up on them yet. That was what she had to hold onto.

Her lack of an immediate response, however, seemed to have encouraged him. He slid closer to her and picked up her hand.

"I have been given a great honor," he said softly. "The honor of being your guide through this journey. I will help you find your way. There is a place that awaits us when we are done, a paradise where we can dwell for eternity. Join me, Samantha, and we will find it together."

More memories that were not hers recognized the texture of his hands and the gentle caress of his thumb against her skin. They had sat like this before, many times, Martouf and Jolinar, finding quiet comfort and solace in each other's company. An ache of longing for the loss of it swelled in her chest.

Sam pulled her hand free, irritated. "Stop it. I know what you're doing, and it won't work. If you think I can't tell the difference between Jolinar's feelings and my own, then think again. And stop trying to play me."

Martouf looked stricken, but she didn't care. She stood up and walked back to the small fire just to be away from him. It had been a long time since Jolinar's memories had surfaced so strongly. The strength of them had caught her off-guard and she needed a few moments to steady herself without the false Martouf hovering inches away.

Unfortunately, he followed her.

"I offer you eternity, Samantha. You. Not Jolinar. Why won't you at least consider this?"

"Because I'm not dead!" She all but shouted it at him. "And nothing you can say or do will convince me that I am." She pointed at the doorway, which was growing dim with the approaching twilight. "The only thing I'm going to do when I leave this place is to look for the rest of my team, because, if I'm not dead, then odds are they're not either." She glared at him. "And if they're alive, I'm going to find them."

"And sacrifice your place in the afterlife?" he pursued, his brow creased, as if what she was saying seemed incomprehensible to him. "You would give it all up — for them?"

She let a steely, determined smile crease her face. She didn't even have to think twice. "Damn right."

He shook his head. "Forgive me, Samantha, but it is wasted effort. If you cannot see that now, you will in time. However —" He held up his hand as she was about to retort. "I will still accompany you, if you will permit me. Then, perhaps, when you realize the futility of your quest, you will accept the great gift which I am offering you."

Sam squelched her first instinct to tell Martouf exactly what he could do with his offer. It probably would have made even the colonel blush. The simple fact was, even though she loathed the idea, she needed someone who knew their way around here. Whatever his motives were, he at least seemed familiar with this place and she probably would increase her likelihood of finding the others if she accepted his proposal.

As long as she didn't allow him to sabotage her efforts. Which, considering how he was still trying to manipulate her feelings, she was almost certain he would attempt to do. His appearance, his voice, everything about him, was Martouf down to a tee. It would be a constant battle to remind herself that this was not the man she had once known.

"Fine," she said. "You can come." And then added, because she felt she should, "Thank you, by the way. For the coat and the boots — and for guiding me back here. I don't think I would have lasted much longer if you hadn't come along."

"Dying here is —"

"Impossible, I know. Because I'm already supposed to be dead. I get it."

"Actually, I was going to say that dying here is called the Second Death. And it is something to be greatly feared. It means that your body is forever separated from your soul and cannot be reunited in the afterlife. In fact, it means that you will never achieve the afterlife and true death will be the end of your existence."

A chill ran through her at Martouf's words. Not that she believed him, but the thought of oblivion, of non-existence…? She'd felt that once. Or something very like it, trapped in the computer of the SGC. A vast expanse of nothing. It had been terrifying.

And something she hoped to never experience again.

"Then I guess we'll try to avoid that," she said curtly, walking away from Martouf and heading toward the door. The need to get some distance from him was very strong. Now that she paid attention to it, she realized why.

"You've got a symbiote," she said, turning back to him in

surprise. "You have one in you right now."

Martouf looked taken aback. "Of course. I am Tok'ra —"

"No." She cut him off before he could spin more lies. "You *were* Tok'ra. It was Martouf who died, but Lantash is still very much alive. The Tok'ra have him in stasis, awaiting a host. If you really were Martouf, and this was some kind of afterlife, you'd be symbiote-free. And you're not." Not that she'd needed further proof, but there it was. Let him try to explain his way out of that one.

Martouf sighed. Sam thought she could sense an edge of impatience in it.

"Samantha, you do not understand the nuances of this existence yet. Lantash will always be a part of me, and it is that which you sense. Nothing more."

Damn, but he was going to be persistent. Fine. It didn't change anything anyway. She still was going to search for the others. And she still needed him to come along.

"Sure. Fine. Whatever," she replied dismissively. There had to be some advantage for him to keep up this charade. She'd figure it out eventually. But she was tired of playing the game right now. Getting out of this place needed to be her first priority. "How long is it dark here?" She gestured toward the door.

"The night is long, I fear. Daylight will not return for many hours." He gave her the same fond look the real Martouf had so often given her. "You should get some rest, Samantha. Our journey will be arduous. You will need your strength."

She was weary, she'd give him that. It was a lot colder by the door so she moved back to the fire, sitting as close to it on the marble floor as she could comfortably get. What little smoke there was drifted up to the invisible ceiling of the mausoleum and dissipated as gusts of wind through the open doorway occasionally purged the smoky air.

"It is safe to sleep," Martouf assured her. "I will keep watch."

Sam merely threw him a doubtful look. What she needed to be most on guard against didn't lie outside in the dark and the snow. She pulled the hood up over her head and sighed. Sleep would definitely not be on the agenda for tonight.

It was going to be a long wait until dawn.

CHAPTER SEVEN

"THIS is everything?"

Freya looked apologetic.

"I am afraid so, General. The Tok'ra retain very few personal belongings. Because we are so often forced to relocate at a moment's notice, burdening ourselves with items that are nonessential would hinder our evacuations needlessly. Besides, many Tok'ra have lived several lifetimes. Retaining trinkets from a previous host might make the present host uncomfortable. For these reasons, our possessions are few."

Hammond looked at the small box on his desk with its meager contents. On the one hand, he felt voyeuristic, examining the intimate items of a person's life. But on the other, he was frustrated that it held so few things, none of which seemed to offer any clues as to who Jenmar was or what his motive for betraying SG-1 might have been.

Carefully he removed each item. A small book. A stone the size of a child's fist with a glyph emblazoned on it. A comb. Three pairs of what Hammond recognized as SGC-issue socks. And a small figurine that resembled something he'd expect to see in Dr. Jackson's office.

"That is the symbol of the home planet of Jenmar's host, Keyleb." Freya indicated the stone with the glyph that he was now turning over in his hand. "It was destroyed by Cronus a few years ago and its people all killed. Keyleb is the last of his race. We assume the symbol is to remind him of his heritage."

Hammond studied it. Mementos, he'd learned, could either be a source of solace or a reminder of loss. For some reason, he suspected this was the latter. Still, it told him nothing, so he set it aside. The comb and the socks also told him nothing, except that perhaps the man had cold feet — or light fingers.

"What about this book?"

"We were able to translate some of it," Anise explained as Hammond examined it. *"It seems to be some sort of, for want of a better term, prayer book."*

Hammond was surprised. "That's a bit unusual for a Tok'ra isn't it?"

"Most certainly," Anise affirmed. *"But not as unusual as that."* She pointed at the small figurine.

If he hadn't known better, Hammond would have sworn it was Ancient Egyptian. Whatever its origin, the statue was worn to the point of almost being unrecognizable, but it appeared to be a woman with a crown on her head. There were markings on the entire length of the statue, but he couldn't tell if they were supposed to be there or simply the result of its obvious age.

"I take it we know what this is," he said, studying it closely. If ever there was a time he needed Dr. Jackson.

"I will be honest, General. Of all the items we found in Jenmar's quarters, that was, perhaps, the most disturbing."

Hammond glanced at her, surprised. Her brow was knit in worry as she eyed the little statuette.

"I assume you're going to tell me why?".

She reached out and took it carefully from his hand, holding it as if it were contaminated in some way.

"As you know, the Tok'ra broke away from the Goa'uld many thousands of years ago. Among other differences, we did not believe in taking human hosts against their will nor subjugating less evolved species by pretending to be their gods."

Hammond resisted the urge to comment on the phrasing 'less evolved species.' It was more important to hear Anise's explanation, after all.

"There was another group which also chose to break from the Goa'uld at the same time," she continued. *"They called themselves the Djedu. Like the Tok'ra, they found the taking of a host against their will abhorrent, but, like the Goa'uld, when they did take a host, they blended with it completely. The Djedu, however, claimed that, because the host was willing, this blending cre-*

ated a whole new being who was neither host nor symbiote, but a perfect merging of two minds and two bodies. They believed this set them apart from both the Goa'uld and the Tok'ra."

Another group of symbiotes running lose in the galaxy? Had the Tok'ra never thought to mention this before? Hammond could feel his blood pressure rise.

"Why have we never heard about these Djedu?" he asked, curtly. Mentally he began composing his phone call to the President and the Joint Chiefs.

Anise handed him back the small figurine. *"Because we believed them to have died out long ago. Their leader was named NebtHet. As a Goa'uld she had modeled herself after one of your Egyptian goddesses."* Anise pointed toward the statue. *"That is her image. From time to time, over the millennia, small groups of Tok'ra, and even some of the Goa'uld, have claimed to be followers of the Djedu cult. They've insisted that the Djedu still exist, in hiding, on a planet called Duat. As with such things, the popularity of these claims peaks and wanes. But the presence of the NebtHet deity among Jenmar's possessions, along with the prayer book, would suggest that he considers himself a follower of the cult. Perhaps over and above his status as a Tok'ra."*

"And do you believe that these Djedu still exist? Could they somehow have decided to come out of hiding and become a threat, like the Goa'uld?"

Anise shook her head. *"They were not militant, General. Domination was never their goal. Their philosophy had to do with exploring the potential that existed within the individual. It was NebtHet's belief, and the belief of those who followed her, that in time the Djedu would be able to shed their corporeal form and ascend to a whole other plane of existence."*

Hammond stared at her blankly. "You're serious," he said finally. "Ascension? Like we saw with the Harsesis — and that Orlin fellow Major Carter encountered?" Granted, he didn't claim to know much about the process, but what little he did made a bunch of navel-gazing Goa'ulds seem the unlikeliest of candidates.

"You may certainly express your doubts, General. Although it was NebtHet's belief that the Djedu could evolve beyond the limitations placed on them by the host/symbiote relationship. The full and complete blending of two consensual beings was thought to be the first step toward achieving that evolution. How far they were able to progress… Well, no one ever knew."

Hammond turned this information over in his mind as he absently gazed at the small figure of NebtHet. He was trying to make the pieces fit.

"So, you think Jenmar has become a member of this Djedu cult?"

"More of a follower, I would think. The Djedu were a closed society. They guarded their secrets closely. But that did not prevent them from making use of the skills of those who hoped one day to be allowed to become one of them."

Hammond couldn't help a humorless chuckle. "And you said they didn't consider themselves Goa'uld."

"Well, there is, after all, a reason why the Goa'uld, and even the Tok'ra, for that matter, consider ascension to be beyond our grasp." Hammond wasn't sure if he detected bemusement or bitterness in her tone.

Another time he would have enjoyed discussing the finer points of that statement, but at the moment he needed to keep his focus on Jenmar and his motives. At least the Djedu did not seem to warrant him picking up the red phone. Yet.

"I take it from this," he indicated the statue. "That you no longer think the Djedu are extinct. Could they be the ones who kidnapped SG-1 on P4C-679?"

"I wish I could say, General. Certainly the evidence points to it."

Hammond felt his frustration mount once again. How could anyone be both helpful and yet unhelpful at the same time? It was like pulling teeth. Deeply impacted teeth.

"Can you think of any reason why these Djedu might want SG-1? Jenmar went to an awful lot of trouble to get them to that planet."

"At present, General, I could only speculate."

He waited, but Anise did not elaborate further. His already thin patience was becoming nearly transparent. His people had been missing for forty-eight hours already. Time was not working in his favor. "Would you care to share that speculation?" There was no point even trying to keep the exasperation out of his voice.

Anise still appeared reticent, but finally Freya spoke.

"Actually, I believe you already have identified the reason, General. Based on the information you have shared with us, SG-1 has the distinction of being the only people, to the best of our knowledge, in the past several millennia to have actually encountered ascended beings. Besides the one calling himself Orlin and the Harsesis child, there was also the being Dr. Jackson described as 'Mother Nature' on Kheb."

Maybe it was the late hour or the fact that he hadn't slept much since SG-1 went missing, but he wasn't exactly seeing the connection.

Showing signs of her own exasperation, Anise took over. *"If I had devoted over three thousand years to the search for the secrets of ascension —"* She sounded as if she was leading a small child through the basics of logical thinking. *"And I learned that there was a group of individuals who had recently had intimate contact with ascended beings, then it is extremely likely that I would do whatever it took to find those individuals and extract from them any knowledge they might possess."*

"So, you're saying the Djedu took my people because they think SG-1 can help them ascend?" It seemed preposterous, but after four years in Stargate Command he'd gotten used to preposterous.

"If it is indeed the Djedu who have them, then yes. I believe that would be their purpose."

"They could have just asked." Hammond harrumphed, more to himself than to Anise.

"*As you are fond of pointing out, General,*" she answered him nonetheless. "*Asking is not something we are particularly good at. And if the Tok'ra are incapable of it, how much more so might be a group that has been in hiding for thousands of years?*"

She had a point, he'd give her that.

"Could they have been taken to this Duat, wherever it is?"

"*If we are dealing with the Djedu, then yes. Duat is where they most probably would be.*"

"And do the Tok'ra have any idea where that planet might be located?" Hammond was pretty sure he already knew the answer.

"*Regrettably, no. There are stories, of course, but to the best of our knowledge, no one has ever actually found its location. As I said. Most Tok'ra have considered the Djedu to be long extinct. Many regard Duat itself as little more than a myth. We will, however,*" she continued, anticipating his next request. "*Make inquiries among our contacts and see if we are able to learn anything which might be of use to you.*"

"I appreciate that." Hammond was sincere. He'd take any lead he could get at the moment. Finding Duat would be no simple task. Without any sort of parameters by which to refine a search, their list of Stargate addresses was pretty much worthless. It was like looking for the proverbial needle in a haystack.

The items scattered about on his desk seemed to have told him everything they could. By the way Anise was fidgeting with her hands, he figured he'd gotten just about everything out of her he was going to for now anyway. He offered her his thanks and nodded to the SF to escort her from the conference room.

Halfway to the stairs she stopped and turned around. "General, there is something else that I think you should know." Freya's face was troubled. "Earlier, I mentioned that none among us knew Jenmar well. His area of expertise — the translation of alien languages — tended to make for an isolated life."

Hammond waited. There had to be more.

"What we did not tell you at the time was that there was one Tok'ra who did, in fact, befriend Jenmar. I do not think it has any relevance to what has happened to SG-1, but I feel, in the interest of full disclosure, that I must share that information with you."

"Do I know this Tok'ra?" Hammond had an uneasy feeling in his gut.

"I regret to say that you do. And that, also, in the end, he proved not to be Tok'ra but a Goa'uld spy."

Hammond could only think of one name. "Tanith."

Freya nodded. "He is, however, dead now, so I do not see how it could have any bearing on Jenmar's actions. Nevertheless, I thought you should know."

Hammond watched her go, unsure whether he should be grateful for the extra information or irate that it hadn't been brought forth sooner. While Freya was probably right — with Tanith dead there wasn't much chance his connection to Jenmar was relevant to SG-1's disappearance — it was still troubling. One more thing to add to his list of concerns.

In the meantime, finding this Duat was his number one priority. The Tok'ra might be his best bet, but it was worth putting in a call to the Tollan and the Asgard as well.

And if he came up empty on all three…?

Well. He could only hope SG-1 would figure out a way home on their own.

CHAPTER EIGHT

SHE wasn't his Carter.

Jack had come to that conclusion about forty-five minutes into their hike through the miserable, chilly rainforest after watching her take point the entire time.

Oh sure, she looked like Carter. And she sounded like Carter. And although he tried not to think about it too much, she even smelled like Carter.

But she wasn't Carter. At least not his version of her. He could tell by the way she moved. Her lack of attention to what was around her. The way she would start when he'd come up behind her quietly and then speak. His Carter moved like a cat. She was always alert, always on her guard. Always ready for the unexpected.

This Carter was none of these. Which really begged the question, who the hell was she?

His mind ran through as many options as he could think of.

She could be another robot Carter. The first one was, well, dead, he guessed, was the best way to put it. And Harlan had sworn up and down that he wouldn't make any more. But could you really trust a guy who stole your DNA when you were unconscious and said Kumbya all the time?

Still, Robot Carter had been a pretty damn good copy, he had to admit. If he hadn't known she was wires and circuits, she'd have passed as the flesh and blood Carter any day of the week. So the chance of this one running on power packs was probably slim to none.

Option two: she was a clone. As far as he knew, only the Asgard had cloning technology, but you never knew. Some Goa'uld could have gotten their hands on one of those things and figured out how to reset it so it didn't pop out little gray-butted aliens every time. But then there was that whole 'down-loaded consciousness' thing, which meant she'd basically be the same Carter she'd always been and he wouldn't be here trying to figure out why she wasn't. So yeah. No clone.

But he did feel a slight headache coming on after trying to sort that theory out.

Option three: she *was* his Carter, just — not. Of all three possibilities, this one scared him the most. Because if she really was Carter, then the 'not' part meant that someone had messed with her in some way, and the thought of that happening to her again made him feel sick in his gut. If some damn snake had wrapped itself around her brain, or some kind of alien entity had taken over her body —

He scrubbed his face with his hand, trying to rid himself of those thoughts. But try as he might, they persisted.

The real question, he supposed, wasn't so much *what* she was but what was he going to do about it. She still hadn't given him any reason not to trust her, and by letting her take the lead, he was able to keep an eye on her. He guessed he'd just have to wait and see what happened — and be ready when it did.

"So how do we know this trail is the one that gets us to this place, anyway?" Jack called out as they slogged through the woods. Branches drooping with the weight of the rain hung low and in Jack's path. He'd stopped batting them out of the way when he realized that doing so only caused the water to backsplash into his face.

"We don't, sir," Carter called back to him. "But it does seem to be the only path available. If we assume that the plaque on the tomb was meant as a set of instructions, then it would make sense that the path would lead us to where we are sup-posed to go."

"I've assumed a lot of things in my life, Carter, that haven't turned out to be true. But we'll do this one your way and see what happens."

She turned slightly and he could see her bright smile.

"Thank you, sir. I'll try not to disappoint you."

Okay. Definitely *not* Carter. He may have been avoiding her lately, but he did know that what had happened on K'tau had eaten away at her the entire three weeks they'd spent there. And still was, as far as he knew. No way she was this chipper. Not these days.

Which left him right back where he'd started: lots of questions, and no answers.

Yet.

"So whaddaya think this Two Halls place is, anyway?" It was worth a try.

"Hall of the Two Truths," she corrected him again. By now the real Carter would have given up. "And I have no idea, sir."

So much for that tactic.

"Except —" she continued, unexpectedly. "I think I remember Daniel talking about it once."

Jack pricked up his ears. Maybe this would be more productive than he thought. "Do tell?"

"Well," she began, apparently encouraged, "if I recall correctly, the Hall of the Two Truths is where the final judgment is made. When you get there, you confess your sins and then have your heart weighed against a feather to see if you are worthy enough to enter the afterlife."

"A feather."

"Yes sir. If it balances, you get to live for eternity. If it doesn't —"

"Yeah. I get the picture." It did sound like some of that stuff Daniel was going on about all the time. And since when did Carter actually pay attention to it any more than he did? "Sounds like some Goa'uld's idea of a good time, if you ask me." Was he imagining it or did he see her flinch slightly at that. "Speaking of snakes, what do you make of all this? Think we're dealing with a bunch of Goa'ulds here?"

She shrugged. "Hard to say, sir."

He waited for more, but that seemed like all she had to

offer on the topic. Right. Maybe he'd have to prod her a bit.

"Well, if you ask me, I'd say we're probably walking right into a trap. It's got Goa'uld written all over it, as far as I'm concerned. In fact, I wouldn't be surprised if that Tok'ra — Jenmar? — wasn't a Goa'uld himself. Hell, I'm thinking we were set up, right from the start."

The smile she threw him was more of a grimace this time. He watched as her whole body tensed.

"That's something of a leap, isn't it, Colonel?" she replied hesitantly. He might even have said flustered. Good. It seemed he had her a bit off-balance.

"Oh I don't think so, Carter." He pressed on. "I mean, look at the evidence. This Tok'ra we've never even heard of before comes and dangles some Ancient ruins in front of Hammond that are just too tempting to resist. The minute said Tok'ra shows up at said-same ruins, we get overrun by a fleet of death gliders. Next thing you know, we wake up in a dungeon — with this same Tok'ra, mind you — where we promptly get ourselves killed by not one, but two, Goa'ulds." He held up two fingers for emphasis. "Only to get brought back to life — in a Goa'uld sarcophagus, by the way — just so we can go on some kind of damn quest to find this Two Halls of Truth."

"Hall of the Two Truths —"

"Whatever." He dodged another low hanging, water-logged branch. "I don't know about you, Carter, but I'm sensing a common theme here."

"I guess when you put it that way —"

"You have another theory?"

It took her a few moments before she replied. "No, sir. I guess not. But it could be that we don't have all the facts yet. Just because we can draw a possible conclusion based on circum-stantial evidence, doesn't mean that it's the correct conclusion. I agree that the series of events that brought us here seem to suggest that there's some degree of Goa'uld involvement. But I'd rather not make any assumptions until we get more data."

Okay, well, that *did* sound like Carter. Sort of. At least, the Carter he'd expect to hear back at the SGC turning over a theoretical problem. But it wasn't the Carter he was used to in the field, the one who knew how to assess a threat and was ready for every contingency.

Which meant that whoever, or whatever, this was in front of him knew Carter well enough to get some of her right — but not all of her.

Just like Jolinar.

He didn't know whether to be sick at the thought, or angry as hell. Maybe he'd just have to go with both.

"Oh, I'd say I've got just about all the data I need," he muttered under his breath, going, for the moment, with 'angry as hell.'

She must have heard him because she looked back over her shoulder and said brightly, "I guess, sir, we'll just have to wait and see."

He tossed her an acknowledging half-smile that barely made it past a sneer.

Somehow he didn't think he'd have to wait all that long.

Bra'tac took the lead, forging into the unknown wilderness with the vigor of a man half his age. Rya'c followed close behind. Teal'c couldn't help but notice that the boy was trying to keep as great a distance from him as possible. He tried not to take the boy's behavior to heart, yet it was apparent that his son blamed him for what had transpired. The blame was well placed, Teal'c could not deny. He had failed Rya'c — and Drey'auc. As an absent father and husband he had not been there to protect those he loved most. The destruction of the false gods and the freedom of all Jaffa must, he had always known, come at a price. He had never intended for his family to pay it.

It was most likely too late for Drey'auc. But he would do everything in his power to restore his son to life. It would be worth any price to know that his son might yet live to see the end of Goa'uld oppression.

And should that day ever come, perhaps Rya'c would then understand why he had done as he had done, and think well of him.

"You are too much in your own thoughts, my friend." Bra'tac had dropped back and allowed Rya'c to take point for a while. The old man now walked by Teal'c's side, stride for stride.

"Is not the point of one's journey through Duat to contemplate the strengths and weaknesses of one's life?" Teal'c rejoined.

"Indeed it is." Bra'tac smiled. "But one must be careful not to dwell too much on what is past. Those pages have already been written. The story cannot be untold."

"Perhaps not." Teal'c's eyes followed the back of the long-limbed youth ahead of them. "But new chapters may yet be added."

"Ahhhh." Bra'tac grasped his meaning. "You are right of course. For one of us, at least, the story will go on." He gave Teal'c a sidelong glance. "Do you not wonder how it is possible to restore one to life, once they have entered Duat?" Before Teal'c could reply, he continued. "Sacrifice, Teal'c, is the only way. A life for a life."

"Someone must die to take Rya'c's place?"

"In a manner of speaking. But we will talk more of this later. Look." The trees had thinned and a vast expanse of sweeping grass stretched as far as Teal'c could see. Bra'tac's voice barely contained his excitement. "Does it not resemble the Cord'ai Plains of Chulak?"

It did indeed bear a striking resemblance to the Cord'ai Plains. To their left, in the distance, rose a range of blue-hued mountains, their ragged peaks muted by low-hanging clouds. Far to their right was a barely discernable line of trees. The High Cliffs and the Chompka Groves.

"Do not be fooled by illusion, Teal'c." Bra'tac seemed to

have guessed where his thoughts had strayed. "We remain in Duat. But our thoughts and experiences have created it for us, so it is little wonder that it mirrors our longing for home." He clasped his hand firmly on Teal'c's shoulder and smiled. "Come, my friend. Now our journey truly begins."

CHAPTER NINE

"HOW goes the great experiment? Are your subjects behaving according to plan?" Aset leaned over NebtHet's shoulder to peer at one of the screens. "Major Carter does not appear to be enjoying the company of her companion, does she?"

NebtHet stiffened. Aset's continued pessimism made her weary.

"Things may not be evolving precisely as we had anticipated, but our people have been well trained. They are adapting to the situation. I am confident they will keep things moving along as planned."

"More confident than I." Aset sniffed. "It is clear that none of them, with perhaps the exception of the Jaffa, have accepted the premise of their own deaths. Without that, the whole exercise is pointless."

NebtHet bristled. "I admit, our subjects have behaved contrary to all models. But it does not mean what we learn from them will be any less valuable. In fact, it may be even more so, once we have had a chance to interpret its meaning."

Aset made a derisive sound. "As I have insisted on many occasions, NebtHet, there are other ways. Faster ways."

NebtHet sighed. She and Aset had debated this issue many times. "Technology is not the answer." She gestured to the storehouse doorway behind them. "We have gathered hundreds of devices created by the best and brightest Ancient minds, yet not one has ever enabled us to ascend."

"Perhaps not. But they could have been used to extract the information we need from SG-1 instead of indulging in this ridiculous drama."

NebtHet studied the movements of SG-1 on the screens in front of her. "I admit, without the technology of the Ancients we could never have hoped to accomplish any of this." She turned to face Aset. "But to use it as you suggest — as if what we are looking for can be found in memories or thoughts alone — *that* would mean certain failure. What we seek is so much more."

"Then, by all means, let us hope your plan succeeds." Aset bowed slightly. "Surely nothing less than the entire fate of the Djedu hangs in the balance."

NebtHet chose to ignore Aset's disparaging tone. Her attention was once more drawn to the monitors. Dr. Jackson and his guide had just emerged from the tent into the desert twilight. "They are departing for the oasis now," she pointed out to Aset. "It is time for you to prepare."

Wisely refraining from further comment, Aset left her in peace. NebtHet shook her head as she watched her go. When the key to ascension was finally theirs, perhaps then Aset would acknowledge that this was the right path to take.

Until then, as long as Aset played her part, NebtHet supposed it was the most she could hope for.

"Look, I don't mean to pretend I understand most of what's going on here, but if you've never been to where we're going, how do you know this is the right path?"

To be honest, Daniel wasn't sure there even was a path. If there was, he certainly couldn't see it. Sha're, on the other hand, seemed to have an uncanny sense of direction, even in the dark. It was an attribute he did not recall her ever having before.

If it even was her, which he was still uncertain about despite what should have been obvious evidence to the contrary.

"It is the right path because it is the only path," Sha're answered simply.

He had to give her that. "And it leads to the Hall of the Two Truths."

He saw her silhouette nod.

"Yes. Where you and I will be judged so that we may gain admittance to the Field of Reeds and never need be parted from one another again."

If only he could bring himself to believe that.

"Here's the thing." He hated saying it, but it needed to be said. "All of those things — Duat, the Hall, the Field of Reeds — they're just stories, made up by the Ancient Egyptians to explain what happened after death. None of it really exists, Sha're. And since it doesn't really exist, then this really can't be it. So it makes me just wonder all the more — what is this place?"

And, more importantly, where were Jack, Sam and Teal'c?

"Why do you doubt so much everything you see?" Sha're slowed down to walk by his side.

"I guess because there have been more than a few times in the past four years when everything I've seen has turned out to be a lie. We have a saying: 'Fool me once, shame on you. Fool me twice, shame on me.'"

"I do not understand."

Daniel sighed. "It means that if you don't learn from your own mistakes, it's no one's fault but your own. I've been tricked before into believing something was true. I won't let it happen again."

"Do you believe I am trying to deceive you, Dan'yel?"

He had no idea how to answer her. She was so very much his Sha're, right down to the hurt in her eyes at his doubts. But if this wasn't real, then neither was she, no matter how much his senses kept trying to convince him otherwise.

"No — at least, not deliberately." He needed to word it just right. "I really do think you believe what you're telling me. I'm just not sure I entirely trust the people who sent me here, or their motives. But, then, I guess I'm suspicious that way."

"You never used to be." There was a tinge of sadness in her voice.

She was right, of course. He *didn't* used to be that way. He had once been quite trusting, expecting only the best out of people if they were given half a chance — believing that the better angels of their nature would win out in the end. When had all that changed?

Maybe he'd been hanging out with Jack O'Neill too long.

Scratch the 'maybe'. He *had* been hanging out with Jack too long. Long enough to finally get some sense knocked into his head about the way the world — heck, the whole galaxy — actually worked. And to realize that his paltry effort to make things better really didn't amount to a hill of beans when it came right down to it.

That part he hadn't learned from Jack. It was, sadly, the voice of experience. Nothing he had done mattered. Not really. All he had to do was look at the woman walking beside him to prove his point. Even if this was Duat, even if he was dead, she had come here long before him because of him. He hadn't been able to save her. Nor Sarah. Not even Shifu, really, who was at least safe and out of harm's way — but solely by the grace of Oma Desala.

As much as he had tried, the universe wasn't any better off for his efforts. In fact he could argue pretty convincingly that, whether it was on an individual or a massive, galactic scale, he'd only ended up making things worse.

"Well, I guess I've changed," he said, finally, in response to Sha're's observation. "Things happened, you know?"

"My poor Dan'yel." She sighed, touching his arm. "You carry too many burdens, even here. You must lighten your load or you shall come before Thoth with too heavy a heart."

"Yes. Well. Easier said than done, right?" Daniel smiled ruefully. If only he could do as she said — shed the things which weighed him down. But how, he had no clue.

CHAPTER TEN

THE SNOW was melting. For that, Sam was incredibly grateful, even if it did mean they had to slog through boot-soaking slush and sole-sucking mud. It also meant she could see the path much easier and no longer had to depend on Martouf for guidance.

To his credit, he hadn't protested when she'd pushed past him to take point. In fact, he'd said little since they'd set out. While Sam doubted he'd given up trying to convince her that this was some sort of journey through purgatory, at least he had backed off for a while and just let her be. It gave her a chance to push him and the effect he had on her to the back of her mind and to concentrate on her situation and the best way to get out of it.

If she could get out of it. Which, if she were honest with herself, she really wasn't sure about. She had too little information to work with and it was frustrating. Martouf most likely knew more than he was telling her, but until he gave up this charade she was pretty much on her own.

Survival 101 dictated that a person first inventory what they had and then figure out what they needed. Sam had long ago discovered that the technique worked with problem solving too. Unfortunately her stockpile of information was fairly sparse. She went down the list, one by one.

Number One. To begin with, she was alive. Always a good place to start, especially given how much effort Martouf was putting into convincing her otherwise. Which brought her to Number Two. Whoever the hell he was, the guy walking behind her was *not* Martouf. She'd sensed the symbiote in him, no matter how much he tried to deny it, and since he definitely wasn't Jaffa, that meant he was either Tok'ra or Goa'uld. Her money was on Goa'uld.

No surprise there. A Goa'uld was why she was here in the first place. And there was her third piece of information. Whatever was going on, probably this NebtHet was behind it. If she was a System Lord, Sam had never heard of her. Daniel had seemed to recognized the name, though. She wished he was around to offer some insight. She wished all of them were.

That brought her to the second half of her inventory: information she needed. Unfortunately, that list was much longer.

First, she needed to locate of the rest of her team. Until she saw absolute proof to the contrary, Sam was determined to believe that they had been revived the same way she had. Maybe they even had their own version of Martouf dogging their steps, trying to convince them they were dead. She wondered how the colonel would enjoy *that*.

Second, she needed to find out where the Stargate was — or if the planet even had one. Sam suspected it did; the Goa'uld rarely occupied planets without them. Sending ships was just too inefficient. If there was a gate, odds were it was close by, since the Goa'uld tended to keep their base of operation near the evacuation point. Score one for Goa'uld predictability.

Third, although earlier she hadn't given much thought as to why this was happening, she realized now that knowing the motive behind their abduction and this whole, ridiculous charade might go a long way to figuring out how to defend against whomever was responsible. The answers lay with Martouf, she was sure. Convincing him to give them to her… Well, that was another matter.

The only other thing she wished she knew was where, exactly, she was headed on this stupid path. She'd had reservations about taking it, especially when Martouf did not object. But with no true sense of where she was relative to, well, *anything*, she hadn't had much choice. Still, she couldn't shake the feeling that she was the rat and this was no more than a large, snowy maze.

"See? Your very presence warms our surroundings, Samantha."

It was the first thing he'd said in a while. Sam tried to ignore him. She'd spent a wearisome night trying to sort out Jolinar's feelings from her own. It had been a long time since she'd had to do that, since what remained of Jolinar had emerged from the far recesses of her mind where she'd so carefully tucked it after Martouf's death. She resented having to deal with it again. Especially now, when she was already feeling like everything she thought she knew about her life was upended—and that was *before* she'd been abducted, killed and left alone on an alien world.

But, as much as anything else, she hated—*hated*—the fact that whomever was behind this had dared to use Martouf in this way. It was tragic enough that he'd died a victim of Goa'uld mind control. Couldn't the bastards have left him alone, even in death? He'd been a good man and a good friend, and having his memory desecrated by this imposter was the final insult.

Sam had an overwhelming desire to punch something. Or someone. Although hauling off and decking the false Martouf would probably be a bit out of line, even under the circumstances.

There really was only one thing she could do, and that was keep on walking. Wherever this path went, it ultimately had to lead her to some answers, one way or another.

But maybe she didn't have to wait quite that long.

"So, what are you? A clone?" she said. The Asgard had cloning technology. It wouldn't be the first time the Goa'uld had stolen something that more advanced beings had developed.

"No—although I can see how you might have thought that. I am a *Ba*."

If the colonel had been there, he'd have had a clever comment right about now. Nothing witty came to mind, though.

"And that is?" Daniel had mentioned something about a *Ba* back in the dungeon. She hadn't given it much attention at the time.

"Ahhh. Well. The *Ba* is difficult to define. I believe the closest thing you might compare it to is the soul." He quickened his pace and drew nearer.

Sam rolled her eyes. She should have realized this would have set him off talking about their so-called journey though the underworld. She was almost sorry she'd asked. "A soul." She tried not to sound skeptical. Not that she was an expert, but as far as she knew, souls didn't walk and talk. Or leave slushy footprints in melting snow. "So, how does that work, exactly?"

He was right behind her now and quite animated as he spoke. "These shapes we assume, which look and feel like our bodies, really are not. They are merely a manifestation of that which we were when we were alive. We're a sort of spiritual double for our real selves. An avatar which makes this journey in our stead."

Again, she wished Daniel were there. First, because he'd probably know exactly what Martouf was talking about, and second, because he'd just eat this stuff up. Not that she didn't grasp the concept herself, and under other circumstances she might have liked to learn more about this whole belief system, but at the moment it was merely an irritating cover-up for whatever was really going on.

She was still going with 'clone.'

"And where exactly are our real selves?"

"Dead, of course."

"Dead." He couldn't seriously expect her to believe this. "So, I'm actually lying on the ground in some dungeon where that Goa'uld shot me, is what you're saying?"

He shrugged. "That is quite possible."

"And the others?" She didn't bother to conceal her scornful tone. "Colonel O'Neill, Daniel, Teal'c — are their *Bas* here too?"

"Regrettably, yes."

"Regrettably?"

"I'm afraid your friends have been classified as 'Enemies of the Gods.' Their fate here has not been… kind."

Sam stopped short and wheeled on him. Martouf nearly ran into her.

"Explain." Even if she didn't buy his ridiculous tale, it didn't mean that her team couldn't be in real trouble.

"Those who have displeased the gods in life, are punished in death. There are places here where such sentences are carried out. They are… unpleasant, to say the least. It is best to avoid them, if possible."

Like hell she would. "Show me."

"Samantha, believe me, you do not —"

"I *said,* show me."

There must have been enough danger in her voice to make him rethink his effort to dissuade her.

"Very well." He sighed with resignation. "Not far ahead, the path divides. We will take the one to the left."

Sam nodded curtly, hoping she'd enforced the idea that lying to her would not be in his best interest, and resumed walking.

"What about me?" she asked after she'd calmed enough to think rationally again. "Why am I not an 'Enemy of the Gods?' I've killed my share of Goa'uld. How come I get special treatment?"

"Because you have an advocate, Samantha. Someone who has come forward to speak on your behalf."

She snorted. "Yeah? And who would that be, you?"

"Actually, yes."

Sam smiled bitterly and turned to glare at him over her shoulder. "Now see, the real Martouf wouldn't be able to do that because he'd be standing right there with Colonel O'Neill and Teal'c and Daniel and myself, proud to be an 'Enemy of the Gods.'" She could feel her anger brimming close to the surface again. "He spent his whole life fighting the Goa'uld," she went on, passionately. "And with his last breath he was still fighting them. So don't try to tell me he'd ever stand here and deny who he was."

"There are things stronger than hatred, Samantha." Martouf's voice was still calm even in the face of her anger. "And what a man may not do to save himself, he may yet do to save another. Especially if that other is someone he carries in his heart."

Okay. There was no way she was touching that. He was obviously still trying to manipulate her feelings, and regardless of her response, she'd only be encouraging him. She left his words unanswered and focused on the path ahead.

Now that she had an actual destination, Sam picked up the pace. It was already warm enough that she'd stuffed the gloves in her pocket and unbuttoned her coat. If the temperature continued to rise at its current rate she'd consider discarding them altogether. Without a weapon, speed might be her best defense if it came down to having to rescue the others. A bulky coat would only slow her down.

Besides. It really wasn't doing her much good against the cold knot of fear that had lodged in the pit of her stomach at the thought that she might already be too late.

CHAPTER ELEVEN

"WHAT an unexpected surprise. How lovely to see you again, Jenmar. It has been far too long."

Tanith's voice made Jenmar's skin crawl. How had he failed to see such duplicity back on Vorash? Perhaps what he had mistaken for friendship had blinded him. In hindsight, all the indications of Tanith's true nature were evident, if only he had been willing to see.

There was little comfort in realizing he had allowed his presumption of a shared purpose to lead him astray yet again.

"I come from Aset a'Teneb." There was no point in drawing this out. The sooner it was over with, the better. He had no desire to exchange pleasantries with Tanith. "She sends a gift for your master. It is a promise of things to come." Jenmar handed over the box Aset had given him.

Opening it, Tanith carefully removed the contents. It was a spiked sphere, small enough to fit into the palm of one's hand. Tanith's eyes widened as he held it up for examination, his smile broadening.

"A most welcomed gift indeed." He returned it to the box, snapping closed the lid before passing it to an attending Jaffa. *"I trust Aset has also provided a list of her terms."*

Jenmar produced the crystal and offered it wordlessly. Where his rage had been before, he now felt only emptiness. It was nearly incomprehensible that he should find himself here, of all places, when a few short hours ago he had aspired to so much more.

Tanith was reading the contents of the crystal at a nearby console. Jenmar stood far enough back to not appear to be looking over his shoulder. Nevertheless, he could still make out some of the writing. The words 'Ancient', 'storehouse' and 'Tau'ri' figured prominently in the text.

"*Excellent.*" Tanith removed the crystal and the screen went blank. "*I will, of course, need to present this to my master, but I am confident an agreement can be reached.*"

The door to the room slid open and two armed Jaffa stepped through, positioning themselves on either side of the opening. At first Jenmar thought they had come to escort Tanith, but when he swept out of the room, and they remained, their purpose became clear.

Tanith paused in the passageway beyond and called back to Jenmar. "*Perhaps, when our deal is concluded, we might toast our renewed alliance.*" His eyes glittered with amusement. "*What is the phrase — 'For old time's sake?'*" Jenmar was certain he heard Tanith's low laugh as the door slid shut.

In his pocket, Jenmar's fingers curled tightly around Aset's remaining crystal. He could guess what information it contained. In the other pocket, his palm cradled the orb NebtHet had given him. The irony that he now stood on the very *ha'tak* she had sent him to find was not lost on him.

Wearily, he took the only seat available in the room — a long, low bench that offered little in the way of comfort. There was nothing to do now except wait. With the guards at the door, he was going nowhere.

Then again, there really was nowhere for him to go.

CHAPTER TWELVE

"THERE is an oasis up ahead. We will stop there and rest," Sha're informed Daniel after another hour or so had passed. He didn't feel so much tired as dry. Even in the cool of night, something about the constant dredging through sand seemed to suck the moisture out of him. He'd tried to ration his canteen, but now he was running precariously low. An oasis would have fresh water and it would feel good to sit for a while.

Daniel found it more than a little curious that Sha're seemed to know what lay ahead. In all the texts of the Egyptian underworld he had studied, he'd never found any which described the exact route through it. They provided no maps to help the deceased navigate their way to the Hall of the Two Truths. It was, as he understood it, not a place defined by geography as much as by experience, with no two journeys ever being exactly alike. Daniel could understand how, if this really was the afterlife, his journey and Sha're's might be joined, but that didn't account for her knowing so much — and he so little. The only way that made sense was if he was correct in his supposition that this was something else entirely.

It took almost another hour of walking to reach their destination. Faint hints of dawn etched the horizon at their backs as the silhouettes of palm-like trees emerged in the distance. By the time they reached them, day had fully come.

They found an outcropping of stone that hung out over the lake — a large, flat rock upon which it seemed many others before them had paused to rest. Both he and Sha're drank their fill from the clear water below before taking out their canteens and refilling them. That task done, Sha're leaned back, arms propped behind her, and lifted her face toward the sun. She looked perfectly at peace.

Daniel couldn't help but watch her. In every way, she was

his Sha're, exactly as he remembered her. Each tendril of hair, each perfect earlobe, each curve of her body which his own still yearned for on long, lonely nights. How hard would it be to let go of his doubts and just accept her as she was? How easy would it be to extend his hand and simply caress her cheek, her hair, her lips —

His musing came to an abrupt halt. Something had moved along the edge of the lake. He hadn't noticed it before. In the shadows, it had been indistinguishable from the landscape. As he watched, whatever it was sidled off toward the darker cover of the nearby copse of palms.

Daniel scrambled to his feet, keeping his eye on the shape so as to not lose it in the shadows. It must have realized it had been seen, because it suddenly sped up, running for the trees. Daniel sprinted after it.

It did not get far. After a few strides, it stumbled in one of the errant sandpits that pockmarked the oasis and fell. Even then the woman — as he closed in, Daniel could see that she was, in fact, female — began to scurry fervently across the ground, as if she might somehow be able to escape before he reached her. With a few more strides he was in front of her, blocking her way.

And trying to figure out what she was.

In form, he supposed, she was human, although, judging by her appearance, she was long past the prime of her life. Her face might have been beautiful in its day. There were vestiges of once-fine features: a proud aquiline nose, brown-speckled eyes, a chin that could be described as haughty. But time had caught up with her. Her cheeks were hollow and her eyes sunken. Matted gray hair hung over her face. Angular bones showed clearly beneath her coppery skin which, despite having the texture of leather, nonetheless seemed fragile, as if at a mere touch it would lose its tenuous hold and slip off her meager frame.

She looked like a living corpse. Or a mummy.

In spite of her appearance, she was still agile. Staggering to her feet, she turned to flee again, only to come face to face with Sha're, who had followed Daniel from the lake. Seeing her only hope of escape thwarted, the old woman sank to the ground again and began to wail.

"Stop, please —" Daniel implored, looking down at her in dismay. He hadn't meant to frighten her, but she was the only person, aside from Sha're, he'd seen since he got here. Questions were going off in his head like flashbulbs.

She did not look at him but only continued her keening, occasionally beating her breast with her fist. Daniel looked helplessly at Sha're, but she only shrugged, as uncertain what to do as he was.

"Look," he tried again, "we don't want to hurt you. I promise. It's just you're the first person we've come upon and we wanted to talk to you. That's all."

"Help me, help me, help me…" she wept, over and over again.

Daniel knelt beside her, trying not to let her appearance bother him. Unfortunately, she smelled as horrible as she looked. "How can we help you? Tell us what to do."

The woman's sobs lessened and she peered closely at Daniel through her tangled, filthy hair. Her eyes widened as if in recognition and she recoiled slightly. Her gaze flitted over to Sha're, and he saw recognition there too, but of a completely different kind.

"I know you!" she cried, flinging herself on the hem of Sha're's robe and gathering it in her fists. "Oh my Queen! Amaunet! Save me!" She reached up a desiccated arm in supplication to Sha're, who tried to back away from her, but could not, as the woman held on with surprising strength. Daniel saw an uncharacteristic flash of anger in Sha're's eyes.

"I am not your queen, old woman," she replied, sharply. "That was the demon who lived within me. The demon who is now long dead. As you too shall soon be, I think."

"Sha're?" He was taken aback by the look of disgust on her face. Daniel wasn't sure he'd ever heard her speak like that. At least, not as Sha're. "Do you know her?"

Sha're at last managed to free herself from the old woman's grasp, leaving her whimpering in the dirt.

"Know her? Yes. Only too well." Sha're nearly spat out her answer. "Her face is forever seared into my mind, even if the demon did possess it at the time." She looked finally at Daniel and her face softened into a kind of grief. "She is the one to whom Amaunet gave my child. She is the one who took him from me and hid him away."

Daniel looked at the woman on the ground and felt an uncontrollable loathing of his own. Yet he had seen the woman who had brought Shifu to Kheb. They had found her, murdered by Apophis' Jaffa, as she fled with the child into the forest. But she had been a Jaffa priestess. This woman—

"I served my Queen!" she hissed at them, suddenly vigorous in her apparent hatred. Out of their two sunken hollows, her eyes abruptly glowed.

—was a Goa'uld.

"*I did as she commanded.*" The old woman's voice was strong with pride. She looked first at one and then the other, her speech taking on the tenor of the symbiote within. "*She knew I would be followed. So she instructed me to find a priestess to take the child far away. To a place that no one even knew existed.*"

"Be gone, old woman," Sha're interrupted her. "Do not bother us further. Crawl off into some dark shadow and die."

As much as Daniel despised the creature on the ground before him, he found Sha're's words harsh. And perplexing.

"Isn't it a little difficult to die here? I mean, if we're already dead—?"

"I speak of the Second Death, Dan'yel. The death from which there is no return." Sha're pointed at the creature on the ground. "See, she has the look about her of one who will perish before her journey to the great Hall is complete."

"I have been cursed!" the woman cried out, managing to look pitiful again. She turned to Daniel this time, the glowing in her eyes now gone and her voice normal. "Please — I implore you. Help me."

Bits and pieces of information were coalescing in Daniel's mind. The Second Death. The fetid smell. The diminished body.

"It is a curse, isn't it?" He knew now. It too was straight out of the Egyptian Book of the Dead. How many times had he pored over the texts as a graduate student, searching them for clues in support of his theories? "You've been forgotten, haven't you? Someone has erased your name from history. Obliterated your memory. No one will ever know who you were, or what you did in life. There is no afterlife waiting for you. Not anymore."

He couldn't help the note of satisfaction that had crept into his own voice as he'd realized the woman's fate. Here was justice at last, or at least a sliver of it. Someone was finally being punished for their part in the crime that had been committed against Sha're.

"Yes," the woman nodded, tears streaming down her face. "It is as you say. And now I will perish. Become nothing. Nothing." She curled into a ball and wept again.

Daniel looked at Sha're whose hard gaze was fixed on the former handmaiden. "It is nothing less than you deserve." Her voice was like ice. "May your bones become as dust." She turned away and strode back toward the rocks.

The Goa'uld looked up at Daniel. Her red-rimmed eyes only made her that much more hideous to look at and he wanted nothing more than to follow in Sha're's wake. But he could not. The old woman held his gaze and he felt as if he were truly seeing the host, not the symbiote within. It was the only thing which kept him from turning his back on her and walking away as well.

"Please." Her voice was barely a whisper. Gone were the hysterics and breast-beating. It was the singular voice of a being in pain. In need. "Please," she entreated him again. "Help me."

CHAPTER THIRTEEN

"SAMANTHA, please. Reconsider."

Sam ignored Martouf's plea and continued the steep climb up the hill, sweating with the effort. The coat was long gone, abandoned a good klick back. Now the landscape was comprised of dead grasses and, on occasion, leafless trees, stunted and twisted in their growth. It was little wonder, considering she'd noticed an intensifying sulfuric odor hanging in the warming air.

It was even worse here. Every breath she took made her want to gag on the smell of rotten eggs — and something else. It was an odor she recognized, but could not place. Not that she really wanted to; her stomach was roiling enough as it was.

Sam could hear Martouf breathing hard behind her as he scrambled up the incline in her wake. The hill itself was more or less barren, save for the mat of ground-hugging grasses that had once grown over it. The path was strewn with rocks, and she'd slipped more than once in her boots. She'd considered ditching those as well — her sandals were tucked in the knapsack on her back — but even though they were overly warm, she figured they offered the better protection.

It took her longer than she would have liked to reach the summit. As she took the last few steps, she came to an abrupt halt, assaulted by a blast of furnace-hot air and a gut-wrenching stench. Both emanated from a vast chasm that was spread below her, the floor of which was covered in a churning, undulating liquid.

Then she heard the sound. It was both human and inhuman at the same time, a painful, wretched noise that made her want to cover her ears to block it out. The pit, she realized, was roiling not only with liquid but with bodies. Hundreds, maybe thousands of people, were crowded together, barely able to move, their cries rising up on the heated air of the sulfuric mud-pit in which they were trapped.

Sam stood there, stunned. She'd seen similar images in depictions of the damned as imagined by artists over the centuries. But to stand on the edge of such a scene, to hear the lamentations of those who were abandoned to so cruel and desolate a place —

Then the true horror struck her. Her team was down there. This was the punishment Martouf had warned her about. These were the 'Enemies of the Gods.'

Sam wheeled on Martouf, who was now standing beside her, looking as horrified as she felt.

"Where are they? How do I get them out?"

He looked mournful. "I have tried to tell you, Samantha. You cannot help them. Their fate has been decided. Their sentence carried out. No one has ever escaped from the Pit of Mutu. If you were to attempt to rescue them, their fate would become yours as well."

"I won't accept that. There has to be a way!"

Frantic, Sam turned back toward the pit, her eyes scanning for a familiar face. There were so many, and they kept in constant motion, climbing over each other or attempting in vain to scale the sheer rock face that surrounded the pit on all sides. Geysers of steam would sporadically shoot high into the air and there would be a cry of anguish from those standing in its vicinity as it rained boiling sulfur down on them. She realized with revulsion that the stench she smelled was that of burning flesh.

She tried looking for Teal'c. With his golden tattoo, he might stand out amongst the others, but there were many Jaffa in the pit — those who, like Teal'c, must have defied the Goa'uld. The rest, though, were humans of all cultures and races. The three faces Sam was so desperate to find were impossibly lost in the midst of so many.

Then she saw the colonel's hat. In that sea of writing

bodies his brimmed baseball cap suddenly stood out. There was no sign of the others, but at least the colonel was alive, even if he was in this hell hole. Now she had something she could do.

Off to her right, Sam noticed that the path led to a narrow footbridge spanning the vast crater. A sadistic catwalk over the theater of the damned, it offered a better view of the interior of the pit and could take her closer to where the colonel was stranded.

"Samantha, no!" Martouf called as she set off at a jog toward it. "You cannot save him!"

Raw fury pumping adrenaline through her veins, she shouted back at him. "I can try! So either help me or shut the hell up!"

The bridge was simply made of corded rope and wooden planks, but it was sturdy. Grasping the rope handholds on each side, Sam strode across it until she was as close to the baseball cap as she could get.

"Colonel!" Sam waved her arms in the air, wondering if it was even possible for him to hear. "Colonel O'Neill! She called his name again and finally he turned.

Her joy at finding him faded as she saw his face. Angry red lesions marred his cheeks and forehead where the heat and sulfur had scalded him. His clothes were burned away in places, revealing bare and blistered skin. When the colonel raised his arm, the flesh was eaten away down to the very bone.

Sam's heart lurched. Even if she could save him, she wasn't sure how long he would survive, not with such terrible wounds. But she wasn't about to leave him there to die in some Goa'uld's demented version of Hell.

Looking around, her hope sank. It was as she feared: all sides of the pit were sheer drops. Even a professional climber would have found it impossible to find any sort of foothold going down or coming up. If she was going to do this, she was going to need a rope.

Except she didn't have one. Neither did Martouf, who'd followed her out onto the bridge. He had nothing with him except his canteen of water — and a knife.

An idea took hold of her. It was crazy. Impossible. Movie-stunt stuff. But it was the only chance she had of rescuing the colonel. Besides, considering what bad shape he was in, she needed to act now. Time was as much a consideration as anything else.

All of which meant it was worth the risk.

Sam eyed the bridge, making the calculations. It was long enough, but she'd have to cut it at just the right point to avoid being submerged in the pit herself. Although, considering how hard she was going to slam into the wall on the opposite side of the canyon, maybe the pit was the better choice.

"I need your knife." It wasn't a request. "And you need to get across the bridge and wait on the other side. We're going to need your help pulling us up."

It took a few seconds for Martouf to catch up to her plan. His eyes widened.

"You cannot be serious? You will die!"

"Yeah, well, been there, done that. At least, that's what you keep telling me. Now give me the knife."

Martouf put his hand protectively over the weapon and shook his head.

"I cannot allow you to do this, Samantha. It is insanity. Please. Just come with me. Let us leave this place."

"I'm not leaving here without Colonel O'Neill," she insisted. "This has a chance of working — a slim one, granted, but one I'm willing to take. So give me the damned knife or, I swear, I'll gnaw through the rope with my teeth."

With great reluctance, he handed her the weapon.

"Now take this, and go wait over there." She pointed to the opposite cliff, handing him her knapsack. For a moment she thought he was going to argue with her again, but he said nothing and instead crossed the bridge and positioned himself on the rock ledge on the other side. He suddenly seemed quite far away and she realized again just how huge a swing she was going to have to make.

"Yeah. That's gonna leave a mark," she muttered aloud.

Looking down she saw that the colonel had managed to stay in close proximity to the bridge in spite of the surging tide of suffering around him. Sam tried not to look at anyone else. The piteous cries of the others, echoing off all sides of the canyon, were overwhelming and she did her best to tune them out. If this worked, it was entirely possible some of them could escape by the same means. Maybe she would be rescuing more than just the colonel.

To have enough length to reach the bottom of the pit, she would have to sever the bridge halfway between its midpoint and where it was anchored on the near side. If she did it right, she could leave the last rope hanging by a few weakened threads in order to give herself enough time to scramble back toward the middle, thereby reducing the arc of her swing and the impact with which she would hit the opposite wall. She regretted giving up the coat now. It would have cushioned her a little at least.

First, though, she needed to make sure the colonel knew what she was planning. The closer he could get to the far side of the pit, the easier it would be to help him up. Sam knew that there'd be a swarm of victims trying to clamber up the bridge-turned-ladder as soon as it fell. She'd have no way to keep them off once they started, and she was concerned that their combined weight would cause it to break, trapping them all in the pit. As much as she wanted to rescue as many people as possible, her first priority was Colonel O'Neill.

"Sir!" This was going to be the hard part. Once he realized what she had planned, he'd order her to leave him there. Well, it wouldn't be the first time she disobeyed a direct order.

When she finally had his attention, Sam pointed toward where she hoped the bridge-ladder would ultimately come to rest. "Colonel, I need you to go *there*," she shouted, pointing with both arms for emphasis. "I'm going to get you out, sir!"

But instead of a vehement head-shake, he only nodded his understanding. Part of her was relieved that he hadn't, for once, argued.

Although another part wondered why.

Not that it mattered. She was going through with it, regardless of what he said. Maybe he knew that.

The knife was sharp and it easily cut through the first two non-weight-bearing ropes. She lashed the loosened end of one of them around her wrist to give herself something to hold onto when the bridge began to tilt. Sam figured her next cut would make that happen.

She was right. The bridge pitched suddenly, anchored now at only three points. Sam held tight to her rope to keep herself from sliding off and with her free hand reached carefully up to cut the other handhold rope. The bridge tilted back the other way and leveled out again, leaving her clinging to the wooden slats and rocking precariously back and forth. Two anchors down. Two to go.

There were shouts from below. Sam peered over and saw another geyser shoot up, high into the air. And another. And another. The mass of people in the pit began to heave and dip like a giant wave as they fled from scalding steam and scorching water. The upward draft of hot air sprayed across Sam, stinging her skin like tiny needles.

The bridge swayed slightly in the super-heated currents and Sam hung on, closing her eyes against a sudden onset of vertigo. Part of her dreaded what she was certain she would see when she opened them again. The renewed and amplified cries of those below were already assailing her ears.

Then she heard him. How the colonel's voice stood out from all the others, she wasn't sure. Maybe its familiarity made it rise above the plaintive din. But he was calling for her. Calling for help. Calling her name.

"Sam! Help me! Sam — please —"

It was… wrong. All wrong.

The colonel would never plead like that. And he'd never call her 'Sam'. Not now. Not even in the depths of pain and agony. And he'd never let her risk her life like this to save his. He'd be cursing at her for even trying, yelling at her to save her own damn ass.

She should have realized it before. But of course, it was all Martouf's doing. He'd completely set her up. And she'd walked into it, eyes wide shut. She'd been so concerned for the colonel, it hadn't even occurred to her that Martouf would try to use him against her like this.

Whoever or *whatever* was down there was as much an imposter as Martouf. They all were. For all she knew, that pit of horror wasn't even real. Maybe, if she tapped her heels together three times, it would all vanish in the blink of an eye.

"Sam… Please, help…"

She could still hear him calling. Even though she knew it wasn't really the colonel, it didn't make it any less painful to hear. She had to get out of there.

With the handhold ropes now dangling uselessly, it would be a treacherous walk. Taking a deep breath, Sam cautiously rose to her feet. The bridge wobbled beneath her shifting weight but overall remained steady. She let her anchor rope drop from her wrist and felt a sudden sense of panic as her only security vanished from view. For just a moment she froze, unable to will a single muscle to move. Finally, with what felt like Herculean effort, she raised her left foot and took a tentative step.

The bridge quivered, but only slightly. She took another step. And a third. She could feel the sway increase with each footfall, but she pushed forward. Halfway across. Three-quarters.

Sam leapt the last few feet onto solid ground and tumbled into Martouf, who steadied her before she could fall.

"Samantha —" He got no farther. His jaw cracked like glass beneath her knuckles and he fell, landing spread-eagle on his back. Blood trickled from the corner of his mouth. The only thing that was more gratifying was the stunned look on his face.

Behind her, Sam could still hear the wails of the people in the pit and the cries of the imposter colonel above all the rest. Even though he wasn't real, it was almost more than she could bear.

Scooping up her knapsack Sam stepped over Martouf and all but ran down the path, putting as much distance between herself and the bridge as she could. Angry tears escaped down her face and she wiped them vehemently away. Damn it all, anyway.

She knew she ought to be relieved, grateful that that *thing* back there really wasn't the colonel. Instead, she felt only a desperate sense of loss and despair. She was right back where she'd started, alone and with no clue as to where she was, or what was going on, or how to get herself out of this mess. The only thing she'd gained at all was the conviction that whoever was behind this had some serious resources at their disposal. Nothing but the highest level of technology could explain what she'd just experienced.

It wasn't much, but at least it was something.

Sam raised her arm to wipe her eyes and face on her sleeve and realized that she'd gained one other thing as well.

She still held Martouf's knife in her hand.

CHAPTER FOURTEEN

JACK heard the waterfall long before he and Carter actually saw it. The unmistakable roar of churning water drowned out the far more gentle patter of the light but persistent rain which hadn't let up once the whole time they'd been walking. The dampness was settling in his bones, thanks to the damn thin clothes he was wearing. He felt like an escapee from the infirmary.

Carter, of course, didn't seem to be bothered by the clothes at all. In fact, she hadn't even mentioned their get-ups, until he'd brought it up during their trek. She seemed to think they were 'burial garments,' which was the last thing in the world that would have occurred to him. Jack couldn't help but think it was the last thing in the world that should have occurred to her either.

Carter was tugging at his sleeve and pointing at the cliffs alongside the waterfall. "There, sir." He could barely hear her above the raging water. "I think that's our trail."

If he hadn't known to look for it, he never would have found the switchback. How Carter had spotted it, he hadn't a clue. Now Jack could see the trailhead at the base of the rock. That was where they needed to go. Unfortunately, the only way to get there was mostly flooded by the rain-swollen river.

Swell. Now they could *really* get wet.

Carter had already begun to pick her way among the swirling eddies. Jack followed. It wasn't long before they had to jump over increasingly large pools of water like some weird game of hopscotch. In sandals. And carrying a P90. He had a feeling this would not end well.

He missed the next jump and his foot went into the water — the icy cold water — ankle deep.

Son of a —

As Jack pulled his foot out of the water, the sandal stayed behind, stuck fast in the mud beneath. Perfect. Mucked up feet along with everything else. He didn't even want to think about what kind of alien parasites might be looking for an opportunistic cut right now.

Jack swished his foot around in the water to rinse it off before reaching down to retrieve his sandal. It took more effort than he expected to pull it out of the mud, and when it finally did give way, he nearly lost his balance. He didn't care much about the clothes; they were mud-spattered already. But he sure as hell didn't want to get any of this oozy crap on his gun.

Straightening up, he saw that Carter had pushed on ahead and therefore missed his narrow escape. She took a zigzag leap to the right and then to the left into what she must have thought to be another shallow puddle, but she lost her balance as she landed in water well past her knees. Before he could even shout, she went under.

All the way under.

"Carter!"

He wasn't even halfway to her when her head bobbed up from its mud-bath and she spat out brown, sludgy water. Streaks of puce muck slid down her face and dripped from the ends of her hair as she raised an equally filthy hand to wipe it out of her eyes.

Had she been fully and completely Carter, he'd have probably made some crack. She might even have laughed, in spite of her embarrassment. But this wasn't Carter, at least not all of her. And she wasn't embarrassed at her predicament, she was afraid. Panic-stricken, in fact.

"Colonel—" She sputtered as she began to flail around in her pit of mud. "I—I'm sinking. Help me!"

Jack started toward her but then stopped. He could keep acting like nothing was wrong, but what was the point? Maybe it was time for the truth. She wasn't in any real danger, after all. But she was stuck. And she needed him. It might be the only leverage he had for a while.

"Colonel, please!" Her voice went up in pitch as she shouted above the din of the waterfall. But even when she reached out a muddy hand toward him, Jack didn't move.

"I don't think so." He cradled the P90 and waited.

If he hadn't been so certain that there was a snake inside her head, the look Carter gave him would have killed him. It was a cross between betrayal and disbelief. For a half second he waivered. What if he was wrong?

But he wasn't. He'd bet everything on it.

Maybe he already had.

"Now see —" He edged just a little closer so as not to have to shout quite so loud. "The Carter I know wouldn't need my help. The Carter I know would know *exactly* what to do in a situation like this."

It was true. They'd been in crap like this before. Or at least something close to it. Carter had known precisely how to get them out of it. It was all about physics or some kind of scientific gobbledy-gook. He hadn't really cared at the time. All he knew was that they'd managed to work themselves out of it with her guidance, even if they had ended up looking like they'd been thoroughly dipped in caramel by the time they'd finally crawled to safety.

"I — It just took me by surprise, Colonel. I only need a little help."

He could see her sinking in deeper the more she struggled. She wouldn't get swallowed up all the way; he was pretty sure that only happened in movies. But she was making it harder to get out with each passing moment.

"Nope. Not gonna do it. If you're the real Samantha Carter, you'll know how to get out of there on your own."

She looked truly terrified now. It took everything he had to stay rooted to the spot. Even if the snake was in control, Carter was still in there somewhere. He hated having to put her through this.

"Jack — please. You have to believe me. I *am* the real Samantha Carter —"

And there was all the proof he needed. It was Jolinar, all over again. He didn't even try to keep the rage out of his voice.

"The hell you are! I know a damned Goa'uld when I see one. Now you either tell me who you are, and what the hell you want, or I'll leave you there to rot!"

Jack had to give her credit. For just a moment he thought he saw genuine bewilderment on her face. Not that he was buying it. Not when the confused look suddenly hardened into one of disdain.

And her eyes glowed.

The P90 was on her in an instant. Even though he'd known what she was, it still felt like he'd taken a blow to the chest. He couldn't find his breath.

Damn. He hated it when he was right.

"*I am Tayet,*" announced a voice that was most definitely not Carter's. It made Jack wince. "*And you would do well to rescue us, human. Unless you wish to abandon your companion as well.*"

The slim hope that what was inside of Carter might be a Tok'ra faded.

"Uh-uh." Jack shook his head. "Not until you tell me what the hell is going on here." The waterfall still made it necessary to shout, but he wasn't going to risk coming any closer.

"*It is only a matter of time before I access Major Carter's knowledge and am able to free myself from here.*" Tayet glared at him. "*However, by then, we may all regret your belligerence.*" Carter's face turned up toward the sky and her eyes closed. It was only then Jack realized that it wasn't just the spray from the waterfall that was soaking them. The drizzle had turned into a steady rain and as he watched, the mud in Carter's hair rinsed away clean. For just a moment she looked like herself again, and he could almost imagine she was simply enjoying the sensation of the rain on her face.

But it was only for a moment because he finally realized

just what the Goa'uld was talking about.

The river was rising. And it was rising fast.

Where Carter had been submerged up to her shoulders before, now she was halfway to her chin. Even on the higher ground where he stood, the water had crept up over his ankles without him noticing.

If he waited too long, she'd drown. The Goa'uld he didn't care a rat's ass about, but no way would he let anything happen to Carter.

"Float," he yelled to the Goa'uld as he splashed over to her. "Stop thrashing around and just try to float on your stomach. The extra water should help you."

She stopped flailing and Jack saw her try to relax. Between the rising river and the downpour of rain it had to be difficult.

"Now, lean toward me." He angled his arm in case she hadn't understood. She tried, but the current was becoming stronger as the river flooded higher. Each time she'd almost get herself tilted, a rush of water would push her back again. The panicked look was back on her face.

She wasn't going to make it. There wasn't enough time.

If he went in after her, he'd end up stuck too. His P90 wasn't long enough for her to reach. He needed a stick.

"Hold on!" Jack splashed back toward the forest. There were plenty of branches scattered about. It was just a matter of finding one long enough and strong enough.

The third one he picked up seemed like it would do the trick. Retracing his quickly vanishing footprints, Jack sloshed back through the mud. The Goa'uld was having a difficult time keeping her head above water now. Damn it. He'd nearly taken too long.

"Carter!" He didn't care what the snake's name was, as long as he got someone's attention. "Grab on!"

Swinging the P90 behind his back, Jack thrust the branch out over the swale where she could reach it. Carter grasped it with first one hand and then the other. The sudden force on the branch nearly wrenched it out of his grip, but he tightened up in time to keep from losing his hold.

"I'll pull, you rock, side to side. And use your elbows if you can." The ground beneath his own feet was anything but firm. Mud oozed over his bare feet and squished between his toes. He'd worry about the microscopic alien parasites later. He had a much bigger one to deal with first.

Jack grunted as he hauled back on the branch, trying to pull her out, hand over hand. To her credit she was doing what he'd told her, rolling slightly from side to side and hopefully loosening herself from the suction of the mud. Nothing happened at first, but finally there was some give in the tension as she made progress.

He stepped back a few feet, trying to regain his footing in the rising water.

"Again!" he called, pulling on the branch once more. He could feel her still making steady progress. At the very least, her head wasn't in any immediate danger of going under now. And she seemed to have managed to work her way so that part of her torso was on solid ground. "Monkey crawl," he instructed. She looked up at him, uncertain. Right. Snake, not Carter. "Use your elbows," he explained, dragging on the branch again. "Crawl with your elbows."

She seemed finally to catch on. Even though he could see them sinking into the mud, the elbows were helping as he tugged her forward, inch by inch. This was good, especially since his arms were really starting to protest.

Finally, the only parts still stuck were her legs.

"Try climbing!" She was closer to him now, so he didn't have to shout quite as loudly. "See if your legs can find something solid."

He saw her twisting, trying to do as he said. If she could find the edge of the mud pit it would help him get her out the rest of the way.

But instead of moving forward, he saw her starting to sink

back again. All that thrashing around had only caused the ground beneath her to become saturated again creating an entirely new mud hole.

"Stop! Stop!" They'd be screwed if she sank all the way in again. "Forget the legs — hold on!"

He took another two steps back and reset his feet. The only way to free her now was for him to physically haul her out himself. His knees were going to hate him in the morning.

Repositioning his hands on the branch, Jack pulled.

Nothing happened. She could have been a lead statue stuck in concrete for all the progress he made, not to mention that his hands felt like they were on fire. In retrospect, a branch without the jagged bark might have been a better choice. He'd happily swap out the Hare Krishna footwear for his gloves about now, even if it meant going barefoot the whole rest of the trip.

Jack tried again. Throwing his full bodyweight into it, he leaned back, using his feet as leverage.

Nothing. And she was still sinking.

"I need you to give me one big push." If she wasn't quite as stuck as before, this could work. "On three." She nodded. He took a deep breath. "One… two… *three!*"

Carter lunged forward as Jack wrenched back the branch with every bit of his remaining strength. For a moment she looked like a graceful dolphin arching above an umber sea, but then she hit the water, splashing down with such force that it spewed mud everywhere, including over his eyes. The tension on the branch gave way and he stumbled backwards.

Wiping the dirt off his face, Jack saw that she was crawling now on her hands and knees, making her way toward him through the rushing water. She was coated in mud from her neck down, except for the areas where the water was swiftly rinsing it away. He automatically reached down to help her to her feet, trying to ignore the sudden weakness in his knees at having her safely back on relatively dry land.

Then he saw her face and remembered.

He may have saved Carter's body, but he hadn't saved *her*.

Dropping her arm, Jack swung his P90 around, training it on her. The expression of relief on her face vanished at the sight of the weapon. Good. She looked less like Carter when she was sullen. It would be easier to remind himself that the snake was in control when she was like this.

"Come on." He waved the gun in the direction of the trailhead. "Let's get out of here. Then you can answer my questions."

CHAPTER FIFTEEN

"SOMETHING lies ahead."

They had been walking across the plain for several hours with nothing but rippling grass before them. Now, on the horizon, Teal'c could detect an object of indistinct shape, directly in their path. As they neared it, the shape took form and finally they could see it was a gathering of tents. There were, perhaps, twenty of them. Even from afar, Teal'c recognized their design as being Jaffa in origin. Most were intact, but some seemed to have fallen victim to the wind, their loosened sides flapping in the steady breeze.

Bra'tac called out as they approached, but the place was abandoned. No life had graced its fires for a great many sunsets.

Teal'c stumbled across the first body — or what was left of it. Although it had no head, its garments identified it as male… and Jaffa.

"Over here!"

Teal'c found Bra'tac standing over not one skeleton but a dozen, scattered across the center of the camp, men and women both, going by their clothes.

There was not a skull among them.

"How is this possible?" Teal'c turned to Bra'tac in confusion. "How can there be death when one is already dead?"

"There is death and there is punishment." Bra'tac looked grim. "Those who have displeased their gods may endure the disgrace of the Second Death — the death from which there is no return." He nudged the headless set of bones nearest to him. "It would seem these wretched beings have suffered this fate."

"There are no gods, only false gods." To hear Bra'tac speak of the gods as if they were real alarmed him. Surely he meant it in another context. But instead of answering, Bra'tac merely smiled, his eyes over-bright with unspoken knowledge.

"There are more here," called Rya'c, who had wandered off

among the vacant tents. "And there." He pointed toward the perimeter of the encampment. "All of them are the same way."

In all they carried twenty-seven bodies to the center of the camp and laid them side by side. Teal'c wished he could have spared Rya'c from such a task; what little flesh remained on the bones had hardened into withered leather. But Bra'tac had argued that the boy should help. "To look upon death is to better know life," he insisted.

Bra'tac also argued against a funeral bier. The grasses, he rightly pointed out, would make excellent tinder and the wind would easily spread the fire to the surrounding plains. Instead, they found a few shovels among the belongings of the dead and together the three of them dug a shallow mass grave and interred the bodies there.

The effort took several hours. Teal'c worked mostly in silence. To talk of other matters in the presence of such carnage did not feel right. Bra'tac and Rya'c must have felt similarly, as they too spoke very little.

When at last the task was completed, they surveyed the vast mound of fresh soil. Not knowing who these Jaffa had been, it was impossible to leave a monument to mark their death. In time the grasses would grow over their grave and even it would vanish from sight.

"No one will ever know their names," Bra'tac pointed out. "It is the ultimate punishment for those who have been thus condemned."

Teal'c could say nothing in response. If what Bra'tac said was indeed true, if for these people there was simply oblivion, then there really was nothing to say. Perhaps, however, even in nothingness there would be peace. If so, then he wished it for them.

The sun was setting behind the distant hills by the time they finished. It seemed foolish to move on with darkness so quickly approaching.

"We have shelter. We have food. There is no better reason to stay here for the night," Bra'tac observed. This was true, and yet Teal'c felt uneasy stepping into the place of the people they had just buried. That Bra'tac should demonstrate no similar misgivings was troubling.

At least they selected the tent farthest from the burial site. It was still intact, except for one corner which the wind had pulled free. Teal'c repaired it with no difficulty, a muted silence descending on the inner space once the wind could no longer penetrate it. They shared the food from Teal'c's knapsack, still saying little to one another, and when they were finished, first Rya'c and then Bra'tac entered into *kel'no'reem*.

Teal'c did not. Too many thoughts assailed his mind to find the state of peace necessary to meditate. Taking in a deep breath he tried again, exhaling slowly, willing the tightness in his muscles to relax, refocusing on the sound of his own breathing.

It was no use. He continued to turn over Bra'tac's comments about the gods in his mind. Something in the old man's voice had made Teal'c's skin crawl. But perhaps he was overreacting. Had Bra'tac not recently taken him through the Rite of M'al Sharran to rid him of his own belief that Apophis was a god? Surely Teal'c must have misunderstood.

There was also the matter of returning Rya'c to the land of the living. Bra'tac had been unusually cryptic about how this was to be accomplished, and Teal'c suspected he knew more than he had yet shared. That he held back knowledge of such importance was troubling as well. In the morning, he would speak to Bra'tac and insist upon answers.

With his thoughts settled on a plan, Teal'c felt some of the tension within seep away. Glancing once more at his son and his mentor, already deep in their own meditations, he took another deep, calming breath and closed his eyes.

When next he opened them, it was morning.

The relief he felt when the tents finally faded from view was less than Teal'c had expected. He was used to death. He had killed many men in his life and had been surrounded count-less times by comrades and friends left dead and dying in the wake of battle. He had seen atrocities inflicted by the Goa'uld that would sicken most people, and he himself had inflicted torment and torture upon those who had been deemed his enemies more times than he cared to remember.

Yet there was something about the headless victims which would not leave his thoughts. Perhaps it was, as Bra'tac had pointed out, that they would be forever unknown. Without their faces or their names, they had been completely stripped of their identity, denied the dignity of their individuality. Nothing of who or what they were would ever be spoken of again. They had truly passed into oblivion. It was the final and most brutal of all insults.

His companions were as reserved as himself this morning. Bra'tac had discovered a staff weapon among the discarded belongings and now used it as a hiking stick. Rya'c seemed even more introspective today and would meet no one's eyes. Perhaps the boy was also troubled by what they had left behind.

Teal'c did not easily find an opportunity to approach Bra'tac in private. Rya'c was always within earshot, and Teal'c preferred he not yet be privy to what he wished to discuss with his old friend. An hour passed. And another. The sun was high over-head, casting small pools of shadows at their feet when Bra'tac finally halted. The old man stretched out the staff weapon and pointed ahead of them.

"There! At last we see it. The end of our journey is in sight."

Teal'c could just make out a stone wall, far in the distance. Considering the height and length he could discern from their current position, it had to be massive. "It is most impressive," he noted, looking to see if there was an end to the wall to the left or the right. He could see none. "What is it we will find when we arrive there?"

"The means by which each of us will continue his own jour-ney." There was that tone in Bra'tac's voice again. It held an edge of danger in it. And excitement. Whatever lay ahead, his old friend was eager to meet it.

No longer could he afford to wait for the most opportune time. Although it would be another hour at the very least before they reached the wall, Teal'c was unwilling to take even one more step toward it until he had spoken to Bra'tac.

"Perhaps, Rya'c, you would like to take the lead for a while," he suggested. "Master Bra'tac and I shall be right behind you."

Obediently, but without much enthusiasm, the boy started down the path and was quickly far ahead of them.

"I sense you wish to speak with me, Teal'c. Without the boy around."

He was not surprised that Bra'tac had read his intent. They knew each other too well.

"Indeed. On many topics."

"So I thought. Very well then. 'Fire away,' as I believe O'Neill says."

Now that he had Bra'tac to himself, Teal'c was uncertain where to begin. Perhaps it was best to address the matter of Rya'c first.

"Do you know how it is we will send Rya'c back to his life?"

"If memory serves, when we reach the wall there will be three gateways. Through one of them lies the passage back to the land of the living. Through another lies the continuation of this path."

"And the third?"

"Ah. The third is the key to the other two." There was that knowing smile again. Somehow it did not give Teal'c comfort.

"I take it there is more to attaining this key than simply opening the third gate."

The smile broadened. "Indeed there is. But we shall discover that when we arrive."

Teal'c had the odd sensation of being once more the pupil and Bra'tac the teacher. There was deeper meaning here that he could not yet comprehend, just as in his youth when the old man's cryptic words would leave him pondering for days. He did not have time for such games now; there were more important matters at hand.

"When we have opened the passage that leads back to life, I wish for you to return with Rya'c," he told Bra'tac firmly, setting aside the matter of what waited for them at the gate. "He will need your guidance, as I once did, as he journeys into manhood. I can think of no one better for my son than you."

"Assuming either of us has a choice, tell me why he would not be better off with his father, instead?"

Teal'c had expected this. "Because his father has pledged himself to the cause of the Tau'ri." Bra'tac had never fully understood his devotion to the SGC. "Even if Colonel O'Neill, Major Carter and Daniel Jackson are dead as well, were I to return I would be compelled to carry on in their memory, fighting side by side with other members of the SGC. If you go, however, I know Rya'c will be cared for and well trained, as I was, so that someday he might carry on the fight in my name."

"Carry on the fight," repeated Bra'tac. "Against the Goa'uld."

"Indeed."

"Against our gods — the very gods to whom we owe our health and vitality, our very existence."

It took barely a heartbeat before the comprehension of Bra'tac's words brought Teal'c's staff weapon up and turned against his old friend. Even then he was not quick enough. With tremendous force the old man swung his own staff downward, striking Teal'c's hands where they gripped the shaft. With a cry of pain, Teal'c dropped the weapon. Bra'tac snatched it up and gave Teal'c a broad, feral smile, pointing both staffs at him.

"Is this the punishment of the gods?" snarled Teal'c, his chest heaving. "Am I now to be sent to oblivion as well? Never to be known or remembered?"

Bra'tac's eyes narrowed. "*Shol'va!*" He spat the epithet. "Would that the name 'Teal'c' *could* be purged from all of history. Believe me. We shall do our best."

Loathing rose like bile in Teal'c's throat. He was beginning to understand. "It was your intention to return with Rya'c all along, was it not? To take back your own life on the pretense of returning with my son. I do not know who you are, but I know Bra'tac would never do such a thing. It is the type of deception only a Goa'uld would attempt."

The old man's smile broadened. "Oh I am Bra'tac, Teal'c. Of that you may be certain. But my eyes have at last been opened. Do you not see? Do you not comprehend, even in death, what is truth?"

"Enlighten me," Teal'c growled. In his heart he still could not believe that Bra'tac, the man who had taught him from his youth that the Goa'uld were false gods, could stand here now and spout such lies.

The old man laughed. "This is Duat, Teal'c. *Duat.* We are dead, but what have we found here? Have you seen great Jaffa warriors feasting at the everlasting banquet? Have you found the spirits of those who have gone before you? Is your father here? Your mother? The many warriors who have fought and died at your side? If the afterlife was as we imagined — as we believed — would these things, these people not be here awaiting us?"

Teal'c could find nothing to say. There was truth in some of Bra'tac's words. Uncomfortable truth, but truth nonetheless.

"This is not the Jaffa afterlife, Teal'c. This is the underworld of the Goa'uld. We were wrong when we said they were false gods. They are not. They reign in the galaxy and they reign here. And we are at their mercy."

There was a terrible logic to his words. And yet, if what Bra'tac said was true, then it meant everything he had done, everything he had worked for, sacrificed for, all these years, was meaningless. In his heart Teal'c was not willing to accept that. Not yet.

"You know I speak the truth, Teal'c. You were wrong. *I* was wrong. I have seen the light, but only just in time. And I fear that it is already too late for you." He pointed with one of the staffs at Rya'c, who was now quite far ahead. "Your son outpaces us with his eagerness for life, Teal'c. If you wish to save him, you must open that passageway; and if you wish to prevent him from suffering your fate, you must allow me to go with him. I will indeed teach him — teach him to honor his god and to serve him. Then, perhaps, one day when he returns to this place, he will be spared your fate and take his place among those whom the gods favor."

"With you by his side, I have no doubt," Teal'c observed, coldly.

Bra'tac nodded, his calculating smile returning. "If I am fortunate, yes. Now let us hurry. The gates await, and your son is counting on you."

CHAPTER SIXTEEN

"YOU lied to me."

She'd vowed she wasn't going to even acknowledge his presence after what had happened at the pit. Her fist had said everything that needed saying. Sam hadn't glanced back once, although she could hear his footsteps steadily following her like some stray dog that didn't know enough to go home. That in itself irritated her. And the more she mulled over the entire situation, the harder it was to keep from laying into him. Again.

"I never said he was your teammate," Martouf replied, as though it hadn't been nearly an hour since they'd spoken. "You assumed he was, and I did not dissuade you. But I never told you the man in the Pit of Mutu was your friend."

"That's the same as a lie." She would not let him off on a technicality.

"I beg to differ with you. It is not. You merely jumped to a conclusion."

That stung. Jumping to conclusions was something she was rarely accused of. Her training had taught her to do just the opposite. His implication that she'd let her emotions cloud her perceptions only heightened her annoyance.

"So what was the point of all that, anyway." She shifted gears. "There are easier ways to kill me than dumping me in a pit of boiling mud."

"Why would you think I want to harm you in any way?"

"Gee. Why *would* I think that?" She stopped walking and turned to face him. "If you really had my best interest at heart, you'd be upfront about what's going on here. But instead, you keep up this pretense that you're Martouf—which is really getting old, by the way."

He wisely said nothing in reply, managing to look somewhat contrite. He absently probed his swollen jaw and she wondered if he'd concluded that there were times when it was better not to speak. She hoped so.

Spinning back around, Sam resumed walking. The path now was easy. Any trace of snow was far behind them and the landscape had evolved into a series of small, colorless hills. They were effortless to climb but they did block the far horizon, and the smattering of trees across them obscured any long-range view. She hated travelling blind, but the path only led in one direction, so it wasn't like she had much of a choice.

"How do you do it, anyway?" she asked after a few minutes.

"Do what?"

"Look like Martouf. Sound like him. Know what he was like? I've seen devices that allow one person to look like another, so I know it can be done. It's just that with the copies there are usually discrepancies. But then, I guess if someone could turn the real Martouf into a *za'tarc*, they could probably figure out how to make a pretty convincing doppelganger for him too." She was fishing. The only device that she was aware of that could do such a thing wouldn't be able to duplicate the knowledge this Martouf seemed to possess. In many ways the whole thing was flawless. Except for the small detail that the real Martouf was dead.

He was silent for so long, Sam thought perhaps he wasn't going to reply.

"What if I told you that I really am Martouf, just not entirely the same as you once knew me," he said at last.

"I know. You're a *Ba*. Whatever the hell that is."

"No — that was a lie. I thought, perhaps, you would find that easier to accept than the truth. "

Sam stopped again, this time so suddenly that Martouf nearly ran into her. Admitting to the lie was the last thing she'd expected from him. Yet there was something in the quietness of his voice that made her hold back her angry retort. "Explain," she said instead.

"When you shot me — killed me — my injuries were too

severe for Lantash to heal. You may not know this, but as a symbiote ages, its ability to heal its host diminishes. Lantash is quite old. Not as old as Selmak, but still quite venerable by Tok'ra standards." He gave a slight smile before becoming serious again. "When it became evident that he could no longer do me any good, Lantash was removed from this host. I was kept alive by machines long enough for that to happen, and as soon as Lantash was safely placed in stasis, it was the intention of the Tok'ra to disconnect my life support."

Sam shrugged off a shudder. "What happened?"

The sad smile returned. "I was given a second chance. A Tok'ra, whom I will not name, found another, younger symbiote. He smuggled me away from Revanna and brought me here so I could be implanted and healed. I *am* Martouf, Samantha, but the symbiote within me now is called Anat."

Of all the ridiculous things he had told her up until now, this, at least, made sense. It fit the evidence too. She had been trying for some time now to speak with the Tok'ra scientists about Martouf and Lantash, but they continued to stonewall her. If someone had smuggled the dying Martouf out of the Tok'ra base, she could see how the knowledge of it would be something they'd want to keep from her.

"That would explain why I can sense the symbiote then," she mused, more to herself. "But I thought there were no more Tok'ra? Without Egeria, how can there be any young symbiotes?"

He hesitated for just a moment before quietly answering. "I did not say Anat was Tok'ra."

Sam stepped back, instinctively, her hand tightening around the knife she still held.

"You're a Goa'uld." She couldn't help the note of horror in her voice.

But he was shaking his head. "Anat is neither Tok'ra nor Goa'uld," he explained. "There are others of the same race who do not subscribe to either philosophy. Anat is one of these."

Right. And Goa'ulds never lied. "How do you expect me to believe you?" Maybe — *maybe* — she could accept that this really was Martouf, but it would take a whole lot of convincing for her to believe that what was inside of him was a benign symbiote. She'd already met this planet's welcoming party. 'Benign' wasn't exactly the word she'd use. "What is this, the second or third story you've tried to spin since you showed up here? You can't blame me for not entirely buying this one either."

"I understand how difficult it is for you to trust me, Samantha. I know I should have explained everything to you from the start. I was worried you might not accept Anat as you did Lantash."

Had she ever really accepted Lantash? It was almost always Martouf who had spoken when they'd been together. In Jolinar's memories, however, the two were inexplicably intertwined. She had loved them equally — almost as if they were one being. But Sam had never been able to make that same connection. Lantash, to her, was mostly hidden. It was Martouf to whom she had become so close. In fact, she had done her best *not* to think of Lantash very often, if she could help it. Which was strange, because she never had a problem with Selmak that way.

So Lantash or Anat — it really didn't make any difference to her — only to the extent that one was Tok'ra and the other was not.

It was the 'not' that was worrying her.

"Could you at least explain why I'm even here in the first place? And where are Colonel O'Neill and the others?"

Martouf looked contrite. "It is on my account that you are all here. You see, there is one disadvantage to my current situation — one that I'd hoped to alleviate by trying to convince you that you had no choice but to remain here with me."

"What disadvantage?" Sam already had a feeling she didn't like where this was headed.

"Because my injuries were so severe, even Anat could not fully heal them. He must revitalize me on an almost daily basis. To do so, he draws on the unique properties of this planet. Were he to leave here, he could no longer sustain me. If I were to leave here, I would most assuredly die."

Sam processed that for a moment. She supposed there could be something unique about the planet that would help Anat keep his host alive, but that was beside the point.

"That still doesn't tell me why I'm here," she said.

"It's simple really." There was that winsome smile again. "I was lonely. I missed you. And I thought, if you believed you were dead as well, you would be content to remain here with me."

Of course she'd always known he'd felt *something* for her — something above and beyond what remnants of Jolinar she still carried with her. But she'd done her best to keep Martouf's friendship from ever crossing that invisible line. Apparently she hadn't been as successful with that as she'd thought. Sam had no idea what to say in response.

"It was, in retrospect, a foolish plan," he went on when she made no reply. "Made even more foolish by its unintended consequences."

She didn't like the sound of that. "Which are?"

"The inhabitants of this planet are a dying race themselves. Their hosts have reached the limit of their lifespan. Because of their dependency on the planet, they cannot leave it to search for new ones. Any new hosts must come to them — willingly, as I did, or… unwillingly."

Now she did feel sick. "So, you brought us here to be hosts?" Sam smiled bitterly. "And you claim you're not a Goa'uld."

Martouf was looking sorrowful. "Because you are my friend, Samantha, at my behest they have left you unjoined. I cannot, I'm afraid, say the same for the rest of your people."

If she'd thought she'd felt stone cold before, she felt frigidly leaden now. The Colonel, Daniel, Teal'c —

Wait a minute.

"Teal'c can't be used as a host. He's Jaffa," she pointed out, trying to quell the panic over the colonel's and Daniel's fate and grasping any straw she could find.

"But he carries a symbiote within," explained Martouf. "The Jaffa, Shan'auc, might have been unsuccessful in converting her symbiote to the ways of the Tok'ra, but there are other means. When it reaches maturity, Teal'c's symbiote will become one of them."

"Like you."

He shook his head. "I have told you, Anat is different. We live in harmony. But there are only a few on this world who share this belief. It is the others who dominate this planet."

"NebtHet." The woman's presence was hard to forget. Martouf looked slightly surprised.

"You remember her."

"Yeah. Kinda hard to forget someone who kills you," she snapped.

"Again, I apologize. It seemed, at the time, the easiest way to convince you this was the afterlife."

Sam's anger was simmering again, along with an urgency to keep moving. If there was even the slimmest chance she could rescue the others before —

"How could you, of all people, even consider this?" she raged at him, needing to channel her fury toward something. And he deserved it. "The Martouf I knew would have died rather than allow others to be sacrificed for his own survival. In fact, the Martouf I knew did exactly that."

He looked chastised, but also somewhat defiant. "And I have told you, I am Martouf—but also, not. It is the price I have had to pay. I do not say it is without regret."

"Yeah." She hoped her sarcasm cut deep. "I can *really* tell."

Sam couldn't stand to look at him any longer. She walked away, letting her anger carry her forward with great, long strides. Behind her, she heard him following again. If only he had been an imposter, she wouldn't feel as nauseated as she did right now at the thought of what he'd become.

"So, now that I know," she called over her shoulder. "What

happens next? You can't really expect me to stay here. And you of all people should know that there's no way I'm going to just give up on the rest of my team." It was time to turn her anger into something productive and start thinking of a plan.

"You must not attempt to rescue them, Samantha. You will only put yourself at risk."

She huffed. "I thought you just told me I was protected."

"You are as long as you willingly agree to remain. If you choose otherwise, I cannot assure your safety either."

Funny how he had neglected to mention that before. "You mean they'll use me as a host too."

Martouf said nothing, but a quick glance behind her and the look on his face was all the answer she needed.

"So, you win either way, don't you? Whether I stay willingly or become a host, you get to keep me around." She shook her head, disgust squeezing her stomach yet again. "You know, it's a shame you didn't die back on Revanna. You're a disgrace to the memory of the Martouf I knew."

Her stride lengthened again as she picked up her pace, trying to put some distance between herself and this mockery of the man she had once known so well. There had to be a way out of this. No way was she just going to accept that she and the rest of her team were fated to be trapped here forever. What she needed was more information.

"What is it about this place that makes it impossible for these symbiotes to leave?"

She heard him sigh. "I do not pretend to completely understand it. But this planet has a very dense naquadah core. Over the millennia the properties of the naquadah have imbued the symbiotes with a very strong healing ability. But it has also become an integral part of their physiology. They need constant exposure to the properties of this naquadah to even exist."

That was interesting. "I suppose it's possible that the naquadah may have become integrated into the food chain, which in turn affected the symbiotes by virtue of their dependence upon the host's physiology to sustain them."

"As I said, I have no idea how it is that they have adapted this way, but the fact is, they have and it is what has prevented NebtHet's people from ever leaving this place, even after they found the Stargate."

She pulled up short and stared at him. "Wait — so there is a Stargate here?"

Martouf nodded. "Yes. Although there was not thought to be one when the Goa'uld banished their brethren to this place. It was only discovered years after their dependence upon the planet's core had become irreversible."

She had been so distracted by the revelation that there was a Stargate on the planet that Sam almost missed a slight movement in her periphery. She raised her hand to silence Martouf, and scanned the area until she saw it again. It was a fair distance from them, but moving quickly in their direction. At first Sam thought it might be a bird or an animal, but as its speed brought it closer she could see it was a man — a young man, little more than a boy, really. Perhaps about Rya'c's age.

As soon as Martouf caught sight of him, he hurried forward to greet him.

"Ne'ban, what news? Why have you come here?" There was an urgency in Martouf's voice. Almost a fear.

"I had to warn you." The boy was nearly breathless. There was panic in his voice. "The plan has been altered. NebtHet has changed her mind. They are coming for her." He turned and stared at Sam, wide-eyed. "They are coming for you now."

CHAPTER SEVENTEEN

HAVING spent a year on Abydos, Daniel thought he knew what
'hot' was. Obviously he'd been mistaken. He might have been
fine had he not been carrying the old woman. The heat from
her body held next to his only made the unbearable temperature even more unbearable. They were travelling much slower
because of her, and Daniel knew they should have sought shelter at least an hour ago. But as there was no shelter, they'd kept
moving toward what Sha're promised would be a place of rest.

Daniel almost didn't care. It had been a long time since he'd
felt such absolute physical exhaustion. He was more stumbling
than walking, his brain nearly numb from the effort of putting one foot in front of the other. And really, what was the
point? If he was already dead, as Sha're insisted, then dying
again wasn't going to be any worse. And if he wasn't dead, well,
dying would be a nice change of pace about now.

Sha're had not allowed his slow speed to hold her back. His
insistence at bringing the old woman with them had not gone
over well and she had expressed her displeasure by making
no concessions to the handmaid's frailty. She was well ahead
of them now, not quite a dot on the horizon but close enough.
From time to time the terrain would rise and Daniel would
lose sight of her as she disappeared over a ridge, but her footprints in the sand always kept him on track. He had called out
to her a few times, asking her to wait, but either she was too
far ahead to hear or she chose to ignore him. He wondered
if she even cared whether he was still following her or not.

He was really leaning toward the 'not' part when he saw
that she had stopped atop a distant hill and was waving at
him. More than that, she was beckoning to him, urging him
to come quickly.

Mustering what little energy he had left, Daniel did his

best to walk faster. He hoped that her enthusiasm meant they'd finally reached somewhere they could stop and rest until dark.

Staggering up the last incline, he barely noticed what lay beyond. It was only after Sha're had offered him her water skin and he'd drank gratefully that his eyes focused enough to see the river valley below. A line of demarcation between the vibrant green of the fertile flood plain and the barrenness of the desert was incredibly clear from their vantage point. And in the far distance, snaking through the midst of it, was the source river. If Daniel hadn't known better, he'd have sworn he was looking at the Nile itself.

"There." Sha're pointed. The sun was so bright Daniel had to squint to see, but at last he could make out a dock at the river's edge. A single barge was moored next to it, the only sign of civilization. "Hurry!" Sha're cried, her voice high with panic. "They will leave without us!"

Daniel wasn't sure he had any hurry left in him, but an unexpected cooling breeze off the distant water offered a promise that the worst of the trip was behind them. If nothing else, the thought of putting his burning feet in the cold, rushing current was incentive enough for one last push. He shifted the semiconscious old woman in his arms for what he hoped was the final time and followed Sha're down into the valley.

It was another half hour or so before they made it to the river bank and the waiting boat. It was a genuine Egyptian barque, long and narrow, with great sweeping lines to its prow and stern. In the midst, a single mast rose, its sail not yet set, although there were two figures standing attentively near it, ready to unfurl it at a moment's notice. Daniel counted eight oarsman — bronze-skinned, bare-chested men with straight black hair who looked uncannily alike, seated in mirroring positions on either side of the boat, their oars raised and brought inside. At the bow another man stood facing forward, up-stream. In the stern, his counterpart, the helmsman, held the shafts of two massive rudders by which to steer.

The remainder of the space was filled with seated people. They were packed like sardines, wedged tightly against one another in neat rows behind the mast. If it weren't for the occasional stirring, Daniel would have mistaken them for statues, they sat so still. No one spoke a word.

The only person not on the boat was a man who waited for them on the dock. He was large — burly, actually. Daniel wouldn't have been surprised to see a tattoo on one bicep. As it was, there was a gold band around his upper arm which looked like it would burst should the man put the muscle to any real use. Unlike the oarsman, his head was shaved and Daniel caught the glimmer of a gold earring in one ear. He showed his teeth to them as they approached and it took Daniel a moment to realize it was meant to be a smile.

"You arrive just in time," he boomed, sweeping his arm toward the boat. "Hurry, please. We have two seats waiting."

Daniel's eyes scanned the barge and saw that there were, indeed, two small spaces still available amongst the already crowded passengers. There was only one slight problem.

There were three of them.

He looked down at the woman in his arms and it must have been only then that the man on the dock realized what he was carrying. A growl of disgust rumbled in his throat and he spat on the ground. "You can't take *that* onboard," he snarled. "Not on my boat."

"Look, I realize it's a tight squeeze, but I'll hold her on my lap. She won't take up any room, I promise."

"I don't care if there wasn't a single other passenger. That *thing* still wouldn't be getting on my boat," the man sneered. "Consider yourself lucky I'm even letting you on after touching it." He spat again.

Sha're turned to him. "Dan'yel, please! This is the only boat that will take us to the Hall of the Two Truths. If we are left behind it will be a long and difficult journey on foot. I beg you. Do not let him leave without us."

Her eyes, her voice, even the way she tilted her head—how could he not believe she was his Sha're? And how could he not step onto that boat and sail with her, simply because she asked him to?

But Daniel didn't move. He wasn't even really sure why. He only knew it felt wrong.

Across the river, far in the distance, he could make out a thin line cut into the rising landscape. It was the continuation of the path they had been following. It would take twice as long, Sha're had assured him, to go by foot. That thought alone was enough to make him give the boat a second glance.

But no. He hadn't carried the old woman all this way only to discard her in this deserted place with no one to look after her.

"Could you at least ferry us to the other side?" He was about to offer some sort of payment when Daniel realized he had absolutely nothing with which to barter. His notebook was meaningless to anyone but himself and the food in the knapsack was never going to seal any deal.

"Dan'yel!" cried Sha're, her voice nearly breaking with disappointment. The boatman merely growled.

"What do *you* think?"

Right. Pretty much as Daniel thought.

"Is there any other way to get across?" The river was wide here, but maybe further upstream it narrowed.

"There." The boatman pointed into the rushes along the river's edge. There was a small raft, half in and half out of the water. Further up on the shore Daniel could see a long pole.

It would have to do.

He turned to Sha're.

"I want you to get on the boat and take it to the Hall."

But she was already shaking her head. "No, Dan'yel. You must come with me. We must go together!"

"I can't, Sha're, I'm sorry. I've brought her this far. I can't just abandon her now."

Sha're's eyes flashed angrily.

"You care more about an old bag of bones than you do me!"

The accusation stung. If only he could make her understand — which would be difficult, considering he wasn't really sure he understood himself.

"No, it isn't that. Sha're, listen —" But she had turned her back on him and was striding down the dock to the boat. The boatman tossed Daniel a look of disdain as he followed her, offering her his hand to steady her step onto the waiting boat.

She never looked back. Daniel saw her gingerly settle into her waiting place and the rest of the passengers shifted slightly to fill the space that had been meant for him. With a final scornful look, the boatman cast off the line and the barque drifted away toward the center of the river. It wasn't long before Daniel saw the oarsman begin rowing just as the small mast was raised, catching the wind and propelling the boat upstream. In no time at all he lost sight of Sha're amidst the crowd of other passengers.

"*You are a fool.*" The voice startled him, coming from the old woman in his arms. She stirred slightly and then was still again.

"Probably," he replied. "And I'll probably end up regretting this too. But I couldn't just leave you here."

She coughed raggedly before answering. "*Why not? What am I to you? She who was my queen despises me for what I did. You should despise me too.*"

"Part of me does."

"*Only part?*"

Well. As long as they were being honest — "Okay, a lot of me. But I'm not doing this for you."

He wasn't sure if what came out of the woman was another spasaming cough or a laugh. "*My host, you mean? You think you are helping her?*"

He really did not want to be having this conversation now. The look of bitterness and betrayal in Sha're's eyes were fresh enough to put him on the verge of regretting his decision. A taunting Goa'uld was not going to improve anything.

Now that she was awake, he set the old woman down and busied himself with securing the raft. It would be easier to navigate from the dock than trying to negotiate all the billowing reeds along the shore, so he towed it to where the barque had been tied and went back for the pole. By the time he had everything ready, he was able to think more clearly. Sha're's face was no longer hovering in his peripheral vision.

Getting the old woman onboard was a challenge, but Daniel finally eased her down off the edge of the dock onto the precariously rocking raft. It was sturdier than it looked, comprised of bundles of something very much like papyrus flashed together with a crude, hemp-like rope. Early Egyptian boats had been made similarly and if he'd had the time he would have enjoyed comparing this experience with the Ancient Egyptian concept of the underworld. But his brain was too tired to do any more than merely make a passing note of it.

Using the pole, Daniel pushed off from the dock. Along the shore, the current was manageable, but as soon as they neared the center of the river, it got a lot trickier. The raft was swept, spinning downstream before he finally got the knack of using the pole. The water was fairly shallow, though, and before long they were actually making some progress across the river.

As they neared the other side, Daniel was able to pole the raft back upstream along the river's edge until they landed at a spot close to where the path resumed. Stumbling through the rushes, they reached higher ground and a small copse of stunted trees, where they both collapsed onto the ground. The old woman was spent, and she simply lay there, unmoving. Daniel crawled toward the trunk of the nearest tree and fell against it, closing his eyes. He was too tired, even to reach for the canteen. It would need to be filled before they could move on, but he had no intention of budging from this place for a long while.

With a sigh, he surrendered to his exhaustion and fell asleep.

CHAPTER EIGHTEEN

IT WAS a good half hour before the terrain began to level off and Jack didn't feel that a misstep would send him tumbling all the way back down to the river. From time to time he could still glimpse its frothy white rapids far below through the trees. Definitely not a fall he'd like to take. It really would mean a swift and permanent jaunt to the afterlife. Although at the moment he wasn't so sure but that this place was a far more accurate representation of Hell.

Now that the ground was more even, the trees began to thin and Jack could make out a vast open expanse not far ahead. Without the thick canopy of trees, the rain was coming down harder on them again, but the open field would be worse. He called for Carter to stop.

"Time for a break." He used his gun to point at a couple of trees that were close enough together to still offer some protection. "Have a seat."

She looked grateful as she sank to the ground against one of the trunks. He sat in front of the other tree, keeping his gun within easy reach as he pulled the knapsack onto his lap and opened it.

"Here." Jack tossed her one of the packets of food, taking another one himself. She unwrapped it quickly and took a bite, grimacing a bit as she chewed. "That bad, huh?" he remarked, taking a small bite out of his own. It tasted like wet cardboard. "Well, you packed it, so don't look at me." Jack washed it down with a swig from the mud-covered canteen he'd reclaimed from her as they'd climbed the switchback. No way was he going to leave their only potable water in the care of the enemy.

He offered her a drink, but she shook her head. Shrugging, Jack put the strap back over his head and finished off the food. Bad as it was, he could have eaten another. But who knew how long they'd have to make what little they had last.

Actually, she probably did.

"Thank you, by the way." She spoke suddenly, taking him by surprise. It was Carter's voice too.

"I didn't do it for you."

She nodded. "Even so, I appreciate it."

"Look, cut it out, okay? I know what you're trying to do, so stop with the games, already. You're not Carter so stop pretending to be her and just be, you know — 'Tayet,' or whoever the hell you are."

Thankfully, the snake complied.

"Very well, Colonel. Nevertheless, I am grateful."

"So, you want to explain what's going on here? I mean, what's *really* going on here? Because if you try to give me that 'you're dead and on a journey to the afterlife' crap again, I'm really gonna lose it."

"You are *on a journey, Colonel,"* the snake replied, placidly. *"And I am your guide. Aside from that, you will have to be more specific with your questions."*

Great. A cryptic Goa'uld. Usually you couldn't shut their bragging up. This one wanted to play twenty-questions.

Jack took a deep breath. "Fine. A journey, you say. To where?"

"As I have already told you, the Hall of the Two Truths."

"Okay then — why?"

She looked slightly impatient. *"As I have also told you before, to have your heart weighed in judgment so that you may enter the afterlife."*

He held up a finger and waggled it. "Uh-uh-uh — remember, I said none of that whole 'afterlife' stuff. There's gotta be more to it than that."

Tayet said nothing in reply.

"Right," he sighed, after a few moments of silence. "Not talking about that, are you. So, Teal'c and Daniel — where are they?"

"I do not know."

Okay. Short and sweet. But not terribly helpful.

"Might they be on a similar 'journey?'" He made quotation marks in the air.

"It is my understanding that they are."

Well there was something, at least. They weren't dead either.

"Any chance we might run into them along the way?" He could really use the help, unless of course Daniel had a snake stuck in his head too, in which case all bets were off.

"All roads lead to the Hall of Judgment," Tayet replied.

Even better, a Zen-Goa'uld.

"So, is that a yes?" he asked, then held up his hand before Tayet could answer. "Never mind. You'll probably say something I wouldn't understand anyway." Jack ran his hand through his hair, wiping off the rain. He noticed Tayet shivering ever so slightly.

"Cold?"

It was Carter's reluctant smile that answered. "A little."

He tried not to let that get to him. "You know, next time you pack for one of these 'journeys', you might want to throw in a little rain gear and some matches." Jack stood up, resisting the urge to extend a hand and help her to her feet. "Come on. Let's see if we can find some shelter. And don't try anything funny, okay?" He motioned her with his P90. She made no reply but walked ahead of him back into the forest.

"Here." Jack passed Tayet the canteen to help wash down the cardboard food. It hadn't been half bad this time. Maybe he was just too tired to care. They'd managed to find enough branches to construct a passable lean-to. It was better than nothing, although a fire would have been nice. Hell, he'd settle for socks, at this point.

When she was done with the canteen, Jack took it back and removed the shoulder strap.

"Come on," he said, indicating her hands. "Let's have 'em."

She looked confused, so Jack shoved both his arms out, wrists up. "Sorry. Not taking any chances." In a way, he *was* sorry. Part of him didn't really think she had any intention of running off or conking him on the head. But he was convinced that was only because she looked like Carter. He had to keep reminding himself that he was really dealing with the snake inside.

Reluctantly she held out her wrists. "*I suppose it wouldn't do any good to tell you that this is unnecessary.*"

He wrapped the strap around them several times and secured them with a knot even Carter wouldn't be able to undo. "You'll forgive me if I don't quite take your word on that." Not that he was going to be able to get any real rest, let alone any sleep.

The snake didn't seem much inclined that way either.

"Can I ask you something, Colonel?" She was sounding like Carter again. He hated it. "How did you know I was not really Major Carter? I had the impression, right from the start, that you doubted me."

"Just a gut feeling." There was no need to point out all the obvious red flags, like the whole 'reading hieroglyphics' thing. "That and the fact that you kept trying to convince me I was dead."

"You rejected that premise right away. Why?"

"Not hot enough."

She took a few seconds to process that one. "I don't understand."

"Ever hear of Netu?"

"The realm of Sokar."

"Yeah. See, that's a little more in line with where I'm headed." He said it as a joke, but he knew better. A guy couldn't do all the damned distasteful things he'd done and expect a halo and harp.

"A place of punishment and eternal damnation."

"Sounds about right."

"And that is the afterlife you think you deserve?"

There was an oddly confessional quality to this discussion, hearing Carter's voice asking questions his second in command never would have dared.

"Maybe. Probably, actually. But then it's really not up to me." He cleared his throat. "Look, can we not talk about this?" The last thing he needed was to discuss his immortal soul with the Goa'uld who was holding Carter hostage in her own body. "Besides. You don't get to ask questions. At least not until you answer some of mine."

"I'll try."

Right. He didn't think his odds were any better this time around, but what the heck? He took a deep breath. "Why Carter?"

"I don't under—"

"Why'd you pick Carter?" He felt a sudden, unanticipated surge of anger. "Why not Daniel? Why'd it have to be her?"

Jack waited for a reply, but there was only silence. Grunting, he shook his head in disgust. Damned snake, anyway.

"Because you trust her the most." The answer came unexpectedly out of the darkness in Carter's clear and quiet voice. It seemed to hang there in the space between them, as if the words themselves had substance and weight sufficient to crush him.

Jack felt sick. The pasteboard food congealed in his stomach, hard as a stone in the very pit of it. There was an all too familiar ring to her answer. One he'd swore he'd never permit himself to hear again.

For this reason, this one was chosen.

Suddenly he was in an isolation room at the SGC, mesmerized by the pen in his hand as the rhythmic snapping of the ventilator mercifully drowned out the voices of self-loathing in his head.

No. Now was not the time to go there. What mattered was

this, right here, right now. He'd find a way to fix it somehow. This time without killing Carter.

Jack suddenly didn't feel like asking any more questions, and thankfully the Goa'uld didn't either. It wasn't long before he recognized the slow steady breathing of Carter's sleep.

At least there was no ventilator this time.

Because you trust her the most.

Yeah. It was going to be one hell of a long night.

CHAPTER NINETEEN

NEBTHET didn't need Aset's critical commentary to know, this time, that things had gone wrong. In retrospect, perhaps it had been a mistake to leave O'Neill his weapon. The analysis of his thoughts and memories had made them confident that he would trust Carter implicitly. It was why she had been selected as the avatar for his Observer. He had been incredibly difficult to read, though, and they had been short on time. Perhaps they should have delved deeper. They must have missed something.

Still, NebtHet had to give Tayet credit for improvisation. She effectively played into O'Neill's assumption that Carter had been taken by a Goa'uld, right down to a convincing, if distasteful, display of glowing eyes, and had salvaged the situation. She had even been able to get them back on the right path eventually. Nevertheless, this most certainly was not the way they had expected O'Neill to behave.

The same could be said for Carter, although Anat had managed, in spite of everything, to still guide her to the Pit of Mutu. NebtHet hoped the injury to Anat's face was not too severe.

The other two seemed to be proceeding as anticipated, although for how much longer, she could not now predict. SG-1 was far different than she had envisioned.

Her eyes drifted momentarily to the screen which displayed the chaapa'ai. It sat in its chamber, motionless and mute. She had not yet heard from Jenmar, and it troubled her. Upon further reflection, their last conversation had been disquieting, as if the trust that had existed between them had been tarnished in some way.

Perhaps she should have shared more of her plan with him. Jenmar truly understood the ideals to which the Djedu aspired, more so, even, than some who had followed her for millennia.

No one was more deserving of the privilege of taking the final step to ascension. In retrospect, she might have entrusted him with more knowledge than she had. When he returned, she would rectify any misunderstanding on the matter.

The monitor in the bottom right corner flashed a live feed of O'Neill and Tayet walking at a steady pace across the Plain of Rosetjau. The colonel cradled his weapon like one might an infant, but at least it was no longer pointed directly at Tayet. It would be several hours still before they reached their destination, but NebtHet had a good feeling now. In spite of the temporary setbacks, this would work. Already she had learned so much by watching SG-1. She could only imagine what their next encounters would reveal.

A thrill of anticipation rippled through her.

A good feeling, indeed.

CHAPTER TWENTY

IF JACK never saw another blade of grass in his life, he'd be a happy man. The stuff was so damned high that he felt like a rat in a maze and definitely at a strategic disadvantage. Worse, he kept losing sight of Carter. Or Tayet. Or whoever the hell she was. The path had so many twists and turns, even when he stayed right on her six she was still out of sight more times than she wasn't. He might have untied her hands, but he still didn't trust her.

"How much longer until we're out of this stuff?" He batted away a swaying stalk that had blown in his face. They'd been at this for what seemed like hours.

"I can't say."

Again with the careful syntax. Wonderful. "Is there anything you *can* say?"

"As with many endeavors, Colonel, there is as much to be gained in the effort as in the conclusion. The journey will be exactly as long as it needs to be."

More with the Zen. Daniel would eat this stuff up. "So, we're almost there, then?" For just a second he caught Carter's smile, until he remembered that it wasn't really hers. He had to quit doing that.

Silence was probably best. She wasn't giving up any more information anyway. Besides, it was easier to remember it wasn't Carter if the damn snake wasn't using her voice.

Jack sensed the movement in the grass before he heard it. Carter — he couldn't help himself, it was technically still her in there somewhere — must have too, because she stopped short, signaling for him to do the same. For a moment he thought maybe it was only the eerie whispering of the grasses brushing against each other in the breeze, but then he heard something else — something that wasn't the random rustle of stem against stem.

The sound had been ever so soft, yet deliberate. Like the careful placement of a foot on grass. There was no mistaking it for the wind or anything else. He glanced at Carter to see if she'd heard it. By the look on her face, she had.

Jack crept closer to her so she could hear his whisper. "Any idea what kinds of things live around here? Are we talking cute little killer rabbits or harmless Giant Sloths?" He'd learned a long time ago that size really didn't matter. At least not when it came to an enemy.

"This is Duat. It is possible for anything to exist."

Okay. No help there. Whatever it was, there was no point in sticking around like sitting ducks.

"Let's keep moving — but quietly." Running might make whatever it was just that much more interested in them.

With every turn of the path, Jack half expected to find someone or something blocking their way, but it remained clear. After a while he tapped Carter's arm and signaled her to stop. Straining his ears, the only thing he heard was the eerie whispering of the grasses. Maybe whatever it was had gotten bored, and moved off.

Then he heard it again. Carter did too. He could tell by the way her eyes widened in fear. So much for giving it the slip. There was no question now, the thing was stalking them.

He motioned for Carter to pick up the pace. There was no point in stealth now. Staying ahead of it was their only hope, and at that a slim one. The tall, reedy grass didn't offer much in terms of a defensive position if and when it decided to attack.

As soon as they began to move faster, so did their pursuer. The sound of it running, off to one side and then switching to the other, mirrored their own jogging steps. If Jack had to guess, he'd say it was toying with them. As close as it was, it could have attacked any time. The fact that it hadn't was almost as disturbing as how closely it was trailing them.

What the hell was it, anyway?

A blurred mass erupted from the brush and slammed into

Carter before disappearing into the tall grass. He caught her as she stumbled toward him, but by the time she'd righted herself and he could bring his weapon up, the creature was long gone.

"You okay?"

She seemed flustered, but unharmed. "Yeah, thanks. But I really think—"

Jack knew it was behind him by the look on her face. Wheeling, he lay down a spray of bullets, sweeping the path behind him, but all he saw was the slightest movement of a tail as it disappeared into the grass.

"Go!" he shouted at Carter. "Go, go, go!"

She ran. He was right behind her. And the creature was right behind him. It jumped back and forth across the path from the shelter of the tall grass, obviously having given up on stealth mode. It moved too quickly for him to see clearly, and what he could see didn't make any sense.

"Keep going!" Jack shouted as he stopped and turned to face it. He brought up his site and took aim. Any second—

It caught him from behind. Razors raked his back and spun him around, sending him sprawling on the ground. The air left his lungs as he hit. For a moment the world dimmed.

The impact had jarred his P90 from his hands and it took a few seconds for Jack to realize that he was lying there, defenseless. The next blow would come at any moment.

Except it didn't. Which gave him just enough time to get to his feet and curl his finger around the trigger. Keeping his site on the spot where the creature had disappeared, Jack carefully walked backward along the path. No way was he giving that thing his back again.

He ached all over. And his back stung like hell. Even so, it could have been worse, and the fact that it wasn't bugged him. Something that powerful should have taken him out the moment he had him on the ground. Just as it should have taken out Carter when it knocked her down. Something about it just didn't fit.

He nearly backed into Carter as he rounded a curve. She was waiting for him.

"Colonel, your back—" she exclaimed in dismay. At least the stinging had died down a little. Except it was replaced by a warm trickle of something that he really hoped was sweat and not blood.

"It's just a flesh wound," he joked, grimly. "Whatever that thing is, it's got a wicked set of claws. What is it, some kind of cat?"

"As I suspected, it is the Ammit."

"The Ammit? What the hell is that?"

"She is the Devourer, the creature that waits for the outcome of the weighing of the heart and consumes the hearts of those who are not worthy. Without your heart, it is impossible to enter into the afterlife."

The thing was more likely to send him *to* the afterlife than be waiting for him there. "So, not a cat, then."

"It's part lion, part hippopotamus, and part crocodile." She was still looking at his back with concern.

"Cuddly," Jack deadpanned.

She gave him one of Carter's patented tolerant looks. He really wished she'd quit that.

"Let's keep moving." He wasn't sure what he wanted to get away from more—the creature, or Carter. "That thing will be back any minute."

She shook her head. "No. Listen. It's gone."

Carter was right. The only sound now was of the swaying grasses. Still, it seemed unlikely that it would just take off.

"May I see your back?"

Reluctantly, Jack turned. The burning sensation was tolerable—just.

"I don't think it intended to kill you." She took the canteen from him. Even though he knew what was coming, it still hurt like hell when she poured the water over the wound. "If it had, you wouldn't have survived the attack."

"My lucky day," he said through gritted teeth.

"Actually, Colonel, it is." She handed him back the canteen. "I believe the Ammit has decided you are worthy of continuing your journey to the final judgment. Not everyone who enters Duat makes it to the Hall of the Two Truths. This is actually a good thing."

Right. Try telling that to his back.

"Maybe next time it could just drop off a nice fruit basket," Jack grumbled. "Understatement goes a long way."

There was nothing understated about the corpse they found twenty minutes later. To Jack's great relief, it was neither Teal'c nor Daniel. Whoever the guy was, his heart was missing from his chest. It did not look as if it had been a painless death.

"The Ammit," Carter confirmed, after examining the body.

"Yeah. I got that."

She stood up and looked around. "We should go and let the carrion eaters have their meal." A group of agitated crow-like birds were fussing in the grass nearby.

When Jack hesitated for a moment, she studied him. "*Do not concern yourself with burying him, Colonel.*" It was the first time the snake had spoken in a while. "*When a man loses his heart, there is little point in salvaging what's left of him.*"

"Don't tell the Tinman," he muttered.

"*Tinman?*"

Carter would have gotten it. "Never mind." He stepped around the body. "Let's just get the hell out of here, okay?"

He pushed past her and back onto the trail, wanting nothing more than to put some distance between himself and the man with no heart.

CHAPTER TWENTY-ONE

THE SHADOWS had lengthened considerably by the time Daniel opened his eyes. For a moment he couldn't grasp where he was, but then he spotted the old woman stirring on the ground a few feet away and it all came rushing back. So, not a nightmare after all.

It took longer than Daniel would have liked to prepare for the next leg of the journey. His muscles protested with every movement, even for something as simple as bending down to fill the canteen with water. The Goa'uld was awake and she watched him silently, accepting the food he offered her without comment or thanks. He didn't know whether it was because she simply didn't have the strength to speak or whether, having made her assessment of him once, she felt it unnecessary to add anything further. Either way, Daniel was glad she kept quiet. He didn't feel much like talking himself.

When they were finished with what had passed for a meal, Daniel helped the old woman to her feet. She sagged immediately against him. Right. More carrying. At least it wasn't as hot as it had been before, and the ground here was firm and easier to negotiate. Large boulders and jagged outcroppings punctuated the landscape while small, low-growing plants hugged the dusty ground. The place was more Mojave than Sahara, which at this point was about the best he could hope for.

Even though the terrain was more hospitable than before, the fact remained that the old woman was a dead weight. The brief rest hadn't been exactly restorative and his muscles still trembled with fatigue as he lifted her. Exactly how much longer he could keep this up, Daniel didn't know. Maybe they'd both end up as vulture food in the end.

The only way Daniel could gauge time was by the passage of the sun. How that translated into hours on this planet, he had no clue. If he went by his level of frustration, however, he guessed he'd been travelling forever.

Maybe the old woman was right. Maybe he was a fool for doing this. Even with frequent stops, Daniel was very near his limit. Maybe this was his fate, to perish out here and never make it to the Hall of the Two Truths. What exactly that meant in terms of the afterlife, he wasn't sure. If this even *was* the afterlife. His doubts about that had grown with each torturous step.

But then, he had brought this on himself. He hadn't *had* to bring the old woman along. That had been a burden of his own making. If he'd just left her behind he would have been on that boat now with Sha're. They would probably already have made it to the Hall, and if this really was the afterlife, they could have entered eternity together.

The old woman was right. He really was a fool.

Daniel spotted the leg first. It was a human leg. Or what was left of it. What hadn't been scavenged by who knew what, was encrusted with beetles — scarabs, by the looks of them. They swarmed across the entire body, their shiny black wings forming a living armor over the corpse.

It was a woman. Daniel could tell by what remained of her clothing and by the strands of long, gray hair that were matted to the fleshless skull. An old woman.

But not just an old woman.

A few meters away he spotted the second skeleton, already bleached white by the sun. If he hadn't known better, he'd have assumed it was a snake. She had been a Goa'uld.

The old woman in his arms moaned slightly. Daniel had been so preoccupied by the grotesque scene that he'd practically forgotten her. He found a sheltered spot for the handmaiden several meters away and carefully set her down. Returning to the skeleton, he gathered stones and began covering the dead woman's remains.

What was left of the symbiote was hardly worth covering. Not to mention the fact that it was a Goa'uld.

But what if he was wrong? It wasn't beyond the realm of possibility that whoever this woman was, she might have been a Tok'ra. There was no way of knowing for sure. Besides. How could he justify judging what this creature had been simply by what it was? The only way to determine what was good and what was evil was by a being's deeds, and Daniel had no way of knowing, in this case, one way or the other.

He had to cover it too. He had no choice.

As he scrounged for a few more rocks Daniel could feel the handmaiden's eyes on him.

"You are a strange man, Daniel Jackson." It was the first time she had spoken since the river.

"How so?" He began piling the rocks on the slender bones.

"You help what you nevertheless despise, both in life and in death."

"Yes. Well. Some would call it more foolish than strange."

She grunted. *"You are not as I expected you to be."*

"Well, that's me." He arranged the last of the rocks. "I'm just full of surprises."

Daniel stood up and dusted off his hands, staring for a moment at the makeshift graves. Usually he would have felt the compulsion to make a few remarks, but this really didn't seem to warrant that.

"We need to keep moving," he said instead.

"I believe I can walk a little, now," she replied, much to his surprise. Daniel looked her over. She still seemed as frail as before but when he helped her to her feet she was able to stand unaided. A couple of steps, however, showed that she was still unsteady, so he gave her his arm for support.

They hadn't gone far when the old woman spoke again. *"Why are you doing this for me?"* There was no bitterness this time, only genuine curiosity.

"You were right before," he admitted. "I did it for the host. I know the Goa'uld have always tried to insist that nothing of the host remains, but I've seen proof to the contrary. And if this is Duat — if we are, in fact, journeying through some kind of underworld — then I have to believe that at some point in this journey there will be a chance to find peace. And if anyone deserves peace, it's a Goa'uld's host."

"*And what about the symbiote?*" The edge of combativeness was back in her voice. "*Do we not also deserve some kind of rest? We are what we are. We can no more choose to survive without a host than can you choose to survive without a heart. Should we be punished for eternity because of our very nature? Somehow that does not seem fair either.*"

"You may not be able to help what you are, but you can choose how you live. The Tok'ra are the same as you, but have taken a different path. Their hosts are willing — they volunteer. And the symbiote does not suppress the host but shares with it equally. There is no dominance of one over the other."

The old woman grunted with disdain. "*I do not think you would care to hear my thoughts on the Tok'ra.*"

"Probably not." The last thing he wanted right now was to debate the questionable merits of symbiotic relationships, Tok'ra or Goa'uld.

"*And yet,*" she continued, to his surprise. "*I do not say there isn't some value in your argument. It could be that something might be gained from a more equitable arrangement between symbiote and host.*"

Daniel was sure his jaw quite literally dropped.

"Like the Tok'ra have," he clarified, but she made a dismissive sound.

"*What the Tok'ra have are two beings crowded into one body, each constantly having to step aside for the other.*" She sniffed. "*No, the arrangement of which I speak is far beyond anything the Tok'ra have ever even dreamed of.*" She took a deep breath as if the effort of talking was draining her. Yet her voice remained strong. "*It is not simply the sharing of one body by two minds, but the complete reforming of the individual by mutual consent, so that two minds, quite literally, become as one. Where before there was host and symbiote, upon complete merging there is now an entirely new being."*

Daniel took moment to process that. He'd never even considered anything like this. Symbiotic relationships could certainly be mutually beneficial in some cases, but not in any way such as she was describing.

"That's a fascinating concept," he answered, hesitantly. "In theory, of course. But I'm not sure it's something I would ever expect to actually see happen. Humans and Goa'uld both desire individuality. I cannot see either being willing to surrender their uniqueness to become something else, something that's shared in the way you describe it. I don't believe it is in the nature of either species to willingly give up their identity to transform into something unknown."

"If that is so, then to what purpose is ascension?"

He wasn't sure he'd heard her correctly. "Ascension?"

"In my life I have heard it spoken of many times," she explained. *"Mostly by the oldest of the Jaffa who dreamt one day of finding Kheb and leaving their physical bodies behind. And of course there are the stories of a race from long ago who also were able to transform themselves into energy and exist solely in that form."*

Apparently he had heard her correctly. "Yes, I know what it is. I just never thought of it as transformative in that way. I always considered it more of an evolutionary step."

"Even so, it is still changing from what is known to what is unknown. Is it not in the nature of your species to desire such a thing, even when what it is remains beyond your understanding?"

In some ways, she had a point. But he felt there was still a subtle distinction.

"Yes, it is. But I would argue that the two concepts are slightly different. Humans are explorers by nature. We've always wondered what lies beyond the next hill, the next ocean, the next solar system. That's different from changing the absolute essence of who we are. Even ascension does not ask us to do that — at least, from what I know. Which, admittedly, isn't all that much. But ascended beings are still the same person. They simply exist in an altered form."

"*And do you desire to ascend, Daniel Jackson?*" The question took him completely by surprise. It was odd, coming from an old Goa'uld.

"I don't know," he admitted. "I hadn't given it much thought, actually. I'm not sure it's something I can just decide on my own."

"*Do you not think it possible for humans to ascend?*"

"Well, considering we recently had an encounter with an ascended being who certainly seemed human, I suppose yes. Possibly."

"*And what about other species?*"

"You mean like the Jaffa?"

"*Or the Goa'uld.*"

Daniel tried to cover-up his incredulous laugh as a cough.

"Goa'uld? Uh, no offense, but I'm pretty sure that as a species they don't quite meet the criteria. At least, not as I understand it."

"*And what is it that you understand?*" There was definite ice in her voice this time.

But it was a good question. What did he really understand about ascension, after all? Very little, if he were being honest with himself. The walls at Kheb hadn't really provided a key so much as they had an ambience from which to gain the enlightenment needed to ascend. Daniel was a long way away from even beginning to understand it. There was no point trying to pretend otherwise.

He sighed. "Probably not as much as I should, to be having this conversation."

There was a small harrumph from the woman. "*So, am I to assume from what you've implied that you believe ascension to be based on one's worthiness? That the desire to ascend is not in itself sufficient, but that there must be some sort of dem-*

onstration of certain qualities in an individual for them to be rewarded with ascension?"

Did he think that? He didn't have a whole lot to go on, but given Sam's recent experience with Orlin, he'd have to say that there was indeed a measure of worthiness involved. And certainly that had been implied by the monk at Kheb as well.

"I guess I'd say yes. I think one has to deserve to ascend. They can't just do it because they want to."

"And how does one 'deserve' ascension? What qualities do you think one should possess to be offered this opportunity?"

Why did he have the feeling this had become more than just a casual conversation? He almost felt like he was being interrogated.

Fine. If she was really looking for truth, he wouldn't hold back. "Well, not taking control of another person's body without their consent would be a good place to start."

The old woman gave him an appraising, sidelong glance. *"You are quick to judge, Daniel Jackson,"* she told him. *"Would you consider that an essential quality for ascension?"*

"Probably not. But then again, I never said I thought I was a candidate."

"Why not?"

Because of Kheb. He thought he had learned so much in so little time, only to discover that it hadn't been him at all, but Oma Desala. He'd been arrogant to think that such a thing was so easily mastered. And if he hadn't learned his lesson well enough there, Shifu had certainly taught him just how far he still had to go. So the answer to her question really was rather easy. "Because I don't deserve it."

She gave him a curious look, but made no reply, and Daniel was grateful that she said nothing more as they walked. The terrain had turned challenging again, and he needed to pay attention to almost every step they took. Daniel was strangely relieved to focus on the physical effort of walking for a while.

Still. The handmaiden's questions had been troubling, not

just for their content but for her uncanny ability to draw him out. He had the distinct feeling that she had been probing for something. Whether or not she'd found it, Daniel didn't know. What he did know was that this little journey across the desert had suddenly taken on a new meaning.

He just wasn't quite sure, yet, what it was.

CHAPTER TWENTY-TWO

"WHAT do you mean, they are coming for her?"

Sam detected an edge of panic in Martouf's voice. She didn't like the sound of this at all.

Ne'ban's eyes were filled with fear. "NebtHet and the others know that you have revealed the truth to Major Carter. They have decided not to wait until you bring her to the Hall, but to take matters into their own hands."

Martouf went ashen. "You are certain? This is what they said?"

Ne'ban nodded. "It is. I swear it."

Martouf placed his hand firmly on Ne'ban's shoulder. "Then I must act accordingly. You have my thanks," he told the boy earnestly. "Now you must go back. And do not let them see you."

Ne'ban threw Sam a terrified look and without another word took off running back the way he had come.

"You want to tell me what's going on *now*?"

Martouf blinked at her, as if he'd forgotten she was there. "The others — NebtHet — believe I will no longer be able to persuade you to come with me to the Hall of the Two Truths."

"Is that where the rest of my team is?"

There was a slight hesitation before he replied. "Yes. That is their destination as well."

"Then I guess NebtHet is going to get what she wants. I told you, I'm not leaving here without my teammates. If that's where they are, then that's where I'm going." It was obviously a trap, but it wasn't like she had any other choice.

"You don't understand, Samantha. There is more at stake here than just SG-1. I have made a terrible mistake, I see that now. Under no circumstances can you go to the Hall of the Two Truths. I must take you to the Stargate, as quickly as possible."

"I'm not leaving without my—"

"No!" Martouf's forcefulness made her jump. "I know you wish to rescue Colonel O'Neill, Dr. Jackson and Teal'c, but it is impossible. Even if they haven't been taken as hosts, you cannot risk going anywhere near them. You do not understand," he insisted, almost angrily.

"Then why don't you explain it to me?" Sam shot back at him. "Just what the hell is going on, Martouf? Tell me everything, and this time I mean *everything*."

He looked around, even up into the trees, as if he felt eyes on him.

"I will tell you," he said, his voice low. "All of it. I promise. But we must keep walking. No place is safe now."

This time they walked side by side. Sam could feel the tension radiating from him. It didn't help.

"As I was saying before, the inhabitants here were banished by the Goa'uld millennia ago."

"Why? Did the System Lords see them as a threat?"

"Yes. But not in the way you might imagine. The System Lords never appreciate anyone who challenges their authority, which is why they've waged war with each other for thousands of years. But it was not because of a power-play that the Goa'uld banished NebtHet and her people. It was because they were too evil, even for the System Lords to tolerate."

The notion that the Goa'uld would find some among their ranks who so exceeded their own lack of moral code that they had to be rid of them was about as ironic as one could get. Chillingly, it was also quite believable.

"The System Lords rounded them up and banished them to this place—Duat. It was thought, at the time, that there was no Stargate here. NebtHet and her people were trapped. Without technology they were doomed, compelled to spend their final days alone and forgotten."

"Obviously that didn't happen."

Martouf shook his head. "No. Ever the opportunists, the

System Lords couldn't even lay aside their feuds long enough to rid themselves of a common enemy. Even as the banished ones were deposited on this planet, the ha'tak that brought them here came under attack. It crashed only a few kilometers from where it had abandoned its prisoners."

"So the banished Goa'uld ended up with a ship?"

"In a manner of speaking. It was not capable of space flight, and most of its systems were irreparably damaged. But it contained a sarcophagus. No longer were the banished ones doomed to live short, miserable lives."

"Instant immortality."

Martouf shrugged. "It helped them to survive and to continue to live and thrive, even in exile. In time they were forgotten, even by those who'd banished them here."

"Then they found the Stargate," Sam prompted.

Martouf nodded. "But by then, they had become dependent upon this planet's core. A few tried to leave, but they always returned, near death, seeking revival in the sarcophagus. It was only then that they determined that their very existence depended on the planet on which they lived. They were still prisoners, after all."

Granted, it was a fascinating story and one that Sam was sure would intrigue Daniel to no end. But it didn't explain what was happening now. "So they remained trapped. And still are, which is why they need hosts. I get that. But what was that all about with Ne'ban?"

The look on Martouf's face told Sam that the worst was yet to come. Jolinar had been right; the man could not conceal his feelings. Self-recrimination was written all over him.

"In your case," he said, "it is not your body they want, Samantha. It is your mind. They know of your brilliance. They know of your work with naquadah. What they want is for you to create a device that will enable them to leave this planet and take their life-giving naquadah with them."

"Good luck with that." Sam didn't bother to tone down the

sarcasm. What the galaxy did not need was another race of Goa'uld even more ruthless than the ones already out there. No way in hell were they using her to get off this planet.

Martouf only looked that much more miserable. "You don't understand. You will do it, willingly or not. If you do not help them of your own volition, they intend to implant a symbiote within you who will take your knowledge and create the device itself."

Sam went cold. Memories of being pushed down into the smallest corner of her own mind while someone else lay siege to her body and her knowledge sucker-punched her. For just a moment she had difficulty breathing. She couldn't go through that. Not again.

"They had promised me…" There was anguish in Martouf's voice. "I… I thought we would have more time. But seeing you again, like this. I find I can no longer be complicit in their plans. You must leave Duat as soon as possible."

"I'm not leaving without the others," Sam told him, when she'd steadied herself. "We don't leave our people behind. Help me rescue them first and then we'll gladly get out of here."

But Martouf was shaking his head. "You heard Ne'ban. They no longer trust that I will deliver you to them. They intend to intercept us before we even reach your friends."

"Then let's get off this damn path and find another route. There has to be a different way to get to this Hall you keep talking about." Sam glared at him. This was no time to be standing around wringing their hands when there was still time to act. "Unless, of course, you plan on changing your mind — again."

Martouf looked chastised. "My only wish now is to protect you, Samantha. You must leave this planet. For your safety and the safety of the galaxy."

Sam wanted to believe he was sincere, but at this point actions spoke louder than words. She'd wait and see exactly what sort of action he was willing to take.

"Then maybe we should get out of here," she suggested. "Quickly."

Martouf nodded. "Yes, yes. First we must make it to the *sebkhet*. When we are safely on the other side, I will take you to the Stargate." He set off at a quickened pace down the same trail they had been taking.

"Martouf, wait." She was jogging to keep up with him now. "I told you, I'm not going to the Stargate until—"

"Sam, you do not understand the terror that would be unleashed on the galaxy should these Goa'uld attain the ability to leave this planet. They will make the System Lords look benevolent by comparison." There was a mixture of sympathy and resoluteness in his face. "As much as it pains me to say it, you must leave the rest of SG-1 behind. If you do not, then you risk everything. The fate of the galaxy — and of Earth — quite literally depends upon you."

CHAPTER TWENTY-THREE

TEAL'C had been wrong. The wall had taken them well over two hours to reach. He was grateful for the extra time. It gave him the opportunity to think.

Bra'tac's words had the ring of truth about them, and yet Teal'c still doubted them. In retrospect, his own experiences since he'd awakened in the tomb contradicted each other so much, he was no longer certain how to interpret them. He was meant to be dead, and yet he felt as alive as he ever had. His throbbing knuckles where Bra'tac had struck them were proof enough that this body was capable of the same wounds and aches as his real one. Likewise, his need to eat and drink, even to relieve himself, all were functions one associated with life, not death. He had fully expected such trivialities to be done away with in the afterlife, and yet it would seem that they were not.

And then there was his symbiote. It still lived within, healing his wounds and giving him strength. Surely in death he would be free from the need of it, and the symbiote itself no longer in need of him? Especially if, as Bra'tac claimed, this was the underworld of the Goa'uld. Should he not have been at their mercy from the moment he entered this place? Where was this punishment Bra'tac believed was due him?

Still. Who knew what may yet lie ahead? Of the three gates, Teal'c knew with certainty what was behind only two of them. The third gate — the one Bra'tac said would lead to the continuation of this same path — was the mystery. If this were indeed the afterlife of the Goa'uld, then perhaps it was there his punishment awaited. If, however, Bra'tac was wrong, or lying, then the path may simply lead him forward, possibly to the places he had believed in all his life, and he would be reunited with those he held most dear.

He would only know the truth when he got there.

Although there was another choice.

He could return to life with Rya'c and carry on the fight. Gods or not, the Goa'uld had to be stopped. If Bra'tac had lost his way—had lost that vision—then Teal'c could not allow him to contaminate his son with the same fear.

Rya'c had halted about a hundred meters in front of the wall and was waiting for them. He seemed uneasy as they approached. At first Teal'c wondered if the boy had seen his confrontation with Bra'tac, but Rya'c's nervous glances were aimed at what, from a distance, Teal'c had taken for oddly stunted trees.

Only they were not trees. They were wooden staff weapons, practice weapons, each planted upright in the ground, evenly spaced as far as they could see to the left and to the right. Atop each staff was fixed a head, dried and shriveling in the sun. Time and the elements had rendered them featureless, except for the faint remains of tattoos upon their foreheads. Undoubtedly they belonged to the Jaffa they had just buried.

Perhaps Bra'tac was right after all. Perhaps this really was the realm of the Goa'uld. And perhaps it would not be long before his own head joined these as a warning to all who would dare to defy their god.

It did not matter. Goa'uld-hell or not, he would not surrender what he had fought so hard to earn. And he would not allow Rya'c to forfeit his freedom either.

"Let us keep walking, my son," Teal'c said, placing his arm around the boy's shoulder and ignoring Bra'tac who had come up from behind. Together they walked past the line of gruesome spikes and toward the wall.

The three gateways stood side by side, each identical to the other. Recessed into the wall and solidly framed in well-hewn stone, they were three times Teal'c's height and at least half that in width. Into the lintel of every door, each in a separate block of stone, were carved symbols. Teal'c recognized them at once. They were the markings that comprised the Stargate address of Chulak, except they were not in the correct order. And there was a seventh, unfamiliar symbol as well.

The door itself appeared to be made of the same stone as its casement. Studying each one in turn Teal'c could detect no way of opening them. There was no handle, no touch-pad, no sign of any technology, simple or advanced. He was puzzled.

And wary. Bra'tac had intimated that opening the gates would be no simple task and Teal'c did not believe the old man had simply been referring to their perplexing opening mechanism. But although the alcoves were bathed in shadows, they were empty of any threat that he could see. No one challenged their approach. He examined each gate unaccosted.

If Bra'tac were to be believed, one gate contained the means by which to open the other two. Yet there was no indication as to which was which. Teal'c placed his hands on each door and touched the nearby pillar stones in the hope that some sign might reveal itself, but they kept their secrets well. As much as he despised doing so, he knew he could not proceed further without Bra'tac's assistance.

Teal'c sensed the threat before he even turned around. Bra'tac had positioned himself in front of the center gate, a weapon in each hand. His eyes glittered with anticipation as he smiled, menacingly. Teal'c understood at once.

"I do not wish to fight you, old man."

Bra'tac's smile was menacing. "I am the Guardian of the Gate, Teal'c. It would seem you have no choice."

"The Bra'tac I know would never attack an unarmed man." Teal'c brought himself up to his full height. If he were to be cut down here and now he would do so with all the courage he could command. Bra'tac would have to kill him, face to face.

"Then defend yourself." Bra'tac tossed one of the two staff weapons he held to Teal'c, who caught it in midair. It was not his. The balance and the weight were unfamiliar, but it would have to do.

The old man's strength surprised him. Bra'tac was a formidable warrior, regardless of his age, but the force with which he brought his staff down upon Teal'c would have been impressive for a man half his years. Teal'c only just blocked it in time, the reverberation of the blow echoing clear to his shoulders. The attack pushed him back two steps, which were just enough to save him from having his feet swept out from under him by Bra'tac's low swipe. Even so, it came close enough that Teal'c lost his balance and stumbled backward, nearly falling over uneven ground.

Bra'tac chuckled. "Teal'c, the great warrior. Perhaps you have left your fighting prowess back in the land of the living."

Within Teal'c, fury replaced conscious thought and instinct took command. The staff weapon became one with him. It spun in his hands and sliced through the air, making contact with Bra'tac's face. The secondary blow uppercut him from the opposite direction. The old man staggered back.

Muscle memory from countless hour of training and battle drove Teal'c forward. Parry. Strike. Sweep. Strike. Again and again, sometimes meeting the force of Bra'tac's staff to block, but more frequently feeling the shudder of his weapon impacting solidly upon soft flesh. There was no mockery on the old man's face now. Only sweat, streaking his dirt-stained face, mixed with trickles of blood from Teal'c's successes — and perhaps, on occasion, the look of fear.

Bra'tac's retaliating blows seemed inconsequential. Teal'c did not even feel them. Sweat burned in his own eyes but he would not wipe it away. The pain only served to drive him harder. This would end. Now.

With all the strength he could command, Teal'c brought down his staff hard upon Bra'tac's neck. There was a sickening crunch and the Jaffa collapsed, his weapon falling from his grasp. Teal'c pinned him to the ground, his staff primed and aimed at Bra'tac's chest. The old man was breathing heavily. Teal'c could hear his labored gasps from what had to be many broken ribs. Blood leaked from the corner of Bra'tac's mouth and his skull cap had fallen off, revealing thin white hair beneath.

"Tell me how to open the gates," Teal'c commanded. Their fighting had pushed them back toward the wall and the three gates now loomed before them.

Bra'tac spat out blood into the dirt and shook his head.

"No."

"I have defeated you in battle. I have won the right to pass."

Bra'tac coughed, attempting to laugh.

"You have won nothing, Teal'c, that you did not already possess. The way home lies before you and you still do not see." He began to cough again, blood and spittle flying from his mouth. When he was done he closed his eyes and lay still, his breath shallow and rasping.

Knowing he would get no further answers, Teal'c retrieved his own staff from where it had fallen at Bra'tac's side and returned to the gates. If indeed he had the knowledge to open them, he did not know what that knowledge was. Yet he did not doubt Bra'tac's words, therefore he had to be missing something. Something that was right in front of him. The only thing he could see remained the out-of-sequence symbols which would, on a DHD, dial Chulak.

A DHD. Teal'c swirled around, scanning the nearby area for such a device. Perhaps the key to opening the gates did not lie within the gates themselves but with another device, just as the DHD was used to open the Stargate.

But he saw nothing. Merely the gruesome sentinels along the perimeter of the wall. And Rya'c, whom Tea'lc had nearly forgotten. There was no sign of anything that might be used to activate the doors.

He turned back and stared at the symbols again. There were two above the first gate, three above the second, and two above the third. Each familiar to him, except the middle one on the second gate. Were this the Stargate, he would presume it to be the symbol of the planet of origin. On a DHD it would simply be a matter of pressing them in the correct order.

Could it be that simple?

Teal'c walked back and forth in front of each doorway, studying them again. There was no way to scale the wall itself. It was smooth and seamless. He couldn't even begin to find a handhold. How could he activate the symbols if he could not reach them?

From behind him he heard Bra'tac chuckle again. "So bold in battle, yet so hesitant now. Do you need your Tau'ri friends to help you help you understand?"

Teal'c felt his anger rise once more and tensed his grip on his staff. He would not allow Bra'tac to goad him into unwise action. And yet—

He looked at his staff weapon; and then again at the symbols.

It would take precision marksmanship to hit each one without damaging its neighbors. But it seemed the only reasonable solution. Casting aside the spare weapon, he took careful aim at the first symbol in the address for Chulak. Holding his breath, Teal'c fired.

The shot was perfect. The symbol shattered, bits of stone crumbling to the ground. He walked to the third gate, where the next symbol was and took aim again. It too vanished in a shower of dust and debris.

Teal'c hoped he was right about this. If nothing else, the silence from Bra'tac was encouraging. There was no mockery now.

Each symbol in their turn met a similar fate until only the unknown symbol remained. Lining up the staff, Teal'c adjusted his aim ever so slightly, glad to have his own weapon back in his hands. Without it, he doubted he would have been able to shoot with the necessary precision. Taking a deep breath, he squeezed off a shot at the final target.

The gate began to move almost at once. Dust rained down

along the edges as it rose, kicking up a yellow cloud from the dirt below, momentarily concealing what lay behind.

As the great gate finally clanked to a halt, it revealed not a passageway, as Teal'c had expected, but an alcove. It was shallow and contained a single pedestal on which rested two objects.

Teal'c approached with caution. The objects were made of stone and identical in their teardrop shape. A center ridge bisected each along its length. One ridge was black, the other red. Teal'c picked up both devices. They were no larger than the palm of his hand.

A rumbling from within the wall shook more debris down from above.

"Father, look!" Rya'c was pointing at the pillar beside the left gate where a small panel had slid back to reveal a compartment. A similar one also opened beside the right gate. Within both was an indentation into which each of the stone keys would fit perfectly.

Now all the remained was to decide which key went where. Neither the gates nor their locks offered any clue.

"Does it really matter?" asked Rya'c when he saw Teal'c's dilemma.

"I do not know. I cannot think that they have different colors for no reason." He considered asking Bra'tac, but he did not think the answer would be of much use. The time had come to act, not think.

"The black one was on the side nearest the left gate. We will use it there. The red one we will try in the right gate."

Rya'c nodded, his look trusting.

Taking the black key, Teal'c placed it in the indentation. With a click it settled into place. When nothing happened, he turned it clockwise until it stopped.

And still, nothing happened.

Perhaps he had the wrong key after all.

When Teal'c tried to reverse the process, however, the device would not move. Whatever he had done, it was locked into place.

There was no choice now but to try the other one. He took the red key and set it in place in the other panel, turning it counterclockwise until it too stopped.

It took a few seconds before the rumbling began and both gates began to rise. Through the churning, falling rubble, Teal'c could see that there was a passageway beyond each of these doors. The way in front of him was filled with an ominous dark red light. The tunnel in front of Rya'c was pitch black.

Above the din Teal'c heard a voice. Bra'tac was calling out to him. He turned and saw that the old man had pushed himself up on his elbows.

"You think you have won, Teal'c, but you have not. Life cannot exist without death to balance it." His smile was triumphant. "One of you must choose death so that the other may live!"

This, then, was the old man's final revelation. There would be no going back now, not if Rya'c were to live. Teal'c did not have to think twice. He would gladly suffer a thousand deaths to save his son. It was simply a matter of choosing the correct gate.

But which one? The path of total darkness seemed as though it would lead to oblivion, yet the other way was bathed in the color of blood, not the red warmth of a life-giving sun. Could he really send his son into something which seemed to him so vile?

No. Red was not the color of life. It was the color of danger. And death. As terrifying as it was, Rya'c would have to go through the black gate.

The ground was still trembling beneath them. Tremors shook even more dirt and stone off the wall and the gateway. Teal'c began to wonder whether the whole structure might collapse if they waited any longer. It was time to act.

He stumbled over to Rya'c and pointed at the opening of the black gate. "Go, my son! You must hurry!" He pushed the boy toward the opening.

A staff blast flew past Teal'c's shoulder and blew apart a small section of the wall behind him. He wheeled, bringing his own weapon up, and saw Bra'tac was on his feet again.

"I am going with him," Bra'tac called. "Get out of my way, Teal'c."

"You are not," shouted Teal'c, positioning himself between his old friend and his son. "You will not poison his mind with your falsehoods."

"I have told you, Teal'c. They are not falsehoods. The Goa'uld are gods. You will learn this very, very soon."

"Perhaps," Teal'c replied, raising his voice above the quaking. "But even if I do discover that they are the divine rulers of the galaxy and the afterlife, I will still have one satisfaction — one which you shall never have."

"And what is that?" sneered Bra'tac, so close now that their weapons were almost touching, tip for tip.

Teal'c could not help his smile. "I. Died. Free."

The sound of both staff weapons activating at the same time rose above the clattering of falling rubble. Teal'c was faster. Bra'tac looked shocked for just a moment before he staggered back, startled by the wound just below his ribcage. Teal'c caught him before he hit the ground and eased him down.

"Send me through the black gate —" he pleaded.

Teal'c shook his head. "Master Bra'tac, I cannot. But it is not too late. Come with me through the red gate. We may find our final rest after all."

The old man's smile was bitter. "Alas, no. I think not."

Teal'c felt Bra'tac shudder and then lay still. His hand, which Teal'c only just realized he held, went slack. Life had departed.

"Father —" Rya'c's voice called urgently from behind him. Teal'c saw the massive stone doors had already begun to descend. There was very little time.

"You must go!" He had to raise his voice over the deafening din. "I will take the red gate, then you must take the black. It is the only way."

The red gate was dropping swiftly. If he did not hurry, he would be shut out and Rya'c would be trapped here. Already the boy was waiting nervously at the edge of the black gate, like a runner anticipating the start of the race. Teal'c had to hurry.

The red passage shimmered ahead. He had no time to think about what he would find on the other side. He only knew he must make it there before the door blocked his way. He could not even spare a farewell glance at his son.

There was only a meter opening left. Teal'c slid his weapon through ahead of him and dove, headfirst, under the dropping gate. There was a peculiar sensation as the air around him rippled. For just a moment his eyes were seared with the brightness of the color that surrounded him, and then, with a sickening sense of weightlessness, Teal'c felt himself being ripped away.

CHAPTER TWENTY-FOUR

"I SEE something — I think." Daniel pointed at a single spot of flickering light which had caught his attention.

The old woman searched the dark distance for a few moments before she too saw it. "*We are nearly there, then.*"

"There? You mean the Hall of the Two Truths?" He hadn't expected to simply come upon it out here in the middle of nowhere.

"*No. Beyond is the Hall. But first one must pass through the gate.*"

"And why do I have the feeling that's not going to be as simple as it sounds."

The old woman smirked. "*Is anything ever?*"

"Of course not." Daniel sighed. He could see now that the distant light was a campfire. Behind it rose the dark shadow of a massive wall that ran in both directions, well beyond his sight.

"So what's the secret for getting through the gate? I take it there are guards of some kind." Daniel kept moving toward the firelight, picking up the pace a little. The sooner they got there, the sooner he hoped to have answers. Perhaps Sha're was even waiting for him at the wall.

The old woman now seemed to have no trouble keeping up with his quickening steps. "*A Gatekeeper and a Guardian.*"

Now he remembered. In the underworld was a series of gates through which the deceased had to pass. The gates were guarded by any number of hideous creatures who demanded one speak the correct password or spell in order to enter. The *Book of the Dead* was supposed to confer upon the deceased all the pertinent information they needed to make it past each guardian.

Too bad his copy was sitting back in his office at the SGC.

As they drew closer, Daniel could see two figures standing near the fire. One was average size, but the other was enormous, towering well above the other. He didn't have a good feeling about either of them — especially the big one.

"Is there anything else you can tell me before we get there?" The old woman seemed to know a whole heck of a lot more about what was going on here than he did. If Jack had taught him anything, it was to go into a situation with as much intel as possible.

"*Only this. The Gatekeeper will ask you three questions. If you cannot answer them, then you must face the Guardian. If that happens, the only way through the gate is by defeating him in battle.*"

"Let me guess. The Guardian is the big guy, right?"

Her nod confirmed it.

"Right." Even in peak condition Daniel knew he was no match for either of them, let alone the Guardian. He better hope he could answer the three questions.

It was probably better to not take the two men by surprise, so Daniel called out as soon as they were within earshot, waving his arm over his head in what he hoped was a friendly gesture. The Gatekeeper spun around at once, scanning the darkness for the source of the sound while the Guardian aimed what looked suspiciously like a staff weapon toward them. Oh yes. This was going to be fun.

"Hey there!" Daniel called again, helping the old woman down the slight embankment until they were only a dozen or so meters away from the campfire. Between the firelight and the moonlight he could see both men clearly.

The Gatekeeper was his height and sported a clean-shaven head. In one ear dangled a gold earring which matched the wide gold collar he wore at his neck. In another time and another place Daniel could easily see him behind the wheel of a chariot, racing across the Egyptian sands.

As intimidating as the Gatekeeper was, it was the Guardian

who made Daniel take a deep breath. Close up he was at least a head taller than the Gatekeeper. More, probably. Bare-chested as well, he made his companion look puny by comparison. And while Daniel could see that it was, in fact, a staff weapon in his hand, somehow he had the feeling that the Guardian would have no need of it should it come down to a fight. Just one twist of his massive hands and there wouldn't be an unbroken bone left in his adversary's body.

Yep. He really did need to answer those questions correctly.

"Who approaches?" It was the Gatekeeper who spoke. Daniel had a hunch the Guardian wasn't much of a talker.

"Hi there! My name is Daniel Jackson and this is —" It occurred to him that he had no idea what the old woman's name was. Now didn't seem the appropriate time to ask. " — an acquaintance of mine." He cleared his throat. "We're journeying to the Hall of the Two Truths and we'd very much appreciate it if you would allow us to pass through the gate there so we can be on our way."

The Gatekeeper stepped forward to meet them as they moved into the perimeter of the firelight. "I am Iqen. Keeper of the Eastern Gate." He bowed slightly.

Daniel returned the gesture.

"Iqen. Hello. Nice to meet you." He smiled, trying to sound casually pleasant. For the moment it seemed best not to make eye contact with the Guardian. "Look, we're terribly sorry to bother you but if we could just —"

"None may pass through the Eastern Gate unless they have proven themselves worthy."

So much for charm.

"I understand, of course. And, um, how does one do that, exactly?"

The Gatekeeper smiled. "Answer my questions. Or, failing that, meet the Guardian in battle."

Daniel tossed another glance at the Guardian. He hadn't twitched so much as a muscle.

"Right. Well, then, I guess I'll give those questions a try." He was still trying to be pleasant. Maybe if he could keep things cordial it would work in his favor.

Iqen inclined his head. "Very well. Follow me." He motioned them toward the gateway. Only then did the Guardian move, reaching into the fire and taking from it a burning stick. He walked ahead of them to the great wall where he lit two torches ensconced on either side of the gate.

Only now could Daniel truly appreciate the height of the wall in front of him. It was at least a half dozen meters of sand colored stone, all carefully cut and placed together, similar in construction to the tomb he'd awakened in. The structure that framed the gate was reminiscent of the great arches in the Valley of the Kings, the opening itself tall and narrow. Two large doors of solid wood barred the way.

Having accomplished his task, the Guardian extinguished the flaming stick beneath his sandaled foot and took up a position firmly in front of the gate, his arms crossed in front of him. The message was obvious. There would be no leeway granted, no matter how nicely Daniel might ask. It all fell to the questions.

Iqen stood a few meters in front of the Guardian and faced Daniel, who stepped forward as the old woman moved slightly off to one side. He felt strangely alone, standing there without her, which he found exceedingly odd, all things considered.

"Daniel Jackson," Iqen intoned. "You have come before the Eastern Gate to beg entry. Three questions I will ask. If you fail even one, you will meet your fate."

Fate stood motionless behind Iqen, his arms still crossed. Daniel took a deep breath.

"I guess I'm as ready as I'll ever be. Shoot."

A puzzled look crossed Iqen's face. Right. Earth idiom.

"I'm sorry. I mean, go ahead, please."

The Gatekeeper nodded and closed his eyes, as if deep in thought. When he opened them, he looked up to the stars, reciting. "Two sisters. One gives birth to the other who, in turn, gives birth to the first."

Daniel really hadn't known what to expect. A spell from the *Book of the Dead*, the half-life of naquadah, a philosophical treatise on Goa'uld expansionism in the Second Dynasty. It could have been anything. But this made sense in a strangely logical kind of way. He smiled.

"That's easy. It's one of the Sphinx's riddles. The sisters who give birth to each other are Night and Day."

Daniel couldn't tell if Iqen was surprised that he knew the answer or not. But it was correct, because the Gatekeeper nodded. Maybe this wasn't going to be so difficult after all.

"A house." Iqen looked straight at Daniel this time. "One enters it blind, one leaves it seeing."

A small twinge of excitement gripped Daniel's stomach. He knew this one too. It was Babylonian. One of the earliest riddles ever discovered.

"That would be a school," he said excitedly. "A place of learning."

Iqen nodded again, still giving no indication of encouragement or congratulations. Still. Two down, one to go.

The twinge of excitement now turned into a knot of nervous anticipation. Daniel hadn't felt like this since the day he'd defended his dissertation and Professor Jordan had told him it was the very last question. He'd nailed it then. Hopefully he'd be just as successful this time.

Iqen studied him a moment. "Those who would walk the Great Path need know but three things."

Daniel waited for more, but that was it. Okay. So obviously he needed to name those three things.

The Great Path. Iqen was talking about enlightenment — and ascension. He *knew* he knew this. The monk at Kheb had said something very similar, Daniel was sure. If only he could remember.

Except, maybe he didn't need to. He'd recorded in his notebook as much of the monk's wisdom as he could recall as soon as they'd returned to the SGC. He just hoped this was one of the things he'd remembered to write down at the time.

"Hold on." Daniel slipped off the knapsack and rummaged through it. Finding his notebook, he flipped open the leather cover and began rifling through the pages. It had been well over a year and a half since Kheb. In some ways it seemed longer, yet also, oddly, as if it were only yesterday. Neither of which was particularly helpful in locating the pages he needed. The poor visibility provided by the flickering torchlight was not helping much either.

There. He recognized his sketch of the glowing ascended being that he'd made in the margin during the debriefing back at the SGC. Sure enough, he had almost two full pages of notes from his time in the temple. The monk had spoken in koans. Daniel hadn't begun to grasp even half of what he'd been talking about, but he'd decided they would be worth mulling over some time in the future. Not that he'd ever actually gotten around to it.

Daniel scanned them until his fingers hit a familiar phrase and stopped. Nailed it. Just like the dissertation.

He looked up at Iqen and smiled.

"Those who would walk the Great Path need know but three things." Daniel raised a finger as he counted each one off. "You cannot know what you do not ask. You cannot find what you do not seek. And you cannot enter where you do not knock." He snapped the book shut with satisfaction.

Iqen's face remained impassive. The answer was right, Daniel was absolutely certain, but maybe it wasn't enough. Maybe no one had ever actually answered all three questions before. Maybe they'd still refuse him passage.

To his relief, though, the faintest, acknowledging smile finally appeared on Iqen's lips and he nodded his head in assent.

"You have indeed proven yourself worthy, Daniel Jackson. For you, the gate opens."

A great groaning sound issued from behind the Guardian and the ground beneath them trembled. The two massive doors parted inward, slowly opening to reveal only darkness beyond. Daniel wasn't sure if it was a trick of the moonlight or perhaps the torches on the wall, but he thought he saw the air between the two now fully open doors ripple ever so slightly.

"Thank you." Daniel bowed slightly to Iqen before turning to take the old woman's arm. The Guardian, however, still stood in their way. By his stance, Daniel knew it would not be a matter of simply walking around him.

"I thought I'd passed the test?" He turned back to Iqen and put just a slight edge to his tone. The terms of passage had been pretty clear and he'd more than met them.

Iqen inclined his head. "That you did. But only you may enter. The one who is with you may not."

Not again.

"Look. She's with me, okay? And she needs to get to the Hall just like I do. So why don't you just let us be on our way."

Daniel could tell by the expression on Iqen's face that his plea wasn't going to do any good.

"Only one may pass, Daniel Jackson."

Right.

"Well maybe you can ask her three questions, then. Let her demonstrate her worthiness to be allowed to pass through the gate as well." He was going out on a limb here. Daniel really had no idea if she was up to the task or not. But perhaps if he could help her —

"She has only made it this far because you chose to help her. Otherwise she would have perished as others of her kind do. We do not offer admittance to those such as her." There was clearly disdain in Iqen's voice now, just as there had been with the Ferryman at the river. And with Sha're. Daniel was getting tired of it, frankly.

The old woman edged up to him. "*Thus is the fruit of your labors, Daniel Jackson.*" There was a triumphant bitterness in her tone. "*For all that you may show compassion, the rest of the universe simply does not care.*"

"I refuse to leave you here." Daniel spun around to face Iqen. "What if I send her in my place? Would that be acceptable?"

Iqen considered this. "Yes. It is your right to choose who enters the gate. If you wish to send another in your place, you may do so. Even one such as she."

Daniel took the old woman's hands. "Look — just take what I'm offering and go, okay?" Many of her bandages had come loose and she looked like some kind of ludicrous cross between a mummy and a scarecrow. But where Daniel had found her repugnant before, he only felt an odd sort of pity now, even for the Goa'uld within. Maybe both of them would find peace this way. He hoped so.

"And if you see Sha're, tell her I'm sorry. Tell her, maybe one day —" He shrugged because he wasn't even sure how to finish that sentence. Maybe he didn't have to.

The old woman didn't appear to be registering what he was saying anyway. She still looked shocked as he gently guided her forward. The Guardian hesitated a moment but finally stepped out of the way as she stumbled toward the gate.

At the archway she paused and looked back, studying Daniel one last time. He tried to smile encouragingly and nodded, willing her to take those final few steps before the reality of what he was doing slammed into him full force. Or Iqen changed his mind.

"*I will say it again, Daniel Jackson.*" Her voice drifted back to him, sounding neither as old nor decrepit as it had before. "*You are a fool.*" And with one last step she crossed the threshold and vanished.

Daniel hadn't realized he'd been holding his breath. He let it out now with a huge sigh as he watched the double doors swing back shut with a sickening clang.

That was that.

"So, now what?" Daniel looked back and forth between the

Guardian and Iqen. Maybe they'd let him answer another three questions.

Or not. He recognized the sound immediately. He'd certainly heard it enough times.

It was of a zat being activated.

In a way, he wasn't surprised. He'd had a nagging feeling that something like this was going to happen sooner or later.

What he didn't expect, however, was the voice that accompanied the sound.

Never in a thousand years.

"You never have chosen the easy way, have you Dan'yel?"

He tried to say her name but before he could even get it out she fired the weapon. Spasaming waves of electricity ricocheted through him and he barely felt the ground as he hit it, still twitching.

As his vision narrowed and the weirdly flickering lights of the torches cast a strange orange light over the swiftly dimming scene, Sha're's face, looking more curious than compassionate, was the last thing to lose focus and fade away.

CHAPTER TWENTY-FIVE

"YOU'RE sure there are only two of them," Sam asked in a low voice. She and Martouf had taken position on the ridge overlooking the vast wall. In the dark there was no way to see it in its entirety, but Martouf assured her that, even in daylight, there was no end of it visible in either direction. What they could see were twin gateways with flickering torches on either side and the two figures who guarded them.

"I am," he replied, equally as quiet. "One Gatekeeper, one Guardian."

"I'm getting an energy signature." She studied the scanner. Lucky thing she hadn't sacrificed the device to start a fire back at the mausoleum. She'd practically forgotten about it, having tucked it in the bottom of the knapsack. When they'd finished off the food, she'd found it there, the batteries still strong. "I think it's coming from the wall itself." She pointed. "Over to the left, it looks like. Although, from this distance, it's hard to pinpoint exactly."

"Do you think those are the controls?"

Sam shrugged. "I'm willing to bet. Most Goa'uld ships have doors that operate on a similar principle. I wouldn't be surprised to find that technology here as well." That was the first thing she'd thought of when she saw the gates, that they looked just like the access doors found in every Goa'uld ship and structure she'd ever been in.

"You can open them."

She sighed. "That's the plan. Unless you think they'll just let us go through if we go out there and ask nicely."

"Regrettably, no. The Gatekeeper will not permit you to pass unless you can pass the test."

Right. The questions. Martouf had explained about those.

"What about the other guy, the Guardian?"

"A hand device. I fear you would not stand much of a chance."

Sam sighed again. "Right. Well, I never much cared for game shows anyway. I guess I'll hotwire it, after all."

Getting to the control panel wasn't the problem. If it was where she thought, it would be easy enough to slip behind the two Goa'uld in the dark and access it.

Hotwiring it was a different story. She hadn't had much luck with technology lately. Just ask the people of K'tau. Or Colonel O'Neill.

And even if she wasn't completely incompetent and somehow managed to get the gates raised, there was still the problem of getting to them. There was no way the guards wouldn't notice as soon as the doors began to open. A hand device couldn't be the only weapon they had at their disposal.

"Once I get them open, we're going to need a diversion," she told Martouf. "Or we'll never make it through."

"I will provide the diversion."

He said it so calmly, she almost mistook his intention.

"No. Absolutely not," she said when she realized what he meant. "We're both going through that gate."

Martouf was shaking his head. "There is no point. At most, I could see you as far as the Stargate, but I would be able to go no further. Anat cannot leave this place and without him, I will most certainly die."

"You'll die if you stay here." She refused to accept his decision. "They won't like it that you've helped me escape."

"True. But if I am to die, then I'd much prefer it to be for ensuring your safety than for any other reason. It is true what I told you before, Samantha. This is not a life I would have chosen. For a while, I had forgotten that. But you have reminded me of who I truly am." His sad smile returned. "I am the reason you are here. Allow me to bring some meaning to this unintended existence by helping you to escape."

"What about Anat? How can you make this choice for him?"

It was a feeble straw she was grasping at, and she wasn't even sure why. An inexplicable sorrow was descending at the thought of him sacrificing himself for her.

"Anat chooses this too. The others would never allow him to live after we betray them. They have been ferreting out the dissidents one by one and would be happy to have an excuse for his execution. He too wishes to die in a meaningful way. We both do."

Sam wanted to argue more, but there was no point. Taking him with her or leaving him behind, his outcome would be the same. This way her chances improved dramatically.

She hated it. Almost as much as she hated the possibility of leaving the rest of her team behind. Sam stared at the two gates. A few simple steps through one of them and she would find Colonel O'Neill and the others. Those same few steps through the other, and she would assure the safety of the rest of the galaxy.

On a cosmic scale, the choice was easy.

She just wished she didn't have to make it.

"Which gate?" Her voice came out choked, in spite of herself. She was doubly glad it was dark now. It was better that Martouf could not see her face.

Sam could tell he took her question as acceptance of his offer. "You will want to go through the gate on the left. It will take you to the Stargate. The gate to the right is the one that leads to the Hall of the Two Truths."

She tried to ignore the sickening knot in her stomach as she marked his words. The control panel was closest to the Stargate doorway. It would improve her odds of reaching it.

"Once I get to the panel, it may take me a few minutes to sort out the crystals." It was better if she focused on the logistics.

His silhouette nodded. "I will be ready."

"Martouf, I —" But she couldn't get anything more out. She wanted to thank him. To stop him. To forgive him.

He touched her arm lightly, his voice quiet and composed. "Goodbye, Samantha."

She waited until he had melted back into the darkness before wiping her eyes. Then, checking her scanner one more time, she slipped away in the opposite direction.

Focus, damn it.

Sam had found the control panel about ten meters to the left of the first gate and with no small effort managed to finally pry off the cover. The glow of the inner crystals had been like a beacon light in the darkness and she'd quickly covered it with the empty knapsack, hoping the two guards hadn't noticed the sudden flash of light.

Now it was simply a matter of figuring out which crystals to switch to bypass the locking mechanism. She'd done it enough times on Goa'uld motherships. It was something she ought to be able to do in her sleep.

Sam stared at the array, but none of it made sense. There wasn't anything extraordinary about it. Compared to other crystal trays, it was relatively simple. But her brain refused to process what she was seeing. She might as well have never seen one before in her life.

Maybe the colonel was right to question her competence these days. If she couldn't even figure out a simple crystal array—

No. She could do this. She had to do this. Everything depended on it. The rest of the galaxy, yes, but also her team. She didn't care what Martouf said, there had to be a way to save all of them.

Sam knew what the colonel would say. Keeping even more Goa'uld from entering the galactic fray would be priority one. She could almost hear him telling her to get her ass off of Duat ASAP, no matter what it took.

She also knew he'd be the first one to dive through the other doorway to rescue his team, even if the odds were stacked firmly against him.

There was no way she could live with herself if she left them behind. No amount of logic or reasoning could lessen the heaviness in her chest when she thought of choosing that first gate. But risking capture and allowing another enemy loose on an unsuspecting Earth — that wasn't an option either.

There had to be a way to do both.

Or at least attempt both. After all, what mattered in the end was that these Goa'uld remain stranded here with no way off. She just needed to be out of the picture, it was as simple as that. There were ways to make sure that happened.

Reaching around, Sam double-checked that Martouf's knife was still secured to her waist with the torn strap from the knapsack. She might need it after all.

She gave her attention back to the crystals. What she wouldn't give for an encouraging hand on her shoulder and a vote of confidence about now. But those were hard to come by lately, even when her team was around.

She'd just have to make do without them. She *could* do this. The only thing stopping her was… her.

With a sudden clarity, Sam knew which crystals she needed to swap. It was so obvious, she didn't know why she hadn't seen it before. Now all she had to do was wait for the signal.

Martouf could have read her mind, his timing was so good. Sam heard a shout in the dark and hunkered down into the deeper shadows at the base of the wall. She saw the guards become instantly alert, the Gatekeeper stepping forward, the Guardian stepping back.

Even though they were relatively near, she couldn't hear everything Martouf said. The Gatekeeper approached and engaged him, probably asking the required questions. Martouf seemed attentive, even thoughtful, as if he were giving careful thought to the Gatekeeper's words.

When the Gatekeeper had finished speaking, Martouf bowed.

That was it. The signal.

Sam switched the crystals and slid the tray back in place.

For a split second, nothing happened. Then everything happened all at once.

Martouf, head already down, plowed into the Gatekeeper's mid-section. The Goa'uld stumbled back and tripped, falling to the ground. With a roar, the Guardian rushed forward just as the gates behind him began to rumble. The sound and vibration caught his attention, but his forward momentum had already propelled him straight toward Martouf who landed, sprawling, on top of the Gatekeeper. Before Martouf could collect himself, the Guardian was on him, pulling him off and swinging him around like a rag doll. Sam heard a sickening crunch as the Goa'uld's fist broke Martouf's nose.

She was so absorbed watching the scene unfold before her that it took her a moment to remember to run. It was a short sprint to the gate. It would only take her a few seconds.

The Guardian saw her. He pivoted away from Martouf and ran toward her, his stride long and swift. Sam could already see that he would intercept her before she reached her destination. She wasn't going to make it.

He was nearly to her when he stumbled. At first she thought it was an accident, but then she saw a bloody-faced Martouf clinging wildly to the Guardian's back.

"Go, Samantha!" he shouted as the Guardian twisted and he lost his grip, falling to the ground with a cry of pain. She tried not to watch. If she lost her focus, all of this would be for nothing.

She was almost to the gate when Sam heard him cry out again. Even though she knew she shouldn't, she glanced over her shoulder, searching for Martouf. In the macabre writhing torchlight Sam saw his face contorted in agony as the device in the Guardian's hand slowly and torturously turned his brain to sludge.

"No!" she cried out, sliding to a stop. Her hand went to the knife at her waist. She couldn't let him do this. He'd died once protecting others, she couldn't let him sacrifice himself again.

But before she could pivot to charge his attacker, Martouf's body slumped to the ground. For one horrible moment she froze, staring at him. She'd reacted too late yet again. He was dead.

Sam was transfixed by the scene until motion in her periphery snapped her back to her precarious situation. The Guardian had turned back toward her. A menacing grin spit his ugly face as he took two long strides in her direction. Behind him, Martouf was motionless. There was nothing she could do for him now. Nothing but make his sacrifice count.

Both doorways were before her, mere steps away. Sam could see the air in them ripple as though they were giving off heat. Something in the back of her mind whispered that these were not just ordinary doorways, but beyond that she didn't have time to think.

The Guardian was nearly upon her. It was time to choose.

Sam took a deep breath and ran. A feeling that was both familiar and strange tore at her as she dived across the threshold, and the last thought that shot through her mind before oblivion took her was, *I'm sorry, sir.*

CHAPTER TWENTY-SIX

"SO, LET me guess. The Hall of the Two Truths."

After a good hour of picking their way across a stony, bramble-lined path, they had finally reached the fortification which had appeared on the horizon at least two klicks back. It stretched in both directions, like the Great Wall — only taller. China barely had a bump, compared to this. And it was solid too. No windows. No openings of any kind, only a single, towering doorway, which was closed.

"Actually, Colonel, no. The Hall lies beyond. First you have to get through the gate." The snake was using Carter's voice again.

"Right." Jack studied the enormous wooden doors. They were featureless, except for the heavy grain that ran through them. "No key, I suppose?"

"Sorry."

"Doorbell?"

Carter shook her head. "There is, however, a Gatekeeper. And a Guardian. You could start there." As she spoke, the doors began to move, parting in the middle just wide enough to allow two figures to walk through.

One was a woman. She was tall. About Carter's height, actually. Except she had straight, raven-black hair that fell below her shoulder. Around her forehead she wore a headband of some kind with a single feather sticking up from the back of it. Her dark eyes were heavily lined, which made them rather striking, in an exotic sort of way. Over an unavoidable form-fitting dress she wore a cape made of feathers that was attached at her wrists, and in her right hand she carried a staff which was taller, even, than the feather on top of her head. Jack had seen her type before — beautiful, graceful, elegant, and one hundred percent Goa'uld.

Although that wasn't what was bothering him most at the moment, it was the second figure which walked by her side. It was neither graceful nor elegant and definitely not beautiful. But it was powerful. He'd have guessed that from the sheer size of it, even if he didn't already have bruises and scratches all over his body as proof.

It was like a lab experiment gone wrong. Saber-sharp claws curled from the dinner plate front feet of some kind of big cat, but its lithe, feline body only went so far. The creature's thickly muscled hindquarters were hairless and leathery, and, instead of cat paws, the back feet more closely resembled tree trunks.

The worst thing, however, was its head. Carter — Tayet — had said it was a crocodile, but it was even uglier than that. The snout had to be a good meter in length. It was gnarled and knobby and encrusted with bits of dried debris, the origin of which Jack didn't want to think about. Atop the bumpy head two slitted eyes stared at him coldly.

"Is that what I think it is?" he asked, under his breath.

Carter nodded. "It is the Ammit."

Wonderful.

"*I am Maat,*" announced the woman with the feather. "*You have come to the Western Gate seeking entrance.*"

Jack's attention went back to the woman. He'd been right. Definitely a Goa'uld.

"Colonel Jack O'Neill." He took a short step closer to her as a distraction, hoping she wouldn't notice as he thumbed the safety off his P90 — just in case. "And yes. If you wouldn't mind opening the gate, we'll be on our way."

Something about her responding smile made Jack cringe. Yeah. No way was it going to be that easy.

"*I will be happy to open the gate for you if you answer but one simple question.*"

"Sure, ask me anything." He tried to project an unconcerned attitude. "Although I should warn you, I'm a whiz at *Jeopardy.*"

Maat stroked the head of the beast next to her and walked over to him. The thing followed her like a well-trained dog. It even wore a collar and some kind of ornamental gold breastplate, like it was a damned pet.

"I should warn you, Colonel…" Her voice was like ice, all trace of the deep Goa'uld voice now gone. "…that if you do not answer correctly, the Guardian will forbid your entry." She glanced for the first time at Carter. "Neither of you will pass the *sebkhet*. Your journey will end here."

No surprise there. He'd known from the moment he saw the croc-thingy that they'd have to fight their way out of here. He just wished he hadn't used up so much ammo on it already. If he could get off the shots, he could probably punch through the wooden gate. He just wasn't sure he had enough to do both.

Jack tried not to let his trigger finger twitch. "Look, I get it. Now, can we just get on with it?" There was no point in polite pretense now.

For some reason his tone brought the return of her smile, which was not entirely unlike that of the creature next to her. They both looked hungry.

"*Very well*," said Maat, turning around. She made a slight gesture with her hand and the beast ambled back toward the gate where it sat squarely on its haunches.

"*Tell me, Colonel Jack O'Neill. For passage through the* sebkhet." Her voice was smooth as glass as she turned, once more, to face him. "*What is the sound of no heart beating?*"

What the hell? "Excuse me?"

"*What is the sound of no heart beating?*"

Great. Where was Daniel when he needed him. He was the one who got this crap. Even the whacko monk on Kheb made sense to him. And that kid too, Shifu. Daniel would've had the gate open in no time flat, and probably learned something 'fascinating' in the process.

But Daniel wasn't there, or Teal'c either, for that matter. And Sam had yet another snake stuck in her head —

The hell with this. The hell with all of it. He was done. "Hey, you know, if a tree falls in a forest and I'm not there to hear it, then I really don't give a rat's ass if it makes a sound or not." Jack gripped the P90 tighter. "And I have no idea what the sound of no heart beating is. Enough of this crap. Just let us through the damn gate."

Maat merely gazed at him placidly. "*The heart may still beat when the chest is hollow, yet the heart may be silent while the chest remains full.*"

Jack had no clue what that meant, and he didn't care. "Why don't you shove your—"

"Colonel…" The half-whispered admonition was so Carter-like that it made him bite back the retort he'd been about to throw at Maat.

Damn. He *wished* she'd quit doing that.

But—and he hated this—maybe Carter/Tayet was right. From a strategic point of view, their odds were better if they could talk their way through the gate. Blasting their way through needed to be the option of last resort. It was worth one more shot at persuasion. Jack cleared his throat.

"Yeah. Well, I'd love to stay and chat some more about hearts and hollows and such, but we really do need to get through that gate. So maybe you could ask me another question."

"*You had one chance and you failed to answer, Colonel. The gate remains closed.*"

"Best two out of three?"

Maat merely blinked at him with her heavily lined eyes and said nothing. Behind her the Ammit had risen to its feet and was eyeing him eagerly. A long string of drool swung from its gaping mouth.

So much for the diplomatic approach. "You know, I had a feeling you were going to be that way about it." Without warning, Jack swung his P90 up and aimed at the gate, his finger squeezing off successive rounds. Wood splintered and flew like sparks from the gradually widening hole. When he could see light coming through from the other side, he gave it a few more shots for good measure.

The hole wasn't big—it'd be a squeeze even for Carter, let alone himself—but it was the best he could do. He hoped he'd left himself a few spare rounds. In a second he had a feeling he was going to need them.

Sure enough, the Guardian leapt toward them. The thing was awkward, but what it lacked in grace it made up for in mass. It came at him like a freight train.

Jack raised his gun, switched to single-shot, and fired.

The bullet tinged off the golden breastplate and ricocheted away. Damn it.

He took aim a second time, but the animal veered suddenly and the shot merely grazed its leathery rump. Only then did he realize where the creature was headed.

Toward Carter.

She was defenseless. No weapon. Not even a stick to beat the thing off with. He saw immediately that she knew the danger she was in, her eyes widening with fear.

Hoping he had at least one shot left, Jack saw there was only one truly vulnerable part left on the beast. Instinctively, he fixed his sight on the creature's eye and pulled the trigger.

Nothing happened. The clip was empty.

A P90 didn't make a very good club, but it was all he had. Slipping the gun strap over his head, Jack charged at the creature, shouting to distract it from closing in on Carter.

It worked. The Guardian turned its huge, ugly head toward him, giving Carter the time she needed to scramble away.

"Go on!" he shouted. The Ammit was focused on him for now, but she was still the closer prey. "Get through—that's an order!" Issuing a command had the desired effect. Carter ran for the gate.

Out of the corner of his eye, Jack saw her pause once she reached it. "Colonel?"

It was so like Carter's voice again that he found it hard not to be distracted. "I told you to go!" he yelled at her. "Get out of here!" He risked one more glance and saw her hesitate again before finally climbing through the hole. Maat, he realized, had vanished. It was just him and the Ammit now.

Jack raised the P90 again and brought it down on the Guardian's head. It was like hitting a rock. The force reverberated through his hands and up to his shoulders. Even more frustrating was that it had done nothing to stop the beast. Jack swung again, catching the thing in the leg. It howled and snapped at him, its fetid breath fouling the space between them. If he hadn't been so busy fighting for his life, he might have retched. As it was, the force of the swing had overcommitted him and he fell to the ground, hitting his shoulder. The P90 flew from his hands.

That's when he knew it was over.

The Ammit was on him in seconds. He didn't even have time to try and roll out of its way. A hundred hypodermic needles pierced his chest. It was fire. It was ice. It was pain like he'd never believed possible.

At least Sam had gotten away. She had a chance, now.

That was worth dying for.

Through the red agony that was fogging his brain, Jack could hear his heart pounding as if it knew its beats were numbered.

What is the sound of no heart beating?

Jack gratefully surrendered into nothingness before he ever knew.

CHAPTER TWENTY-SEVEN

THE FRESH air felt good, as did the brisk walk through the portico to the Great Hall. NebtHet breathed deeply as she let her long strides carry her forward. She had learned so very much these past few days, more than she'd ever thought possible. In many ways, she had never felt so alive.

There was still much to be discovered, true, but all in good time. Final preparations still needed to be made. She would take care of those shortly. Now, however, she had a small window of time and other matters needed her attention.

Most importantly, she needed to contact Jenmar. She had been in the Observation Room so long she had lost track of how many days had passed since she had sent him away, but it was certainly too many now. His silence had her concerned. This was most unlike him.

The communication device was in her pocket. Pausing outside the entrance to the Great Hall, NebtHet removed the small box and retrieved the orb. It activated at her touch.

Nothing happened at first. Golden mist swirled, indicating the device was functioning, but Jenmar's image did not appear. Finally the drifting smoke resolved into a blurry shape, and gradually a familiar face came into focus.

There was still something wrong with the device. Jenmar's face looked pinched, his eyes overly wide. The audio made him sound as though he were stammering.

"NebtHet a'Eshe —" It was almost as if he were whispering. Perhaps she had caught him at an inopportune moment. He appeared nervous. *"I — I did not expect to hear from you."*

"But I did expect to hear from you, Jenmar. Tell me, what have you learned? Do you know who it was who attacked you on Teranu?"

The image was unstable, making it difficult to read his face, or even to hear him.

"*No...*" The audio cut in and out with the image. "*None of... sources know... behind... There... eems... be... deal... infight... since... death... Apoph...*"

NebtHet pieced together his transmission the best she could. It did not surprise her that chaos had ensued in the wake of Apophis' death, with System Lords squabbling over the remains like vultures over a carcass. Perhaps, then, the attack had merely been a fluke, a coincidence that had put SG-1 in the wrong place at the wrong time.

"Very well." She tried to speak clearly and slowly, hoping her message would be comprehensible through the interference. "SG-1 is nearing the end of their purpose here. I will require your assistance in helping to escort them back to Teranu so they may return to Earth. After that, it will be time for you to come home."

The image suddenly stabilized in the sphere. Whatever had been causing the interference had stopped. Jenmar looked confused.

"*Home?*" he repeated.

Perhaps the transmission had still not been clear. She nodded. "Yes. Home. You must return to Duat."

"*To stay?*"

"Of course. You have served me well, Jenmar. The Djedu are finally near the end of our journey. You must join us for this, our final step."

The device was experiencing problems again because it looked as though all color had drained from Jenmar's face.

"*I — I am honored, NebtHet a'Eshe.*"

"No. It is I who honor you, Jenmar a'Keyleb. We look forward to welcoming you home soon." She swept her hand over the sphere and deactivated it. Jenmar's image faded at once.

At least she did not have to worry about the Goa'uld. That was, admittedly, a great burden lifted from her shoulders. Now she could devote her full attention to SG-1 and the final journey that lay before them all.

The sphere shattered as it hit the metal floor, shards scattering everywhere. The semi-liquid core pooled into a quivering gray puddle, dull and silent.

What had he done?

Jenmar replayed NebtHet's words in his head, hoping he had misunderstood. But, no, there was no other interpretation. He, Jenmar a'Keyleb — granted, at long last, the privilege of a full Djedu name — had been summoned home.

Home to Duat.

Home to the Djedu.

Home to NebtHet.

The very home which Tanith would soon leave orbit to attack, destroying both SG-1 and the entire Djedu race.

Jenmar could scarcely breathe.

What had he done?

He should have trusted NebtHet, but his anger and disappointment had blinded him. It was only too clear, at last, that he had allowed Aset to play upon his worst fears — and now everything was in ruins.

He had no one to blame but himself.

If only he had severed the connection with NebtHet when he had the chance. How much better to have never known what she offered him, to be blissfully ignorant of everything he had just thrown away.

Now, not only would he be the instrument of her destruction, but he would be forced to witness it firsthand. Tanith's was to be the lead ship in the attack. His master — *their* master, now, he supposed — would then move in for the final kill.

The unsuspecting Djedu would have no chance — unless they were warned. But there was no way, not without the sphere.

There was, of course, the chaapa'ai…

But that meant he would have to leave the ship. Tanith had dismissed the guards once Jenmar had relinquished the second data crystal, so he was, in theory, free to go where he pleased —

But, no. Even if he could ring back down to the planet, Jaffa were already massing at the chaapa'ai, awaiting the order to invade Duat. Getting past them unseen would be impossible.

Unless it didn't matter whether he was seen.

NebtHet had called him resourceful. Perhaps he was. Perhaps there was a way out of this, after all. He had talked the Tau'ri into exploring a worthless pile of ruins. Convincing some Jaffa he was on a mission for Tanith would be child's play.

At least, he hoped so. Whatever happened, if he could save the Djedu and SG-1, it would be worth the risk. Even if NebtHet found out what he had done, even if she denied him ascension. Even if he died.

He had to at least try.

CHAPTER TWENTY-EIGHT

"Oy."

Not again.

At least there were no steel drums pounding in his head this time, only a slight buzzing sound which, now that he focused on it, Jack realized were insects of some kind. Alien crickets. Very loud alien crickets. Very close by. In the grass.

Grass. So that was what was making his ankles itch. Actually, it was a nice change of pace from waking up in a black pit or a stone crypt. Tayet's people got bonus points for not repeating themselves. And of all the possibilities he could think of, waking up lying in grass listening to crickets wasn't the worst of them.

Tayet.

Carter.

Jack's eyes flew open and he pushed himself up with his elbows. It was dark. Night, then. That would explain the crickets, or whatever they were. Above him were dim stars, none of which he recognized. Still not Earth. No surprise there.

The last thing he remembered was Carter/Tayet vanishing through the gateway, just before that crocodile-lion thing had taken him down.

Instinctively Jack felt his chest. No gaping hole. Good. His heart was still intact then. For the most part.

Carter, however, was nowhere in sight. It was just him. Alone.

The rest of him seemed in one piece, so he stood up. Someone had given him a new tunic. The other one had been pretty well shredded. Still with the sandals, though. Seriously, what did these people have against decent footwear?

Now that his eyes had adjusted, Jack could make out what was around him. The large, black shape immediately ahead of him turned out to be the remnants of a collapsed wall. In fact, there were partial walls on all four sides. It was a room of some kind, or what was left of one. The roof was long gone and only a single, arched stone doorway remained.

Wherever it led, it was too shadowy to see.

What Jack *could* see, though, was his empty P90 along with the canteen and knapsack neatly piled by the archway. At least they'd sent his stuff along with him, worthless though it was.

Their placement couldn't be random. They might as well have slapped an 'Exit' sign over the archway. Fine. He'd play along.

He needed to find Carter anyway. And save her, if he still could.

When Jack picked it up, the knapsack seemed heavier than it ought to. Reaching inside, his fingers curled around something of familiar size and shape.

Son of a —

It was a clip. And a full one, judging by the weight of it. How convenient.

Jack replaced the empty one in his weapon and double-checked the safety before settling it into its familiar position across his chest, which, as it turned out, was still a bit tender after all. There wasn't much comfort in knowing that someone had thought he'd need the extra ammo. Especially considering how that had turned out the last time.

Edging around the corner of the doorway, Jack scanned for sign of anything. It was clear — just a big open grassy area, surrounded by more half-broken walls. The darkness made it difficult to find the doorway in the opposite wall, but after letting his eyes skim up and down it a half dozen times, he finally spotted it.

Jack felt vulnerable as he jogged to the other side, like maybe someone was watching him. He kept glancing up at the tops of the walls, scanning for the slightest movement, but there was absolutely nothing there. At least, not that he could see.

This doorway was identical to the first one, and the chamber it opened up into almost the same as the one he'd just left. He'd seen some stupid science fiction show once where the people would leave a room by one door and walk right back into it from the opposite side. Probably not what was happening here, but it sure as hell felt like it.

Overhead, the faintest hint of turquoise was tingeing the sky and the stars seemed to be fading quickly. Not so much night, then, as nearing dawn. Good. Once he had enough light, the rules of this game were going to change. He was sick to death of getting led around by the nose.

Although how he planned to change them, Jack hadn't figured out yet. He'd leave the details to Cart — To later.

Right now, there wasn't much to see. In fact, there was nothing, so he pushed ahead to the next chamber.

Finally. Something different.

For a moment, Jack thought he'd made it out of the ruins and into a forest. In the dim light he could just make out the thick trunks of enormous trees, stretching far beyond the range of his vision. Only they weren't trees. Jack was in the midst of them before he realized they were nothing more than staggered rows of massive stone pillars in yet another vast but roofless room. And the shadows were still deep enough that he'd lost track of the boundary walls. Without them, he had no sense of which direction he'd come from, or where he needed to go.

Crap.

He hadn't meant to get turned around like that. Usually he was pretty good at keeping on a straight track. This place though — well, it was as confusing as hell. Everything looked the same as everything else.

A faint rustling noise reached him on the cool, dawn air. Jack froze. Visions of the Ammit stalking him made his heart rate spike for a few beats. But it wasn't the right sound. This was more controlled, more cautious. More human.

"Carter?"

A shadow emerged from behind a pillar. He raised his gun as a precaution.

"Ah, no, Jack. Actually, it's me."

"Daniel?" Okay, so not quite who he'd been expecting. Not that finding Daniel was a bad thing. That is, if it *was* Daniel. Jack wasn't ready to trust anyone in this place. Not without proof.

"Yeah. Hi." Daniel had put his arms up in the air when he saw the weapon, but he gave a little wave in greeting.

Definitely Daniel.

Still. He'd been fooled before. Carter had seemed okay at times too, until her eyes glowed.

Jack kept the gun raised. "How do I know it's you?"

"Um, I don't know," Daniel replied, with just the right hint of mystification in his voice. "Who else would I be?"

"I assure, you, O'Neill, that he is truly Daniel Jackson."

Jack spun to his left as Teal'c's voice came from the shadow of another nearby pillar. The Jaffa strode forward, staff weapon in hand, and came to stand beside Daniel.

"It is good to see you, Daniel Jackson." Teal'c sounded sincere. He even bowed his head in a very Teal'c-like way.

"Yeah. You too, Teal'c. It's nice to see a friendly face," Daniel beamed.

As much as Jack wanted to lower his gun, he still held it at the ready. He needed to be very, very sure.

"Hey!" From his right, Carter also emerged from the forest of pillars and made to join the group. "Am I glad to see you guys!"

"Hold it right there." Jack swung the gun from Daniel and Teal'c and took a bead on Carter. She froze in her place.

"Colonel?" Uncertainty tinged her voice. She sounded so like herself that he'd have been fooled too, if he didn't know any better.

"Just — don't come any closer." Jack motioned her away from the other two with the tip of his gun. "She's a Goa'uld.

Her name is Tayet."

Shock drained Carter's face of all color. Even in the weak light Jack saw her go pale as a ghost. "What? Sir, I swear —"

"I do not sense a symbiote within Major Carter," Teal'c said. He gazed calmly at Jack.

"You sure?" He wanted to take Teal'c's word for it, but, under the circumstances, knowing just whom to trust was a tough call. The only thing Jack knew he could be certain of was that T himself wasn't a Goa'uld.

Although that didn't mean he couldn't be compromised in some other way. They'd had proof of that recently enough.

"I am quite certain," Teal'c replied, just as calmly as before.

"Jack, you want to put that down, please?" It was Daniel this time. Teal'c had vouched for him too. It all came down to how much he trusted Teal'c's word.

Carefully, Jack lowered the weapon.

"How'd they get it out of you so fast?" he asked Carter. Jack knew enough about the extraction procedure the Tok'ra were working on to know that he didn't want to know. From what he'd heard, though, it was a risky and complicated procedure. He hardly expected to see Carter up and walking around so soon, like nothing had ever happened.

"Sir?"

"The snake, Carter. How'd they get it out?"

She looked completely perplexed. "Colonel, I have no idea what you're talking about. I just got here."

"So you don't remember the quicksand and that whole business with that croco-lion thing that wanted to eat our hearts out?"

Carter's eyes grew big as he spoke and she shook her head. "Sorry, sir. I was stuck in some place with Mar…" Her voice trailed off and she looked uncomfortably between him and the others. Taking a deep breath she went on. "With someone who looked and acted an awful lot like Martouf."

"Martouf is dead," Teal'c pointed out, a bit too bluntly. Carter winced.

"I know. Which is why I'm sure now that it wasn't really him. But whoever he was, he was awfully convincing."

"They all were," said Daniel, thoughtfully.

"Excuse me?" Jack could see Daniel was having one of those light bulb moments. There was a look of barely controlled excitement on his face.

"They were all convincing." He pointed at Jack. "You, I take it, had someone who looked and acted like Sam." He turned to Carter next. "You had someone who convinced you he was Martouf. And I—" Daniel took a deep breath before continuing. "I had Sha're—and an old woman who claimed to be the Goa'uld who took Shifu from Amaunet and gave him to the Jaffa priestess to hide on Kheb," he added in a rush. "But, that's neither here nor there."

"My companions were Bra'tac and Rya'c," added Teal'c, reflectively. "In retrospect, I do not believe they were authentic either, although at the time I thought otherwise."

"Wait—so you're saying that the Carter I just spent the last two days thinking was a Goa'uld, wasn't?" That headache was starting to come back.

"Oh she probably was a Goa'uld, she just wasn't—you know—Sam," clarified Daniel. "None of them were real. Or, at least, they weren't the people they pretended to be. I'm pretty sure they were real enough otherwise."

"So, how do we know we're all the real us now?" Jack looked from face to face. Now that he'd caught up, what Daniel said made sense. If he really was Daniel, which he was if Jack trusted Teal'c. Who probably wasn't compromised, but could be. In which case, then Carter maybe wasn't herself either.

Yeah. His head was definitely hurting.

The others were all looking at one another. Finally Daniel spoke. "I guess we don't, Jack. We're just going to have to trust each other."

Jack looked at each one of them: Teal'c, Daniel, Carter. Familiar faces, acting and talking like he'd expect them to. It felt right. Not like before, when everything had felt wrong.

Fine. He'd go with his gut on this one. He just hoped to hell his gut was right.

Lowering his weapon all the way, he rested one arm on top of its stock.

"Okay. I can do that." The smile came fairly easily. "By the way, good to see you, kids."

Carter's face relaxed into a slight smile as well and Teal'c inclined his head. Daniel, Jack could tell, was already a million miles away, his brow creased in thought.

"Well, the good news is, I guess we're not dead after all," Jack pushed on. "So anybody have any idea what the hell is going on here?"

Daniel raised a finger. "I think I do."

Why did that not surprise him? "Care to share with the rest of the class?"

"This all started when we were 'killed' back in that cavern by those two Goa'uld."

"NebtHet and Aset," provided Teal'c.

Daniel nodded. "NebtHet was an Ancient Egyptian Goddess of the Dead. According to mythology, she and Aset welcomed the dead to the underworld and stood guard at either end of their funeral bier in the tomb. If you think about it, there's a certain logic between those personas and what happened here. Obviously, they're the ones behind all this."

"But what exactly *is* this?" Carter sounded just as confused as Jack felt. Good. At least he wasn't the only one not quite tracking.

"Sha're — the fake Sha're — kept insisting we were on a journey to the Hall of the Two Truths."

That sounded familiar. "Yeah, what is that?" Carter asked. "Martouf kept talking about it too."

"It's also from Egyptian mythology. It's the Hall of Judgment where the deceased were to be deemed worthy or not to enter the afterlife."

"Except, we're not the deceased. Are we?" Jack added. The fake Carter had finally given that up, but still, it didn't hurt to check.

"I'm pretty sure a sarcophagus was used to revive us all, sir," the real Carter replied. "That is, if we were even dead in the first place."

Jack shoved the images from the cavern back into the dark corners of his mind. Oh yeah. They'd been dead all right.

"Whatever happened to us," Daniel went on, "I'm fairly certain we were meant to believe we were dead, and on some kind of journey through the underworld."

"Bra'tac told me that I had died. As had he and Rya'c," Teal'c offered solemnly. There was just a touch of something in his voice that made Jack give him a sideways glance, but the Jaffa appeared as stoic as ever.

"Yeah, Sha're tried to convince me I was dead too," mused Daniel. He looked at Carter. She was nodding.

"Martouf said the same thing." Carter looked like she was about to say more but decided against it. In the near dawn light, Jack thought he saw her face redden slightly. He could only imagine what kind of mind games they'd tried on Carter if they'd conjured up Marty's ghost. Bastards.

The others were looking at him, he realized, to confirm their theory.

"Well, you know me, I always believe everything Carter tells me. So, yeah, I thought I was dead there too. For a while. At least until her eyes did that whole glowing thing." He cringed at the memory.

"But *how* did they do it?" Carter's face was taut with concentration. "I get that they were able to make themselves look like people we knew, but how did they get everything so accurate? All the information? Stuff no one would ever know unless they *were* the person they pretended to be?"

Daniel was shaking his head. "I don't know, Sam. But the more important question, I think, is why? What do NebtHet and the others want with us, that they'd go to these lengths to get it?"

"Does it matter why?" asked Jack. "Look, we're all together now. I say we just find a way off this rock and the hell with the Hall of the Two Whatevers."

"Two Truths," Daniel corrected.

"*Whatever,*" Jack threw back.

"If Martouf — the fake Martouf — is to be believed, then there is a Stargate on this planet," Sam said. "There was a gateway that supposedly would have taken me there."

"But you ended up here instead?" Daniel asked.

Carter flushed a little. "Long story." She gave a rueful smile. "Look, the colonel's right. We need to just get out of here. Martouf told me that the Goa'uld who live here can't leave this place — their physiology is dependent upon the naquadah in the planet's core." She took a deep breath. "Apparently they need someone who can design a way for them to leave and still survive, and they're willing to use whatever leverage they can to make that happen. We need to get through the Stargate before they find out we've managed to escape. According to Martouf, these guys make Apophis and the other System Lords look like guardian angels."

Daniel, Jack noticed, was shaking his head again.

"I don't think we did escape, Sam," he said in that solemn voice that always preceded what was sure to be bad news. "And I wouldn't trust the story Martouf told you either. I think there's something else going on here, something we haven't figured out yet. I'm pretty sure this is just part of the whole journey. They wanted us here, like this, so we can all go to the Hall of Judgment together."

"For what reason, Daniel Jackson?" said Teal'c.

"I honestly don't know, Teal'c," Daniel shrugged. "I guess we'll find out when we get there."

"No. We won't," said Jack, curtly, shifting his weapon. "Because we're not going." He didn't give a damn about the 'why'. It was obvious now — they were nothing but rats in someone's maze. Well, he was done being a lab rat. And his people were done too. "If Carter's right, and there's a Stargate on this planet, then *that's* where we're headed. The Hall of Two Truths, or whatever the hell it's called, is going to have to wait until I'm really dead."

"But Jack," Daniel objected, "we have no idea where the Stargate is. Last thing I knew, I was in a desert — and suddenly I woke up in some place that looks like the ruins of a gothic cathedral. Who knows where the gate might actually be?"

There was a simple answer to that. "Carter knows. Right?"

Jack saw her grimace. That was never a good sign.

"Sorry, sir. But no, I haven't a clue. There doesn't seem to be any rhyme or reason to this place and I honestly wouldn't even begin to know which way to go."

"But you said there were two doorways — so if one came here and the other went to the Stargate, let's just go back and take the other one." It seemed straightforward enough, but by the look on Carter's face Jack had a feeling it wasn't going to be that easy.

"I don't think we can, sir. They weren't ordinary doorways. I think they had some kind of transporter mechanism in them. When I went through, it was a similar sensation to using the rings." She looked apologetic. "I don't know what happened after that. I woke up back there just a while ago." She indicated the general direction from which she'd come. "I think, maybe, I was out for quite a while."

"I too experienced a similar sensation when I chose the Red Gate," Teal'c told them. "The experience was unusual, but as Major Carter pointed out, not unlike the transportation rings. I would not be surprised if they shared a similar origin."

"Ancient technology," Carter clarified.

"Indeed."

She nodded. "That would explain a lot."

Jack was lost. "Carter?"

"Sir, we know that the technology the Goa'uld use is only a fraction of what the Ancients must have constructed. I mean, look at the Ancient Repository of Knowledge. Its contents are so vast the human brain is incapable of containing all of it, let alone comprehending it."

"Tell me," he inserted, dryly. She smiled a bit.

"Who knows what else the Ancients might have developed, or what the capability of that technology might be? Daniel was in a desert; I woke up and found myself in the middle of a blizzard." She looked at Teal'c.

"I was in an environment that very much resembled Chulak."

"Yeah. Well, I woke up in Vancouver. It rained almost the whole time," Jack said, irritably. "What's your point?"

"I'm just saying, sir, that whoever is behind all of this — and whatever their purpose is — I'll wager they're using Ancient technology to make it all happen."

Jack sighed. There were days when he wished he had retained even a fraction of what the Asgard had taken out of his head. Maybe then he could at least keep up. At the moment, though, he still wasn't sure where this left them.

"Good for them," he tossed out, wryly. "But again, I ask — what's the point? So they used Ancient tech to gaslight us. How does that help us find the Stargate?"

Carter looked crestfallen. "I guess it doesn't," she admitted. "But my point was, since I think we're now talking about some kind of transporter device being used in those gateways, then the Stargate could really be anywhere. Anywhere on the entire planet."

"Ah." Well. That certainly took the wind out of their sails. Jack took a deep breath and released it slowly. It sounded like it was time for Plan B.

If only he had one.

"Look, I know you don't like the idea, Jack, but I think our only option is to keep playing along and see where this all ends up,"

Daniel said. "Once we find out why this has happened to us, then maybe we'll be able to figure out a way to get home. But until we know the purpose to all of this, I think going off half-cocked is only going to make the situation just that much more difficult."

Daniel probably had a point, even though it didn't sit particularly well with Jack. Something about being some Goa'uld's lab experiment just rubbed him the wrong way. He looked at Carter.

"What about you? You're the one with the story about the uber-evil Goa'uld. Won't we be playing right into their hands if we keep heading to this Two Truths place?"

Carter thought for a moment. "I don't know, sir." She sounded tired. "At the time, Martouf's explanation made sense. But given what Daniel said, I'm pretty sure now that all of it was a lie. I shouldn't have let myself fall for any of it."

Jack's anger simmered again at how the Martouf doppelganger must have manipulated her. Sons of bitches.

"I agree with Daniel Jackson," offered Teal'c, in the awkward moment that followed Carter's admission. "There is a purpose to all of this which we must uncover. It would diminish the ordeal each of us has been through were we to never understand why we were forced to endure such difficulties."

"Et tu, Teal'c?" Jack groaned, but the Jaffa merely looked at him somberly and he remembered again what Teal'c had said about believing Rya'c to be dead. And Daniel had just spent the past few days with his dead wife.

In retrospect, maybe he'd gotten off easy, all things considered.

And maybe finding out who was responsible wouldn't be a bad thing either. He'd have a word or two to say to them, when he did.

"Fine. We'll follow the breadcrumbs." Under his breath he added, "Let's just hope we don't end up in someone's pot of stew."

At least the light was better now. Dawn had brought up the

dimmer switch as they'd been talking. However, it did nothing to illuminate which way they needed to go. After several days of having only a single path to follow, it was odd that this, of all places, should have none. The four of them made short recons, all within hailing distance — Jack wasn't about to lose track of them again — but there was no obvious path anywhere.

"West," said Daniel finally. "I think we should go west."

"Random?" Jack asked.

Daniel shook his head. "No. In the Ancient Egyptian belief system, the west was always the direction of the land of the dead. Toward the setting sun. So it makes sense that we ought to keep going west if we're going to reach the Hall of the Two Truths."

Jack looked at the other two for input, but Teal'c seemed to have no opinion and Carter just shrugged.

"Great. Then west it is," he decided. It wasn't much, but at least it was something.

"Um — you do know that it's entirely possible that on this planet the sun may actually set in the east," mentioned Carter. "It completely depends on the direction of rotation of the planet. I'm just saying," she added when the others simply stared at her without comment.

Oh yeah. It was Carter all right. No doubt now.

"Does that make a difference, Daniel?" Jack asked, just to be sure.

"Mmm. No. It shouldn't. I think we're safe in assuming that the direction of the setting sun would be enough of a guide, regardless of whether it's actually called west or not. In fact —"

"Good." Jack cut him off and strode past him, keeping his back to the rising sun. The sooner they got to this Hall the sooner they'd know what they were dealing with.

And then, maybe if they were *really* lucky, they could all go home.

CHAPTER TWENTY-NINE

"I think it's a maze."

Sam could practically hear the colonel's eyes roll.

"*Really*, Daniel. Thank you. I had no idea."

"I'm just saying," Daniel continued, unperturbed. "That the concept of a maze or a labyrinth as an obstacle to a certain goal is very, very old. In fact, the first depiction of a maze was found as a petroglyph on a stone at Goa in India, dating back four or five thousand years."

"Fascinating," deadpanned the colonel. "And does that help us at the moment?"

There was the slightest beat before Daniel answered. "Not really, I suppose. Except —" he added hastily, "it suggests that we made the right decision coming this way. Why go to the trouble of constructing something this elaborate unless there's a purpose to it? In Greek Mythology, King Minos had the famous Cretan Labyrinth built to contain the Minotaur. After killing it, Theseus was only able to escape by means of a single strand of yarn he'd unreeled behind him as he made his way inside of it."

"Minotaur?" The colonel again.

"Yeah, half-man, half-bull. Completely mythical, of course."

Sam wasn't sure but she thought she saw the colonel shudder slightly.

"Let's just keep moving, all right? Carter, what does it say?"

Sam looked down at the scanner, which, like Teal'c's staff weapon, Daniel's notebook, and the Colonel's P90, had somehow made the trip through the doorway with her. She studied the energy signature again. "I'm still getting a reading," she reported. "We need to work our way in that direction." She pointed off to the left and a little forward. "About ten o'clock, sir."

"Better than a ball of string," she heard the colonel mutter to himself as he walked by her. Or maybe it wasn't to himself. There was a slight twist to his mouth, almost a smile, as he said it. She hadn't seen that in a while.

"Is there a maze connected with the Hall of the Two Truths in Egyptian mythology?" she asked Daniel as she fell into step behind Colonel O'Neill. Daniel was right behind her, with Teal'c bringing up the rear.

"Not that I can recall, although it was believed to be surrounded by concentric walls. I suppose, in retrospect, that could be interpreted as a sort of maze."

"Here," called the colonel from up ahead. "How's this one?"

He was standing by an opening that led to another walled passageway, indistinguishable from the one they were currently in. "I can see another opening just up ahead," he reported back after having reconnoitered it for a few seconds. Sam nodded.

"Looks good, sir."

He nodded. "Let's mark it, Teal'c."

Teal'c obligingly activated his staff weapon and aimed two short bursts at the wall, marking the way they'd just come.

"Better than a ball of string," she echoed quietly as she walked past the colonel toward the next opening. She wasn't sure but she thought she heard him chuckle softly.

They'd been at this for a while now. 'West' had brought them, eventually, to a sandstone wall with a lone doorway so low that Teal'c had to duck to pass through. It had led to what was little more than a passageway, open to the sky but narrow and curving, with high walls on either side and no other doorway immediately in sight.

Sure enough, the same energy signature she'd detected at the gateway with Martouf was here too. Based on her readings, it was straight ahead, *through* the wall. Concluding that there must be a way to reach it, they picked a direction and began working their way inward. It hadn't taken long to realize that getting out again would be a nightmare unless they marked their way — which was when Teal'c's staff weapon had become quite useful.

Without a weapon of her own, Sam was glad to at least have the device to focus on. It took her mind off the past two days and Martouf. The *false* Martouf. She couldn't believe she'd fallen for his story about being rescued from Revanna and implanted with a new symbiote. She should have known it was bogus from the start — which had been her first instinct anyway. But she'd let her guard down, let him play on her guilt over what had happened to the real Martouf. To say she resented some Goa'uld dredging all that up and using it to manipulate her was an understatement. It made her as mad as hell.

Sam glanced up at the colonel's back as he scuffed along the path in front of her. He hadn't said much about his experience with her doppelganger. Teal'c and Daniel weren't sharing either. If their encounters had been anything like hers, she didn't blame them. She didn't exactly want to go into details herself.

What made her curious, though, was how their captors had managed to pull it off. She'd seen technology, even entities, that could perfectly duplicate someone's appearance, so that part was easy. Relatively speaking. But the intimate knowledge of her history with Martouf that his replica had demonstrated was frighteningly accurate — almost as if they had been able to harvest not only her memories but also her deepest thoughts and emotions associated with those memories. The Tok'ra Memory Recall Device could access these to some degree, but not independent of the subject's own consciousness. This had to be something completely different, maybe based on the same theory but far more advanced than anything she'd ever seen or even heard of. The implication of having something that could tap so deeply into someone's psyche was frightening.

"Carter?"

The colonel's voice snapped her out of her musings. She hadn't even noticed they'd stopped walking and he was looking at her, impatiently, for directions. Sam quickly refocused on the device in her hand.

"Sorry, sir," she said after getting her bearings. "It looks like we're moving away from it now. We probably needed to go in the other direction."

With a dramatic sigh, the colonel made a little spinning gesture with his finger and they all turned around and headed back. It had been this way for a while, playing hot and cold with the energy signature. Sometimes they'd actually come to dead-ends, even though the signal strength would be at its strongest where the passageway was walled up. The first time this happened, Teal'c had simply wanted to blast through, but she and Daniel had argued against it — Daniel, because he felt that they really needed to work through the maze as part of their journey, and she because there was just no way of knowing what ramifications blasting through a wall might have. In the end, the colonel had told Teal'c to save the shot for when they might really need it and they'd reversed course.

Finally they came to another opening in the wall and at the colonel's raised eyebrows, Sam rechecked the scanner and nodded. Teal'c marked it with the staff weapon and they entered the next level of the maze.

This time the scanner showed the signal strongest to the right.

"You sure?" the colonel asked, skeptically. "Because, you know, you said 'right' last time and we still had to make a u-turn."

"It's because the signal is getting stronger, sir. It's getting harder to differentiate direction the closer we get to the source."

"Closer?" He sounded unconvinced. "You mean we're actually making progress?"

"So it would seem."

"Okay then," he said, matter-of-factly, as if he hadn't just questioned her ability to read the data in front of her. "Except, I think we'll go left instead."

Or, maybe he did question it. "Sir —"

"I know what your doohickey says, Carter, but humor me. We're going left."

She shot Daniel a look, but he merely shrugged. Teal'c was already several paces down the path ahead of the colonel.

Okay, then. Left it was. Sam watched the signal strength weaken with every step they took.

It was almost down to being barely readable when they came around a curve in the path and discovered the doorway to the next level. The colonel was smiling smugly.

"Sir, how did you —?" she began, but her scanner distracted her. The moment she'd passed through the doorway a whole new set of indicators started flashing. "There's a massive surge of some kind of energy from close by, but it's not like anything I've seen before."

"Could it be the one we've been following? Maybe we're just right on top of it?" Daniel asked.

She shook her head. "No. This is a completely separate signature. And it's putting out massive amounts of energy." She stared incredulously at the readings. "I have no idea."

"Well then, perhaps just standing here isn't the wisest choice," said the colonel. "Let's keep moving."

They went right this time, although Sam wasn't paying attention to the original signal any more. The new one commanded all her attention. It was slowly, but consistently, growing in strength after the initial spike, like something had been suddenly powered up and now was generating additional energy that it was holding in reserve. Unless it had infinite capacity, as some point it would be forced to release all that energy. Sam could only speculate about what needed that kind of power, and why. A ship, maybe? Although the more likely candidate was some kind of weapon.

Sam hadn't noticed they'd reached another doorway until she nearly ran into Teal'c, who had stopped to mark their route. The colonel had once again guessed correctly which direction to take. Apparently he no longer required her help, which was fine. She could give all her attention to the new signal, which had finally slowed in its rate of increase, even if it hadn't stopped. Although this might not necessarily be good news either. Once it had leveled off, it made sense that whatever it was meant to do, it would start doing it.

It was not a comforting thought.

On the other side of the doorway, the colonel was choosing left again.

"What was that?" The concern in Daniel's voice brought them all to a standstill.

"What was what?" asked the colonel, but Daniel shushed him.

"Listen," he whispered.

Sam strained her ears. She heard nothing. The colonel didn't either, if she went by the impatient look he was shooting at Daniel. Teal'c, however, had furrowed his brow in concentration.

"There!" exclaimed Daniel, again in a whisper, looking from one to the other for confirmation. Sam hadn't so much heard it as felt it, a slight trembling in her feet that for a moment gave her a sense of vertigo. Teal'c and the colonel had felt it too, she could tell by the sudden jerkiness of their movements as they tried to maintain their equilibrium. Small pebbles from above skittered down the wall and into the dirt at their feet.

Sam's first instinct was to look up. A mothership taking off or landing was capable of shaking the ground just this way, but the sky above was clear. Anyway, nothing that size could be that close without them seeing it. Unless it was cloaked.

The ground shook again, more violently this time and with an accompanying rumble that emanated from deep underground. The unexpected upheaval threw Sam off-balance and sent her tumbling into the colonel. He caught her around the waist, keeping her from spinning into the dirt. Their combined momentum slammed them into the wall behind. For just a moment Sam had the wind knocked out of her.

"It's an earthquake, sir!" she shouted after she got her breath back. The rumbling now was nonstop.

"Ya think?" he called back, ducking protectively over her as dust and more debris showered down from overhead. It took her a moment to realize he still had his arm wrapped around her waist. He seemed to realize it too and let her go.

"I don't think standing here is a good idea —" It was Daniel shouting now. He was right, they should probably keep going. A moving target was less likely to be hit.

Cringing away from another, larger piece of falling wall, Sam checked the device. The energy level had dropped to its initial baseline, but had started another upward climb. "That was just the first quake, sir. There's another one coming. We need to find someplace away from these walls."

"Go! Go!" the colonel shouted, motioning her and the others to move, but his voice was drowned out by yet another thunderous growl from below. Sam felt the earth suddenly give way beneath her and scrambled backwards. Daniel, across from her, did the same. Between them a huge crevice appeared, separating herself and the colonel from Daniel and Teal'c. Sam watched in astonishment as the ground vanished into the ever widening rift, pushing the other two further and further away until it was impossible for them to even think about trying to jump across. If that weren't enough, another crack was appearing, perpendicular to the original chasm, sending a new fissure right toward the middle of the path on the other side.

"Carter! Come on!"

The colonel was pulling her back. Sam had been so fixated on the spreading chaos at Daniel and Teal'c's feet that she hadn't noticed the matching fissure moving just as quickly in her and the colonel's direction. The collapsing earth spewed a cloud of dust in the air and she lost sight of both Daniel and Teal'c. She tried calling out to them, but the rumbling was so loud now she could barely even hear herself. She thought she could make out two indistinct forms moving through the haze, about a half dozen meters away. Hopefully they were no worse off than she and the colonel.

Beside her, the colonel coughed raggedly. Sam squinted at the scanner in her hand, wiping a layer of dirt off the digital readout. The next shockwave was still building strength, but they were running out of time. The walls on either side had already been weakened by the first quake. Another strong one would bring them down. At the very least they needed to find the next doorway. It would give them some measure of protection. Not a lot, but it was the best they could do.

"Sir, we need to go. These walls—"

What felt like an enormous hand thrust Sam backwards as the ground buckled and heaved. She landed next to the colonel, both of them dazed. Through her slightly foggy state she heard the colonel curse.

The sickening sound of crumbling stone made her focus. The upper ledge of the wall on their right was swaying in and out of her field of vision. Any second, gravity would claim it—and she and the colonel were right in its drop zone.

"Colonel, watch out!" Sam shot to her feet, grabbed his arm, and pulled him up. The huge stone block landed right where his head had been, the collateral fallout of smaller stones and pebbles catching them both in the back as they stumbled out of the path of the collapsing wall.

Ahead of them, along the passageway, more sections of the wall swayed dangerously. Sam exchanged a look with the colonel. Going forward was going to be just as dangerous as staying put, but neither of them had any better ideas.

"How long until the next one?" he said.

The energy reading had dropped back to its baseline, but this time there didn't seem to be any indication of another surge building up. At least, not yet. "I don't know, sir. It seems stable, for now."

"Right. For now. In that case, why don't we—"

They both felt it at the same time. The ground began to

vibrate, only slightly at first, but with ever-increasing intensity. "I thought you said —"

"It's not a quake, sir," she insisted. The readout showed the energy level as unchanged.

The ground under their feet continued to shake so much that her teeth started to rattle. Sam felt like she was standing on a jack-hammer.

"C-c-c-c-art-t-t-ter?"

There was a terrible cracking sound. Sam looked up, expecting to see another chunk of the wall breaking loose, but she couldn't find where. She felt a tapping on her arm. It was the colonel. He was pointing.

The fissure that had opened during the first quake had spread. They could see it, like a zipper, slowly but deliberately splitting the earth in two. It had already covered half the distance to where they stood and it didn't give any indication of stopping. If anything, it was speeding up.

"Sir, I think we'd better —"

"Yeah."

Dodging the fallen sections of wall, the two of them sprinted down the passage, away from the fissure. When they rounded a curve, Sam and the colonel drew up, both breathing hard. They were a safe distance away from it now, well out of its path.

Or not.

Unbelievably, the fissure appeared to be following the curve of the passageway, leaving an ever growing cloud of dust in its wake. Its path was too precise to be random.

"Is it me, Carter, or is that damned thing chasing us?" the colonel panted.

"Actually, sir, I was just thinking the same thing. I don't think it's a natural phenomenon."

"Let's not stick around to find out."

It was getting more difficult to see as they ran. The passageway acted like a channel, keeping the thickening air contained within its walls. An umber fog enveloped them and Sam could feel the grit of fine sand in her eyes.

"There!" the colonel shouted, suddenly shoving her through a doorway that had appeared on their left. Their momentum hurled them against the far wall as they tumbled through and they leaned against it catching their breath again.

But only for a moment.

As if it had some kind of malevolent consciousness guiding it — and Sam was almost certain now that it did — the fissure rounded the corner with ease and followed them into the new passageway. For just a heartbeat it seemed to pause, as if waiting, and then, with another round of violent shaking, began heading toward them again. As they ran, the unmistakable sound of crashing stones told them that the walls themselves were crumbling in its wake.

Ahead of her the colonel stumbled, but righted himself before he fell. Sam's heart thudded in her ears. She knew his knee could be unreliable at times. If it were to suddenly give out now—

Sam refocused her thoughts. Deal with problems when they came up. Not before. The only thing she needed to be thinking about now was how to get out of this. Turning corners hadn't really slowed the fissure down much, but it was the only strategy they had until they could get to where they were going. Wherever the hell that was.

She saw the next doorway before the colonel did and yelled for him to turn. Instead of listening to her, however, he shook his head and grabbed her arm, preventing her from going through.

"Dead end!" he shouted in response to her disbelieving look. "There's a pattern. I've been keeping track—" His voice was raspy. They were both getting winded easily in the filthy air. "We'd have been goners if we'd taken that way."

So that was how he'd known which way to go. She should have guessed. Although she wasn't sure what surprised her more, the fact that he'd actually discovered a pattern to the maze, or that he'd managed keep track of it in all this chaos.

When the next opening appeared on their left, he pointed and they managed to cut swiftly into it, this time without colliding with the wall. The colonel dragged her to the right just as the collapsing ground rounded the corner behind them.

"Sir, we need to get to the end of this maze." Sam raised her voice so he could hear her. "I can't explain why, but I think if we can make it there, we might be safe."

"My thoughts exactly," he hollered back. "Look — go there!" He was pointing at a doorway to yet another level. "Take a right!" he added, just before they skidded through.

Sam did as he told her, trying to regain her stride once they'd taken the corner. She didn't see the wall until she nearly crashed into it. It was a dead-end.

She didn't need to hear the colonel to know what he said; the curse was readable on his lips as he pounded both fists on the solid rock.

The fissure had only just entered the passage where they were. Maybe it was her imagination, but it seemed to have turned this corner more slowly than before. Something about that nagged her. In fact, the whole thing was bothering her, although she couldn't put her finger exactly on why — apart from the obvious, of course. Death by fissure wasn't exactly how she planned to go.

"Carter, are you listening to me?"

Turning around Sam saw the colonel had laced his fingers together and was making a step for her with his hands. His intention was obvious. He wanted to boost her over the wall.

She looked up. With his help she'd barely have enough reach to get herself up the rest of the way.

Sam shook her head vehemently.

"Damn it, Carter. Get up there. That's an order!" He was shouting at her now, his face a dark cloud of irritation.

"I wouldn't be able to pull you up, sir," she shouted back. "But maybe you can pull me." If he were atop the wall and she could get a good enough grip on the bare stone, she might be able to climb up far enough for him to reach her. Sam laced her own fingers together and held them out for him to step into.

"Carter, this isn't open for discussion!" the colonel yelled.

"Exactly, sir!"

He glared at her and cursed again, but finally the colonel stepped into her hands and Sam boosted him up the wall. The sudden weight was more than she anticipated, and for a moment she worried she couldn't lift him high enough, but finally Sam felt his other foot find her shoulder and then his weight left her altogether as he struggled to pull himself up to the top.

Sam looked over her shoulder. The fissure appeared to have moved in the opposite direction, away from them. But as she watched, it changed course and was heading back her way. She had a minute, at most, before it reached her.

The likelihood of the colonel being able to reach her was slim at best. Part of her had known that when she'd sent him up first. Rock climbing had never been her forte. She'd never make it high enough for him to get a hold of her.

There was another option, though. If she acted quickly, there still might be time to jump over the fissure before it got too wide and go the other way. It was as much of a long shot as trying to scale the wall, but it was better than just standing there, waiting for the chasm to swallow her up. And maybe — just maybe — it would follow her instead.

She couldn't risk telling the colonel. It would be better if she just took her best shot. If she made it, he could chew her out later. If not —

"Carter!"

Sam looked up, squinting into the bright light, and saw that the colonel was reaching down with some kind of cloth in his hand. It took her a second to realize it was his tunic, which he must have taken off, because now she could see he was bare-chested, hugging the top row of stones.

Stretching, she could just touch the edge of the sleeve with the tips of her fingers.

Close. But not close enough.

Cracking earth and tumbling rocks sounded behind her, and Sam turned back to see that the fissure had advanced even closer. In those few seconds she'd lost the option of trying to leap over it. If nothing else, it made the decision easier.

Putting as much power as she could into her tired legs, Sam jumped. The tunic fluttered away from her grasping reach and she landed empty handed. Trying to keep her eye on it, she jumped again. This time she managed to get her fist around it, but not with enough fabric for a sustaining grip. Frustrated, Sam slipped back down the wall to her feet, feeling the fissure's vibrations through the bottom of her sandals.

She had one more try before it would be over. Above her, the colonel was hanging precariously off-balance in order to lower the tunic as much as possible. He wasn't even yelling at her to keep trying. They both knew it was this time or never.

With what little room she had, Sam backed up to get a running start. Even if she managed to grasp the dangling sleeve, this was going to hurt.

The fissure was almost to her. Time was up.

Two long strides got her there. She leapt up on the last one, using her momentum to give herself greater height. For one horrible moment Sam thought she'd misjudged her reach, but then she felt the coarse linen fabric against her hand and she grasped desperately for it.

She was rewarded with a handful of cloth a split-second before she slammed into the stone wall. Her grip faltered momentarily, but only slipped a bit before she clutched the sleeve again and held on. Below her she could see the ground collapse into the ever widening chasm that had reached the base of the wall.

For what seemed like an eternity, she swung there, taking deep, steadying breaths. Already she could feel the perspiration on her hand. Any time now, her grip would start to fail.

Above her, Sam heard a groaning noise, and there was a sudden jerking on the fabric. The colonel was trying to pull her up from his already compromised position, but all he'd succeeded in doing was setting her to swinging a little harder.

Sam felt the fabric slide through her fist just a fraction more.

"A little help, here, Carter!" the colonel grunted down at her.

Pulling herself up as best she could with her one hand, Sam swung her free arm up and managed to grab onto the tunic just below her other fist. That felt a lot more secure. Looking up again she realized just how impossible it was for the colonel to do anything except hold the makeshift rope in place. How he hadn't fallen himself, she had no idea.

"Sir, just anchor it. I think I can do the rest."

"You might want to hurry." He was looking past her.

Craning to glance down, Sam saw that a large crack had already begun to work its way through the first course of stones. As more ground gave away, it would be only a matter of time before the whole wall would cave into the abyss.

Twisting around, Sam kicked out toward the wall and managed to find some purchase with her feet. With that as support, she scrambled, hand over hand, toward the top.

Sam was so focused that the colonel's hand appearing suddenly in her field of vision startled her. Grateful, she grasped it and allowed him to pull her up the final few feet until she could swing her legs over the top and straddle it.

He was breathing almost as hard as she was. Sam could see sweat beading at his temples and running down his neck to his chest, where a dozen or so bright red puncture marks dotted the area around his heart. They looked relatively fresh, the skin around them still raw.

As he half-turned away from her to shake out his tunic, Sam caught a glimpse of other fresh scars on his back. Two rows of stripes, like something sharp had raked across his skin. The tunic covered them as the colonel pulled it over his head and she quickly looked away so he wouldn't catch her staring. He hadn't mentioned getting hurt, but then, of course, he wouldn't. At least they looked as though they were healing.

"Thank you, sir," she said, when they could both finally speak again.

He brushed her comment aside. "We'll call that one even. Come on. Let's move, before this wall goes down and us with it."

Sam gave a cursory look around her. Damn. She'd hoped that, if nothing else, the wall would give them a view of the maze that would help them navigate it more efficiently. Apparently the pattern the colonel had picked up on didn't hold true for the entire structure, since he'd just led them into a dead-end. But there were so many dust and dirt particles suspended in the air that it was little more than an amber fog, even up here. Sam couldn't see a thing.

"Carter?"

The colonel was already hanging off the other side, ready to drop to the ground. Right. No time to gawk.

With movement that hurt a whole lot more than it should have, Sam landed in a crouch next to the colonel. The crack in the wall was already waist-high. Beneath her she could feel the trembling of bedrock as the fissure pushed its way beneath the wall's base.

The colonel tossed her a look she understood immediately. Keep moving.

"I thought I'd broken the damn thing." Hammond watched as Dr. Cameron Balinsky carefully rotated the sections of the small statue of NebtHet that Anise had left with him. "But then I saw those, and I wondered if they meant anything."

The last thing Hammond wanted was to explain how the statue might have been damaged. He rarely allowed his frustrations to show, and taking his aggravation out on inanimate objects was not his normal practice. In this case, though, it may have yielded an unintended benefit.

The newest addition to the SGC's team of archeologists picked up the magnifying glass and squinted through it. Maybe he was getting old, but the red-haired young man didn't look a day over sixteen. Hammond wasn't even sure he'd started shaving yet.

Balinsky still hadn't spoken, so Hammond kept talking. "I'm no expert, but it looked like hieroglyphics to me — or at least some kind of writing."

The archeologist was examining the back of the statue now and gave a low whistle.

"Doctor? Any idea if it's of significance?"

Balinsky blinked up at him. "Yeah, I'd say so." He offered the glass to Hammond but held on to the statue. "This is very cool. I've never seen anything like this before. Certainly not this old."

He positioned the artifact behind the glass so Hammond could see where he was pointing. "It's really a puzzle of sorts. The statue is made up of different sections, all of which can rotate."

Balinsky demonstrated by twisting the statue at various places. Because of the symmetry, it still looked perfectly normal — except the markings Hammond had seen earlier were no long distinguishable. "But, when you align them just so…" Balinsky twisted the statue again. "You've got a word. Or, in this case, a name."

"What name?" Hammond was trying hard to be patient.

"NebtHet. She's the Egyptian goddess of —"

"I'm familiar with who she is, son. Thank you." It wasn't much of a discovery after all, then. Anise had already told him who the statue was meant to represent.

"But sir, here's what's really amazing about this." Balinsky's voice went up a bit in excitement. "When you line it up to say 'NebtHet' on the front, look what happens on the back." He turned the statue over and offered it back to Hammond to examine. At first it just looked like random indentations on the surface, but when Hammond held the magnifying glass to it, he saw something else.

"Doctor, am I seeing what I think I'm seeing?"

Balinsky grinned at him like a kid on Christmas morning. "If you think you're seeing gate symbols, sir, then yes. And there are six of them. It's a gate address."

CHAPTER THIRTY

THE COLONEL'S directive to keep moving was easier said than done. There was a definite uphill grade to this path. Sam felt it not so much in her legs, although they were getting fairly tired, as in her lungs. The same foul air that had been impossible to see through was just as impossible to breathe. She could even taste the dirt in her mouth, the grittiness of it scratching the back of her throat. It didn't take long before she and the colonel were wheezing as they ran.

If there was any good news, it was that they seemed to have outpaced the fissure for the time being. The wall had slowed it down, or maybe it was the uphill climb. Although the more Sam thought about it, the less sense either explanation made. Regardless of what was causing it, the act of physically splitting open the ground shouldn't require any extra effort in the presence of a wall or an inclined slope. That nagging feeling was back. It was almost as if —

"Sir, I was just thinking." It took her a moment to get her breath. "None of this makes any sense."

"That's not exactly a news flash, Major."

"What I mean is, why kill us now? They had plenty of opportunities before. Why bring us back together only to kill us this way? There's no logic to it."

Sam saw the colonel shrug before a fit of coughing overcame him. When it had subsided, he wiped his mouth with the back of his hand and she realized that he had a fine layer of dust covering his entire face — in fact, he was entirely coated with dust. Looking down at her own arms, she saw she was too. Little wonder they were having a hard time breathing.

"Maybe the experiment is over," the colonel offered, finally. "Instead of outright killing us, they just open up the ground and let us fall in."

"That's an awful lot of energy and effort just to kill off four people."

"Yeah, well, you're the one who said it didn't make any sense." He spat out more dirt.

"What if they're not trying to kill us?"

The colonel looked skeptical.

"What, then? It's just playing tag?"

"Well, not tag, exactly," Sam replied. How to explain what she was only just piecing together? "But what if this is still just part of the experiment? I'm pretty sure I saw the fissure slow down when we were trapped at that dead-end. It was almost like it didn't want to catch up with us, like it wanted to give us time to find a way out."

"How considerate."

"What I'm saying, sir, is that we might be able to slow down without increasing our risk. If it's intention isn't to harm us, then it should keep a safe distance."

The ground shifted beneath them with no warning and a loud crack reverberated like a single gunshot. She'd forgotten about the earthquakes. It was as if someone was still determined to shake the whole place into nothing but a pile of ruins.

Sam heard the colonel shout, but it came a split-second too late. The silhouette of the falling wall darkened the ground in front of her a heartbeat before it came crashing down. She'd half-turned, a reflex to both the colonel's warning and the looming shadow, which was all that saved her from being crushed. Instead, a chunk of rock clipped her left shoulder, spinning her around and knocking her into a section of wall that had already collapsed. As she landed, Sam half-heard, half-felt the sickening crunch of bone just before her left side went momentarily numb. Her vision dimmed for a few seconds and a freight train roared in her head.

Through the fog she saw movement. Strong hands were lifting her off the rocks, guiding her to her feet. A face resolved into focus, close in front of hers.

"Come on, Carter. No lying down on the job."

She shook her head and instantly wished she hadn't. The numbness was replaced by a sharp, piercing pain, stabbing her left side. Each breath Sam tried to take felt like inhaling shards of glass. Cracked ribs. Maybe a punctured lung. It was hard to tell with the air already being so hard to breathe.

"Sorry, sir," she muttered, finally. Something flickered in his eyes for a moment — concern, maybe? — but it was replaced by a critically assessing gaze. He'd had enough broken ribs himself to recognize the symptoms, she was sure.

"We've gotta —"

"You go, sir. I can't run. I can hardly —" She took a deep measured breath in order to get the last word out. "Breathe."

"Good thing we caught a break then. Come on. I've gotcha." The colonel positioned himself on her right side and brought her arm up to his shoulder. Sam felt his left arm go around behind her, supporting her back, his hand careful to avoid the tender spots on her left side. She appreciated his gesture, but there was still no way they could outrun the fissure like this. She would only slow him down.

The ground was still trembling with aftershocks. But it wasn't until the colonel guided her away from the wrecked wall that Sam realized they weren't continuing through the passageway. Instead he was carefully picking their way over the very rocks that had nearly killed her. When she looked up, Sam saw why.

It wasn't just the wall next to her that had collapsed. It was as if someone had tipped over a row of dominoes. Wall after wall had tumbled down, knocking against the wall in front of it. The entire maze, or what was left of it, had been destroyed. Across the piles of rubble, no more than an eighth of a klick away, was a small building that had to be their destination. It was the only thing still standing.

"Look, company." The colonel nodded off to their left. Sam could see two other people working their way through the ruins toward the building.

Daniel and Teal'c.

The colonel called out and both men turned toward the sound. They seemed to have fared slightly better. At least they were both walking unaided.

Sam could breathe a little easier now. As long as she didn't try to talk too much, the pain in her side was tolerable. She disengaged from the colonel's shoulder and tried a few tentative steps on her own.

"I'll be okay, sir, thank you," she said in response to his questioning look. "I just had the breath knocked out of me, that's all."

Whether he believed her or was just letting her save face, Sam had no idea. He nodded and moved off, but only a little way. Close enough to be ready in case she went down again.

Not that she'd let that happen.

It took a lot longer than it should have to reach the building, but finally they staggered up to the last debris pile. For something as impressive sounding as The Hall of the Two Truths it was a lot smaller than she'd imagined. It was relatively plain, too, made out of the same stone they'd found in the rest of the maze. One single, tall doorway stood right in the middle, flanked by two massive stone pillars which rose up to a flat canopy over the entrance. The large wooden door was closed, giant hinges on either side suggesting that it probably opened inward. There was no sign of a lock.

Daniel and Teal'c were still working their way through their own labyrinth of broken walls. Both of them were covered with umber dust, not a single glimmer of gold visible on Teal'c's forehead. Flecks of shattered stone clung to Daniel's hair.

Another strong tremor sent everyone staggering. Daniel nearly lost his balance, but Teal'c steadied him before he went sprawling. Sam took a moment to appreciate the scene. It was only hours ago that she'd thought she might never see them again.

"Uh, Carter?"

The tone of the colonel's voice brought her back from her momentary lapse of attention. But he wasn't looking at her. He was looking at the ground. Pebbles and tiny bits of dirt were vibrating around his feet. The low rumbling, which had never really stopped, was getting stronger again. But it wasn't the sound she'd come to associate with the quakes.

It was the other sound. The one that had been chasing them for the better part of an hour.

She and the colonel both looked behind them.

"Crap."

That was an understatement.

"It's a legitimate gate address, sir. The computer matched it with one from the Ancient database. We just can't get it to connect." Harriman had dialed the gate three times already. Hammond was about to order a fourth attempt.

"The Goa'uld will keep a gate open during an attack so that no one can dial out," Colonel Reynolds pointed out. His team was geared up and standing by in the gate room. "We've seen that happen before."

"Or the gate could have been destroyed," offered Harriman, immediately looking like he wished he hadn't spoken.

Hammond turned to Reynolds. "If someone's keeping the door jammed open, that only works for thirty-eight minutes." It might be the very last straw he had, but Hammond was going to grasp it. "I want that address redialed every five minutes for the next hour. Maybe we'll get lucky and beat them to the punch." With a sigh he clicked on the microphone. Seven heads swiveled in his direction at the sound.

"SG 3 and 16, stand by. This could take a while."

The fissure had returned. And it seemed to have met up with its other half, the part of it which, Sam guessed, had been pursuing Daniel and Teal'c. The two rifts had devoured everything in their respective paths, and now, as they rejoined, they made an enormous arc across the maze.

As the ground began to shudder violently, everything behind the conjoined fissures began crumbling. It was like watching the sinking of a ship. Bit by bit, getting nearer and nearer, the land disappeared from sight, plummeting down into an ever expanding canyon.

It would reach them in minutes.

The colonel was already waving Daniel off but Daniel continued to stumble toward them. The roar of splintering rock and crumbling soil made it nearly impossible to hear, but the colonel yelled at him anyway.

"Get the hell out of here, Daniel!" He gestured vehemently again toward the structure. "Just go in the damn building!" The colonel took a step forward just as the ground beneath him buckled. Sam saw him go careening back, off-balance.

The wave hit her a second later and with it another nauseating sensation of vertigo. There was nothing solid beneath her feet. The ground just vanished, leaving her and the colonel suspended, for one impossibly long second, in midair.

Everything moved in slow motion.

A low, mangled shout came from the colonel as he windmilled his arms, trying to regain his balance. Sam could feel the updraft of the collapsing soil spraying against her back as the gaping maw opened beneath them. Together they began to fall back into the bottomless chasm.

Until two strong arms seized them.

Teal'c stood there, legs spread wide for balance, grasping each of them by the arm. For a terrifying moment Sam was afraid that their backward momentum would pull Teal'c in as well, but he was strong enough to withstand the force. With evidence of only a little effort, he pulled them both back to solid ground.

There was no time to thank him. Sam could still feel the instability of the soil under their feet. In a moment this section would give way too. They had to get to the building. It was their only chance.

Daniel, for once, had listened to the colonel and already made it to the door. With the full force of his weight he was trying to push it open.

The ground was quite literally falling away from their heels as they ran. The stabbing in Sam's side returned with a vengeance as her lungs demanded more air, but she pushed past the haze of pain and focused on Daniel. They were almost there.

A single stone step was all they needed to reach to make it to safety.

Or, at least, what they assumed would be safety. If the building also began to collapse —

Daniel had managed to open the doors so that one person at a time could squeeze through. It was good enough.

One more earth shaking rumble rattled Sam's teeth. All around them — all around the entire building — the ground fell away. All that remained was the building in front of them, perched on what she could only guess was an island of rock in the midst of a vast canyon.

They'd run out of time. They'd run out of space. The last bit of soil was disintegrating under their feet.

They dove for the step.

For one horrifying moment she thought they hadn't made it. But then Daniel's hands were pulling her forward followed by grunts and exclamations from Teal'c and the colonel as they piled onto the steps after her.

Blowback from the falling ground made it nearly impossible to see, and even more difficult to breathe. Between spasms of coughing, the colonel was shouting for them to get inside. Half feeling her way, Sam followed the shape that looked like Daniel and squeezed through the partially open door. There was a familiar, lurching sensation and she tumbled forward onto a floor that was hard and cold and solid. More importantly, it was absolutely motionless, with no indication that it was going anywhere at all.

And laying there with her fractured ribs piercing her side so excruciatingly that she couldn't even speak, not going anywhere was all Sam really cared about.

CHAPTER THIRTY-ONE

IT TOOK Jack a few minutes to adjust to the dim light. And the silence. After the roaring and rumbling destruction they'd just escaped, the absolute stillness in this place was downright creepy.

The other thing that was creepy was that he was pretty sure that they'd ended up someplace besides the other side of the doors they'd just stumbled through. It was like Carter had said, kind of like using the rings — only not. That would explain the sense of vertigo he had when he finally hit the floor after what seemed like just a second too long in the air. And why there wasn't a single tremble from the homicidal earthquake that had chased them here.

Beside him, Carter moaned. If the pallor of her skin was any indication, those ribs had to hurt like hell. But Daniel was already seeing to her, so Jack accepted Teal'c's outstretched hand and pulled himself to his feet.

"You okay, Carter?" She'd pushed herself up to all fours, although that looked like it had taken some effort. Nevertheless she nodded.

"Yes, sir. Just give me a minute."

"Uh, Jack —?" Daniel was looking past him, frowning. Teal'c too, was staring. Jack had a feeling he wasn't going to like what he saw when he turned around.

He was right.

It wasn't the high ceiling with its sunlit windows reflecting light off the blindingly white pillars. It wasn't the marble floor which gleamed as if no foot had ever before stepped on it, or the matching marble walls which made the place feel like a cross between a tomb and an art museum. It wasn't even the long center aisle lined on either side by a row of life-like statues, or the elevated dais at the far end.

It was who was waiting for them *on* that dais.

Goa'ulds — what else could they be, in those get-ups? — about a dozen of them, give or take. And something else that made Jack's blood chill. The Ammit was there, sitting patiently like some perverse dog next to what appeared to be a giant set of scales.

"Oh this does so not look good," he muttered under his breath.

He raised his P90 just as Teal'c brought up his staff. Out of the corner of his eye, Jack saw Carter reflexively reach for a zat she didn't have.

Teal'c unexpectedly shifted his aim toward the left row of statues. Daniel gasped quietly.

"I believe it is actually worse than it appears, O'Neill." Teal'c spoke without taking his eyes off his targets. "The statues are alive."

Shit.

Teal'c was right. Jack could now see that they weren't statues at all. As far as he knew, statues didn't move. But these did. More Goa'ulds, like the rest of them, and each and every one of them was staring at SG-1.

No wonder he'd felt uneasy. Jack counted twenty-one pedestals on either side, plus the dozen on the dais. And the Ammit. Yeah. Quite the welcome wagon.

It was hard to know where to aim, so Jack kept his site on the group on the other side of the hall. They appeared to be the ones in control.

"Carter," he said quietly. "What's your condition?"

"I'm good, sir."

Good enough, Jack translated, which was the best he could hope for at the moment.

"Wait — Jack!" Of course it was Daniel. "I know what this is. This is where we're supposed to be, it's the Hall of the Two Truths."

"And?"

"And I don't think we really want to come in here, weapons blazing."

"Do you see me firing, Daniel?"

"No, but—uh-oh."

Now what?

"Daniel?" Carter was on her feet now. She sounded marginally better.

"If that's what I think it is—"

"Daniel?" Jack repeated Carter's question, adding an extra edge of irritability. He didn't like it when Daniel sounded worried. It usually meant things were a hell of a lot worse than he already thought.

"It really is right out of the Book of the Dead—everything. This place, what we've been through, it makes perfect sense, now."

"I take it that's a bad thing?" Carter said.

Daniel grimaced. "Not if you're actually dead. The final step in the journey to a blissful afterlife is the weighing of the heart."

"You're talking about a metaphorical weighing, though, right?"

But Daniel shook his head. "I don't think so, Sam." He glanced up at the dais where those scales were. "To the Egyptians, the heart was the center of everything—thought, will, love, hate. It was the only organ left inside the body when it was mummified. It was believed that, at the end of the journey through Duat, the heart was quite literally weighed against a feather. If it was free from sin then it was light and balanced with the feather. If not—well, see that rather hideous thing waiting there?" Daniel pointed at the Ammit. "Let's just say, they didn't call it The Devourer for nothing."

Jack shuddered. He'd seen what that thing could do. He had no desire for an encore. "Any chance we could just walk out of here?"

"I don't think so, sir," Carter answered for Daniel. "Even if we wanted to, I'm pretty sure we came through one of those transporters. I don't think they go both ways."

Without warning, and before Jack could stop him, Daniel stepped forward, his arms raised in front of him.

"I am Daniel Jackson," he spoke in a loud voice. It filled the entire hall. "This is Jack O'Neill, Samantha Carter, and Teal'c. We have endured the trials of Duat and humbly ask for admittance into the Hall of the Two Truths. We stand before you, clean of heart and unfettered by any sin."

Jack grabbed Daniel's arm and jerked him back. "Daniel, just what the hell are you doing?" The last thing they needed was to end up at the other end of the room with their hearts on that scale.

"When a person enters the Hall of the Two Truths, one is expected to make a sort of 'negative confession'," Daniel explained in a half-whisper. "To show that one is worthy of entering the afterlife."

"But we don't want to enter the afterlife, Daniel. At least, not today."

"Just trust me, Jack. It's a ritual. I think we should go through with it and see what happens."

"What happens is that we end up down there with someone's hand in our chests!" What part of this picture was Daniel not getting?

"I admit, it looks bad —"

"*Looks?*"

"I don't pretend to understand exactly what this has all been for, Jack. But my gut tells me that we need to finish the journey. The whole journey."

Jack glared at him for a long minute before screwing up his face in distaste.

"Fine. But if they make one move toward any of us, all bets are off, do I make myself clear?"

He wasn't sure it was exactly a nod, but Jack knew Daniel got the message. He'd go down fighting before he'd ever let any of his people set foot on that dais.

Daniel stepped forward again and spoke to the people seated on the pedestals.

"I am Daniel Jackson. Hear me, oh judges of Duat. I stand before you and make my confession. I come to you with a clean heart. I have not lied. I have not stolen. I have not killed without cause. I have not taken food from orphans. I am not evil—"

Oh for crying out loud. This was ridiculous. Jack had heard enough. And frankly, he'd had enough. There was a time to play along and a time to put an end to the game. He wasn't going to play anymore. He didn't care what Daniel said.

Dropping his weapon so it banged against his side Jack passed Daniel in three long strides and didn't stop until he was halfway down the aisle. He could feel the gaze of every Goa'uld on him. Their faces were completely devoid of expression, but their eyes revealed their curiosity. When he reached the midpoint, Jack stopped and turned in a circle.

"Look." He spoke to the rows of faces staring at him, and to the cluster of people who were also watching from the dais. "I could walk down here and feed you a bunch of crap about how perfect I am, how perfect all four of us are. But it would be a lie. Not that what Daniel here just told you wasn't true— I can personally vouch for the fact that he has never taken food from orphans in all the years I've known him." Jack paused, but there was no reaction from any of them. Tough crowd.

"And hey, if it's lies you want, then fine. I can tell you exactly what you want to hear. But if you're here to judge us — really judge us — then judge us for who we truly are.

"Sure, I've done a lot of stuff in my life that I'm not proud of. I've lied. I've stolen. And yeah, I've killed. Many times." Jack waited, but there was still no response. "So maybe that makes me a bad person," he pushed on anyway. "I don't know. One day, I probably will, but I don't think it's up to you folks to decide. Because I don't think you're in any position to judge anything."

"Jack, what are you doing?" Daniel had joined him in the middle of the room.

"Just telling it like it is, Daniel." Jack turned directly to the people on the dais. Now that he was close enough, he recognized one of them. It was the Goa'uld from the cavern. The one who'd shot them all at the outset. NebtHet.

"You." He pointed at her. "You kidnapped us, and then killed us, and then brought us back to life just so you could send us on adventures in your twisted little wonderland here. Let me tell you — if you want to judge someone for doing right and wrong, then maybe you ought to start by looking at yourself." His anger was getting the better of him again. "If there's anyone around here who needs to make a confession and get their own heart weighed in that scale there, it's you."

Jack could feel the disapproval radiating off Daniel, but he didn't care. It was time to end this.

The woman on the dais — NebtHet — stepped forward. She was in a long robe which, considering the fashion tastes of most Goa'ulds, was a bit on the plain side. Her headdress, however, was another matter. It was an elaborate piece that seemed to balance high on her head, like an upside down stovepipe hat. She removed this, however, and set it beside the scales before descending the steps from the platform. Jack held back reaching for his gun. Behind him, he heard Teal'c shift his staff weapon.

"You are correct, Colonel O'Neill, that it is not necessary for you, for any of you," NebtHet spoke around him to the others, "to confess your sins." She smiled. It was not a smile he took much comfort in. "We already have witnesses who are prepared to come forward to speak on your behalf."

She nodded and from the crowd on the dais, six stepped forward. Jack heard a collective intake of breath from Daniel and the other two at the back of the hall. He knew why, of course — while he didn't have a clue who the others were, there was one among the six who was completely recognizable. He even took a quick look over his shoulder to make sure it really wasn't Carter standing there.

But no, she was still with Teal'c. Jack wondered what she made of her doppelganger, but it was difficult to tell from here. No doubt they were all amazed at the likeness. Maybe now they'd understand why she'd been so convincing.

NebtHet motioned Carter and Teal'c forward to join them. When Carter was finally standing next to him, he whispered, "See what I mean?" But she only gave him an odd look in response. She had, he realized, been fixated on one of the other witnesses.

Teal'c too had a peculiar expression on his face, except he wasn't looking at the fake Carter either but at the first two individuals who had lined up opposite them. Daniel's face had momentarily lit up as the witnesses approached, but then settled into something that Jack could only read as a sort of regret.

"Teal'c," announced NebtHet, when the six had gathered. "These are Aqti and Ahi, whom you have known as Bra'tac and Rya'c." The two individuals reached out toward Teal'c's head. Jack had his weapon up in a flash and they froze.

"Hold it, right there."

"Jack." Daniel put his hand on the P90. "I think it's okay. Let them do it."

Jack let the weapon be pushed down slightly. Maybe he was being too jumpy, but only because Daniel was being his usual, overly trusting self.

The two witnesses touched Teal'c's head at the same time and Jack saw the Jaffa's eyes grow wide with surprise as he caught his breath.

"Aqti and Ahi, speak to us of the one called 'Teal'c,'" NebtHet invited them. The two men smiled.

"We have never before met anyone so brave," the one named Aqti proclaimed.

"To stand against one whom you have always held in highest esteem," continued Ahi, "takes valor of more than just the body. In your heart you know Truth, and you live by that Truth, no matter the personal cost."

Teal'c, who seemed to understand what they were talking about, bowed his head in acknowledgement. Jack wondered how he managed to look both proud and humble at the same time.

"You also demonstrated great courage in choosing the red gate," Aqti pointed out. "Few walk so bravely toward death when life remains an option."

Again, Teal'c seemed to understand, even though he did not reply. Jack was more surprised by the admiration the two clearly had for the big guy. Whatever he'd expected to happen when NebtHet called her 'witnesses', this certainly wasn't it.

"Thank you," continued Ahi, reaching out and clasping Teal'c's arm, Jaffa-style. Aqti did the same. "We have learned much from you," he added, bowing. Teal'c returned the gesture one more time and stepped back.

"Okay, could someone please explain what just happened here?" Jack asked. First these guys were trying to kill them and now they were all smiles and gratitude. Somewhere he'd missed something.

"Just wait, Jack," Daniel shushed him. "I think it'll become clear in a minute."

"Carter?" Jack asked, hoping she at least was as confused as he was. But she was still staring at one of the other witnesses who persisted in smiling back at her.

"I don't know, sir," she answered, distractedly. "But I think I'm starting to understand."

Jack threw up his hand in frustration as Aqti and Ahi returned to the row of witnesses. NebtHet was still looking serene.

"Daniel Jackson," she said. Daniel looked up, expectantly. "This is Khemy, whom you have known as Sha're. And perhaps you remember Aset, whom you have seen since as well."

The two women walked forward and touched Daniel's head in the same manner the others had touched Teal'c. Daniel's eyes also grew wide, although Jack had the distinct impression that whatever it was he saw was not too much of a surprise.

"Nice to meet you — again," Daniel said, smiling.

"And you, Daniel Jackson," replied Khemy.

"Khemy and Aset, speak to us of the one called 'Daniel Jackson,'" instructed NebtHet.

Khemy spoke first. "It is easy to offer kindness to those one cares for. It is more difficult to do so when someone for whom you care deeply disappoints. And it is most difficult to demonstrate kindness to one whom you abhor. Daniel Jackson has done all three."

The one called Aset nodded. As all smiles as the first Goa'uld was, this one looked like what she had to say would leave a bad taste in her mouth. Jack could almost hear her gritting her teeth.

"I will admit that I was skeptical at first." She spoke tersely, as if she couldn't wait to be done with it. "Not only of you, Daniel Jackson, but of this entire endeavor. But in spite of how you feel about the Goa'uld in general, and who I was in particular, you nevertheless acted with a degree of feeling I had never thought possible." She glanced at NebtHet briefly and Jack thought he saw some kind of unspoken exchange between them. Whatever it was, it seemed to prompt Aset to reluctantly add, "And you showed a level of compassion that exceeded anything we have ever before seen."

"Thank you," Daniel replied, looking slightly embarrassed. Maybe he hadn't picked up on the fact that, in spite of everything he probably had done, this Aset still hated his guts.

"No, we thank you, Daniel Jackson," replied Khemy, leaning forward and kissing Daniel on the cheek. He went beetred from the neck up.

Jack knew Carter was next. Maybe it was the way Mr. Smiley was twitching in line.

"Major Carter," intoned NebtHet, once the two women were back in line. "This is Anat, whom you have known as Martouf."

Anat came forward and touched Carter's head. Actually, it was more of a caress. Jack saw him smile as whatever had happened to the others happened to her as well.

"Wow," she said, under her breath, shaking her head slightly. Anat's smile broadened.

"Anat." For once Jack was grateful for NebtHet's interruption. "Speak to us of the one called 'Samantha Carter.'"

"Hello again, Samantha." Anat's voice was smooth and very similar in tone to Martouf's, Jack noticed. "In my many years of existence, no one has ever shown me the meaning of the word 'duty' until I met you. In spite of your personal feelings for your fellow teammates, and even for Martouf, for whom you once held affection, you nevertheless chose the greater good, no matter the personal cost."

"But I didn't." Carter was shaking her head. "At the last minute, I chose the other gateway. I went to save my team, not find the Stargate."

Anat, however, merely smiled. "I know. Ultimately, you listened to your heart as well as your head. You believed you could accomplish both and took the risk. By this, you have taught me that duty without feeling has no purpose. For this lesson, I thank you."

For just a moment, Jack thought Anat was going to kiss her, but after a slight pause he merely bowed and backed into his place in line. Carter appeared slightly flushed. Jack scowled. Maybe this little show and tell was almost done and then they could get back to the SGC. He wanted her in the infirmary as soon as possible.

"Colonel O'Neill."

Finally.

Carter's double stepped forward. Why no one else was staring at her, he couldn't figure out. Side by side they were indistinguishable.

"This is Tayet, whom you have known as Major Carter."

"Yeah. Hi." Jack plastered on a smile. Tayet reached out and with two fingers touched his temple.

It was like someone flipped a switch.

"Whoa!"

Stepping back instinctively, Jack saw Tayet smile. She was a complete stranger. How he'd ever mistaken her for Carter —

Wait. He'd had this experience before, with that stranded alien they'd encountered — the one who'd passed himself off as Lt. Tyler. But this was no Reol. The woman in front of him was of indistinguishable age, neither young nor old, sort of like the rest of the Goa'uld in the room. More importantly, she looked nothing like Carter.

"Tayet," said NebtHet. "Speak to us of the one called 'Jack O'Neill.'"

"Colonel O'Neill." Tayet studied him, as if unable to decide what to say. Daniel was fidgeting on one foot in the awkward silence. It was to the point of being just a tad uncomfortable when she finally continued. "Your reputation here had preceded you, and yet I was quite unprepared for what I discovered."

"Well, that's me. I'm full of surprises," Jack quipped. Her stare was making him uneasy.

"Yes, you are," agreed Tayet, narrowing her eyes as if contemplating exactly how to phrase what she would say next. He raised one eyebrow at her in anticipation. "It was not expected that you would distrust someone whose opinion you so highly value. So when you began to suspect that all was not right with your Major Carter, I was forced to improvise. Little did I know that this would prove to be the far greater lesson for us than the one we had set out to learn."

"You had the whole techno-babble thing down pretty well, you know," he felt compelled to point out. "But — and forgive me for saying this — as a soldier, you sucked. Carter never would have made rookie mistakes like that. I figured something was up."

"Yes. And I used your assumption that Major Carter had been compromised by a symbiote and adapted."

That she had. And damn well, too. Although he wouldn't

give her the satisfaction of telling her that.

"And what big revelation did you learn from me?" Jack asked casually, not certain he really wanted to hear the answer, or anyone else to, for that matter. If they'd known enough to choose Carter as his guide, who knew what else they might have figured out.

"Sacrifice," Tayet replied, without hesitation. Jack relaxed a bit. "The willingness to surrender one's life so that another might be saved. Even if," she added, "by such an act, a mortal enemy is saved as well."

"Yes. Well. No offense, but as far as I was concerned, the Goa'uld was just along for the ride." He refused to be praised for something he hadn't done. There was only one reason he'd sent Tayet through that gate, and they both knew it.

"While this is true," she acknowledged, "there are those in this galaxy who would not have missed an opportunity to strike down an enemy, even at the cost of a treasured ... comrade. It would be, by many standards, an acceptable loss."

"Well not by mine." Jack let his irritation get the best of him.

"So we have seen." There was that appraising look again. "As I said, it was a most valuable lesson. For this, we thank you." Tayet leaned forward and for a disturbing moment Jack thought she was going to kiss him as Khemy had Daniel. Instead she whispered, "I have seen the depths of your heart, Colonel, and I know what lies within. Deny it to others if you will, but do not deny it to yourself." She stepped back, and with a pointed look at Carter added aloud, "You have my envy — and my pity."

Bowing slightly, Tayet rejoined the others.

Jack struggled to keep his indifferent expression in place, although he felt like someone had just jolted him with a cattle prod. So, maybe she had managed to dig a little deeper into his head after all. He just hoped...

Risking a sideways glance at the rest of SG-1, Jack was relieved to see they merely looked bewildered. For once, that was a good thing.

NebtHet, mercifully, drew everyone's attention back to her. "These witnesses have spoken on your behalf and provided testimony as to your character. We will conclude, now, with the rite." She turned and, with the six witnesses, walked back up the steps and resumed her position on the dais. NebtHet placed the upside-down stovepipe thing back on her head and clapped her hands twice. Nearby, the Ammit stirred slightly and inched forward. It looked hungry.

"Now wait just a doggone minute —"

"Just… hold on, Jack." Daniel put his hand on Jack's arm. "Give it a minute."

Jack glared at him. "We might not have a minute, Daniel."

Daniel's look was patient. "Look around," he said. "Do you see a single weapon, anywhere?"

Jack's annoyance level ratcheted up another notch. Maybe there wasn't a zat or a staff weapon in sight, but that didn't necessarily mean anything. Zats were entirely concealable. And Goa'ulds had other, less obvious weapons. The Ammit wasn't exactly a lapdog either.

"What's your point, Daniel?" One of the minions on the dais was hurrying toward NebtHet carrying a pillow. There was a white feather on top of it.

"What I'm saying is, if they really meant to harm us, don't you think they'd have taken away your P90 and Teal'c's staff? The only people in here, at the moment, capable of doing harm are us."

"You sure about that?" Jack growled. "Then what's that about?" He jerked his head toward the dais where NebtHet had placed the feather on one tray of the enormous set of golden scales. The tray dipped ever so slightly, but the balance remained intact.

For his part, Daniel had the decency to look confused. Jack saw Teal'c's grip on his staff weapon tighten while Carter was studying the scene as if was a puzzle. She had that look of concentration on her face she got when she was in the same breathing space as her high-tech doo-dads, although what that meant, at the moment, Jack wasn't quite sure.

He was more concerned with that feather and the fact that NebtHet had turned once more to face them.

"Now that each of you has completed your journey and been admitted to the Great Hall, one final step remains."

Yeah. That's what he thought.

"Oh I don't think so." Jack had his weapon up now. Teal'c too had raised his staff again. "You're not touching a single one of my people. And you're definitely not weighing any of our hearts on that thing there." Jack jerked his head in the direction of the scales.

NebtHet had become very still. There was enough arrogance in her to not actually look afraid, but he could detect the sudden tenseness in her stance. Good. At least now he had her attention.

"Jack, I think —"

"So help me, Daniel, if you tell me one more time that we ought to just let this play out —"

"Actually, sir, I think it'll be okay." Carter's words caught him off-guard. Even more so when she stepped forward. "I'll go first," she told NebtHet.

"Carter?" For a second he considered ordering her back, but there was something in the tentative half-smile she threw him that said she knew what she was doing.

He hoped to hell she did.

Carter climbed the steps to the dais and seemed to know where to stand before NebtHet could show her. The Goa'uld nodded approvingly and stepped aside. A different Goa'uld came forward, one Jack hadn't noticed before — which was a surprise, since he looked like nothing less than a Goa'uld Liberace. The gold and jewels on his cloak probably weighed a ton, and to finish off the look he wore a headpiece that resembled some sort of monkey. Maybe a baboon.

Another time, Jack might have cracked a joke about the

wardrobe and the headgear, but the somber-faced Goa'uld was unusually dignified, even if he did look like an MGM extra. Besides, that was Carter up there. Now was not the time to say anything stupid.

"That's Thoth," whispered Daniel. Jack had no idea who that was, although obviously it meant *something*. At least he'd know what name to put on the report when he had to sort this all out for Hammond.

If he had to sort this all out for Hammond. Whether Carter's confidence was justified or not remained to be seen.

Baboonhead — Thoth — was incredibly focused. Or maybe it was just hard to keep that thing balanced on his head. He positioned himself at the base of the scale and spread his arms.

A column of light snapped on from overhead, engulfing Carter. She closed her eyes against the brightness of it and Jack saw her stiffen slightly. Very slowly she began to revolve beneath it — not because of the light, he figured out, but because the part of the dais where she stood was turning. She'd probably spotted it when she walked up there, which was how she'd known where to stand. She must have seen something else too, something he hadn't. Maybe it had to do with that beam she was standing in. Somehow he had the feeling it wasn't just an ordinary spotlight.

It was taking an excruciatingly long time to make one full rotation. Carter didn't look uncomfortable standing there, but then she didn't exactly look relaxed either. Whatever the hell they were doing to her, Jack just wished they'd get it over with.

As soon as she'd made one full revolution, a second column of light appeared over the waiting scale pan. It quivered for just a moment and then, within its beam, a slightly rounded object took shape. Jack couldn't make out what it was at first, but then Daniel gasped softly.

That's when Jack figured it out.

It was a heart.

Carter's heart.

His own stopped for a few seconds until he understood just what he was looking at: it was a hologram. He could actually look right through it as it revolved on the scale at exactly the same pace Carter was turning in the beam of light.

And it was beating.

Jack could see the slightly rapid rate of its pulsations, the rhythmic contraction of its chambers. It was probably his imagination, but he swore he could almost hear it in the absolute silence of the Hall. And despite the fact that he knew that the real organ was still safe and sound inside her body, it seemed vulnerable and defenseless, nevertheless.

He wanted them to stop. Now.

The monkey-man had turned to NebtHet and was giving her a solemn nod. The column of light around Carter vanished and half a beat later the avatar of her heart did as well. NebtHet stepped up and guided her forward.

"Your heart has been weighed against the Feather of Truth and you have been found to be *maa-keru*."

"True of voice," translated Daniel before Jack could even ask.

NebtHet was actually beaming. "Go now, in peace." She gave Carter a final bow.

Looking a bit unsteady, Carter rejoined them. She was pale, but her eyes were bright with discovery.

"It's kind of like the Asgard technology, sir," she explained, under her breath. "Only far more sophisticated. It doesn't hurt, just tingles a little bit."

"Which one of you will be next?" NebtHet extended her arms in invitation.

From what Jack could tell, Carter didn't seem any worse for wear. If she said it was okay, then he'd go with it. With a sigh he gave Daniel and Teal'c the go-ahead.

T went next. NebtHet led him to the same spot on the dais and a moment later he too was slowly revolving as his holographic heart appeared on the scale.

"Your heart has been weighed against the Feather of Truth and you have been found to be *maa-keru*," pronounced NebtHet. "Go now, in peace."

It was the same with Daniel. His holographic heart balanced the scale and was apparently found worthy as well.

Finally it was Jack's turn.

Carter was right. It did tingle a bit when the beam hit him. It wasn't unlike how the air was charged during a thunderstorm, only inside of him. He could almost tell the exact moment when his holographic heart appeared on the scale, even though he was facing the other direction at the time. When he revolved around to where he could see the scale, sure enough it was there.

Jack really didn't want to look at it. Not that he was squeamish. It was just another body part, after all, and a holographic one at that. He'd figured out by now that all this was just for show. Of course a hologram would weigh nothing. Still, he couldn't shake the notion that his might somehow tip the scale. As hearts went, he was sure his was heavier than most.

But when the column of light vanished, there was NebtHet proclaiming him *macarena* and telling him to go in peace as well. Just as he thought, all for show.

Not that Jack expected anything less from a bunch of Goa'ulds. Even a very odd bunch, which this group clearly was.

The show being nearly over, Jack hoped, NebtHet came and stood before them again.

"People of the Tau'ri — and Teal'c," she added, inclining her head toward the Jaffa. "We have learned much from you and for that you have our eternal thanks. You are now free to return to your world. Aset will show you the way."

The four of them stood there, confused. That was it? Three days of hell only to be patted on the head and sent home? No explanations? No apologies? Just 'Thanks, you can leave now'?

He didn't think so.

"Just hold on there a doggone minute." Jack called after NebtHet, who had already started to leave with the others. "Nobody's going anywhere until someone explains what the hell just happened here."

Next to him, Daniel spoke up. "I think what Jack is trying to say is, we've been through an awful lot these past few days and we really feel as though we deserve some kind of an explanation."

Okay. More diplomatically put, but Jack wasn't feeling particularly diplomatic at the moment. No one used his people like this and just walked away. He'd get answers if he had to wring it out of NebtHet with his bare hands.

For a moment, he thought she was going to just keep walking, but after apparently giving it some thought, she returned. This time she even came down off the dais.

"You are correct, Dr. Jackson. You do deserve an explanation. Old ways of secrecy are often difficult to lay aside. Even now." She glanced over at Aset again, who scowled slightly. "We are the Djedu."

"Goa'ulds," clarified Jack. Just because they hid behind some fancy name, it didn't mean they weren't snakes.

"We are no more like the Goa'uld than are the Tok'ra," she corrected. "As they separated themselves from our common ancestor, so did we, millennia ago, although for a far different purpose."

"Which was?" Jack prompted.

"Spiritual enlightenment, Colonel. We had no interest in galactic domination. We had no desire to fight in any conflict. We have sought one thing and one thing only through all these long, arduous years: ascension."

"A Goa'uld cannot ascend," Teal'c pointed out. "The monk on Kheb told Bra'tac as much."

NebtHet smiled sadly. "And so the monk would appear to be correct. As you can see, we are all still here, despite our best efforts to follow in the footsteps of those who have succeeded in the past."

"Wouldn't that be pretty hard to do?" Daniel asked. "Especially since they're all, well, ascended?"

NebtHet nodded once. "Exceedingly. Which is why, millennia ago, we turned to what others of our race have fallen back upon in the hope that what we could not find within, we might find without."

Jack had gotten lost back at "ascension", but luckily Carter seemed to be keeping up.

"Technology," she supplied, nodding to herself in apparent understanding. Good. He was glad someone was getting it. "Just like the Goa'uld and the Tok'ra," Carter went on. "You hoped to advance beyond your limitations through the use of someone else's technology."

"Yes," replied NebtHet. "We have spent our entire existence searching for technology that would unlock the secret to ascension. But nothing we have found has been of any use. Not even the technology of the Ancients."

"Wait," interrupted Carter. "Are you saying that you've been collecting Ancient technology from around the galaxy — and that you can get it to work?"

NebtHet nodded.

"Is that how you were able to create everything we experienced these past few days? How you were able to tap into our memories and make everything so… real?"

Again NebtHet nodded. "The scope of technology left behind by the Ancients is impressive. Yet, ultimately useless to us. Until now."

"Why now?" Jack wanted to know. He knew Carter wouldn't ask — the thought of a warehouse full of Ancient tech had distracted her completely. He didn't deny that it gave him a bit of a rush to think that maybe, at last, they'd found something that would help them in the fight against the Goa'uld. Assuming it turned out to be all that NebtHet seemed to be saying it was.

"Because it enabled us to study you, in ways we never could have without it."

"Explain." This came from Teal'c. Jack could hear just a tinge of challenge in his voice.

NebtHet took a deep breath and exhaled it slowly. "When it became apparent to us, after eons of research, that there was no technology which would enable us to ascend, we began to lose hope. Many Djedu accepted that ascension was something we could never achieve and they began to willingly embrace death. Slowly, but steadily, our numbers declined. We were — we are — indeed, a dying race.

"But then we received word through one of our acolytes that members of the Tau'ri had come in contact with beings who had ascended. We learned that Kheb had been found and its secrets uncovered. We heard how the Asgard had proclaimed the Tau'ri worthy of joining the Four Great Races that once populated the galaxy. And we came to believe that you, more than any other race in the galaxy, held the key to ascension."

"Except, we don't," pointed out Daniel. "I mean, not really. I studied the temple at Kheb — I'm still studying it — and I have to tell you, there is no magic formula. It's something that has to come from within."

NebtHet smiled.

"Of this we are aware, Dr. Jackson. In fact, the more we learned of the Tau'ri the more it became clear to us that, as a people, you are completely ignorant of your potential. However, it does not mitigate the fact that the potential remains. We also learned that the very things we ourselves lacked were those essential human qualities which, as a race, we have never understood or demonstrated. At least, not very well." She sighed. "It is the chain which has held us bound to this existence."

"So you weren't trying to convince us we were dead so you could get information about ascension from us?" Carter was still trying to sort this out the same way Jack was. For her part, NebtHet looked bemused.

"No offense, Major Carter, but your knowledge of ascension is of little interest to us, compared to the millennia we have been studying it."

"Then I still don't get it," Jack interjected. "If you weren't trying to pick our brains, why all the 'underworld' mumbo jumbo?"

"The journey through Duat is the final test for all who die, Colonel," NebtHet said simply. "What better way, then, to learn the mettle of a person than how they walk toward Final Judgment."

"So you were less interested in what we knew than how we behaved when we thought we were dead?"

Now, see, even Daniel was confused. Jack found that oddly comforting. But NebtHet was nodding, which meant that whatever the hell Daniel had just said must have been right.

"Death is a great liberator, Dr. Jackson. We hoped if we freed you from your mortal concerns and responsibilities we could more easily understand what makes each of you so unique. SG-1 has, after all, had more contact with ascended beings in the past few years than has been reported by anyone for centuries. We assumed there must be a reason for this, and with the help of the technology at our disposal, we created scenarios so that we might study certain aspects of humanity which we believe we are lacking. Each of you was placed in a different situation so that we could better understand your unique qualities in ways that were concrete rather than theoretical."

"In other words, we were lab rats," Jack scowled. Just as he'd thought. They could rationalize it all they wanted. It still didn't make it right.

"As I understand the analogy, then, yes, I suppose that's one way to view it, Colonel. Although, if it is any consolation to you, we have found the experience to be most illuminating."

"I bet you have," muttered Jack. Damned, arrogant snakes. They were all the same, no matter what they called themselves.

"Really?" Daniel was asking, although he sounded more curious than irked. "In what way? I mean, aside from what you've already told us about duty and sacrifice and such?"

Jack resisted the urge to roll his eyes. Leave it to Daniel to want to discuss the finer points of the experiment with their captors.

A commotion interrupted NebtHet before she could reply. Shouts were accompanied by the rapid approach of running feet. Jack saw several Djedu scurry out of the way as someone hurled themselves into the Hall.

Jack recognized him. It was Jenmar.

"Colonel O'Neill!" The Tok'ra's words came out in great, heaving gasps. "NebtHet!" he added looking around the room. "They will be here any minute — you must all leave at once!"

"Jenmar?" NebtHet stepped toward him, confused. "What has happened?"

He bowed low before her. "Forgive me, NebtHet. It is all my fault. But you must flee, or prepare to defend yourselves. It is the Goa'uld — they are about to attack!"

As if on cue, there was an explosion and the entire chamber shook. Dust rained down from overhead.

"Too late," shouted Jack above the sudden eruption of cries and chaos. "Looks like they're already here."

CHAPTER THIRTY-TWO

"PLEASE tell me there's a Stargate on this planet."

Another explosion nearly pitched them off their feet. There was no mistaking the blast of a mothership. By the frequency of the hits, Jack figured there had to be at least two in orbit.

"Yes," shouted NebtHet over the din. "It is in the chamber behind this one. Aset will take you."

Aset, however, did not budge. She merely stood there, dust falling around her, looking insolent. Jack grasped the situation a heartbeat ahead of NebtHet.

"Aset — no." NebtHet stared at the woman, incredulous. "Why?"

"Do you really have to ask?" Aset shot back. "You who are so wise, yet see nothing! We have been rotting here for thousands of years while our species — our *kindred* — have ruled this galaxy." She smiled bitterly. "Once I believed you, when you said it was possible for our kind to ascend, and I followed you for thousands of years, NebtHet. But to what end? Only to decide that we should become like *them*?" Aset gestured toward SG-1, her face twisted in disdain. "I will not become something less than I am out of some pathetic hope of immortality. We have immortality right here, right now. And power, if we choose to use it. I will not waste another day on this planet when I can take my place beside our fellow Goa'uld and rule over the pitiful likes of these." She spat toward Jack's feet.

Another blast rocked the Hall. Up on the dais the golden scale with its white feather toppled over, clanging against the marble floor. People were running about with no purpose that Jack could see. It was readily apparent that they'd never come under any kind of attack before. Everything was in utter chaos.

NebtHet looked stricken. Jack almost felt sorry for her. But this wasn't any of their business. Who did what to whom was entirely beside the point now. He just wanted to get his team home. They could blow each other to hell, for all he cared.

"Hey, you!" He pointed at Jenmar. "Can *you* get us to the Stargate?"

Jenmar seemed not to have heard him. The Tok'ra was pale as the proverbial ghost. He looked as if he would pass out, which was what Jack thought he was about to do when Jenmar sank to his knees. But in fact the Tok'ra was actually throwing himself at NebtHet's feet.

"This is all my fault, I am the one who has truly betrayed you, NebtHet. I am the one who brought the Goa'uld to Duat. I — I thought you would not share the secret of ascension with me. After everything I had done for you, I feared you would leave me behind. Forgive me."

Okay, Jack hadn't seen that one coming. Apparently neither had NebtHet. She looked down at Jenmar, uncomprehending.

"I do not understand. You did this? In league with Aset?"

The Tok'ra nodded miserably. Another ground-rattling shot reverberated beneath their feet and dust began to rain down from the ceiling. NebtHet took no notice. She rounded on Aset, her face equal parts sorrow and rage.

"What have you done?"

There wasn't time for this. Someone had to act, or they'd still be standing there when one of those motherships hit a bulls-eye.

"Look," he interrupted, stepping between the two women before Aset could speak. "I don't know about the rest of you, but the four of us would like to get the hell out of here. The sooner the better."

"We've got a bigger problem, sir," yelled Carter over yet another large explosion. "It's the Ancient Technology. We can't let it fall into the hands of the Goa'uld."

Carter's words got NebtHet's attention. Her eyes narrowed and she glared at Aset.

"This is what you promised them, isn't it? The devices of the Ancients."

That insolent look was back. Jack had a sudden urge to wipe it off her face. He had the feeling NebtHet did too.

"They were quite pleased with my initial gifts — a sample of the infinite treasure that is wasting away in our storehouse. And when they take possession of the rest, there will be no question as to their success. And mine," Aset added, triumphantly.

There was an all too familiar egomaniacal glint in her eyes. Jack half expected them to glow.

"Yeah, well, I hate to break it to you, but I wouldn't put a lot of faith in what those Goa'ulds promise," he said, sarcastically. "Believe it or not, snake-heads can lie through their teeth. Go figure."

"I'm pretty sure she knows that, otherwise she would have turned everything over to them already," Daniel jumped in. "The only thing that stopped you was because you knew once you did, they'd have no use for you."

"The only thing that stopped me, Dr. Jackson, was making sure the full value of what I had to offer was completely understood — and sufficiently rewarded."

"Oh, you'll get your reward, all right. Trust me," Jack sneered.

"Indeed I shall, Colonel. Especially since the technology of the Ancients isn't the only thing of value on this planet."

"Us," Carter surmised. "We're your insurance policy. If they want us, they have to take you too."

Aset's smile confirmed Carter's deduction. Gee, a Goa'uld not trusting another Goa'uld. He sure hadn't seen that one coming.

The room shook again with another nearby hit.

"You do realize," Jack felt it was worth pointing out, "that there are four of us and only one of you. You really can't expect us to just come quietly."

Aset merely shrugged. "Feel free to take me into custody,

then, Colonel. I assure you, it won't be for long."

"If the Goa'uld have already activated the Stargate, O'Neill, we will not be able to escape," Teal'c pointed out.

The triumphant tilt of Aset's chin pretty much confirmed that. Jack knew the drill. Thirty-eight minutes to hold the gate and then hope like hell they could dial out faster than whatever Goa'uld was behind this could dial back in.

Of course, they actually needed to *get* to the gate first.

"Jenmar, take them to the chaapa'ai — please." NebtHet still looked stunned and slightly unfocused. For his part, the Tok'ra seemed surprised that she'd even spoken to him, let alone asked for his help. He glanced nervously at SG-1 as he got to his feet, and then back at NebtHet before beckoning Jack and the others to follow.

"Sir." It was Carter again. "We can't just leave. The Ancient tech —"

"We will not allow the Goa'uld to take it, I assure you," NebtHet interrupted. "We will destroy it ourselves first."

Jack looked at Carter and saw his own doubts about NebtHet's ability to make good on that promise written all over her face.

He also saw the answer.

Right.

"Daniel, Teal'c — go with Jenmar and find the gate. The minute the damn thing shuts off, dial the Alpha Site and get your asses through." Jack glanced at Carter who nodded in agreement.

"Dial back when you get there and keep it open as long as you can," she added. "By the time it shuts down, we should be done and good to go."

There were a hundred and one things that could go wrong with that plan, but at the moment it was the best they had. Plan B would have to come later — if they needed one.

"Oh, and since she offered," Jack pushed Aset in Teal'c's direction. "Take this piece of garbage with you." Teal'c wrapped Aset's arms in his viselike grip and frog marched her ahead of him in Jenmar's wake.

"So." Jack turned to NebtHet. "I'm presuming that in addition to all this wonderful technology you have something that can blow it to hell as well?"

For a moment the Djedu looked distracted again. Maybe she didn't have it in her to do this. After all, she'd just had quite the sucker-punch. Two, actually.

"Yes — yes. I believe we have the very thing you will require." She looked at Carter when she said it. "Hurry, though. I do not think we have much time."

For the briefest moment Sam envied her dad. Selmak would have had these ribs healed by now. But it was only for a moment. All she had to do was look around to remember why the experience with Jolinar had been more than enough. She'd take unhealed ribs jabbing her in the side any day.

Still, they were hard to ignore, especially while running. But she didn't have the luxury of coddling them now. They were on the clock.

NebtHet guided them through a maze of corridors until they found themselves outdoors on what otherwise might have been a lovely day. The flowering, manicured garden surrounding them belied the congealing cloud of smoke behind them. The air was acrid and filled with cries of grief and loss.

Sam did her best to ignore them. If they didn't destroy the technology the Djedu had collected, a whole lot more people than those on Duat would suffer. Whichever System Lord this was, and neither Jenmar nor Aset had mentioned a name, putting this much Ancient technology in their hands could make them too powerful for even the Asgard to handle. The Protected Planets Treaty would be worthless and Earth would be right in the crosshairs.

"Whatever it took, that couldn't be allowed to happen.

NebtHet led them away from the worst of the bombardment, moving swiftly through a series of narrow alleys until they came to a small, insignificant-looking building. Hardly the vast storehouse Sam had expected, especially when, once inside, there was only enough space for the three of them to move comfortably around. She shot the colonel a puzzled look, but he was staring at a bank of video monitors that took up one entire wall of the room.

There were about two dozen of them, each with a feed from a different location. The colonel seemed fixated on one showing a raging waterfall. It didn't look familiar, but the scene on the monitor next to it did. It was the Pit of Mutu — empty now, of course. Beside it was a view of a vast sun-baked desert, and the one beneath it showed several abandoned tents in the midst of a windswept plain.

Sam couldn't suppress a shudder. So this was how they'd been watched. Every action, every word, manipulated and studied like lab rats. Just as the colonel had said.

"Carter."

Sam looked up. The colonel had moved to what she'd taken for a darkened window at the back of the room. Only it wasn't dark now. NebtHet waved her hand over a spot on the wall and illuminated what was behind.

Or more precisely, what was below. The window overlooked a vast underground bunker. It was huge, at least several thousand square feet. But that wasn't the most impressive thing.

From their vantage point Sam could see dozens, maybe even hundreds, of artifacts in various sizes and shapes. Things she had never seen before and couldn't comprehend just from looking at them. Thousands of years of collecting, from all across the galaxy, assembled in one location. It was incredible.

"Wow." If she only had time to study even one of them…

But no. They had a job to do.

NebtHet moved her hand again and a doorway slid open beside the window, revealing a long flight of steps down to the storeroom.

The technology was even more impressive from below. Sam

wished Daniel were with them, just so he could translate some of the writings. It would be nice to know what it was they were about to blow up.

"Carter…" The colonel nodded at an enormous golden box.

"A sarcophagus." Sam couldn't suppress a shudder.

"Well, that explains a lot." He glanced ahead to see if NebtHet was out of earshot and lowered his voice. "I want you to know this is breaking my heart, Carter."

Sam nodded, sympathetically. In all their years of exploration they hadn't even scratched the surface of discovering usable technology, compared with what this room held. The potential benefits to science, medicine, defense, and their overall knowledge of the universe… It was mind-boggling.

Maybe there was another way. Maybe they could hide it. Or set up a defensive perimeter.

"Forget it, Carter."

The colonel was shaking his head, as if he'd been reading her thoughts. He was right, though. There would be plenty of time later to regret what they'd done. She had to keep the bigger picture in mind. Preventing the Goa'uld from getting their hands on this was their first and only priority. Whatever NebtHet had planned, Sam hoped it would be powerful enough.

As soon as she saw it, she knew it was — or would be, if rigged the right way. And rigging it was something Sam knew how to do.

Next to her, the colonel pulled up short. "Is that what I think it is?"

"Yes, sir." Sam looked at NebtHet. "Where did you get it?"

For once the Djedu looked abashed. "We have become experts at salvaging what others leave behind, Major. As to which planet, or when, I really couldn't tell you. Am I correct in assuming that it will be sufficient?"

Sam looked at the naquadah reactor and frowned. "Actually, there's a slight problem, sir."

"Of course there is." He sighed. "What now?"

She studied the device. "I can hotwire it to overload, but the timing mechanism is missing. There's no way I can set it on a delay to give us enough time to get back to the Stargate. Once the overload starts, we'll have about five minutes to get as far away as we can. But it won't be enough."

"Five minutes ought to give all of us enough time to get out of here."

Sam shook her head. "If we were only blowing up the generator, then yes. But given all the unknown technology in here, there's likely to be a number of secondary explosions, possibly even more powerful than the first. The shock waves may even reach the gate. I can't say for sure."

The colonel furrowed his brow, thinking. She knew what was going through his mind, because the same thing was going through hers. Someone was going to have to stay.

"Show me what to do," NebtHet said.

They both turned and looked at her.

"I have lived for over three thousand years," she said calmly. "And I have spent my entire life seeking enlightenment in the hope that someday I might achieve an immortality that did not depend on the use of technology." NebtHet closed her eyes briefly and took a deep breath. "This day, I have come as close to understanding ascension as I have in the past three millennia and I see now that it is something neither I, nor any of my kind, will ever be able to achieve." She looked between them, earnestly. "Please. Allow me to do this. Allow me to give you the opportunity to try to accomplish what I cannot. For what I have put you through to enable me to come to this understanding, let me pay this debt."

It was the last thing Sam had expected to hear, the colonel either, going by his expression. Maybe there was more to NebtHet than they'd given her credit for. It didn't excuse what she had done to them, but Sam could certainly see why the Djedu had followed her for all these years.

"Show her, Carter."

Sam knew him too well not to recognize the unspoken regret in the colonel's tone. NebtHet might have literally put them through Hell, but even in the colonel's eyes she didn't deserve this. There had to be another way.

"Sir, maybe I could—"

"We're out of time, Major. Just prep the damn thing and let's go."

Sam wanted to argue, but she had no other option to offer. Pushing aside the part of her that already mourned this woman, she gave her attention to the reactor.

Sam's heart sank when she opened the casing. The timing mechanism wasn't the only thing missing. Someone had attempted to modify the device since it had left the possession of the SGC. Whatever it was they'd been trying to do, most likely hadn't worked. The alterations were jumbled and confused. Nothing was at all where it should be.

"Oh boy," she muttered under her breath.

"Something wrong, Carter?"

Sam looked up and met the colonel's eyes. She'd been going to explain the problem, but changed her mind. "Nothing I can't handle, sir," she said instead, giving her attention back to the device.

Rewiring the reactor back to specs would take longer than they had. But she didn't have to completely rewire it. She just had to fix it enough to blow it up.

Visualizing the wiring diagram in her mind, it only took Sam a few minutes to reroute what was needed to activate the overload. She left one wire unattached.

"Give us a ten minute start," she told NebtHet as she passed her the lone wire. "It should be enough." At least, she hoped so.

NebtHet looked at the wire in her hand and then up at the two of them.

"I have one favor," she said, her eyes boring into the colonel.

"When you see Jenmar — Jenmar a'Keyleb," she amended. "Tell him… I forgive him." Her look softened slightly. "And tell him that, someday, I hope he can forgive me as well."

The colonel held NebtHet's gaze for several seconds before he nodded. "I will." For just a moment Sam thought she glimpsed a look of grudging admiration on his face before his standard, brusque detachment dropped into place. "Come on, Carter. Let's go."

They had only taken a few steps when the colonel stopped short and turned. "You know, NebtHet, this whole ascension thing…" The colonel paused for a moment, searching for the right words. "I'd say you're a lot closer than you think."

Before the Djedu could respond, he'd wheeled around and was striding toward the stairs, not looking back. Sam hurried to catch up, but not before she glimpsed the gratitude on NebtHet's face. She wished the colonel had seen it.

By the time Sam got to the top of the stairs she was winded, and the pain in her side was worse. There wasn't time to stop and catch her breath, but she couldn't help it. The colonel was almost out the door of the building before he realized she wasn't right behind him.

Sam swiftly dropped her hands from the doorframe she'd grabbed for support, hoping he wouldn't notice.

"You okay?" The colonel eyed her suspiciously.

She took as deep a breath as she could without wincing and nodded. "I'll be fine."

His eyes narrowed in skepticism and she waited for the accompanying reproof, but all he said was, "Come on. We gotta move," and pushed out the door.

Good. Arguing over whether she was in good enough condition to beat the clock probably wasn't a productive use of their time anyway.

When Sam stepped outside, he was waiting. As they retraced their route back toward the Hall, it was evident that the bombardment hadn't abated in the least. If anything, the attacks had escalated. Only the area in the vicinity of the bunker was unaffected — of course. Aset would have told the Goa'uld where the Ancient technology was kept. They'd have been careful to avoid it.

There was a certain irony in the fact that the safest place in the whole compound was the one they themselves were about to destroy.

Breathing became more challenging the closer they got to the main part of the compound. What air she managed to take in made Sam's lungs burn just that much more. The colonel had been pushing ahead at a steady jog, but stopped when he saw she'd fallen behind again. She hated that she was slowing them down, but each pounding step felt like a knife thrust into her side. Finally she had no choice but to stop.

Leaning over, Sam put her hands on her knees and coughed. Blood spattered on the ground.

That wasn't good.

A pair of dusty, sandaled feet appeared in her range of vision. Looking up she saw the colonel's eyes go to the bloody spittle at her feet.

"Sorry, sir. Go on ahead. I'll catch up," she promised, before he could say anything.

He scowled. "Yeah. I don't think so. Come on."

Reluctantly she let him pull the arm on her good side around his neck, as he had back in the maze. There was no point in protesting. He wouldn't have listened anyway, and she didn't have the breath left to argue.

"Let's go." He tried easing her into a moderate gait which, despite his care, still drove spears into her ribs. All of her concentration now was simply focused on not passing out. She was vaguely aware that they were approaching a large building. Was it the Hall already? The colonel's voice seemed distant, fading. She heard him say 'No time!' and 'Get out of here!' and then, with a swift, sickening pull she went careening into a darkened doorway.

She heard a roaring. Part sound, part bone-rattling vibration, it thrummed through her just before the shock wave lifted her off her feet. For an eternity she couldn't breathe as all the air was sucked away, and then, like a rag doll flung by a petulant child, she was hurled to the floor. Something heavy crashed into her and groaned a curse.

For one brief, excruciating moment every inch of her throbbed in agony. The space around her spun like a vortex as her vision narrowed. Without further protest, Sam slipped willingly into the darkness.

CHAPTER THIRTY-THREE

THE ATTACK hadn't lessened any, as far as Daniel could tell, although it didn't seem to be having much of an impact on the Duat version of the gate room. While debris and dust and the occasional small chunk of rock were dislodged by the nearby explosions, for the most part the room remained undamaged. He pointed this out to Teal'c.

"I do not believe the Goa'uld are targeting this building, Daniel Jackson. If the Stargate is damaged, they would have no way to send through their Jaffa warriors, who are no doubt waiting for the signal to proceed."

Daniel looked involuntarily at the wavering event horizon of the Stargate, as if one of those warriors was about to emerge. But no. They wouldn't come yet. The *ha'tak* was still hard at it. When the overhead attack stopped, that's when they'd have to worry.

As if there wasn't already enough to worry about.

At least the DHD was still intact. Somewhere in the back of his mind Daniel had harbored a fear that they'd get here only to find some chunk of ceiling had smashed the dialing device. Now all he had to do was dial out quicker than the Goa'uld could dial in. Sure. No pressure.

"I have the utmost confidence in your ability, Daniel Jackson," Teal'c assured him, as if sensing Daniel's concern. He still had Aset firmly by the arm and was forcibly guiding her to a location away from the gate and out of the sightline of the address for the Alpha Site. Leave it to Teal'c to think of that.

Watching Aset gloat even now, Daniel found himself wondering what would become of her. He could only imagine the number of people who'd be interested in her if she was brought back to Earth. He'd be surprised if she ever saw sunlight again.

Once, that would have bothered him more than it did now, especially considering all the time they'd spent together crossing the desert. He wouldn't go so far as to say that they'd developed a bond, but in the Hall of the Two Truths he had thought, for a while at least, that she had been sincere.

Obviously not.

They could, of course, simply leave her behind. If Sam and Jack were able to destroy the Ancient technology, she'd lose the only clout she had with whomever it was up there blasting the Djedu to extinction. Maybe justice would be better served if, when the gate shut down behind SG-1, she was still on this side of it.

So much for his so-called compassion.

Maybe he really had been hanging around Jack too much.

A particularly close hit brought down more bits of the ceiling and the chamber's high windows rattled precariously. The bombardment was picking up pace. The explosions were nearly nonstop. Daniel couldn't even imagine what it was like out there. Even through the thick walls of the structure he could hear cries and shouts. At this rate, when the Jaffa finally did make it through the gate, they wouldn't have much left to do. The Djedu would be wiped out.

Daniel glanced at Jenmar, standing, dazed, a few feet away. As much as he hated to admit it, Jack had been right about him from the very beginning. Yet, for all the Tok'ra had done, Daniel didn't get the impression that true malice lay behind it. He was just someone who, somewhere along the line, had lost his way.

Jenmar must have felt Daniel's eyes on him because he raised his own to meet his gaze. Daniel could see they were red-rimmed. The Tok'ra looked haggard, his youthful appearance having aged in the course of the past three days.

"All I ever wanted was peace," he said, a slight quaver in his voice. "Not this. Never this."

Daniel felt sympathy for him. "I believe you."

"For decades I had sought the Djedu. There had been stories—legends—that they rejected both the way of the Goa'uld and of the Tok'ra, and sought only their own enlightenment, their own inner-peace." He wiped at his eyes. "I was so tired of fighting, tired of the relentless subterfuge and sabotage in the conflict between the Tok'ra and the Goa'uld." His voice broke and Daniel waited as he regained his composure. "At last I found NebtHet and became her follower. Her words… When she spoke, I could hear the same longing that was within me, and I thought, here is someone I can follow. Here is someone who will help me find peace."

"You know, sometimes we follow a certain path, or a person, who seems to have the answers we need, and there's nothing wrong with that." Daniel wasn't sure this was going to help, but he had to try. "Eventually, though, we have to take charge of our own destiny, even if means choosing a different way from those we've always trusted."

"I trusted *her*." There was anguish in Jenmar's voice. "I believed that when the Djedu discovered the secrets of ascension she would share this knowledge with me, and I could join her and the others. But in the end, I lost faith. And that is no one's fault but my own."

"Fear makes us do all sorts of things we might think we never could—or would." Daniel glanced at Aset. He had little doubt who had played on Jenmar's fears. "I'm not saying that what you did wasn't wrong, but I think I understand how you got there. And in the end, you tried to do the right thing. Believe me, that counts for something."

Jenmar shook his head and Daniel understood there was nothing he could say that would ease the Tok'ra's guilt. There was only one person who could really give Jenmar the absolution he sought, and it was a tough call as to whether NebtHet ever would.

Cries of fear swelled through the hall as another blast struck, sending tremors through the great room. More and more Djedu were crowding into the ever shrinking space. People continued to run in and out, but what Daniel had initially taken as confusion he now realized was a rescue operation. Teams of Djedu, many of whom he'd seen in the Hall of Judgment, were returning with survivors of the attack. Many were injured. All looked disheveled, frightened and in shock. No sooner was each group brought in than the teams headed out again, despite the fact that the bombardment was picking up in intensity. Those who remained behind, and were able, began tending the injured in their midst.

Above the growing din, Daniel thought he heard a familiar whine of engines. The staccato of weapons fire and smaller explosions confirmed his fears. Death gliders. Daniel's eyes met Teal'c's and he could see the Jaffa had arrived at the same conclusion. Ground troops wouldn't be far behind.

Daniel turned back to Jenmar, who'd remained perfectly still in spite of the escalation of the attack. "Which System Lord is responsible for this?" It was a question they hadn't had time to ask, before. With so many of the Goa'uld vying for position now that Apophis was dead, Daniel could easily think of a handful without trying.

"I do not know," Jenmar answered, dully. "I was never told his name."

That made no sense. System Lords were never hesitant about declaring their superiority or their intention to seek power. Modesty was not one of their character flaws. "You had to have had a contact," he persisted. "Someone close to him. If we had a name, we might be able to figure out —"

The hall was plunged into twilight as the Stargate whooshed and the wormhole vanished.

Thirty-eight minutes were up.

"Okay, our turn." Daniel frantically began dialing the address for the Alpha Site. One by one the symbols lit up on the DHD and the inner ring spun, locking each one in place.

"Come on, come on," he muttered under his breath, pressing the last panel and leaning on the red orb in the middle. He worried when the last symbol wouldn't lock at first, but with a loud *ker-chunk*, it finally slid into place and another wormhole erupted into the chamber. Daniel sagged against the DHD in relief.

Teal'c came forward, dragging Aset.

"I knew my confidence was not misplaced, Daniel Jackson." Teal'c smiled at him as together they stared at the rippling event horizon. Daniel shot him a dubious look.

"Well, then you're far more certain than I was." He studied the wormhole. That little last minute stutter in getting the lock worried him a bit. "I *think* I did that—"

"We shall soon see," replied Teal'c, firming up his grip on Aset. "We should proceed to the Alpha Site as O'Neill instructed."

Daniel listened to the now persistent firing from the death gliders outside. Once they found they couldn't establish an incoming wormhole to Duat, the Goa'uld would begin landing troops. The Djedu would soon be overrun.

"Listen, Teal'c, you take Aset and go. I'm going to wait here for a while until Jack and Sam make it back. Maybe we can evacuate some of these people before whoever that is up there ends up destroying this whole place."

"Those were not our orders, Daniel Jackson," Teal'c pointed out, frowning. Daniel shrugged

"Yeah, well, you know me and orders, Teal'c."

"Then I shall remain as well."

"Teal'c, no. Someone's got to get through to the Alpha Site and —"

Daniel was pitched to the floor by the most powerful blast yet to roll through the chamber. It jarred his bones, rattling him down to his very teeth. Even his ears were ringing. Around the chamber, everyone else had been thrown to the ground with him, including Teal'c. Amid the muffled cries of fear and alarm, Daniel recognized a distinctive cracking sound. Before he could even look up to confirm his worst fears, the high windows exploded inward, launching the shattered glass across the entire room.

Daniel covered his head, protecting his face and eyes as the cascade of razor-sharp shards sprayed over him. More cries of pain and terror filled the hall as it was thrown into darkness yet again.

The blue light was gone. The wormhole had shut down.

Teal'c was most surprised to find himself on the ground. It had to have been an explosion of enormous force to send him sprawling. No Goa'uld mothership could have caused such an impact without making a direct hit, and as far as he could tell, the building was still structurally intact. The only reasonable conclusion, therefore, was that O'Neill and Major Carter had been successful in their attempt to destroy the Ancient technology.

Looking around, Teal'c saw that everyone had been knocked to the floor, including Daniel Jackson. As his friend picked himself up, shaking off bits of shattered glass, he looked Teal'c's way. Reflected in his face, Teal'c could see the same concern he too felt for the safety of O'Neill and Major Carter. Apparently Daniel Jackson had surmised the cause of the explosion as well.

Realizing that his left hand was now empty, Teal'c looked around for Aset. She had been thrown to the ground with him. He remembered her cry of fright as the glass pelted her from overhead. Amidst all the crying and dazed occupants of the hall, however, he could not see her. Several bodies remained motionless on the ground and Teal'c hurried to check them. Most were dead. None were Aset.

She had escaped.

Anger at his own carelessness burned in his chest. He should have been more attentive, gripped her more tightly. Being caught off-guard by the explosion was no excuse for allowing her to reclaim her freedom. She would have been a valuable prisoner from which they might have learned much.

He was tempted to go in search of her, but there was no time. They must reopen the Stargate before the Goa'uld could dial in.

At least they had been fortunate in that the DHD had not sustained any damage. A massive metal window frame had narrowly missed crushing it; however the frame now leaned precariously across the top of the device, blocking access to the keypad. It was too big to move alone. "Daniel Jackson, I require your assistance."

"Uh, Teal'c, not right now —"

Daniel Jackson was kneeling on the ground. He had torn off more of his already ragged pant leg and was attempting to use it to apply pressure to a large gash in Jenmar's neck. Teal'c could see the effort was futile. Blood was quickly soaking the cloth and Daniel Jackson's hands as Jenmar's face turned deathly gray. Not even the symbiote within could heal such a wound. On the floor beside him, Teal'c saw the bloodied piece of glass which had pierced the Tok'ra's artery. There was no helping him now.

Teal'c squatted beside Daniel Jackson. "His injury is grave. I fear there is nothing that can be done." He glanced up at the silent chappa'ai. "It is more important that we reopen the Stargate."

Daniel Jackson nonetheless continued his efforts and Teal'c knew he would not stop until all hope was gone. It would not take long.

Jenmar's eyes fluttered open and Teal'c saw that he knew only too well that death was near. But instead of the fear he was accustomed to witnessing on the faces of men in such circumstance, this Tok'ra showed only relief. With a trembling hand which he could barely raise, Jenmar reached over and weakly pulled Daniel Jackson's arm away, stopping his ministrations.

"No more, please," he whispered, his voice rattling as fluid filled his throat. "I welcome death."

Daniel Jackson said nothing but grasped the still reaching hand in his own. "I'm sorry."

Jenmar managed a barely perceptible shake of his head.

"This is best," he gasped. "Please, just tell NebtHet that I died her humble servant —"

The Tok'ra closed his eyes and with one final, release of breath was gone.

Daniel Jackson sighed deeply, sinking back to the ground, his hands still covered in the Tok'ra's blood.

"Now is not the time to mourn, Daniel Jackson." Under normal circumstances Teal'c would have respected his friend's need to grieve over what had just transpired, but such sentiments would have to wait. "We have lost the connection to the Alpha Site. It must be re-established before the Goa'uld can dial in again and prevent our escape."

Daniel Jackson appeared weary, but he allowed Teal'c to pull him back to his feet and staggered over to the DHD.

"When we get this cleared off, you go through," Daniel Jackson told him as they struggled to shift the heavy frame off the DHD. "I'm waiting for Jack and Sam."

"That was a powerful explosion, Daniel Jackson," Teal'c reminded him, solemnly. As much as he hated the thought, the likelihood that their friends were still alive were slim. "We must face the possibility that they did not survive."

"Oh I wouldn't go and count us out just yet, T." O'Neill, supported by Major Carter, was limping toward them through the debris. O'Neill's knee appeared injured and Major Carter was struggling under the colonel's weight, although she made no complaint. With a final push, Teal'c heaved the window frame to the floor, hurrying to take her place as O'Neill's crutch. The gesture earned him a brief, grateful smile before she placed her hands to her ribs and winced.

"Are you injured, Major Carter?"

"I'll be fine, Teal'c. But the colonel's knee took a hit when we were caught in the shock wave."

"It's just a flesh wound," muttered O'Neill.

Teal'c saw his eyes light on the body of Jenmar. An emotion he could not interpret briefly crossed O'Neill's face, but just as quickly it was gone.

"Dial it up, Daniel." O'Neill gestured toward the DHD. "They'll be landing those motherships before you know it."

"Where's NebtHet?" Daniel Jackson asked, looking around as he began dialing.

Biting her lip, Major Carter just shook her head.

Looking grim, Daniel Jackson turned back to the DHD, but before he could press the final symbol it activated on its own.

It was an incoming wormhole.

Next to Teal'c, O'Neill cursed.

"We're too late," Major Carter said.

O'Neill raised his voice so the whole chamber could hear. "Listen up, everybody — take cover!"

There were so many, Teal'c was uncertain there were sufficient places for them to conceal themselves. In his periphery, however, he saw them tighten together in their groups, crouching low and trying to stay out of the way.

"Teal'c —" O'Neill indicated the staff weapon which Teal'c had set down next to Jenmar's body. He retrieved it and together he and O'Neill each took refuge behind one of the chamber's enormous pillars. Whoever came through the gate would be caught in a cross-fire of staff-blasts and P-90 ordinance. It would give SG-1 at least a momentary advantage.

Major Carter and Daniel Jackson also sought cover. Without weapons they would be unable to assist. Likewise, none of the Djedu appeared to be armed, as no one else came forward to join them. It would all depend on O'Neill and himself.

Except for the unmistakable thrumming of the wormhole, the chamber fell into an uneasy silence as they waited. Teal'c tightened his grip on his staff, aiming carefully at the optimal height for incapacitating the first person to emerge from the Stargate.

A tell-tale ripple in the surface of the wormhole caused him to tense, his finger poised, ready to fire. But instead of the tattooed head of a Jaffa warrior, a familiar metallic shape appeared, pausing momentarily on the edge of the event horizon before continuing its slow, treaded descent down the stone ramp.

It was a MALP.

"Hold your fire!" O'Neill shouted.

Teal'c could almost feel his teammates heave a collective sigh of relief. Limping forward, O'Neill met the device as it rolled into the midst of the chamber and stopped.

"General, sir? I sure hope that's you on the other end." O'Neill leaned over and spoke into the camera mounted on the front. From the built-in speaker a welcome voice responded.

"*Colonel, I can't tell you how good it is to see you're in one piece.*" General Hammond's Texas accent was indeed good to hear.

"Yes, sir. But we won't be for long. We need you to shut down the gate, General, and let us dial out of here. This place is about to take the full brunt of some Goa'uld wrath and we'd rather not be here when it does."

"*Understood, Colonel. Until we can sort this out, report back to P4C-679 and SG-3 will meet you there.*"

"Copy that, General." O'Neill patted the MALP as if it were an old friend. "Glad to know you left the light on for us, sir."

If General Hammond made a reply, no one heard it. The chamber exploded with falling debris and the Stargate went dark. The Goa'uld had scored a direct hit.

Teal'c ducked, as did the others, giving their backs to the shrapnel as a portion of the roof was obliterated. More screams and more cries came from the Djedu, and through the fog of smoke and dust Teal'c saw many bodies crushed beneath chunks of collapsing pillars.

The Goa'uld were no longer avoiding the Stargate. It had become their final target. Perhaps Aset had made good on her threat after all.

"Carter!" bellowed O'Neill. He had no need to say more. Major Carter scrambled through the haze of yellow dust to the DHD and began dialing. Teal'c did not realize he had been holding his breath in anticipation until the last chevron was locked into place. He exhaled with relief as the large plume shot out, instantly cleansing the air in its path. The way to the Stargate was clear.

"Go, go, go!" O'Neill shouted, making a waving motion with his arm. Daniel Jackson moved first, but not toward the Stargate. He ran, instead, to O'Neill, coughing as he gestured toward the Djedu who were still alive.

"Jack, we've got to take them with us." He raised his voice above the escalating barrage of noise. With part of the roof gone, the whine of death gliders was relentless.

"They're *Goa'ulds*, Daniel—" O'Neill roared back, disbelief on his face.

"I know, but—"

"They *kidnapped* us, Daniel!" O'Neill's face became even harder in light of Daniel Jackson's persistence.

"I know—"

"They put us through *hell*, Daniel. *Literally*—" O'Neill added, jabbing his finger for emphasis. Daniel Jackson, however, would not back down. Teal'c had seen this determination in him many times.

"I *know* all that, Jack!" he shouted back. "But they're all going to be destroyed in a few minutes if we leave them behind."

"Do I *look* like I care, Daniel?" O'Neill was growing red in the face. "If you want to invite them, fine. Invite them. But I am not holding that gate open a second longer than I have to."

"Sir—" All eyes turned to Major Carter. She likewise had failed to comply with O'Neill's order and instead was standing at the Stargate itself, her hand partially submerged within the wormhole.

Teal'c saw O'Neill comprehend. *She* was holding the gate open. Not just for SG-1, but for all of them. For a moment

O'Neill hesitated, some struggle Teal'c could not decipher playing out across his face. Then he turned and faced the surviving Djedu, who had reformed into small groups amidst the ruins and their dead.

"Anyone who wants to get out of this place before those motherships blow us all to hell, get your asses over here now."

Not one Djedu moved.

"You don't understand," Daniel Jackson implored. "If you stay here, you're going to die."

"Not die, Dr. Jackson." Khemy, the Djedu who had portrayed Sha're, stepped from the midst of the others. She was covered in dust, and in blood which did not appear to be her own. "We know our fate, and we do not believe it is death. Not anymore."

Teal'c saw comprehension illuminate Daniel Jackson's face. O'Neill, too, seemed to grasp the meaning of her words. He pulled Daniel Jackson by the arm.

"They've made their choice, Daniel. It's time to go."

For just a moment Daniel Jackson looked as if he might argue, but did not. With a nod of regret toward the Djedu, he allowed O'Neill to push him toward the Stargate where Major Carter still waited.

"Teal'c—" O'Neill called to him, as the other two entered the event horizon. "Time to go."

Gazing out over the calm faces of the Djedu, Teal'c felt great compassion for them. Many Jaffa, after all, clung to the very same hope. And while he did not share their certainty of the future which awaited them, Teal'c could not help but admire their resolve. Behind Khemy he saw Aqti and Ahi, disheveled yet serene, even as the sound of weapons fired came menacingly closer.

"Teal'c?" There was added urgency in O'Neill's voice. They were out of time.

With a final bow to those who remained behind, Teal'c stepped through the gate.

CHAPTER THIRTY-FOUR

"ACCORDING to Dr. Fraiser, there's trace evidence of the same residual markers in our brains as when we encountered the Reol."

Major Carter's report brought Hammond back to the topic at hand. For a moment he'd been more focused on how his people looked than on the debriefing. If he could have, he would have postponed all this for another twelve hours to give them a chance to rest up, but he knew it was better to get the full story while the details were still fresh in their minds. Not to mention that the Tok'ra had been demanding specifics about Jenmar almost from the moment SG-1 had returned to Earth. Normally he wouldn't have danced to their insistent tune, but Hammond felt he owed Anise a favor, considering what she had done for him. Anything to keep her from getting into further trouble with the High Council.

All four members of SG-1 looked as though they could do with a good night's sleep, at the very least. Something he'd insist on, in fact, once this meeting was over. Hammond wasn't even sure Major Carter should be out of bed. By the way she was favoring her one side, he was pretty sure Dr. Fraiser would corral her back to the infirmary as soon as possible.

Sitting beside the major, Jack sat hunched over, his hands folded in front of him on the table. The colonel had been uncharacteristically subdued upon his return. Part of it, Hammond was sure, was simple fatigue. But he sensed there was more to it than that. Not that Jack would ever say. The best Hammond could hope for was to read between the lines once he got Jack's final report. On the other hand, perhaps there were things he was better off not knowing.

Dr. Jackson was unusually quiet as well. According to Major Carter, he had been the one who'd tried to encourage the Djedu to return with them through the Stargate.

Knowing Dr. Jackson as he did, Hammond could only imagine that their refusal and subsequent deaths were weighing heavily on the man. As he understood it, the individual who had acted as Dr. Jackson's guide on Duat had assumed the persona of Sha're, and that had to have taken a toll as well. Little wonder he was sitting there, distracted, absently playing with the pen in his hand.

Of all of them, Teal'c seemed the least affected by what he had been through, but then Hammond didn't find that surprising. Even so, he couldn't help but think that the Jaffa looked unusually pensive. Teal'c's description of his experience had been as brief and lacking in specifics as Jack's. Studying his inscrutable expression, Hammond wondered if he'd ever get the full story at all.

From any of them.

"The Tok'ra have been working on developing a synthetic version of the Reol pheromone," Major Carter was saying. "But as far as I know, it's still in the testing phase."

"Considering Jenmar's involvement, I think it's safe to say he may have had something to do with how the Djedu got their hands on it," Dr. Jackson offered. "He must have been passing them information about us for quite some time, otherwise NebtHet would never have singled us out as her test subjects."

"Lucky us," muttered Jack, under his breath. Major Carter gave him a sympathetic glance.

"Well that explains how you all saw people you thought you knew," Hammond said, thoughtfully. "But some of the other experiences you had… I'm not sure how to begin to understand those."

"If I had to guess, sir, I'd say that most of what happened to us was made possible by the technology the Djedu had gathered over thousands of years." Major Carter rallied a bit. "We've already seen devices that can affect weather and climate. And the Asgard have hologram technology that's eons ahead of anything we've even begun to conceptualize. If the Djedu were collectors of anything and everything that the Ancients left behind, who knows what they may have discovered? We are talking about the people who built the Stargates, after all."

"Well, it's all gone now," Jack pointed out.

"Are you certain all of it was destroyed?" Hammond looked from one to the other. In spite of what had happened to each of them personally, he also had to be concerned with the greater picture. "If whoever attacked Duat were to get their hands on even one piece of Ancient technology—"

Jack deferred to his second in command. "Carter?"

"We can't be absolutely certain, no, sir. But when a naquada reactor overloads, it typically doesn't leave much behind. I doubt the Goa'uld were able to salvage anything."

"Unfortunately, that doesn't mean they walked away empty handed," Dr. Jackson added, grimly. "Whatever Aset had already turned over to them, it must have been significant enough to pique their interest. Which is sort of a scary thought."

"And do we have any idea who this Aset was working for?"

Dr. Jackson shook his head.

"According to the Tok'ra, it wasn't any of the major System Lords. They're all tied up elsewhere, duking it out amongst themselves now that Apophis is dead. No one has any idea who it might have been."

Hammond looked at the only member of SG-1 who hadn't spoken. "Teal'c, any thoughts on who we might have been dealing with here?"

"I have none, General Hammond. We saw no ground troops. There were no distinguishing markings on the death gliders. And unfortunately, I allowed Aset to escape before we could interrogate her further."

Hammond should have known that, out of everything that had happened, that incident would disturb Teal'c the most.

"Don't beat yourself up over it," Jack consoled him. "Chances are, she never made it off the planet anyway. Not that I'm sorry. If you ask me, she got what she deserved."

"Have we tried dialing the address again, General?" Major Carter asked. "I know the chances are slim that there are survivors, but still—"

Hammond shook his head. "We did, Major. We couldn't get a lock. We're assuming that the gate was damaged or destroyed after you came through. I'm sorry."

The major chewed on her lip and nodded.

"So the Djedu really are extinct now." There was bitterness in Dr. Jackson's voice.

"You say that like it's a bad thing," the colonel shot back.

"Jack, come on. It's not like they were Goa'uld."

"It's *exactly* like they were Goa'ulds, Daniel! In fact, they *were* Goa'ulds. Dressing them up and pretending they had these lofty, spiritual goals doesn't make what they did to us right. In fact, it makes it just that much worse. They *used* us for their own personal gain." Jack's eyes were blazing. "Sure, maybe it wasn't to grab power from a bunch of other Goa'ulds, or to go out and conquer half the galaxy, but it was just as self-serving. And if you can sit there and tell me that you had a great time wandering through the desert with someone pretending to be your dead wife, then maybe Doc Fraiser better have another look at your head."

The room fell deathly silent. Major Carter studied her hands. Teal'c was looking straight ahead through the window overlooking the gate room. The colonel and Dr. Jackson glared at one another across the table and Hammond could feel the tension in the room rise palpably. In the corner the SF sat up a little straighter, alert.

No one spoke for several very long seconds until Dr. Jackson heaved a huge sigh and leaned forward on his arms.

"You're right, Jack. You're absolutely right. They did use us. And no, I would not consider my encounter with that Sha're to be one of the high points of my life—" Hammond heard his voice catch slightly. "But that doesn't make me any less sorry that they're gone. And not because of the technology they had, but because they were on the verge of accomplishing something truly amazing."

"Oh for crying out loud, you're not going to tell me that you think they actually ascended." Jack's eyebrows creased together with annoyance.

"I honestly don't know," Dr. Jackson replied. "But can you tell me, with absolute certainty, that they didn't?"

Jack said nothing but merely glowered at Daniel. Hammond wondered if he should intervene, but Dr. Jackson continued before he could.

"That place where we ended up — the place every one of our guides kept telling us we had to get to — was the Hall of the Two Truths," Dr. Jackson spoke hurriedly, as if he were afraid Jack might jump in and say something. "In the Book of the Dead it is also known as the Hall of the Two Maats. Maat was an Egyptian goddess of Truth and Order. In Ancient Egyptian culture, Maat represented the principle of balance and harmony, which is why the feather of Maat was used in the weighing of the heart."

Hammond could tell Dr. Jackson had already given a great deal of thought to what he was saying. For his part, the colonel continued to look unconvinced, although he was letting Daniel continue.

"To the Ancient Egyptians, the heart was the location of the soul. It was also where they believed all thought and decision making took place. It's why, of all the internal organs, it, and it alone, was returned to the body before mummification." Dr. Jackson pushed on, perhaps encouraged by Jack's lack of rebuttal. "When the dead arrived at the Hall of the Two Truths, the final judgment of whether or not they were truly worthy of eternal life was when their heart was weighed against the feather of Truth, because it was believed that the heart could hide no secrets. That one's deeds — good or bad — would win out in the end. *Those* are the two Truths, Jack. The truth of one's words, and the truth of one's deeds."

"All of that is *fascinating*, Daniel." Jack's tone was still irritable. He cast a sidelong look at Major Carter, which she did not see. "Except for the fact that *we* were the ones up there getting our hearts weighed, not the Djedu."

"I know, Jack." Daniel closed his eyes. Either he was searching for patience or the right words. Quite possibly both. "It's just — The point I'm trying to make is that the Djedu must have had very strong ties to that belief system. And if, in the end, their deeds came into balance with their words, then it's very possible they were able to find the afterlife they were looking for."

"You're saying, what they learned from us changed them enough that they were able to ascend," clarified Major Carter.

"They did face the certainty of their fate with great courage," Teal'c observed.

"And NebtHet sacrificed herself so that we could make it back to the gate," the major added, looking thoughtful.

Jack was shaking his head. "Fine. If you folks want to believe they all drifted off to some higher plane of existence," he fluttered his fingers in the air like a sideshow magician, "then go right ahead. And maybe they did ascend. You're right, Daniel. I don't know." His voice was calmer now. He glanced at Major Carter again. "NebtHet did seem to be on the right track there, at the end," he conceded. "But it doesn't excuse what they did to us. That's all I'm saying."

"No. No it doesn't. It's just —" Dr. Jackson slumped back in his chair. "Well, it'd be nice to think something good came out of it, in the end. But I suppose that's just me."

No one said anything, and for a few awkward moments the only sound in the room was the ticking of the second hand on the wall clock. Hammond wasn't sure what had just happened, but he sensed there were deeper ramifications to Dr. Jackson's comments than he was able to grasp just yet.

Finally Jack cleared his throat and turned toward the head of the table.

"Not that we're not all enjoying this immensely, sir." Jack's tone was just on the edge of sarcasm. Hammond could hear the fatigue behind it. "But I'm not sure there's anything more we can tell you at the moment."

There was a silent plea implicit in Jack's words which Hammond understood. They'd had enough. He was inclined to agree.

"I think we can let you all rest for now," he replied, pushing his notes back into the folder on the table in front of him. "And I'm sure you'll each provide me with a thorough and complete written report, when the time comes."

"Absolutely, General." Jack's palms smacked the table. "You know me. Thoroughnicity and completeness are my middle name when it comes to reports. Or is it 'names?'" His brow furrowed in feigned confusion.

"Thank you, sir." Major Carter made to stand, but Hammond waved her back to her seat.

"I have a feeling Dr. Fraiser would like you back in the infirmary ASAP, Major."

"I'm fine, sir. Really."

"Oh, Carter, you're about as fine as I am. Fraiser'll hunt us both down if we don't go back." Jack pushed himself to his feet. "Besides. I hear they've got Jell-O on the menu today."

Back in his office, Hammond watched his people as they filed out of the briefing room. Major Carter wasn't the only one who was going to need a little down time. Teal'c had already expressed a desire to visit his son, and by the way Jack was limping, he wouldn't be going anywhere soon. Well, they'd more than earned it. He wouldn't deny it was a relief to have them back again, all in one piece — more or less.

The statuette of NebtHet was still on his desk. Hammond picked it up, studying the worn image. Whether the Djedu had succeeded in ascending or not, he supposed they'd never really know. SG-1 hadn't exactly been forthcoming on what, precisely, NebtHet and the others had learned from studying them, but personally, he couldn't think of any finer examples of humanity than the four individuals who'd just left the room.

Hammond watched his people disappear down the stairway at the other end of the conference room, talking amongst themselves. He could never condone what the Djedu had done, of course. But if the unintended consequence was that SG-1 had regained some of the confidence and rapport that had been missing these past few months, then perhaps he owed this NebtHet a begrudging nod for succeeding where he had failed.

If for no other reason than that, Hammond hoped Dr. Jackson was right. Maybe, when all was said and done, they'd all found peace in the end.

At the very least, it was nice to think so.

ACKNOWLEDGMENTS

FIRST and foremost, I would like to express my deepest and most heartfelt gratitude to Mara Pheonix for suffering through every chapter of this book as it was conceived and written, and for the many (many!) hours of discussion which helped me so much along the way. I could never have accomplished this without her input, encouragement and enduring friendship.

This book would still be languishing on my hard drive were it not for the efforts of Marian Trupiano, whose persistence made this happen, and Diana Dru Botsford, whose insight and guidance helped make it a better story than it otherwise might have been. Of course none of this would have seen the light of day without the support of Sally Malcolm, who took a chance on a new writer and ever so graciously taught her that less is oftentimes more.

My passion for and understanding of the Stargate universe has also been greatly enhanced by innumerable enjoyable conversations with my Gateworld friends: Melissa McDonald, Jane Rawson, Amy Sharpe and Megyn Stacey. And I would especially like to thank Jennifer Fischer, for always making me dig deeper, Mary Boyle, whose own determination and perseverance continue to inspire me, and runway aficionado, Claudia Henry, for being my technical advisor on all things USAF.

Finally, I would like to thank my parents, Wilfred and Doras Parker, for believing this day would come, and most especially my family, Jim, Thomas and Claire, for putting up with — and occasionally indulging — my science fiction obsessions.

Ad astra per aspera.

www.ingramcontent.com/pod-product-compliance
Lightning Source LLC
Chambersburg PA
CBHW011158190726
48286CB00009B/2837